THERE WERE NO WINDOWS

Persephone Book N° 59
Published by Persephone Books Ltd 2005

First published 1944 by William Heinemann
© The Estate of Norah Hoult
Afterword © Julia Briggs 2005

Frontispiece photograph of the author taken from the
1946 Readers Union edition

Endpapers taken from
'Treetops', a screen-printed cotton and rayon furnishing fabric,
designed by Marianne Mahler,
produced by Edinburgh Weavers 1939–40
© Manchester City Art Galleries

Typeset in ITC Baskerville by Keystroke,
Jacaranda Lodge, Wolverhampton

Colour by Banbury Litho

Printed and bound by Biddles, King's Lynn

ISBN 1 903155 495

Persephone Books Ltd
59 Lamb's Conduit Street
London WC1N 3NB
020 7242 9292

www. persephonebooks.co.uk

THERE WERE NO WINDOWS

by

NORAH HOULT

with a new afterword by

JULIA BRIGGS

PERSEPHONE BOOKS
LONDON

Norah Hoult

Man is not a windowless monad.
Count Hermann Keyserling (1938)

THERE WERE NO WINDOWS

PART ONE
INSIDE THE HOUSE

CHAPTER ONE

She had been living quite happily because importantly in
the old house, when a sudden loud explosion arrested her
attention, and tugged it to that No Man's Land territory in
which she found herself marooned between the old house
and the new, the past and the present. Yet marooned is not
altogether the word, for it suggests a state lacking the capacity
for motion, whereas the odours, the voices and the thoughts
of the past rushed to coalesce with dubious newcomers intrud-
ing from the present, causing whirling eddies of confusion
in her head. And, violently agitated by this confusion, she,
a woman to whom life must be expressed by movement,
however painful, immediately ran to the window, stared out
unseeingly at the street, then ran to the door of her bedroom
and listened, and, finally, ran downstairs calling angrily: 'What
is it? What was that noise?'

At the bottom of the staircase the silence about her made
her pause and try to remember from whom she should seek
an answer to her question. Where was Caxton? No, Caxton,
her faithful maid for years, had gone; she was left with some
new people – a cook. For the moment she couldn't remember
the name of the new cook. No matter, she would be able to tell

her what had caused that horrible noise. And, 'Cook,' she called loudly.

There was no answer. She went to the head of the basement stairs and called again more imperiously. This time she heard a rustle, and then a low voice said: 'Kathleen, she's calling you.'

An Irish voice shouted: 'What is it now?'

She remembered which cook it was. It was the pretty, bad-tempered one with the clear pink skin and the glossy black hair whose name was Kathleen.

'What was that noise, cook?'

Kathleen's face appeared at the bottom of the staircase. 'Ah, it was nothing, nothing but a time bomb going off. It was streets away from here. Aren't you making your bed?'

She went down the stairs eagerly. 'A time bomb? Is that a new kind of bomb? Do you suppose anyone was hurt?'

'Ah, no one was hurt,' said Kathleen, barring her way. 'They moved the people away yesterday. Why don't you finish doing your hair? You look a terrible sight with it the way it is.'

What rudeness! She put up her hand to her head, and felt a strand of her hair on her shoulder. Yet it wasn't the place of a servant to remark on this! But, at the same time as the rudeness stirred her to anger, her consciousness reminded her of something familiar in that rudeness. It had happened before, and there was some reason why it should go unrebuked. Though what possible reason could there be for a servant to speak in that way to her mistress?

Over Kathleen's shoulder she saw a neat, pale, middle-aged woman sitting at the deal table on which was a pot of tea and two cups. 'Who is that sitting there?'

'You know well enough who it is. It's Mrs White, who comes every Monday to help with the washing.'

'Of course it is. I MUST speak to her.' She brushed past Kathleen. 'Good morning, Mrs White.'

'Good morning, Madam.'

The woman had half-risen from her chair, her elbow propped on the table. The gesture was awkward, but intended to be respectful, and therefore to be rewarded by graciousness.

'I hope they are making you comfortable?'

'Yes, thank you, Madam.' The woman's gaze had shifted away from her to the tea-pot. She was probably feeling rather guilty to be caught sitting there drinking tea instead of doing the washing.

'There's a lot of work for you to do, I know. Kathleen, have you given this lady the sheets off my bed?'

'They were changed yesterday. It's a wonder you wouldn't see them, and you making your bed. But I suppose you haven't made your bed yet. Hadn't you better go and finish it?'

More impertinence! A servant asking her mistress if she had made her bed and practically ordering her to go and do it! Topsy-turvy! Gilbertian! Really funny! But it would be no use pointing that out to Kathleen, for she remembered someone remarking that the real breach between oneself and the working classes was that they never appreciated irony. Of course there was the cockney understatement, but that was different. . . .

'I'll join you in your cup of tea, Mrs White. There's something so cosy, isn't there, in women sitting together gossiping in the morning . . .' she hesitated a moment, wondering if it were morning or afternoon, but Mrs White's calm gaze reassured her . . . 'when all the men are at work or at least out of the house. Kathleen, bring another cup!'

'There's no tea left, or nothing but a mouthful that's stewed to death,' said Kathleen, taking off the lid from the brown teapot, peering inside, and then slamming it on again. 'And you don't want tea now: you only had your breakfast an hour ago.'

'I do want some. Really, cook, I think I know whether I want some or don't want some better than you do.'

'The kettle's off the boil. You'll have to wait so.'

'I will wait,' she said excitedly. Now she was a little girl again, defying her nurse, defying her governess. You could generally get the better of people paid to serve you if you exerted all your energy, and set your will against theirs without relenting. Governesses didn't like you to scream, because that brought your mama into it. A strained look came into their plain and worried faces, making them still more plain and worried. But if you didn't fight them then they would override *you*.

But when she looked round with triumph Kathleen wasn't there any more. She had gone into the back kitchen, and now Mrs White was moving away from her, carrying cup and saucer in her hand.

'Where are you going?'

'I'm going to start my work, Madam.'

'Oh, please wait just a moment. You can wait a moment, can't you? Till Kathleen brings me my tea. Do let's have a little conversation. How's your husband? Didn't you tell me he was ill or something?'

'He's dead, Madam. He died eight months ago.'

'Oh dear! How stupid of me to forget. I remember perfectly now. Aren't you terribly lonely without him? I know what it is to lose a husband. My husband went off with another woman, you know. But I believe he's dead now. Yes, I'm sure he's dead. But the loneliness of it! How do you stand the loneliness?'

'I miss him, but then there are the children. And they keep me pretty busy, besides other work. Then with the war, and everyone having their troubles. . . .'

'Oh yes! The war. I know there's a war on. Everybody keeps harping on it. Really it's rather silly to make so much of it.'

'It's a very dreadful war, Madam,' said Mrs White in a faintly shocked voice. 'These air-raids! That one on Saturday night was dreadful the damage it done.'

'Yes, I dare say. Was there one? But talking about it all the time the way some people do, one common woman that comes and sees me does, is very tiresome. It interrupts con-versation, don't you think? There always have been wars, and always will be, and to let oneself be obsessed is to make oneself a person of one idea. Was your husband killed in the war?'

'Oh no, he was too old to go. It was a stomach ulcer, and the pains of it wore 'im out.'

'How shocking! But people often die in shocking ways. Do you remember the Irish playwright, Synge, writing that death should be a poor, untidy thing, though it's a queen that dies? No, perhaps you wouldn't.' Kathleen came into the room carrying a cup of tea. 'But you should, Kathleen, being Irish. You've heard of Synge, haven't you?'

'No, I have not. Here's your tea. And when you've drunk it, will you go and make your bed? You're interrupting us in our work.'

'Make my bed! Why should I make my bed? Don't you make my bed?'

'You always make your bed. Because you complained that it didn't suit you the way I did it. As you know very well.'

'It must have been that you didn't turn the mattress. Oh, I remember, you'd never tuck the blankets in at the bottom, and my feet got cold.'

'That's a lie,' said Kathleen coldly, turning away. 'But please yourself what you say. I'm used to it by now.'

Kathleen had gone, but she had left a phrase behind her. She called out: 'Yes, I shall please myself what I say. It's my own house.'

She started to sip her tea. It didn't taste nice. It was half cold. 'Cook, this tea is not drinkable. It's dreadful!'

There was no answer except the clatter of cups and saucers from the other room. This wasn't what she had planned at all. She had thought the three of them might have an interesting talk by the kitchen fire, because a writer must always sacrifice her dignity to the possibility of obtaining copy. And sometimes servants could . . . look at George Moore and *Esther Waters*. She pushed her cup petulantly away, calling out: 'I won't and can't drink this.'

Still no answer. She got up and pulled the door of the back kitchen open. Kathleen was stooping, emptying tea-leaves into a bucket; Mrs White was poking at sheets which lay in a great tub of soapy bluish water. Their backs turned to her and the stir of activity they suggested discouraged her, and she turned away.

'But how extraordinary that I can't get a cup of tea in my own house,' she said, going quickly up the basement stairs. She said it again in the hall, half-hoping that one of the doors would open, and a sympathetic face appear. And she muttered to herself as she mounted higher and higher till she arrived at the door of her own bedroom once more.

But as she passed over the threshold and stared expectantly about her, the interest of arriving in a fresh setting drove the painful significance of the reiterated grumble from her mind which now dipped and swooped like the flight of a seagull, having lost, or nearly lost, the habit of moving in a groove formed by the sequence of impressions. This room which had been her bedroom for so many years had the quality of being transported, like a magic carpet, to other settings, but in time rather than in space. Thus the half-made bed now suggested to her that she was living in that period when, her father being ill and requiring extra service, she had volunteered to do her room herself. As she pulled up the blankets and tucked them tidily in, there therefore entered into the snug place of routine the expectation of visiting her father in the next bedroom, and inquiring, after a dutiful kiss, what sort of night he had spent. In the composure induced by that anticipation, she finished the bed carefully, smoothing out the creases in the counterpane, pulling up the eiderdown with hands that were sensitive to its taffeta softness.

Moving over to the dressing-table, and peering into the glass, she perceived with surprise that her hair was hanging untidily about her face. Even as she took up the comb and seized hairpins, she became aware that she had also received a disagreeable impression, disagreeable enough to cause her to pause, and then take up the hand-mirror.

Why, her hair was quite white! That was what had disturbed her. Naturally enough! Her father would be disappointed because he had always praised her fine chestnut tresses. Had she received some shock, so that it had turned white in a night?

The phrase seized upon her attention, becoming thereby divested of its previous significance. *Hair that turned white in a night* was surely one of the most stupid conventions of the melodramatic novelist. In her own experience she couldn't remember such a thing happening. For herself, she remembered plucking out one white hair after another till the time – had it come or not? – when they had got the better of her. No, it was one of the conventions, one of the many that novelists shook carelessly out of their bag of tricks, like that one about innocence and goodness . . . what foolishness! As if the innocent could ever be truly good! She remembered discussing that with the Scotsman who had been so shocked when she had told him that she wasn't a virgin. What was his name? Then there was that popular rather clever man who wrote such nonsense about the sinister quality of the Chinese, thus making the uneducated and the untravelled, in a word the whole of the British lower-middle class, believe for ever and ever that the Chinese were sinister and in-scrutable, leading on to the notion of the Yellow Peril. Yellow Peril, Scarlet Woman . . . Blue Lagoon, how they loved colours!

Like a dowdy chapel audience having to be cheered up in their drabness by imaginations of the flames of hell . . . her thoughts went scampering on, till a cold current crept down her back, arousing her to an impatient sense that she mustn't waste any more time. There was something she had to do, somewhere she had to go. Where?

Yes, to go and see her father, and ask him how he did. She went on her usual quick light step out of her big front room at the top of the house across the landing to knock at the door of the adjacent one. There was no reply, so she went in.

The bed with its thick honeycombed white counterpane to which her eyes immediately turned was empty. So was the room, which carried the musty smell of long disuse.

She stood still and tensely watchful, as was her habit during the rush of transition from past to present, or imperfect present.

Of course, dear papa was dead! He had died years and years ago. How could she have forgotten when she remembered so well the ominous sound of the coffin being carried down the stairs, while she did her best to distract her mother's attention by pretending the wine she was drinking had gone to her head and made her a little tipsy, so that she talked feverishly of one thing after another.

Yes, how could she have forgotten? Because she was losing her memory. They were always telling her that. And behind the reminder, uttered by falsely smiling or bored or impatient faces, there was always the sense of threat. For what did they do to those who had entirely lost their memories? They shut them into asylums. That was why she had to be so very careful. All the time. Supposing anyone had seen her just now knocking at the door of an empty room because she thought her dead father was lying there ill? That might be enough for some people! She had to be very careful . . . all the time she had to be most careful.

From this monstrous thought she must plunge into action, but with the addition, as even a woman with the utmost need to hurry out snatches up her cloak, of caution. She must remember exactly what she was supposed to be doing that day, so that they would never suspect that she had lost as much of her memory as she had. Where was her secretary who knew her engagements? Miss Phillips, dear Phil, always such a rock. She must go downstairs immediately and see if she had arrived.

There was no Phil in the first-floor room, now used as a study. But there was the typewriter, and she went over and removed its cover. 'Not that I think this will be one of my writing mornings,' she said aloud, addressing the keyboard. 'I can't collect my thoughts.' And until one had collected one's thoughts, how impossible to withdraw from them, like a shining jewel, *le mot juste*. *Le mot juste* that her husband had agonised to find, that so many artists had striven for at the cost of such self-torture.

She fluttered about the room, taking up books from the table and bureau, opening them, and putting them back almost unseeingly. Nowadays she had lost the power of reading with any concentration beyond a very few pages of the novels that Miss Phillips sometimes brought her from the library, but the sense of being surrounded by books, some of them fashioned of the stuff of literature, renewed within her the sense of her position as a literary woman. Their covers held for her much of her life, that life of the mind which with her had as its arbiter taste. It was the manner of a book that was so much more important than its matter. Not what you say, but how you say it. That was the faith her husband and his friends had held with such fervour . . . how long ago was it? She had forgotten.

It was then as a woman of letters that she went with slower tread down the stairs, and looked into the dining-room, and then into the front room. Shaking her head, she went to the head of the basement stairs once more, and called: 'Kathleen, hasn't Miss Phillips come? Why is she so late?'

'Miss Phillips isn't coming,' Kathleen shouted back. ''Tisn't her morning.'

'Why isn't it her morning?'

There was no answer but a despairing groan. Then: 'Because she can only come on Saturdays now. And Mrs Jessup has left.'

'Mrs Jessup! That's who I mean. Why isn't she here?'

'Because she's left,' Kathleen said, appearing at the foot of the stairs. 'And small blame to her. She's not coming any more. Now do you understand?'

'Do you mean that I have no secretary? How am I to get my work done? Why did she leave? I paid her a pound a week just for a couple of hours every morning, and I should think that's good pay enough.'

Kathleen put her hands on her hips, and spoke slowly.

'With the war she can get more than that. Anyone can get more than that. What's more, she would have had a nervous breakdown if she'd stayed with you a day longer. Now have you got it into your head, and now will you leave me in peace? I can't spend my whole morning shouting up the stairs to you.'

'And what about me having to shout down the stairs to you? Because if I ring the bell you don't come. Kindly remember you're a servant, and paid to be respectful.'

Trembling with anger she awaited a reply. But it didn't come. Kathleen had disappeared. It would be useless to call again, and after all she had had the last word.

Back along the hall she retreated, muttering angrily: 'The impertinence! I shall really have to get rid of her. It's no use.' In the dining-room she paused a few moments by the sulky fire, noticing it for the first time. Yes, of course, she and Mrs Jessup usually worked here in the mornings. And now that woman had said that Mrs Jessup wasn't coming any more. Something about a nervous breakdown? No, nonsense! It wasn't true! She remembered perfectly: Mrs Jessup had come to her and explained that she had been offered a good post in some Ministry – war-time always produced Ministries for some unknown reason, and so a lot of dull people got quite good jobs – and for the sake of her little girl who had to be kept at some boarding-school, she felt she couldn't very well refuse. And she had told Mrs Jessup that she had understood perfectly, that she wouldn't dream of standing in her way . . . had she actually said that? It was rather a *cliché*, but one had to speak to these people in words they understood.

And Mrs Jessup, while good-looking in her rather common-place way, was not really very bright. They must get somebody else for her. She must ask Kathleen about it.

But at the door she paused: that awful woman had been rude to her when she had asked her a sensible question about Mrs Jessup, and if she asked her something again she would be still ruder. She wrung her thin, cold fingers, and then grew still, looking about her, and sensing that behind the furniture, under the table, everywhere about her, were the frightening apparitions of Suspicion and Tragedy.

Yes, they were watching her, knowing that she had absolutely no one to talk to, that she was left alone at the complete mercy of an illiterate Irish cook who bullied her and shouted at her, and implied that she had nearly given Mrs Jessup a nervous breakdown. The situation was extraordinary because it had happened of all people to Her, a Woman who had known Everybody, every writer of eminence in England. And an artist in her own right. If she hadn't been an artist she might not have perceived the tragedy. She might have looked at the play as some women sat in the theatre and looked at *King Lear*, their fingers searching in the dark for bon-bons, or their sexual feelings titillated by the proximity of their male escorts. Yes, there were plenty of dullards who wouldn't know how fearful and monstrous . . . how *grotesque*, grotesque was the word, as a maimed or idiot person is grotesque, was the situation in which she found herself. They would sink without a murmur into long, lonely senility to the click-clack of their knitting-needles.

If she could have sat there quietly, perceiving the tragedy

and suffering it, she could have come to terms with it by the only way in which we can come to any terms with misfortunes, by acceptance. So her inward life would have had its opportunity of resurrection. But her mind, which all her life had run eagerly forward, seeking stimulus from outside, and now in its disorder was even more impelled to take flight, would not let her be still.

No: since she considered the situation intolerable, she could not sit still and alone in its presence: she must find someone; there must be something, some way of relief. She stared round her, and then in a flash remembered. Of course, her cat! Where was Lisa? She must have Lisa.

Kathleen, busy making a pie for their midday dinner in honour of Mrs White, heard her voice once more at the head of the stairs: 'Cook, is Lisa down there? I can't find Lisa. I've looked everywhere.'

Kathleen glanced at the hearth-rug. No, Lisa wasn't there. But, asked this question a dozen times a day, it was her procedure to take the chance of her mistress not coming further and reply in the affirmative. If she said 'No', there'd as likely as not be ructions with herself rushing out into the street looking for her, and stopping passers-by with questions: 'Have you seen my beautiful cat? . . . I'm so upset; I've lost her.' And her charge was to keep her indoors as much as possible. So she called back: 'Yes, she's here all right.'

'I want her. I'm coming down to fetch her.'

Kathleen took her hands out of the basin and went quickly to the foot of the stairs. 'What do you want the cat for? She's happy where she is. Leave her alone, can't you?'

'I want her. That's enough. It's my cat. And I'm determined to have her.'

Warned by the hysteria in the voice that there was no stopping her, Kathleen returned to her pastry. Busily engaged in kneading, she said without lifting her eyes as footsteps paused by her: 'The cat's not there now. She must have hooked it away when my back was turned.'

'Why did you say she was here then? I've told you before not to tell me lies in my own house.'

'Don't excite yourself. It's no lie that the animal was there a minute since, and is not there now. She's having a run out somewhere, and why not?'

'I told you not to let her out in the street to be run over. Those were my instructions. I shall never forgive you if anything happens to Lisa.'

'What should happen to her? I expect she's flew upstairs to your bedroom; she has a fancy to go there now and again.'

'I'll go and see. But are you sure she's not here? Is she in the other kitchen?'

'Go and look, if you want,' said Kathleen. As she rolled out her pastry, she listened and heard:

'I'm looking for my cat . . . oh, it's Mrs White, isn't it?'

'It's not here, Madam.'

'Oh dear! You see, I'm so terribly lonely that I simply must have my cat with me. You understand, don't you? I suppose you have a husband?'

'My husband's dead.'

'Then you will understand. Aren't you terribly lonely? To have no one to say "good night" to!'

'I have my children.'

'Children! But they're different, aren't they? I never had any children. And if I had, they'd have grown up and left me by now, wouldn't they? I'm an older woman than you are. Do you know my hair has gone quite white?'

Mrs White made no reply to what seemed to her an obvious statement. Kathleen turned to hear: 'The cat's not there. Do you mind if I look in your bedroom?'

'No, the cat's never let in my bedroom, and I'm not going to have you poking into it. That's definite now. My bedroom's for me alone, as I've told you times without number.'

Taken aback by the sudden fierceness, her mistress took a little time to rally. 'Well, I only asked. Because you told me the cat was down here, didn't you?'

'I told you it was here, but it wasn't here now. That's what I told you.'

'Is it upstairs, or has it gone out?'

'I don't know. Will you kindly allow me to get on with my work in peace?'

'I don't want to interrupt you, cook. There's no need to be so bad-tempered. I'll go and search for Lisa. Poor Lisa! I do hope she's not got run over.'

She went upstairs in the uneasy mood of the vanquished who feel that if only it could be found there's a reason why they should not have been vanquished. Of course cooks hated to be disturbed when they were cooking, and Kathleen, she remembered, was Irish, and the Irish were notoriously hot-tempered, and wasn't it true, too, that the Celts were not kind to animals. . . .

18

Opening the front door, she shouted into the cold January morning: 'Lisa, Lisa . . . Puss, come here, Puss . . . . Lisa, Lisa!'

There was no Lisa, and no Lisa when she went down to the gate and opening it stared up and down the road. She would look in her bedroom, and then she would have to go out and find it. But she must put on a coat before she went out in the street, or that bad-tempered cook would shout at her, as she remembered that she had shouted at her once before. As if it were her business! But life had turned topsy-turvy!

Trailing up the first flight of stairs, she stopped to look with curiosity at the signed photographs of celebrities that lined the walls. She had so often pointed them out with little bits of scandal attached to each, but now there wasn't anyone to show them to. And what use were they, was the unformulated thought at the back of her mind, when they were no longer exhibited? For what, she thought, as she arrived on the first floor, did one entertain and be entertained, for what did one garner memories, listen attentively to gossip, savour the spice of scandal, form apt judgments, and carry along with one as portable luggage revealing incident after incident of bedroom, boudoir, dining-table and drawing-room, if at the end one had no one whom to entertain by relating these things? For what had one taken all the pains one had taken to *know* people if, at the end, there was no one to impress; no, *intrigue* was a better and less vulgar word, intrigue by one's knowledge?

The celebrities themselves, those who had been flattered by seeing themselves on her walls when they came to dine, could they all be dead? Dear Henry, yes, he certainly was dead. But she couldn't remember if BJ was dead. If he wasn't

dead, then he had neglected her scandalously, for she was quite sure she hadn't seen him for months, maybe for years. And yet he had been in love with her. He had even told her so, when he brought her back from some party. He had wanted to stay the night with her, of course. But she had only laughed. A good brain, she supposed. In his own line. But stolid, matter-of-fact, taking everything *au pied de la lettre*. It would have been like going to bed with one's butler.

Still even he, if he could be found and asked to dine, would be better than no one. Much, much better than nobody at all. She must remember to ask her secretary. Her secretary was that rather good-looking but very wooden female who had divorced her husband, named Jessup. But wasn't there something . . . was she still coming?

If she wasn't there that morning, and certainly she didn't seem to be, why then she must speak to cook, however bad-tempered the woman was. She must ask her if there were any arrangements, if someone was coming to dinner or not. Mostly no one came any more; she was quite aware of that. And there weren't any invitation cards on her mantelpiece. But if no one was coming, surely she could ask *someone*, surely there was someone in the whole of London whom she might ask to dinner. The cook was a good cook even if she was bad-tempered.

'Cook!' she called at the top of the basement stairs, 'Cook, I want to speak to you, please.'

Mrs White, just going out of the back door with a basket full of washing to hang up on the clothes-line, felt a nudge of her back, and turning saw Kathleen.

'I'm coming out with you to give you a hand. That old devil's after calling me again, and if she says another word about the cat, I wouldn't trust myself. She's doing it out of spite, do you know?'

Her mistress, seized by a sudden apprehension of the silence below stairs, went down, and ran from front kitchen to back kitchen, and then stopped, listening intently. There wasn't anybody there. She remembered the maid's bedroom, and knocked at the door, and then opened it. A peep inside showed her that it, too, was empty, and some consciousness that someone would shout at her if she was discovered looking in made her close the door again hastily. Back to the kitchen she went, and stood staring round, trying to ascertain if there were any evidences of recent occupation. There was a fire, but they might have lit it and then gone off.

Was she alone then? Was she quite alone in the house without a soul near her? Oh, pray God, it wasn't so, she appealed, her hand going to her heart. For this was the most fearful bogey, the worst shadow of all, the mainspring at the back of all the shadows, colouring them, making them gibber before her. She saw the back door was slightly ajar, and she rushed to open it, and stare out. With an intensity of relief which caused her hands to fall loosely to her sides, she saw the figures of the two women, one with her arms stretched holding some garment, the other looking in a box on the ground for a peg. And as a child who has been lost spies a familiar figure and runs towards it, she hastened into the garden.

Kathleen saw her first, and murmured: 'Oh, my God,'

causing Mrs White to glance round surprised. Then, turning squarely upon the advancing old woman: 'If you're looking for the cat, she's not here, so you're only wasting your time!'

'I wasn't looking for the cat; I was looking for you. I thought you'd gone. Where is the cat then?'

'I don't know. What did you want me for now?'

There was a moment's hesitation before the reply, and then it came out triumphantly: 'I wanted to ask you about the arrangements for the day. You told me my secretary wasn't here, so you're the only person I have to ask.'

'What do you mean, *arrangements* for the day?'

'Why, is anyone coming to dine? Or . . . no, I don't think I have any engagement, have I?'

'Not that I know of.' Kathleen turned her back, and started to help Mrs White, who was pegging a sheet.

She said sharply, angered by the movement: 'Please pay attention, cook, when I ask you something.'

'Ask me something that has sense then. I've no time to be answering the questions of a mad woman.'

The forbidden word was out, out in the full light of Monday washing morning: the wet sheet flapped it at her; it was written on the grey London sky. Here was danger, which her instinct directed side-stepping: 'Really, cook, to tell me I'm mad, because I ask you who is coming to dinner, is quite ridiculous. It is you who must be mad.'

'All right then, it's me. And the answer is that no one's coming to dinner, nor at any other time. Are you satisfied now?'

'Certainly, I'm quite satisfied.'

She walked away from them with dignity, her head up. It

was really too much: whenever she spoke to that awful woman there was a brawl. And to be called . . . but she mustn't think of what she had called her.

She went upstairs, and then struck by a sudden notion went with stealth into the small back room next to the bathroom that looked out into the garden. Standing cautiously at the side of the curtain, she peered out at the two women. Their heads were near together, Kathleen talking, Mrs White listening. Talking about her of course! She would be a fool to expect anything else. Servants always talked scandal about their employers. But why had Kathleen said *Mad*? So long as she wasn't trying to persuade the other woman, to draw her into some dark plot. It was preposterous to think of it, but servants did plot. There was that terrible French governess that Sheridan Le Fanu had written about, and the end was a hired chaise, or motor-car it would be now, and a hand over one's mouth muffling shrieks. Servants hanging out washing in a Kensington sooty back garden could be spectres of evil from that dark world which lay under a black or red sky, carrying the immediate threat of thunder and lightning, lightning like a silver dagger piercing the world. In that monstrous world, which was a world of melodrama and stage properties and yet was also a very real world, servants could betray as Iago betrayed his master, one could be starved and tortured, shut away behind barred windows where no one could hear one's cries. Or if they did, the cries would be explained away: 'You see, she's raving mad.' A monstrous explanation, but one that always satisfied, always quietened the most kind-hearted. A world of melodrama, yes, but it existed, as Shakespeare knew, as the eighteenth-century novelists knew . . . even today in the nineteenth century, or was it the twentieth century?

Yes, it was the twentieth century. But what year? Her mind relaxed from its tension as she tried to puzzle out the date. There was a war on, and the war started in 1914. But, no, this was, they kept saying to her, a quite different war. It was therefore much later than 1914. Yes, it must be in the twentieth century.

Her attention was recalled by the sense of movement in the garden below. The two women were going back to the house, an empty clothes-basket held between them. Kathleen was looking up at the sky; she was quite a pretty woman, her colouring set off by the pink overall she was wearing. But she was a cruel woman, and perhaps a wicked woman. She was seeing her now as the doubting Othello saw the beauty of Desdemona: *O thou weed, who art so lovely fair and smell'st so sweet that the sense aches at thee . . .*

Not, of course, she thought moving impatiently away from the window, that there was any real comparison between Kathleen and Desdemona. Kathleen was decidedly not 'of so gentle a condition'. She was a virago, an Irish slut. Moreover, Othello had been wrong in suspecting Desdemona, and she was not at all sure that she was wrong in suspecting Kathleen.

But she had been thinking about something else. What was it? Something to do with time. Euclid, she recalled, was all wrong now, and that made everything more insubstantial. Yet there were still dates, and it was important – since that woman had had the audacity to come right out with the statement that she was *mad* – that she should know what date

it was. No doubt that was one of the questions they would ask. And if she didn't know, they might consign her straight away to Bedlam. There must be a calendar or almanac of some kind in the house. She would go from room to room and search for one.

Upstairs and downstairs she wandered, her eyes going round the four walls of every room. It was extraordinary that there shouldn't be a calendar somewhere, for at Christmas so many people sent one calendars, some in atrocious taste that one threw immediately into the fire or gave to the servants. But there were generally one or two that could hang in the lavatory at least, and, of course, there should be one in the study. She lingered for some time at her desk, turning over old cuttings till her fingers became stiff with cold, and she paused to wonder what it was she was looking for.

She was looking for a date, but what date? If someone asked her suddenly, what are you looking for? she would say more prettily: 'I am looking for time.' For it was foolish to divide time into days. You must divide it into phases, like 'the gay nineties', when oneself had been gay with the years. It was then that she had defied Mrs Grundy and supped in Soho with journalists and often come home alone by hansom. It was then that she had experienced her *grande passion*. Oliver Manning. Say his name now, and it still meant more than any other name. But how badly he had treated her . . . when his wife had at last died marrying that old Frenchwoman without looks, without even much money. Why, why? She still after all these years couldn't understand. 'You are a woman to whom love brings unhappiness,' he had written. And: 'We will make

each other unhappy as well as happy.' And why not? Because
he was a coward, as all men were cowards. But she hadn't
protested, she had been very ill, and then she had gone to Paris
with that painting Irish countess, and sat in the cafés watching
people and visiting the Morgue . . . oh those windows with
their perpetually running water! Yes, it was stupid to count
time by days. There were periods when your heart was cut
out of you, and then long periods when it grew again. Only
to be cut out once more, because when she was amusing and
gay and quite the fashion, Wallace had come, and threatened
suicide. And she had fallen victim to that stupidity of women,
the stupidity which made them believe that they could save
men.

Middle-aged, she had been then. But it was nothing to be
middle-aged. One could still dance and flirt as she had danced
and flirted. But to be old, that was terrible. Because then it
was unseemly to open wide and thoughtful eyes, holding the
gaze that looked at you, till his eyes began to hold interest,
till the something passed between that said: 'Yes, you are
a woman and I am a man.' When had that stopped? that was
what she wanted to know. When had *his* gaze, whoever it was,
spelt nothing but polite attention? Or else, worse, had flickered
away in a kind of gauche embarrassment?

That was what she would like to ask God, if there were such
a person. Why did women spend years learning to be women,
becoming adept in flattery and charm? And then for years
one was an old woman with white hair and hollow neck whom
men did not desire to love. Well, she had held them still,
by conversation and by always having a good cook. But then

another trick had been played against her; her memory had gone astray, had cantered up hill and down dale, with the result that one was no longer very amusing, one was, in fact, a bore. How now, God? Was that altogether fair?

No, it was so unfair that she couldn't help but imagine that there was some conspiracy against her. Her enemies, people she had annoyed by saying amusing things about, but things which, of course, had been indiscreet because naturally they were repeated, her enemies had got together and delivered her into the hands of her cook, a cruel and vulgar woman, of whom all that could be said was that her savouries were quite good. So no more conversation, no more parties, no more flirtations, nothing except that she was still as light as she had ever been, and so she could still dance, even if it were all by herself.

And just to prove it, holding up the skirt of her thin black dress, she started to dance, humming to herself the refrain of *The Merry Widow* waltz . . . on and on she went, skirting the foot of her bed, swaying her hips ever so slightly, inclining her head now and again, imagining that she was holding a fan, imagining that a man's arm clasped her tiny waist, that the band was seductive, that the floor was excellent, that her partner was beginning to be just a little in love with her, and was murmuring something about the fineness of her eyes. She paused for breath, and then glided and swayed once more, dancing on and on to the music that had played in other years.

CHAPTER TWO

I

A voice was calling her name, calling loudly and imperatively. From the chair in which she had come to rest and listen with surprise to the beating of her heart, she considered the voice, and wondered who it was that called so impatiently. As it came nearer she heard its intonation, an un-English one. An Irish woman, she decided. Ireland! She had never had an Irish beau; it was poor Kitty O'Shea whose life had burnt to a sudden flame, and then petered out for long years in Brighton because of an Irishman. Poor Parnell; yet surely he had been more fortunate, for with him the blaze had been so bright and so brief. Illicit love, Cyprian love that made for tragedy. . . .

The door of her bedroom opened violently, and a voice said: 'So here you are! Didn't you hear me shouting for you? The sirens have gone, so you'd better come downstairs. Mrs White thinks you should come, though I don't believe myself you're safer in one place than another.'

Sirens! What song the sirens sang? She stared blankly back at the face, which gradually assumed a familiar aspect.

Why, it was Kathleen, the cook whom surely she had reason to believe was bad-tempered. But for the moment she seemed quite kind: she was saying: 'Isn't it a wonder you wouldn't be cold up here! Come on now. There's a plane right overhead.'

She rose eagerly, remembering that Kathleen usually refused to allow her near the kitchen except at meal-times. 'You mean it's lunch-time.'

'Lunch will be ready in about twenty minutes; I suppose you'll want to have it with us,' said Kathleen, leading the way downstairs.

She went too slowly for her mistress's liking; moreover, a well-trained maid naturally stood back to let one go first. 'Do you mind, Kathleen, if I go first?' she asked, permitting just an inflexion of irony in her voice to remind the woman of her place.

'In a hurry, are you? Is it afraid you are?' asked Kathleen, with real curiosity, for the air-raids seemed to have a different reaction on the queer one, as she thought of her, every time. She stood back, and then saw that it was only just the pushing nature of the queer one, who asked with real bewilderment: 'Why should I be afraid? No, you must really remember to let your social superiors precede you, Kathleen, or you'll never be considered a well-trained maid.'

'Is that so?' inquired Kathleen, trying a little irony on her own account, and with as unsuccessful a result, for she was not even heard: her mistress had turned the corner and was running down the stairs into the basement to be greeted by Mrs White:

'You're right to come down. It's safer when one of them things is about.'

'What things?'

'German airyplanes. I said to Kathleen I was sure it was a German when I heard it overhead before the sireens went.'

'Sireens? What are they?'

'You know. Didn't you hear them?'

'No,' said Kathleen, who had arrived and answered for her. 'She didn't. She never hears anything that you'd expect her to hear.' She gave her mistress a dark look, as from one adversary to another who has scored for the present, but is not going to be allowed to go on scoring. 'You'd better sit down here.' She indicated the basket chair on the other side of the kitchen-range, and then slammed open the door of the gas oven: 'There, my pastry is burning with having to bring you downstairs!'

'It's a Zeppelin raid, isn't it, Mrs White?'

Kathleen, seizing a cloth to take out the pie, said loudly and angrily: 'No, it isn't then. Them things only happened in the last war.'

'What is it then?'

'German airplanes dropping bombs, or trying to drop bombs.'

'Well, it's the same thing, isn't it? Whether you call them Zeppelins, or German airplanes. I suppose you're nervous, are you, Kathleen? That accounts for . . .' she broke off, observing the thunder on Kathleen's face, and feeling that perhaps she'd gone too far in defiance.

'It's not me that's afraid. It wasn't me that scuttled down the stairs like a rabbit.'

'I really don't know what you mean.'

It was no good talking to Kathleen, for she was off to the back-kitchen. Moreover, her attention was suddenly diverted by the sight of the cat lying on the hearth-rug, but with open eyes turned upon her, and she started to caress it. 'Dear Lisa, where have you been? I've been looking for you the whole morning. Naughty pussy to stray.' When Kathleen came back and started to lay the cloth, she informed her: 'Lisa's come back.'

'What do you mean "come back"?' cried Kathleen, rendered quite unscrupulous by the necessity she felt to put her mistress back in her place. 'She's been here the whole blessed morning.'

'I don't think she has.' But she spoke in a low voice, for she didn't quite remember. It might have been yesterday morning that Lisa had got lost. She stooped down, and lifting Lisa on her knee held her closely.

Lisa, preferring the hearth-rug, resented the action. As soon as the arms holding her relaxed, she stood up arching her back. Then she made a sudden jump, landing back on the hearth-rug.

'The poor cat, she likes to be left alone,' said Kathleen, who had observed with approval this gesture of rebuff.

'No, she doesn't; she generally loves being nursed. What's Mrs White doing?'

'She's doing her work, of course, in the other room. What else should she be doing? Do you want her?'

'No, I don't want her. I only wondered where she had suddenly disappeared to. She was here a moment ago, I'm sure.'

'Would you please mind moving your chair further back. I'm just going to dish up, and you're in the way.'

She moved her chair back, watching helplessly the bustle of protective movement with which Kathleen surrounded herself. The oven door was opened and shut, and opened again, just when one had thought that Kathleen was finished with it. Then she lifted a saucepan of potatoes, and took them into the back kitchen, closing the door behind her so that one just heard whispering voices. Just as she was half out of her chair with the intention of walking in on them herself, Kathleen came back and took down a dish from the dresser, darting a look at her that seemed to say: 'I know you're trying to listen.' What she should say to Kathleen, she thought, as the door was slammed once again, was: 'Do you mind making rather less noise?'

Kathleen finally returned, followed this time by Mrs White, who was drying her hands on her apron. Such ugly fat red hands, thought the watching woman, who next heard: 'Lunch is ready. Will you sit here?'

Really, the woman spoke to her as if she were a schoolgirl instead of being her mistress. Mrs White, on the other hand, looked ill at ease, as if she recognised that it was rather odd for her to sit down at food with the mistress of the house who paid her. She decided that though Kathleen was to be discouraged, Mrs White, who seemed a worthy kind of creature, should be set at her ease. Therefore she started to eat without for once criticising the food, though she knew that thereby she was letting one of her weapons against cook rust. For, she remembered now, Kathleen took a great pride in her cooking, and got quite red with rage if one made the least criticism, or left most of it on one's plate.

So she took a few mouthfuls, glancing around her with vivacity, as she waited for her hostesses to speak. For that was what in fact they were. But there was nothing but that engrossment with food, Mrs White staring intently at her plate, Kathleen eating with an absent air, and then staring out of the window. It was evidently left for her to break the ice. She would ask Mrs White some sympathetic question about her family.

'Does your husband have to work very hard, Mrs White? Do tell me. What does he do?'

Mrs White gave a despairing glance over at Kathleen, who went on staring out of the window. Carefully finishing what she had in her mouth before answering, she said: 'I told you, Madam. He's dead.'

'Dead? Oh yes, of course you were telling me. How very sad! My husband's dead, too, I think. I still get his press cuttings, but I think someone told me that he's dead. Oh yes, he died in . . .'

'Hush!' said Kathleen, raising a finger. Faintly a wail came on the air; then grew stronger and stronger.

'All clear!' nodded Mrs White. 'I'm glad I didn't go home, as it wasn't much of one.'

'What a ghastly noise, isn't it? Thank heavens, it's stopping. All clear. What does that mean exactly? That the Zeppelins have gone?'

'You'd have been a fool to have gone home,' said Kathleen, answering Mrs White. 'It's the gunfire that's more dangerous than the bombs these times. That was only one raider, I expect. Nuisance raids they call them. Nothing to talk about, if you stay indoors.'

'I know,' said Mrs White. 'But even one plane, and there are them that get killed.'

It had started again. What she couldn't bear! People talking to each other at her own table as if she wasn't there. And often saying things that she couldn't quite understand. The only way to stop them was to talk oneself.

'They really shouldn't be allowed to make such a ghastly noise, whatever the reason. Why do they do it? How do they make such banshee sounds? Why not blow trumpets for the "All Clear", that's what you called it, isn't it? Of course the English are not a musical people like the Germans, but really, they needn't go quite so far in the other direction.'

Kathleen said nothing, but Mrs White smiled sympa-thetically, and said: 'It's a terrible noise, I think, myself, but I suppose they have to have it that way. Only I think there did ought to be more difference between the Warning and the All Clear; I know there is a difference, but I mean really a difference.'

'They wouldn't want the bother of fixing up two different sets of instruments, that's why,' said Kathleen, cutting across her mistress. 'Some more potatoes, Mrs White?'

She ought really to have asked *her* before she asked Mrs White; it was true she still had some on her plate.

'No, thank you. It's a nice bit of meat, isn't it?'

'Not bad.'

'Kathleen is a very good shopper. But she can't get any cream, and that's a thing that I do miss. I used to live on cream practically. Can you get cream?'

'No, Madam. No one can get cream. The Government don't allow it.'

'Why don't they allow it? Because cream is so good for people, especially thin people like me.'

'It's the war, you see,' started Mrs White. Kathleen said impatiently: 'I've told her that dozens of times. It's no good trying to make her understand. She refuses to.'

'I understand perfectly, cook. It's not very difficult. I know quite well there's a war on, and so the Government makes all sorts of rules and regulations. I'm only saying that this regulation is a ridiculous one, because cream happens to have food value. We got cream in the last war.'

Kathleen pushed back her chair and started to collect the plates. 'Have you finished?' she asked her mistress, staring at the plentiful remains on the plate.

'Yes, I think I have. The meat is really rather tough, isn't it?'

Making no reply Kathleen took the plate, banged it on top of the others, and left the room. Alone with Mrs White, she said in a low voice:

'You see how she treats me? Either she doesn't answer when I speak to her, or she is shockingly rude. What am I to do?' She stopped with her finger on her lips to indicate that Kathleen was just coming back. And just to cover up an awkward situation in case Kathleen had guessed she was appealing to Mrs White, she hailed the appearance of the apple-pie with vivacity: 'Oh, doesn't that look nice! Kathleen makes very good pastry. You'll enjoy it, Mrs White.'

Setting a portion in front of her, Kathleen said inexorably: 'I'm glad to hear it. Only the other day you were saying that the pastry I made was only fit to give a dog to poison it.'

Momentarily nonplussed, she heard Mrs White say: 'You

can't get the fats now. It's a long time since I made pastry. But I was lucky last week; I got some suet, and I made a lovely boiled pudding for the children. I had some treacle specially saved.'

'I've got treacle, and I've got Atora suet,' said Kathleen. She was going on to say something else, when she lost her turn:

'Isn't it curious, Mrs er . . . Mrs White, that though I've often been complimented on my taste in food, and that though I've generally managed to keep a good cook, I've never known how to do much except make an omelette myself. And I can make quite a decent cheese savoury. There was a time long ago, because I'm going back now to the time of my first real *affaire*, in fact the only real *love* affair I've ever had, because my husband was rather different, it was more maternal, pity rather than love. You know what I mean. I should describe it as a sentimental occupation, full of loving-kindness rather than passion. But in those days to which I am referring when I really was in love, I did cook little suppers for us both on a gas-stove in a tiny flat where we used to meet without any-body knowing. You see, one didn't have one's *affaires* openly in those days, as you may remember. One's reputation counted then. It doesn't now, does it? People do anything.'

'Have another helping?' Kathleen asked Mrs White, who was laying down her spoon and fork and looking at them with intentness.

'A small piece. If you can spare it. Thank you very much. It's very good; I don't know how you manage to get it so rich in war-time.'

Kathleen passed Mrs White's plate over to her without, she

noticed, apologising for stretching in front of *her*. So when she was asked, if you can call so uncouth an utterance being asked: 'I suppose you don't want any more,' she replied promptly: 'No, thank you. But do help yourself, won't you, cook?'

She put in the last bit just to underline the oddity of the cook having the impertinence to act as if she were entertaining two visitors, instead of being merely a paid servant. Then she turned to Mrs White: 'That's a rather nice piece of china you're eating your tart off. . . . Not Sèvres, but it has worn so much better than most women wear. I remember we have had that dinner service since I was a child, and now it is all broken except that one dessert plate.'

'It's not all broken,' said Kathleen. 'If you look, you'll see that you're eating off the self-same pattern yourself.'

'That's not so, cook. It may look the same to you, but actually the texture is quite different. I know we have only just the one dessert plate left of that set, and so I was interested to see you give it to this lady.'

Kathleen pushed back her chair noisily, saying to Mrs White: 'I'll just put the kettle over for a cup of tea. I know you'd like one.'

'Not that I've ever cared greatly for collecting *things*. Not the way my sisters did. They just grabbed everything they could when my mother died, pieces that I knew she wanted me to have. I could have gone to law about it, but I didn't. Besides, I was then very troubled about my husband. He had started to make love to one of my best friends. And when a woman's affections are concerned, nothing else seems to matter a great deal. That is one of our weaknesses, don't you

think? But now that I've suddenly grown into an old woman, I find that everything becomes part of one's life. That William Morris table in the dining-room, you must have noticed it?'

'Yes, I think I have.'

'Of course you have. You could hardly have come to dine here without noticing it. I put my hand on it, and I think how can I bear never to see it again. And then the bureau! I say to it: "You know, Robert Browning once used you; he sat and wrote a letter, and my mother gave him a stamp." It was something he wanted to send off immediately. I expect it was a note to some duchess. He adored duchesses, you know. And then my father's pictures! I lie awake at night and think how sad it is that I have no one to leave all my dear and valuable possessions to. All the continuity will have gone. They will be scattered among strangers, and in time no one will know that Robert Browning sat at that bureau. He wanted to write a letter to a duchess, you know.'

'Haven't you any relatives to leave your things to then, Madam?'

Kathleen, coming into the room with a tray of cups and saucers, replied for her: 'Of course she has.'

'I have nieces, if that's what you mean, cook. As dull as ditch-water, both of them. I shouldn't dream of leaving anything to them.'

Kathleen went over to the stove and took up the kettle: 'Think shame of yourself to speak that way,' she threw over her shoulder. 'Very nice ladies, the both of them,' she added, speaking to Mrs White.

'It's really quite amusing the way my cook corrects me at

every moment, isn't it? Well, of course, they are "nice". Quite worthy, both of them. But I find I haven't anything to say to either of them. It's just like talking to a wall. I should hate to think of them having my Dutch cabinet.'

Kathleen came back to the table, and began to pour out the tea. 'They're no worse than any other relatives, and what will it matter anyway, and you in your grave?'

'But I'm not in my grave yet. That's the point. I can still anticipate the future, and that with the gloomiest forebodings, as my husband said. Cook, what are you giving me now?'

'Tea, what else?'

'I should think we might have coffee. This is luncheon surely, and we have a visitor.'

'Lunch or dinner or whatever you like to call it, we always have tea after it. You have your coffee in the evening and for breakfast. And Mrs White prefers tea, don't you?'

'I must say if it's the same to everybody else, I think there is no beating a good cup of tea for putting energy into you.'

'Does it put energy into you? How interesting! I don't want any. Isn't there something else?'

'There isn't anything else. You don't expect me to make coffee *and* tea in war-time, do you? Just for three women.'

'I don't expect anything, cook. Apparently it's what *you* say, extraordinary as it may seem. I suppose it's the servant shortage that accounts for it.'

'Are you satisfied with your butcher?' Kathleen asked Mrs White, who withdrew a fascinated gaze.

'Not altogether. He's better than some. But he favours. There's no doubt he favours. There's a woman I know gets liver, and the best calf liver at that, from him regular, but, oh no, he never has any for me.'

'You should get him to favour you,' said Kathleen.

Mrs White shook her head, and her lips drew together. 'I know too much about him,' she said. After a moment's hesitation, she added: 'I know why he favours, see?'

'Why does he?'

Mrs White glanced sideways to indicate to Kathleen that now was not the proper moment for confidences. But she observed that the old lady's eyes had closed. For the moment, having eaten a much heavier meal than was her custom, she had been overtaken by drowsiness.

Kathleen followed her gaze. 'Go on. Don't mind her.'

Mrs White sat forward, suddenly exhibiting unexpected dramatic talent.

'They say there's hardly a woman that's registered with him that doesn't go with him,' she hissed across the table.

'Why, is he that good-looking?'

'It's not that, but that's how they get an extra bit of meat or something fancy like liver, see?'

'And do you believe it?'

'Believe what?'

'That it's true that that's what they do for it. More likely that it's a packet of cigarettes, or a quarter of tea slipped across. I've seen a woman pass half-a-crown myself, and there was a man sacked over in Queensway for giving one woman more rations than she should have coming to her. The manager came out and caught him in the act, do you know. But even in this country, I wouldn't believe . . .'

'You don't believe because you don't know the party in question. And you don't know the way certain women go on now that their husbands are away, or even, and I know one case, and her husband – though they say that it's not really her husband – is not away.'

'Ah well, you can't believe everything.'

'I believe it because I seen it.'

'Seen it?'

The old woman's eyes had opened as the surprise in Kathleen's voice startled her into attention. But, unnoticing, Mrs White proceeded:

'Last Friday I went to the pictures with a lady friend. It was black as black when we come out, no moon, you understand. Even with my torch, for she hadn't one, it was bad-going getting home. And another thing, when I did show my torch there was a nosey-parker stopped me. "Keep your torch low," he said. "And it's too bright," he said. "You know very well," he said, "you should have it dimmed with tissue-paper. Correct that," he said. The cheek of him!'

'Was he an air-raid warden?'

'I couldn't say. How could I see when I was as good as told not to use my torch?'

'Well?'

'Well, my friend, she was for taking a short cut back up an alley-way, sort of, that isn't used much. I wouldn't go it by my-self at night. Well, going on ahead, do you see, and not having a torch, see, she walked smash into a pile of sandbags. "Let's have the torch, duck," she calls to me. And I switch on, and I see figures. I can't make out who. But she sees. Oh, yes, she sees.'

'What?'

'Her butcher, and my butcher, too, and the butcher, for that matter, of most of us round our way. And she sees who's with him, too.'

'Who?'

'That woman that I was telling you of. 'Er that's living with a man that's not 'er 'usband. And 'as children by him, too.'

'And they were . . .?'

'They were . . . right there, trusting to the dark, of course, not to be seen.'

'But how extraordinary! Do you mean that they were actually holding the court of love in the public street?'

Mrs White experienced horror. The old lady had awakened! She coughed and looked over at Kathleen, but received no help.

'That's what my friend saw,' she answered reluctantly.

'And who was the man, did you say, a butcher or something?'

'The butcher our way. That's what she said. I didn't see myself.'

'You don't mean our butcher, dear old Mr Lang, who once asked me if I would chaperon his daughter for a season?'

'Oh no, Madam. Nothing to do with Langs. This butcher is a man in a small way, see? And I wouldn't even like to say it were 'im, because I didn't see myself. I was too taken aback.'

'No, it couldn't have been Mr Lang. I'm sure Mr Lang would never have misconducted himself like that. For I did understand you to say that they were misconducting them-selves?'

'It was what my friend saw. I didn't, Madam.'

'But your friend saw it all. She really saw a respectable tradesman – in my time, tradespeople were always called respectable, and before my time, too. Do you remember old-fashioned novels usually had a reference to some minor character, "Mr A, a respectable tradesman of the town of B, happened that night to be looking out of his window, and saw . . ." and so forth? So you see, the tradition that trades-people are respectable characters is a long-established one. But you tell me that it is no longer so, and that in a public street in broad daylight . . .'

'No, Madam. It wasn't daylight. It was long after the black-out. And it was up a side turning, where some houses were blitzed as a matter of fact. . . .'

'Even so, people were passing, and didn't you say your friend stumbled right into the two of them engaged in their . . . what shall we call it? . . . amorous pastime?'

'Will you have some more tea, Mrs White?' asked Kathleen. Mrs White, passing her cup, was aware from Kathleen's voice that she disapproved of the conversation between herself and the old lady, and tried to give it a more general turn.

'It's the war, you see. Awful things happen in war-time. Families broke up. There's some women just can't seem to resist anything in trousers, and then with all these foreigners come into the country, what can you expect? I don't think we should let them in the way we do.'

'You mean, Mrs White . . . it *is* Mrs White, isn't it? Thank you! I knew it was! You mean that people's morals are so loose in war-time that they commit the act of love even in the streets at night-time. Of course, I've seen people, common people, making love in Hyde Park, and on the beaches. That is to say they'd lie in each other's arms and not care who saw them. In one way I used to think that if it wasn't so ungraceful, it was rather sweet. But now they've overflowed from the parks on to . . . sandbags, wasn't it you said?'

'You are getting it all wrong, and should think shame of yourself for thinking such badness,' said Kathleen. She pushed back her cup and saucer and rose.

'All the same,' said Mrs White, still smarting under Kathleen's attitude of disbelief, 'there's plenty of things that'd shock anyone, any decent person, I mean, going on. Husbands away fighting for their country, and their wives acting a fair disgrace. I know what I'm talking about, I can tell you.'

'Oh, do tell us.'

But Mrs White, hearing the clatter Kathleen was making with the crockery, was aware that it would be ill advised for her to do so. Shaking her head she, too, arose and began to help to clear away.

Was there *anything* she could do to postpone these destructive activities that hindered what had really turned out to be a most interesting conversation? 'Kathleen, don't take away the tea-pot: I'll have another cup, and I'm sure Mrs White will join me, won't you?'

'You said a while back that you wouldn't touch it: now there's no more left.'

'But can't you make some more?'

'No, I can't. We have to get on with our work.'

'But Mrs White can surely rest a minute.' She groped for the thread of the conversation; if she could only detain Mrs White,

then she could postpone the time when she was pushed back into the twilight of her own thoughts as Kathleen was waiting to push her chair back, and herself out of the room. She fixed Mrs White with her eyes. 'You see . . . as I was, I think, telling you, in my day our *affaires de cœur* were all under the rose. Our lances at Mrs Grundy were tilted with due discretion, and we paid lip court to her. Of course everyone knew, for naturally one confided in one's most intimate friends, and naturally one's most intimate friends told it to just one other person, and so it went all round the mulberry bush. But if it rose up above the mulberry bush, if you understand me, there was a measure of social ostracism. I know all about that, I can tell you. And my own sister never speaks to me even to this day.' She saw Mrs White, who had been listening patiently, stoop down and take up a plate, and sought eagerly for words that would halt her exit from the room: 'But you were saying . . . it's not like that any longer . . . something about sandbags?'

Kathleen, returning, judged it time to interfere: 'We don't want to have that all over again. It's time for you to go upstairs now, and have your rest. There isn't room for anyone to sit around here.'

'It *was* sandbags, wasn't it, Mrs *m'm?*'

'Yes, Madam.'

'I've seen them of course. Why, the house next door but one has simply piles of them. Why they should think that they'd be any protection against air-raids I can't think. But nature that abhors a vacuum has evidently found a use for them. For I remember perfectly what you were telling me just

now. Respectable tradespeople who most decidedly are no longer respectable! In my time it was more difficult. The man had to provide a flat; or, of course, the more abandoned kind of women went to certain places that cater for that sort of thing. Above a restaurant. But usually it was a surreptitious visit to a flat or his chambers, and the servant was sent away for the night. One might say, to adapt Shakespeare – I'm thinking of the sandbags – that we did it with a better grace, but the lower orders do it more natural.'

'Hadn't you better go out and fetch the handkerchiefs in, Mrs White?' Behind her hand Kathleen whispered: 'I'll never get rid of her as long as you stay in the kitchen.' Aloud she added: 'They should be quite dry by now, I'm thinking.'

'I saw you say something behind your hand, cook. Don't let her send you away. She is terribly rude, and one can only get along by ignoring her lack of breeding.'

'It's my washing, you see, Madam. If you'll excuse me.' Mrs White hurried out.

Kathleen seized the table-cloth, and went to shake it out at the back door, humming to herself. The watching woman decided that she had taken the table-cloth just to humiliate her; to make her feel that she's out-staying her welcome and committing a socially shameful offence, of talking so much that everyone had crept away pleading other engagements. Now Kathleen was piling the dishes up in the back kitchen, still humming to herself. Should she go and speak to her; tell her that it was really too much? And if she answered back, then dismiss her: give her a week's notice . . . her mind wavered;

there was some reason for that being a too high-handed action. What could the reason be? The domestic shortage? Probably. So many girls in munitions, she remembered hearing. But she would really tell Miss Phillips when she came. Meanwhile, looking round the room, she sought for some immediate cause that would make Kathleen stop her humming.

She found it in the cat, who chose this moment to rise from the hearth-rug, and stalk towards the open door. She followed: 'Lisa, come here, Lisa.'

But the back door was also open, and Lisa disappeared through it, advancing towards Mrs White and the clothes-line.

'Now see what you've done! You've let the cat out into the back garden.'

'And why shouldn't it go into the garden if it wants?'

There was no immediate answer to that. She hurried out after the animal, calling: 'Puss! Come here, Lisa. Puss, puss! Good pussy, come to your mistress!'

But it wasn't a good pussy. After loitering a moment beside Mrs White it ran quickly to the bottom of the garden, and jumped on the wall.

'Oh, Mrs White; look where Lisa has got to!'

'Yes, Madam. She is a one!' Mrs White passed her going with hasty steps towards the house.

'Lisa, come down from there. Puss, puss!' And then she stopped suddenly, and turned away, hearing the echo of her own voice, and pierced suddenly by a sharp sense that her whole life was resolving itself into a ridiculous pursuit of a cat. Moreover, a stray cat who had attached itself to the household, a mongrel cat, quite different from the cat she had really and truly loved, Josephine, who was a cat of dignity who never, never or hardly ever, ran away from her mistress.

'All right, stay there, you beast, and wash your face,' she said to the cat, and crossed over the draggled winter grass towards the back door. Kathleen and the woman who did the washing . . . White was her name, Mrs White, were standing together at the sink washing up. She had the feeling that they'd been talking about her the moment before she entered.

'I don't know why you don't train that animal better, cook.'

Kathleen said, giving an effect of weary patience: 'What do you mean, train it? Who ever heard of training a cat?'

'Of course cats are trained. Trained to be clean, for one thing.'

'That's more than. . . .' Kathleen stopped, and turned back to the sink. 'Aren't you going to have your rest?' she said in a quieter voice.

'I'm going upstairs. I don't expect I shall rest. In any case if anyone telephones will you please let me know at once. Don't send them away, like you sometimes do.'

Kathleen made no reply, but presumably she had heard her instructions, and she decided to go on upstairs. With some idea that Kathleen's intention was that she should go right upstairs to her bedroom, there to be out of the way, she entered the dining-room. The fire had slack piled upon it, and she meditated going back to the kitchen and asking for some coal. But perhaps she had better not. That same instinct that had spoken before warned her that she had gone far enough. If she did ask her, she'd probably be told, 'I'll come when I've finished the washing-up'. For that was Kathleen's way. She never, never did things when you asked her to; she might do them, but only in her own time. 'And yet, I pay for her time, don't I?' she asked herself, and shook her head.

She found herself yawning, and was surprised. She really was sleepy. It must be because they had had some guest to dinner . . . she'd forgotten her name, but there had been someone. And there had been a good story about sandbags. Trying to remember the full details, she fell into a light half-slumber.

II

'A sleep will do her good,' said Mrs White when the sound of the footsteps had ceased.

Kathleen was still listening. 'She's gone into the dining-room,' she said. 'That's to spite me. Because she knows she's supposed to go upstairs and rest in the afternoon. The doctor told her she must rest more, do you see?'

Mrs White, whose legs were tired, sat down on a three-legged stool, and started to rub up the silver. Watching Kathleen dip the knives into a bowl of clean water after she had washed them, and thinking in one part of her mind how particular the woman was, she said: 'What beats me is why she's always on to me about my husband that was. That's what I can't understand.'

'It's the badness that's in her, that's why,' answered Kathleen decisively. 'She wants to talk about men, that's all. She wants to talk about her own husband, though she was never married to him, that's what I've heard, and that's what she admitted to me more than once. In a sort of way. Rambling on she was.'

Mrs White did not feel this to be a satisfactory explanation. 'But over and over again! I tell her that he's dead, and the next moment she's asking me again.'

'That's because her memory's gone altogether. Tell her a thing, and it's just water off a duck's back. Haven't you heard her yourself?'

'Yes,' said Mrs White doubtfully. It still seemed to her strange that the old lady, even if she were funny in the head, should, whenever she saw her, bring up the question of the late Mr White. Besides, she didn't altogether want an explanation. There was something that captured her imagination, something exotic, in this extreme curiosity. She liked to muse over it, as a botanist muses over a strange flower.

Sensing something of this, Kathleen, after dipping a vegetable-dish, made haste to prick the bubble: 'You don't realise the badness in her nature, old as she is. It's the men that she always wants to be talking about and thinking about. When she sees a woman, it's what her man is like that interests her. Any excuse to get talking on the one subject. Didn't you notice the artful way she pretended to be asleep, and then sat there drinking in every word of what you were talking about? And then she had to betray herself and join in, because her ears were falling out with delight just because it was something dirty.'

'So she wasn't asleep?'

'Of course not: often she does that, closes her eyes, and the next moment, when you think, well, at last she's off, and there'll be a bit of peace, down she comes on you as sharp as sharp. That's the kind of madness hers is, do you see? You'd be hard put to it, or someone who doesn't know, you see, like yourself, would be hard put to it, to distinguish between when the madness ends and the artfulness begins.'

Mrs White dried the vegetable-dish with a thoughtful air. Kathleen started again: 'Did you hear the barefaced way she boasted to you about cooking for a lover, a man she was living with, in a little flat unbeknownst to anyone? She doesn't mind who knows about her wickedness. Those are the two men she loses no chance of talking about, the one she had before she pretended she was married, and then the one she pretended she was married to, who ran off and left her for another woman.'

'She's had a very sad life then,' summed up Mrs White, drawing a different moral from the one that Kathleen had intended.

'All her own fault. What do you expect, and she carrying on with men that were married? Both of them were married, you know. And the badness of her mind continues to this very day, as you can see for yourself, when she's about eighty years of age. I'll tell you another thing that shows her up for what she is. When Harold came here on a week's leave . . . oh, I didn't tell you, did I? We've decided to get married.'

'No, you never told me. My word! So you're going to do it again?' said Mrs White, speaking as from one widow to another.

'I gave way, because I got no peace otherwise. "I can't go on the way we are," he said, all upset. You know what some men

are. "Why won't you marry me?" he said. So as there was no
reason against it really, and then you have to think of the
allowance I'd get, d'ye see, so . . . but what I was telling you
was about *her*.'

'Yes, doesn't she want you to get married?'

'As if I'd ask her permission! Oh, no, I'll stay on here, if it
suits me, till the end of the war. Unless she gets too much for
me altogether. I can be collecting a few things for my home,
too. But it was the way she seized, like the old harpy she is,
on Harold, that I was saying. He says he's afraid for his life of
her.'

'Why should he be afraid of an old woman like 'er?' queried
Mrs White a little tartly. 'She may talk funny so that you don't
understand what's she saying, but you can see she's educated.
And she don't act violent.'

'Oh, doesn't she?' said Kathleen. 'The way she pushes past
me at times and yells screaming at me is violent enough for
me, I can tell you. But it's the never leaving you alone, not
for one minute, that is worst of all. Harold said he didn't know
how ever I could stand it. "There's no one else would!" he
said. And that's true. I wouldn't, only the way it is I'm used to
mad people, and don't mind them.'

She laid a saucepan on the board, which Mrs White took
up and wiped. 'I'd be afraid,' she said after some cogitation,
'that she might be setting fire to the house.'

'She might, too,' said Kathleen calmly. 'I wouldn't put
anything past her.' She listened for a moment, and then said:
'She's keeping pretty quiet up there. I wonder if I'd better go
up and see what's in the air.'

She wiped her hands on the roller-towel, and went rapidly but quietly out of the kitchen. Mrs White, hanging up the saucepan, pondered on the conversation. She felt an obscure resentment against Kathleen, and decided that Kathleen was 'funny'. Perhaps because she was Irish, and everyone knew they were 'funny'. Look at the way she'd made so little about getting married to Harold, and had seemed to doubt her word about the butcher and his carryings-on. On the whole, she decided, she was sorry the poor old lady had someone like that. Yet, of course, it was true that she wouldn't find many that would put up with her.

Completely unaware of such criticism or its possibility, Kathleen came back, her eyes bright with interest. 'Wonders will never cease. She's asleep there by the fire. A thing I've not known the like of for days and days.'

Mrs White said nothing. She wished Kathleen would finish the other saucepan, and then she could get to her ironing.

'It's the good dinner she ate,' Kathleen decided after a moment's meditation. 'She ate more food today than she's done for a long time past. That was because you were here, and she got it into her head that you were some sort of a visitor, you see.'

'I thought she didn't remember who I was once or twice.'

'In the ordinary way it would make you sick, and spoil your appetite on you to see the way she does be playing about with what's on her plate, asking: "What's this?" and grumble, grumble, grumble, and scraping her fork around as if she were a two-year-old.'

'The poor old lady, it's really only a baby she is.'

53

'Worse,' said Kathleen taking up the saucepan and wiping it vigorously. 'Does any baby make as much mess as she does? Not if a child is properly trained from the beginning. Did you hear her say about a cat should be trained to be clean, and me nearly giving way to the temptation to ask, what about herself then? Well, you know yourself what it is. You saw the sheets and the bits of underwear. I did say to her, "Aren't you ashamed to expect anyone to wash after you?" I spoke to her another time, but she burst into tears and spent the whole evening crying and taking on, so I do try not to say much. But that's really the reason why her last secretary, you know the one, left.'

Mrs White, who had dried the last saucepan and sponged the draining-board, turned to wipe her hands on the towel. She considered her swollen knuckles with momentary attention as it occurred to her that she could hardly remember the time when her hands hadn't been employed in washing out clothes for someone. She had been the eldest of a straggling family, and had started off with helping with the babies' napkins. Then she had done laundry work; then there had been marriage and her own children, and her ailing husband. And now she went out or did washing at home for several families. All the degrees of dirt were familiar to her, all the consequences of mankind's physical frailties in sickness and in health. She had long known that for her it didn't do to be too particular; and known, too, that those who were particular were the ones that could afford to be. Like Kathleen! Kathleen could cook, and therefore she could give herself airs about what she wouldn't do. Now turning back towards her, she said: 'She's an old, old lady, and they can't always help it, you know.'

Kathleen emptied the basin of dirty water into the sink, and then replied: 'Can't help it! Don't tell me she can't help it. It's not as if she were ill, or taking medicine. She's strong as a horse, or else how could she be rushing up and down the house all hours of the day and of the night, the way she is. Do you know she'd rouse me from my sleep till I had to lock myself in? And the only way I can be sure of not having her pry and poke in my own bedroom is to have raised such blue murder when I found her in there that at her maddest she doesn't dare venture. Did you hear though the way she asked me if she might go in this morning when she was chasing after the cat?'

'Yes. She's desperately fond of the cat, poor thing. I suppose it's because it's the only thing she has to be fond of.'

'I wouldn't say she's fond of it. She forgets it for hours, and sometimes days. And then every minute she's on to it. It's just part of her contrariness . . . are you going to iron in the kitchen?'

'Yes, I could be starting on the handkerchiefs and serviettes.'

'I'll get the ironing-board out for you in a minute. Yes, it's the dirt she makes is the worst for the person that has to live with her. And they don't go with all the grand airs she gives herself.'

'She's proper old-fashioned in the way she talks about the lower-classes, isn't she?'

'Well, you see, she *is* a lady. A real lady,' Kathleen added

with emphasis, for this factor was a necessary part of the creation she had formed of her mistress. 'Her grandfather was someone very high up in the Protestant clergy, and her sister married a title. That makes it all the more terrible, the way she's bent on disgracing herself in every possible way. Didn't you hear her yourself admit that that same sister wouldn't speak to her because of her wickedness and disgracing the family?'

Mrs White nodded. Then she moved away and into the kitchen.

'I see you want to be on with your ironing.' Kathleen followed and set up the board. 'And I tell you what I'm going to do. I'm going to give my hair a wash and set, for it's not often that I can feel she's out of the way for a few minutes. I'm going up to the bathroom, because the water's nice and hot. And if she comes down here, tell her you don't know where I am, and don't encourage her to talk, or you'll never get rid of her.'

III

A door closing, though it closed gently enough, disturbed her from her light slumber, and she sat up, looking round her apprehensively. Where was she? She turned her head, and behind her was the tall window hung at each side with dark plum-coloured curtains; and in front was the sideboard that carried its familiar burdens. It would seem that she was safely in her own place, but one could never be sure. For while one slumbered the enemy could enter, and *they* might

– one couldn't be certain – have rigged up a room to look like one's own dining-room, but in reality one might have been transported miles away. The thing to do, as she was always reminding herself, was to look out of the window, to note if it were barred, to see if the outside scene were also familiar.

In a moment she was out of her chair, standing by the window and staring out with eyes that only gradually recognised the accustomed landmark. She was looking, certainly she was looking out on to a strip of back garden in which washing had been hung. It was a horrid garden, she decided, in the instant before she accepted it as her own; a garden that had been for so long uncherished that it wore an air of desolation, making it the fit and proper region for the furtive occupations of stray cats who prowl across dank grass and lurk among dusty evergreen bushes. A waste ground, but a respectable waste ground, as the cat is a domestic as well as a wild animal, for the stone house which looked down upon it, and the three walls and door which enclosed it on the other sides, ensured its respectability as a piece of private property.

The washing, too, was the sign and seal of its being private property. She peered at the sheets, and decided that they must be her own sheets. Then in all probability it was Monday, washing day, and that seemed to make it all secure enough. With triumph she remembered that they had a woman in to do the washing whose name was Mrs White. Quite a nice respectable sort of creature. She must go and see if she was still there. But the cook, who was so disagreeable, hated her to talk to Mrs White, so first of all she had better speak to her.

She hurried out of her room, and hastened to the head of the basement stairs: 'Cook!'

No one answered. She called again: 'Cook!'

There came the sound of an iron being clamped down in its metal holder. Then a voice said: 'She's not here, Madam.'

'Oh, where is she? I'm coming downstairs . . . you're Mrs White, aren't you?'

Mrs White took up her iron once more. 'Yes, Madam.'

'Where is Kathleen? It's not her afternoon off, is it?'

'No, but I don't know where she is. She's not down here.'

'What can she be doing? I'd better go and find her.'

'I believe she might be washing her hair. She said something about it.'

'Washing her hair? At this time of the day? What time is it, could you tell me?'

Mrs White looked round at the alarm clock. 'Ten-past three.'

'Ten-past three of Monday afternoon, washing day. That's what I thought. It's not Kathleen's afternoon off, so really it's rather impertinent to rush off and wash her hair. She ought to be helping you, oughtn't she?'

'It's all right. I can manage.'

'I'll go and find her and see what she is doing.'

Mrs White, remembering Kathleen's injunction, said: 'If there's anything you want perhaps I could get it for you.'

'I did want something. I forget. What was it? Oh, I know. I wanted to know if anyone is coming to dinner this evening?'

'I don't think so.'

'Well, then, I must ask someone. I can't bear to be left evening after evening all by myself. Could you bear it?'

'It is very lonely for you.'

'I know whom I can ask. *Faute de mieux*, I'll ask my dull and wooden secretary. She's better than no one. Now she's left me because she has a better job, and more money. I'll ask her to dinner, and then she can tell me all about it. Not that she makes anything that has happened to her very interesting, but still . . . as I can't remember things I can no longer choose whom I know. Will you please telephone her for me?'

Mrs White looked horrified. After a moment she said: 'I'm sorry, but I'm no good at the telephoning.'

'Aren't you? What a nuisance! I tell you; you can find the number in the book. Jessup is the woman's name, and she lives at some Bayswater address. Then I'll tell the Exchange. You don't mind, do you? You see I can't be bothered looking through all that small print. I forget what I'm looking for and then I can't remember the number when I take up the receiver. That is what makes telephoning so impossible, so that I'm entirely cut off, and have no one to speak to. Come along, will you?'

It was no good, thought Mrs White. Kathleen would have to deal with this. 'I expect Kathleen will know the number, Madam, if you ask her. My eyes are not very good.'

'Aren't they? Why don't you wear glasses? Never mind, come and help me. I don't want to ask cook, because she'd say there wasn't anything for dinner and make difficulties. I tell you what, if you keep saying Jessup to me, then when I've found the number in the telephone directory, I'll tell it to you,

and you keep saying it, so that I shall remember to tell Exchange. Isn't that a good idea? You see, though I've lost my memory I still retain plenty of common sense in an emergency. Come on. Leave those . . .'

'But . . .' started Mrs White feebly. It was no good. The force of energy impelling her was superior to her own feeble powers of resistance. After all the old lady was her employer, even if she wasn't quite right in the head. She went slowly out of the room and up the stairs, wondering how it was that old as she was Mrs Temple could run like a young girl. In the hall she remembered that Kathleen would probably hear them, and come down.

Kathleen did hear. She was just arranging her wet hair in a pompadour style like everyone was wearing to see if it would suit her, when she became aware that two people were in the hall. She stopped to listen, and heard her mistress's clear voice say impatiently: 'There's no need to bring Kathleen into it. She's my cook, not my secretary . . . now who is it we are going to speak to?'

'You said Mrs Jessup.'

'Of course. A, B, C, D, E, F, G, H, I, J . . . J, after I. I've got H . . . now, here's J. Ja . . . James. What a lot of people called James there are, aren't there? B, James, photographer, we don't want him, do we?'

'It's not on that page, Madam.'

'Isn't it? Oh, do you mind looking for me. When I see all those names of people living in the suburbs or keeping shop or working in the City, and all of them doing different things, I feel my brain going round and round. You look, will you?'

'How do you spell it?'

'Spell what?'

'This . . . Jessup, isn't it?'

'Jessup . . . Mrs Jessup. Of course, that's whom we are calling. To ask her to come to dinner.'

Oh, are you, thought Kathleen, tying a towel round her head in preparation for descent, while Mrs White mumbled: 'J e s, I suppose?'

'That's it. Jessup.'

'Here's Jessup. What's her other name?'

'Do you mean her initials? I don't know. She's the kind of woman one just calls Mrs Jessup. She's never *done* anything, you know. Her husband was an explorer, or something, but she's divorced him. She's quite a nobody herself. I never called her anything, really.'

'Do you know where she lives then?'

'Yes, of course I do. She lives somewhere near Whiteley's, the Universal Provider man. In a square. I went to tea with her there, and the cake was quite uneatable. There was another rather frowsty sort of woman there who . . .'

'There's a Jessup at Powys Sq, W2, and that has a Bayswater number. Mrs H Jessup, she is.'

'That's the one! How clever you are. Her husband was Henry Jessup. I could never quite make out why she divorced him. She's got a lover, I believe. What is the number? No, don't tell it me till I take the receiver up.'

As she did so, Kathleen, who had been waiting unperceived just behind the top of the stairs, came swiftly down. 'Who do you think you're ringing up?'

'Oh, it's cook, wearing a towel as a turban. Please don't interrupt . . . Yes, just a moment, Exchange. Now give me the number.'

'If it's Mrs Jessup, you can ring and ring and there'll be no answer, because she's at work.'

'*You* don't know. The number, Mrs White!'

But listening to the conversation Mrs White had lost the place. She murmured: 'Kathleen says she's out.'

'I can learn that for myself. Oh dear, let me look.' As she put the receiver down on the table, Kathleen picked it up and replaced it.

'What have you done that for? Now you've gone and lost the connection, you fool!'

'Fool yourself! Who do you think you're ringing up?'

'I am ringing up Mrs Jessup,' she answered with triumph. 'Have you got the number now, Mrs White?'

'It's Bayswater 4760,' said Mrs White in a low voice. She put down the telephone book with some determination, and moved down the passageway leading to the kitchen. She felt she had done her duty towards both parties. Behind her she heard a clear voice demanding: 'Exchange, are you there? Please give me Bayswater 4760.'

Kathleen judged it time to act. Mrs Jessup was likely to be out, but suppose her daughter or someone answered the telephone, and said they'd give the message. Then Mrs Jessup, who was kind-hearted, and, Kathleen's mind added the rider, knew that she would probably get quite a good meal for wartime, might conceivably turn up. And she, Kathleen, had other arrangements for that evening.

'Mrs Jessup asked me specially to tell you that she wasn't to be rung up,' she said, and with a quick movement snatched the receiver from her mistress and hung it up. 'I'm not going to have you make a fool of yourself, see?'

'You devil, how dare you! Will you please go back to your work and leave me alone.'

'I certainly will,' said Kathleen. She started to ascend the staircase slowly. Suppose her mistress did remember the number again?

But she didn't. She sought for it, and all sorts of numbers chased each other around her mind, but she couldn't be sure which was THE number. It was Mrs White who had found her it before. 'I'm going to ask Mrs White,' she muttered.

Kathleen heard and turned: 'Don't think you can worry Mrs White any more; she's just going home, and she won't stand for being taken from her work. Besides it's all nonsense. You don't know who you're calling; and you don't know the number. You're only making a fool of yourself, and anyone would think you were mad.'

'How dare you speak to me like that! You're dismissed. Leave the house instantly.'

Kathleen descended a step, and stood looking at her steadily, making a pool of silence in which the words said were given time to be realised at their full import. Then she said softly: 'Would you mind saying that again? I just want to be sure I heard what you said.'

The gaze she held wavered before hers, and the eyes looked into a darkness when there would be no one to call, no one to get her breakfast, no one to lie in the same house with her at

night. She would be quite alone, and then, she knew, madness would indeed come and greet her for its own. She would be impelled to lose all dignity and run crying into the street, asking passers-by for help. And then an ambulance, or a police car, or a black van. . . .

'I said that you had no right to come and interrupt when I am telephoning. What right have you? I can surely still ring up people if I want to.'

'I just wanted to stop you being disappointed since the lady in question wasn't at home,' said Kathleen airily. 'I was trying to do you a kindness, and that's all. But it's small thanks I get, God knows.' She went on up the stairs, slipping the towel off from her dark hair as she went.

Utterly confused now, the old woman in the hall stared after her. It might have been that she *was* going to make a fool of herself, and that Kathleen *had* done her a kindness in stopping her. On the other hand her intuition sensed that in some way she was being cheated, that the lower order had assumed the reins. 'I'm going out; I'm going to see into all this,' she shouted after Kathleen, who merely slammed the bathroom door in reply, and with trembling hands and muttering to herself, she pulled on the old black coat that hung on a peg at the back of the hall.

IV

The afternoon was grey and dull, a sky hiding under its neutral grey all its knowledge of sunlight and depth of wild scurrying clouds and white clouds that drifted across the blue

as peacefully as a dream; a sky content to be a lid across the world. Like an angry child who has sobbed itself into a condition when it no longer knows the cause of its grief, but only that grief, and resentment at that grief, were part of its being, the old woman padded rather than walked down the hill which led to Kensington High Street. She padded because she still wore her bedroom slippers of thick black felt.

People turned to glance at her with the expectation of amusement that is aroused by any manifestation of eccentricity in the modern world, but their amusement was halted on its way. She was not, it became plain, what they had first thought her, a crazy old beggar woman. She walked even in the slippers with too much determination, even arrogance, and the bare head with its fine white hair knotted behind was held too high. And they went on their way more uneasy than amused, for the truth they were glimpsing, whether they knew it or not, was that here was a woman who, unlike those who have not been gently nurtured, had no defences. Those whose lives have been an exercise in the pitting of their wits, or the selling of their talents, time and strength, to those who pay the piper, can, even in their old age, even with their wits partially gone, automatically practise defences, and appeals for aid. But not so those who have never asked, who have never bargained.

Unnoticing of the stares she received, she went on till the energy of resentment which had driven her from home had been partly dissipated. As one that has received her sight, she saw, suddenly, the red London buses below her; and, approaching nearer, the plate-glass windows of the big stores. In the next moment she felt there was something she should be carrying. Yes, her bag! She had come without her bag containing her purse; they generally left a half-crown in her purse divided into sixpences and coppers, but this afternoon, because she had come out in such a hurry without telling Kathleen that she must have some money, she had nothing. Nothing at all.

She edged across the High Street, avoiding the traffic by intuition and luck rather than by observation, and came to a stop before Barker's grocery window. What she had really wanted to buy, she thought with sudden eager desire, was a bottle of whisky. They hardly ever had anything to drink in the house now, and they pretended it was because she was too poor to afford wine or whisky. But whether it was the truth, or whether it was just that behind all the supervision there laboured a cruel malice, she could not tell, and her head was now too confused to start trying to solve that eternal problem.

Certainly they had managed to deprive her of all the delights of shopping, so that she hardly ever went into a shop unless she went out with her secretary or Kathleen, when they went to buy food in the mornings. They said, too, it was something to do with the war, and there was a whole business when you asked for something of saying: 'But you're not registered here', or 'Have you the points?' It sounded a most frightful tyranny, but everyone took it for granted. And a dull tyranny. A tyranny that just said 'No', so that you didn't do it the courtesy of trying to understand what it was all about.

But other people walked into the shops, pushed through the revolving doors. If she had even a very little money she

would go too. Perhaps it was true that she was terribly poor. If she were, it was because of all the money she had spent on *his* children. Really he ought to pay it back to her. So that she could buy just a bottle or two of whisky.

Impatiently she turned quickly away from the contemplation of the window, colliding with a middle-aged man. He turned and raised his hat: 'I do beg your pardon.'

'Please don't apologise. It was my fault.'

He answered her smile with another bow before going on. She turned to glance after him, thinking that there were so few gentlemen now left in the world that one looked at them as intrigued as a child by the spectacle of the giraffe in the zoo. The incident flattering to and fluttering her still lively femininity renewed in her a more lively consciousness of herself and her surroundings. She put her hand to her head, and was disturbed by the realisation that she was hatless. 'I look a sight,' she thought, catching a half-glimpse of herself, and decided that she would go home, and perhaps come out again when she had got some money from Kathleen and powdered her face. Supposing she met someone she knew, they would report that Claire Temple was straying about looking quite a spectacle these days.

As she went up the hill, walking more slowly now, she looked about her, watchful of faces. But all the faces she saw were strange; there were two girls in blue uniform, and, really, she decided, though perhaps the lower classes were improved by having to don something that made them look neat and orderly, she didn't approve of uniform for women, for it robbed them of all individuality. Those two girls now, she'd never

recognise them if she met them the next minute. But why was there no one about whose face was familiar? The big block of flats towards which she was advancing provided her with some answer. Strangers and interlopers everywhere; those flats, for example, had only been put up within the last few months or few years. Ah, now, she was coming to a house whose inmates she had known. The big singer man, what was his name? He had given parties and she had been invited. Then there had been some scene and they said that when he was drunk he had fallen down the stairs and hurt himself badly. Anyhow, years and years ago he had disappeared, a too gay bird for the grey plumage of Kensington. Yet gay birds had alighted in Kensington: despair and grief and laughter and noise had yet run like an underground stream from house to house, so that those who heard the scandals like herself, one whose own tears and defiances had watered the stream, could never walk up its hills and along its terraces without pointing a reminiscent finger. It was here that that fair woman had poisoned herself; her husband was unfaithful; it was there that the Douglases had tried to entertain, but they had no money to speak of really; the debts they left behind when they flitted; tradesmen ringing the bell; she herself had told one man: 'They have gone; it's no use your ringing.' 'Do you know their address, Madam?' 'No, I don't.' And, adding to herself the rider: 'And if I did, I shouldn't tell you. It's not one's business to act as common informer.'

And one night just as they had turned this corner, they had heard a woman's scream. It had come from that house. They had stopped, and then he had gone on at a slightly faster pace.

'Oughtn't we to do something?' 'Why, what?' 'We might be able to help that poor woman.' He had replied: 'Let it alone. Let it be for us just the sound of a woman screaming in the night.' His was the mind that moved slowly and nourished quietly, while she had always rushed to do, and to know. A misalliance.

She shook her head and threw all the thoughts and memories they had roused in her back at the closed gates, for they were fatiguing and depressing. Passionate Kensington, as that clever woman had called her book, had turned for her into dusty Kensington, into decayed Kensington. There was a song that a male impersonator used to sing: 'They are turning Park Lane into flats.' Now it also applied to Kensington, and if she looked into the gutter she would find pieces of orange-peel and bits of dirty paper.

She descended from the pavement to look in the gutter, but could find no orange-peel or paper. In fact, it was all surprisingly clean. Raising her eyes she encountered a familiar face approaching, and she sought for the name: 'Good afternoon!' 'Good afternoon, Madam.' *Madam*, that gave her the key.

'It's Mrs White, isn't it? Have you been working for me?'

'Yes, I'm just going home now.'

'You saw me looking in the gutter, didn't you? You must have thought it strange, but I was so surprised at finding it so clean. No orange-peel, none of that ugly dustbin clutter which man, proud man, dressed in his brief authority, leaves behind him everywhere he goes.'

After a moment's thought, Mrs White explained: 'It's the

war, you see, paper being so scarce, and oranges. We are not even supposed to throw away our bus tickets any more.'

'Really? How extraordinary! Must you go? Oh, of course, you said you were going home. Have you been paid?'

'Yes, Madam. Kathleen saw to it.'

'Kathleen? Oh, the cook. It's hardly her business. But I suppose it's a good thing, because I've come out without my bag.'

'It's quite all right. Good afternoon, Madam.'

'Did they give you some tea?'

'I'll get that when I get home. I have mine with the children.'

'How nice. I have no one to have tea with at all. And very soon I suppose your husband will be back from work. What shall you give him? To eat, I mean. A kipper or something?'

The troubled kindness with which Mrs White had regarded the old lady disappeared, and her face closed up. She said stiffly: 'I must go now. Good afternoon.'

She stared after the retreating woman. Why had she broken off a pleasant casual conversation, as between employer and worthy employee, so abruptly? It wasn't as if she had said anything she shouldn't, was it? What had she said? She had merely asked after her husband. What could be wrong in that?

She paused before her own gate, and after closing it behind her felt for her bag. Oh dear, had she come out without it? Now if cook had gone out, there would be no one to let her in.

She rang the bell and knocked loudly. To her relief it was answered almost immediately. 'A dreadful thing has happened, cook. I was so afraid you wouldn't be in. I've either lost my bag or else I went out without it.'

'You left it behind you. It's on the table.'

'Oh, thank you so much.'

It was evident to Kathleen that the walk had done her good. Her mistress had gone out like a roaring wolf and returned, as sometimes happened, a lamb. Well, for her own part, she was ready to return mildness with mildness. She had had the afternoon to herself, her hair had set beautifully, and she was looking forward to this evening.

'But it *was* tiresome. I was quite unable to do my shopping.'

'What matter? There was nothing you wanted to buy, was there?'

'Oh, yes, there was. I wanted to buy some wine. And a few bottles of whisky. There's an extreme lack of spirituous comfort in this house: anyone would think we were Dissenting tee-totallers.'

'Miss Phillips said you can't afford it. I'll poke up the fire for you. Now there's a nice blaze. I'll bring up your tea for you in one moment. Oh, and there's the cat to keep you company.'

It was true. Lisa advanced, sociably purring. She consented to rest on her mistress's lap, and went on purring as her golden fur was stroked. When Kathleen brought up the tea-tray, they were sitting peacefully together, and she also heard a gracious: 'Thank you very much, cook. That is most kind of you.'

But when she came up half an hour or so later the scene was less decorous. Her mistress had filled a saucer of milk for Lisa, and one way or another a lot had got spilt on the carpet.

Also a piece of half-eaten buttered toast was lying on the coal-scuttle, and too hastily poured tea had made a big stain on the newly ironed white tray-cloth.

Kathleen noticed all these things with a shrug. She made merely a mild expostulation: 'What a mess you've made with that milk . . . it's a pity you didn't eat much of your toast, for that was real butter on it.'

'What do you mean *real* butter? Butter is as real as anything else, I suppose. As a matter of fact, I put it down looking after Lisa, and then I couldn't find it again. And now it's all dirty.'

'If you put good food down by the fire there, it will be dirty.'

'Never mind. There was something I was going to ask you. Is anyone coming to dine here tonight?'

'No, no one at all,' said Kathleen cheerfully. She added: 'You had your dinner in the middle of the day, if you remember. With Mrs White and me. So I just thought of doing you sardines on toast, apple and custard, and coffee for your supper. Will that be all right?'

Waiting for the answer, Kathleen took a peep at her new coiffure in the overmantel, and felt pleased with what she saw.

'I suppose it's enough if that's all we've got, cook?'

'It is all we've got,' Kathleen nodded, and took herself and the tray off humming 'The Rose of Tralee'.

Left alone, Mrs Temple said to the fire: 'My cook goes about singing and staring at herself in the looking-glass over my head.' She was silent a moment pondering her own words.

They seemed to carry some purport which she had not intended. Stroking the cat, she added softly: 'It looks as if she is in love, or expecting a beau.'

But was that altogether seemly? Should one's cook entertain a young man? Because she would be certainly entertaining him at *her* expense. And yet she had announced that there was only a sardine for *her* evening meal. Why? Because of course she was cooking for him, and so her mistress was supposed to be such a fool that she could do without.

But she wasn't such a fool. She started to listen. For the next half-hour she was up and down from the door, opening it and shutting it, but noiselessly. Each time she was disappointed, for she heard no sound of a man's voice or arrival, but only Kathleen washing up, and when she had finished washing up apparently moving a chair. Then she heard her singing. She was quite sure that Kathleen was expecting someone. It would be that soldier, who had been before, and whom Kathleen had introduced as 'my fiancé'. The lower classes used such unsuitable words these days. Why not 'intended'? She forgot for five minutes her vigil, and, afraid when she remembered that something had happened in her absence of mind, went right to the head of the basement stairs to listen. Her ears were rewarded by the sound of Kathleen drawing the curtains. Down there in the kitchen, she thought, returning cautiously to her own chair, it was snug, warmed by life and expectancy. But in this room, in this dining-room which was moving into semi-darkness, there was no such warmth of expectancy. If only someone, it didn't matter who, was coming to dinner. . . .

Unable any longer to sit still, she rose clutching the cat in her arms, and still noiselessly, for though she had forgotten the reason, she felt there was some necessity for Kathleen not hearing her, she left the room and went tiptoe up the stairs, and into the study. There she stood by the window, watching the opposite pavement, bending forward when anybody came into sight, and watching them intently till they disappeared. If only someone would cross the street, would come through her gate, and mounting the steps, ring *her* bell!

'I am like Tennyson's Mariana of the moated grange,' she thought, turning away with a shiver: *'"He cometh not," she said; "I am aweary, aweary. I would that I were dead!"'* And she wished she were dead, too, but *pour être mort il faut mourir*.

She moved into the back room, and there it seemed so much darker and so, so much more deserted that she was seized by a macabre fancy. Since this room was never used these days – it had been *his* study – was it not more than probable that its emptiness contained an invitation to spooks? Spooks was a childish word, of course; earth-bound spirits was what that woman who had been the fashion years ago, and might, for all she knew, still be the fashion, would call them. Or theologians would no doubt dub them the *damned*. Anyhow *damned* was the older word, the word which found its response in our secret recognition of the dark and evil places of life. She clutched Lisa so closely that, the next moment, the cat wriggled in her arms. 'You don't want to stop here, do you, Lisa? All right,' and she let the cat down on the floor, and saw it prowl through the door.

Immediately, she went after it, and took it up into her arms again. Lisa, she thought, had probably seen something in the back room. Perhaps damned children who had wanted to pull her tail. That was an idea: damned children! Henry James had never said what happened to the little girl in *The Turn of the Screw*: perhaps she, or her like, had wandered into the room she had just left, and taken up her abode . . . .

She stood by the study window once again, but now she was not staring into the street. The impulse had flickered up: write a story about a woman left alone in a house to which the damned came. At first they entered timidly. She saw them at the back door, peeping as she went to take up the bottle of milk which the milkman had left. But they scampered away so quickly – children, a little boy and a little girl, lovely, but the horror of damned souls looking out of their eyes – that she couldn't be quite certain she had seen them. Gradually, they would become bolder; gradually they would fetch other playmates, and start their childish tricks. As she raised the brush to her hair, it would be snatched from her; when she went to bed they hid her nightgown . . . the next night they were in her bed, and there was no room for her. In the end there was no room in her house at all for her; the damned children had taken complete possession. Perhaps she would have to find her place at the last in the hell of the grown-ups. . . .

She started with fright, for she heard steps coming up the stairs. Now who was that? It couldn't be spirits. They wouldn't be so bold. They had paused, and she heard the sound of the curtain being drawn across the landing window. Of course, it was one of the servants. She went to the door, and peered, then called: 'Who's that?'

'Oh, there you are! What are you doing up here in the dark? Why don't you go back to the fire?'

'I wanted to be up here.'

'Please yourself. But if you stay up here, I shall have to do the black-out for you.'

'No, don't draw the curtains.'

Kathleen switched on the light before replying: 'I'd better draw them, because you always forget and turn on the light and leave it. Don't you remember the last time, and the air-raid warden coming?'

'But I don't want the curtains drawn; there's a lovely dark blue colour that came suddenly when you turned on the light.'

'I'm sorry, but it's not what you want these days, but what the government says,' replied Kathleen. She drew one curtain with a firm hand, while her words aroused a misgiving, the shadow of a fear that had to be voiced:

'Why, I'm not ruled by the government. I'm in my own home, aren't I?'

Kathleen drew the other curtain before she replied: 'Of course you're in your own home. But your home's not your castle these days.'

'Why isn't it?'

Kathleen didn't reply. She was occupied in seeing that the curtains overlapped. Satisfied, she turned away, and went through the door, proceeding upstairs:

'Where are you going?'

'I'm going to do the black-out in your bedroom.'

As she descended again, she saw her mistress still standing by the door, and remarked: 'I'd come down to the warm if I were you. I shall be bringing your supper in presently.'

'I'm coming down with you. I would like to have my supper with you, please.'

Kathleen sighed internally. On some evenings she didn't mind, but it wouldn't do tonight with Harold coming in about ten minutes' time. Assuming a shocked and respectful tone which she found useful on occasion, she said: 'Oh, no, you couldn't possibly do that, Madam. I'll bring a nice tray to you in the dining-room.'

'If I'm to be left quite alone, I must have Lisa. Where has she gone? I am sure she was in my arms a minute ago.'

'She'll be down in front of your fire, you see if she isn't.'

Hurrying downstairs after Kathleen, she found with relief that the cat was there. But she surveyed the quiet room with dissatisfaction, and left it almost immediately to go down into the basement.

'Cook, your kitchen is so much cosier than the dining-room. I won't be in your way if I sit here, will I? Just for a minute or two?'

Kathleen decided that the situation called for her last remedy: 'If you go upstairs and sit quiet by the fire, I'm going to bring you up something special,' she said.

'What?'

'You were wanting whisky this afternoon, weren't you? Well, I've got a little put away, and I'll bring you a glass.'

'Oh, how nice! I do love whisky.'

'But you must go upstairs, for when I've brought it, I have to get on with my cooking.'

'I quite understand that cooks mustn't be interfered with when they are cooking. Do be quick, won't you?'

Back in the dining-room, she told Lisa with satisfaction the news. 'Nobody is coming to dine, but you and I are going to have an *apéritif*.' She held up a finger. 'She's bringing it now.'

It was a good half-glass of whisky that Kathleen brought, and whisky that for once was undiluted. Kathleen said mildly: 'I'd put some water to it if I were you,' but went off without seeing that she did so.

She raised the glass to her lips and savoured the contents with deep satisfaction. It was really extraordinary the effect that spirits had of calming one's fears expressed and those not to be expressed, of shaping the world into a ball that could be manipulated without much difficulty. George Moore, she mused, had said something profound in one of his earlier books – *The Mummer's Wife*, she was nearly sure it was – when he made one of his characters observe that whisky and gin had saved more people from throwing themselves into the river than had driven them to the river. He was talking, of course, of the London of their youth, that gas-lit London with its twopenn'orth of gins, the fog and the down-and-outs that huddled together on the Embankment, and to whom, poor wretches, the murky waters of the Thames were a temptation. But then there were a few coppers to be obtained from holding a horse's head . . . now what did they do for their coppers? And gin, and whisky, cost so much more. Oblivion or

courage could no longer be purchased for the price of an old song.

V

Kathleen was delayed with the supper-tray by the arrival of Harold. When she came in her mistress said to her: 'I've been thinking of George Moore and one of the things he wrote. Of course his last books were atrocities, but I don't think he altogether merited the scathing criticism of my old friend, Henry James, who said, do you remember: "I found him consecutively, consistently, and unimportantly foolish." Delightful, isn't it?'

'Yes, Madam. I see you've drunk all your whisky.'

'So I have. You might bring the bottle up. There's no need to decant it, as I'm not having anyone to dine.'

'There's hardly any more.'

'Well, bring what there is, please.'

Kathleen said nothing, but went out of the room. When her mistress got into this mood, which she called her grandee mood, the easiest temporary way was to ignore her, to rely on her forgetfulness. But soon, she felt, sterner methods might be required.

They were. In five minutes she heard a voice from the head of the stairs: 'Cook, have you forgotten my whisky?'

'Oh, give the old cow her whisky and keep her quiet,' murmured Harold.

'Cook, is there somebody down there with you?'

'I'm coming up in one minute, Madam,' called Kathleen

with angry impatience, and with relief she heard the footsteps going back to the dining-room.

A few minutes later, the very spirit of incarnate determination, she entered the room carrying another half-glass of whisky: 'Now, Madam, this is the last time I am to be disturbed. Are you aware that this is my evening off?'

'No, I wasn't aware of it. Do you mean that I have to wait on myself?'

'You've had all the waiting on you want. You've eaten your supper, haven't you? Don't you want any apple?'

'Yes, I think I would like a little.'

'Well then I'll leave it, and I'll clear the rest.'

'What about coffee?'

'You said you didn't want coffee. Now I've brought you this whisky . . .' Like a conjuror, Kathleen produced the tumbler from the sideboard where she had concealed it. 'But I don't know that I should let you have it.'

'Don't be silly, cook. I'm not a child.'

'It's against the doctor's orders that you should have it. That's what Miss Phillips told me.'

'I can deal with Miss Phillips, cook. It's not your responsibility.'

'Now do you remember what I just told you?'

'What?'

'That it's my evening off. And I'm not to be disturbed. It'll be no good your coming shouting after me. . . .'

'I know quite well it's your evening off. Presumably I told you you could have it?'

'Yes, you did.'

'You're entertaining someone, aren't you?'

'My fiancé is visiting me.'

'Really, how very nice for you. Do I know him?'

'Yes, you have met him. And the once is enough. It's my kitchen, and I want a little bit of peace at the end of the day.'

She had to make an effort to say the words, for Kathleen's behaviour was really almost threatening. But such an assertion could hardly be passed.

'Excuse me, cook, you are rather inaccurate. It is after all *my* kitchen. I pay you to work there. I'm very glad to have you, but . . .'

'If you're glad to have me, you'll let me alone this evening. Otherwise I shall just walk straight out of the house, and leave you alone. Understand?'

'I don't quite . . . really I do wonder why cooks are so hot-tempered. Is it the pepper and spices that get into their blood?'

'Never mind what it is,' said Kathleen, piling dishes on the tray with a ruthless hand. 'Maybe they have plenty of reason to be hot-tempered.' She raised the tray, and went to the door. There she turned to say: 'And don't be pulling the curtains back, or anything. Even if it's a back room some neighbour might see, and be after informing the police. And you know yourself that you've been warned twice. The next time they'll put you in prison. Do you hear that?'

'I'm not deaf, cook. You are behaving exactly like a prison wardress yourself.'

'All right. Then that's the way I'm behaving,' said Kathleen.

Balancing the tray on her hip, she pulled the door to behind her.

Kathleen's crustiness had banished her pleasant mood of literary reminiscence. Momentarily overlooking the tumbler in front of her, she sat thinking. Of course the whole point of cook's fiery and unsuitable behaviour was that she wanted to be left alone with her lover. All right. She was no spoilsport, no stern moralist. At the same time, and considering that she paid cook to be a cook and not to spend her evening committing fornication or adultery, for most probably her soldier swain was a married man, it was most decidedly a breach of manners. She must tell her that this evening must be an isolated occasion of sin. Then if she were impertinent, she would speak to Phil. She would put it lightly: 'Cook is sinning so much that I only get sardines for supper . . . it has quite spoilt her soufflés.' After all, the sins of the lower classes could never attain to romance. There had never been a single romance in history which concerned people who had been humbly born. Antony and Cleopatra, Tristan and Iseult, Héloïse and Abélard, Dante and Beatrice, the Brownings . . . well, there *was* something middle-class about the Brownings. But it was hardly a romance since it ended in a happy marriage. Romances, like causes, had to be lost or they were misnamed . . . Kathleen, of course, was Irish, and would pretend that she wasn't sinning. Parnell and Kitty O'Shea were the only great pair of Irish lovers, and Parnell was of quite good family. Oscar, of course, had been Irish. . . .

She saw the glass in front of her, and raised it eagerly to her lips. 'Poor Oscar,' she murmured, as she set it down a second time, and now thinking of Oscar she felt an impulse to weep. But the moisture that came was not unpleasant; she was indeed, her feelings numbed by alcohol, in the position of an acquaintance of the family who attends a funeral, and feels less moved by the poignancy of an individual loss than overtaken by that autumnal mood of sadness which is the scent of *memento mori*.

And: 'Poor Oscar,' she murmured again, for of all the men and women she had known in her long life, this tragedy was the one which had most touched her imagination. Had not Oscar, or so she believed, once, long, long ago, asked her father if he might propose to little Claire? He was therefore the first man in her life. And if he had asked *her*, and if she had said 'Yes' – which was very unlikely, for she had been too young then to think of marriage with any sort of desire – would she not have made him a far better wife than the woman he did marry? His wife was too cold, too stern, too intolerant. Perhaps the tragedy would never have happened if she had married him.

And then even if it had, she would have waited for him when he came out of prison. Or would she? Her mind hesitated and recalled with real pain a stain that her conscience had also borne for many many years. Once again it retraced that episode at Boulogne, as we are impelled to turn mechanically down a street which holds part of the story of our lives, or so that we may pass by a house we have never forgotten that someone has told us was haunted.

He came down the hill, looking so well, so rubicund, more like a country squire than an aesthete. And the way his face lit up when he saw me . . . oh, I would have gone on and met him with outstretched hand, but for that woman, the wife of the American dentist, holding me back: 'You mustn't bow to him. Come away at once.' And I went, but not before I saw his poor face with the light gone out of it like a blind drawn down. I shall never forget it.

No, she had never forgotten her own betrayal, and she turned her glass uneasily, till she saw it still contained some whisky. She drank, and when she looked up the room seemed to have grown dim about her. Where was . . . where was the cat? She peered round disturbed and saw it lying on her arm-chair, and a little unsteadily she pushed her chair back and sat down in the easy-chair with it in her arms, looking unseeingly into the low-burning fire.

After a while, she roused herself to listen. She thought she had heard a man's voice laughing. Of course it was the vile-tempered cook entertaining her lover in the kitchen. Mistress Doll Tear-sheet sort of scene. Her mind, charged now by a subconscious draught of jealousy, aroused itself to seek an answer to the old, old question: why had she been so un-successful in love? It had been her fate to be attracted by intellect and personality, but not the strong silent personality, if such existed. Kitchener perhaps? More than anything she had wanted conversation; what was it she had written? – that love was a crystallisation or localisation of the gregarious instinct: 'When Wallace left me I was lonely, but I got over McFarlane because our *affaire* was a compound of passion and domesticity.' Yes, Edith was right in telling her that she was not a sensual woman; you had to sit still, you had to know how to wait to be sensual, and she had never been able to do either.

No, she had wanted to talk, to be amusing, to dance and to flirt most of all. And now she saw again in her imagination the polished dance-floor, the raised orchestra behind the tubs of flowers or palms, the tuning-up, everything thin at first, so that one must always remember to arrive rather late, when the pulse was beginning to beat strongly: and then, when it was all gay, the violin suddenly becoming plaintive, and thereby somehow – that was its secret – turning mere gaiety to joy, ecstatic music. And that was the moment when one looked more closely into one's partner's eyes. And then the popping of corks . . . though one never needed champagne in those days, for one was drunk without it. It was just the luxury that must always be there if one had completeness . . . come to think of it, the century had died to the sound of a valse.

Her mind stirred: no, somebody had said something better than that: it had been said at her own table, and they had all applauded. *The Victorian age had been scattered by motor-cars.* For herself she hadn't really noticed its dispersal because the motor-cars had still taken her out to dine and sup, and had brought people to her house. When was it she had started living . . . wait a moment, there was a correct phrase for it . . . in reduced circumstances? For years she had been living in reduced circumstances, ever since Wallace had gone, for it was then she felt loneliness. And the more lonely she was the fewer people came and went. *From him that hath not, shall be taken away even that which he hath.* How cruel the Bible was! she thought suddenly, sitting up in a rush of indignation. The most cruel book that had ever been written!

Her movement disturbed the cat, who jumped off her lap, and went to the door, where she stood mewing to be let out.

Even the cat didn't want to be with her. It was with some difficulty that she roused herself from her chair to cross the room. 'Go on out then, Lisa, if you want to.'

Yawning, she decided that she would go downstairs and see what cook was doing. If she was in a good temper she might allow her to stop with her a few minutes. She would say, for she always had to have some excuse for going: 'Lisa wants to be down here with you, cook. She prefers your company.'

But the door at the head of the stairs was closed. When she opened it, she heard a man's voice, and then Kathleen's laugh, and it all came back to her. Of course cook was entertaining her young man, and had strictly forbidden her to enter her own kitchen. She went back to the dining-room, and stumbled over a chair as she groped her way back to the fire. There she sat crying softly, for her brain had dulled, and she was only conscious of the cruelty of it all: people were having a party, and she was not allowed to go.

At last a phrase she had repeated before found its way back to its groove in her mind. She was in such reduced circumstances that she was shut up in her own dining-room to suit the convenience of her cook. How had it come about? How had it come about that she was in such reduced circumstances? When had all the parties to which she was asked stopped? She couldn't remember, so it must have been gradual, as gradual as the turn of the tide. For some waves always outran the others, so you had the delusion that the sea was coming in still . . . but there had been the point . . . if she could only

remember when it had turned for good and for ever and for ever, and left her on a desolate beach, on a waste place, on the deserted shingles.

The word struck a last spark, recalling a line of poetry: *Retreating, to the edge of the night-wind, down the vast edges drear and naked shingles of the world.*

Whoever had written that had understood something of the horror of the aftermath of life. Matthew Arnold! That was the man. Poor Matthew Arnold, who had run away from his Marguerite pretending that it was 'God's tremendous voice, that had boomed: "Be counselled and retire."' She had never run away; she had always run forward, but whether you ran or whether you didn't run or, as he did, ran away, it was the same in the end . . . cold, naked shingles.

She stirred the fire with the poker, and then let it drop with a clatter which she didn't hear. For she was suddenly overwhelmingly tired, and her head dropped. The whisky had at last, after exciting her mind, brought it a temporary repose. She slept, but in her sleep she sobbed.

When nearly an hour later Kathleen opened the door, her eyes bright from Harold's farewell embrace, she saw, as she had expected to see, a sleeping woman. But she awoke as soon as Kathleen approached:

'Who are you? Oh, it's the cook, isn't it?'

'Yes, it's the cook,' said Kathleen good-temperedly. 'I've just come to see you off to bed.'

'What time is it?'

'It's past midnight,' said Kathleen mendaciously, for if she said a late hour it would be easier to get her upstairs.

'Come on now, and I'll give you a hand. I've put your hot-water-bottle in the bed, and you'll be lovely and warm.'

The old woman came quietly enough with her, murmuring something about never being warm again, because she had got to the naked shingles of the world, which, of course, she didn't pay heed to.

But she did pay heed when, guiding her into her bedroom, she heard her say: 'Well, I hope, cook, you have enjoyed your hours of dalliance.'

'I beg your pardon!'

'The embraces of love you have exchanged with your young man.'

'You're only showing up the badness of your own mind,' said Kathleen. 'Come on now; stand still, while I undo your dress for you.'

'I hope you didn't surrender the final citadel. Because, you know, I expect he's married.'

'That'll do,' said Kathleen. 'I'm not listening to that sort of talk. Here's your nightgown now. Put it on over your head.'

She got her into bed and turned out the light with a decisive hand. Going downstairs she decided that with the wickedness of her mind it was no wonder the queer one had got the way she had got.

PART TWO
OUTSIDE THE HOUSE

CHAPTER THREE

Having bestowed her ticket inside the receptacle provided, Edith Barlow alighted from a 27 bus and started to walk very slowly up the hill. She went slowly not only for the reason that the long journey by bus had tired her: she was not looking forward to her fortnightly Sunday luncheon with her old friend, Claire Temple. Her *oldest* friend, that indeed was what continued to keep her faithful to a tryst which had now become merely a trial to flesh and spirit. 'Poor Claire,' she murmured to herself, her thoughts going forward to the ordeal ahead, but her heart did not stir in pity with the thought, and in exculpatory realisation of this, she added: 'to think of her becoming such a bore, and such a dreary lachrymose bore!'

Edith Barlow was two years older than her friend: she was in fact approaching her eightieth birthday, and she was aware that she had withstood the long, slow, but remorseless pressure of the years with a respectable fortitude. As a writer she was still held in esteem: her satirical study of the women in Shelley's life which had appeared in the year before the war had been noticed appreciatively by the few critics and papers that still mattered. Mr Desmond MacCarthy had devoted the

whole of his column in *The Sunday Times* to a favourable review which maybe was as much concerned with Shelley as with the book, but no matter. It was true she had made little money during a lifetime waged in the service of literature as biographer and short story writer; and six years ago she had accepted the Civil List pension without the least reluctance, knowing that in her case, the case of a talented, sincere and non-prolific writer, the labourer was well worthy of his hire. That in fact her worth exceeded the modest sum of a farm labourer's pre-war wage that was now hers. The war had finally put *finis* to her literary work: the added strain with the care of an invalid sister was too much even for her stoical will. But she didn't complain, she got along and she got about; she could see and hear; her intelligence still functioned admirably. As for her appearance, that, she knew, was, in the main, an improvement on the plain, gawky and sallow girl she had once been. Then no one took any notice of her; now people looked at her respectfully, registering something like 'an English gentlewoman of the old school'. Men were gallant to her; she had just been helped most respectfully off the bus by the conductor; then they had never taken any notice of her; and it had been her own instinct to shun their attention. 'Edith Barlow is a virgin born, but, of course, it all comes out in the wash,' Claire Temple had said, referring thus coarsely to her friend's partiality to writing tenderly about the famous strumpets of the eighteenth century. The remark had, needless to say, been repeated by a common friend; but Edith had only registered it as an example of the feminine disability to separate the masculine mind from those reserves of the flesh which were natural to some women, among them herself.

But if at first Claire had seemed the more picturesque figure, having more money, more looks – debatable as Edith herself considered these to be – and most of all the gift of getting herself talked about – by dint, Edith considered, of indefatigably talking about herself without the least sense of decency or reticence – yet now that they were both old women, and indeed for many years past, Edith Barlow might be said to have caught up and easily passed in the race. If she had not disliked hackneyed quotations, Miss Barlow might have remarked that the whirligig of time brings in his revenges, but something of the sort was certainly in her mind as she neared her friend's house. She would be met no longer by the allegedly amusing Claire Temple, but by a drooling, not too clean, semi-deranged old woman.

Edith Barlow, a faithful camp follower for so many years of the glorious Age of Reason and Enlightenment, did not believe in God, but as she turned in at the gate of her friend's house, she prayed: 'God, give me patience.'

Kathleen, in a clean white apron over a black dress, and with the curtain of demureness behind which she veiled her face when Miss Barlow and the few other callers visited the house, opened the door. But immediately there was a quick scurry of feet behind her:

'Is that you, Edith?'

'Yes, how are you, Claire?' said Miss Barlow, advancing to kiss the other's proffered cheek.

'Oh, my dear, it's dreadful. I won't tell you how dreadful

because I know how bored you would be. Are you cold? Come in to the fire.'

'Give me time to leave my coat and hat, will you?'

'Of course, darling. Can I help you?'

But there was no need to shake her head. Claire fluttered helplessly round waiting merely, Edith thought, to seize rapaciously upon her never-ending tale of woe. The one thing she envied her was her extraordinary capacity to keep warm. It was a cold day in the beginning of March, yet for all the thin dress she was wearing, Claire's nose was not in the least red, as she was conscious that her own was. And she was glad to see that the so-called cook, really, of course, the general servant, had prepared a blazing fire.

When she went to warm her hands, Claire said: 'I've no sherry to offer you. Either I can't afford it, or they just refuse to get any. There is some wine, just *vin ordinaire*. It used to be two shillings; now it's four-and-six.'

'I've told you before not to bother about wine for me. I can never afford it for myself, as you know.'

'All the more reason for me to give it to you when you are so kind as to come all this long way to see me. But it's not only the wine; my cook behaves so brutally about everything. Sometimes I think I shall die of her cruelty.'

'Of course you won't die. Let's talk about something else for a change, shall we? I've been reading a most interesting book by Guedalla . . .'

'It's no good talking to me about books. Or theatres. I can't concentrate any more. It's the loneliness that's driving me . . . that's making me so unhappy. I know you won't understand

94

this, but then you see it's so different for you; you have your sister.'

The rumbling of the service lift which connected with the kitchen saved Miss Barlow the necessity of replying. She knew from experience that the best way of getting the dishes off the lift and her dinner set before her while it was still hot, was to do most of the job herself, and she set briskly to it. There was a small nicely browned joint of beef surrounded by roast potatoes; there was cauliflower, there was sauce, there was an extra tureen of gravy.

Having set the dishes properly on the table, she turned to capture her hostess: 'Now, Claire, if you'll sit down and carve we can get our food while it's hot. I like it hot, if you don't.'

'I'm looking for the corkscrew; I can't find it anywhere; she hides away all my things; I don't know what she does with them; I used to know where everything was, but now . . . And do you know what she does?' In her excitement at the sudden recollection, she flitted away from the sideboard and sat down at the table, leaning towards Miss Barlow: 'She has a soldier in about once a week. And he stays till midnight. Of course they misconduct themselves. And I have to pay for the supper she gives him. It's not altogether . . . I mean, is it?'

'If you're not going to carve that nice-looking piece of beef, shall I do it? I don't want to sound greedy, but I've come a long way.'

'Have you really? How kind. Where have you come from?' Mrs Temple took up the carving-knife and fork and started to carve.

'I'm living in the same house as I've lived in for more than twenty years, Claire. If you don't know where it is, you never will. Why don't you stop to think before you ask these foolish questions?'

Intrigued, Claire stopped carving. 'But never in my life have I stopped to think. If one did, would one do anything? One would be like Balfour, wasn't it? who just couldn't make up his mind to get out of his bath.' She passed the plate containing a very scanty portion.

'I'll have a little more, please.'

'Oh, certainly, I'm so glad you're hungry. . . . Now is that enough? Will you help yourself to everything?'

'Thank you. Now you cut yourself some.'

'I don't want much; it's so tough. I can tell it's tough.'

'It's not at all tough. Do you mind if I start? Hurry up, or you'll be left behind. Now let me give you some cauliflower.'

'Thank you very much. You are so brisk and efficient, aren't you? Is that because you are used to looking after your invalid sister? Does she like it? Oh, I know. We want some wine. Where's the corkscrew?'

'Wait a moment, and I'll find it. Here we are. Shall I draw the cork for you?'

'If you would be so kind. It's only *vin ordinaire*; it used to cost two shillings, but now it costs four-and-six. I get it from that funny old dear in Wardour Street. It's only *vin ordinaire*, but it costs four-and-six . . .'

'Yes, you told me. Of course wine costs more than it used to. It will go up and up till we shan't be able to get any. You see, we don't get any more from France, so we have only our existing stocks, and they will get scantier and scantier as the war goes on.'

'How interesting! And sad. We should never quarrel with the French, because we are so dependent on their wine. Their exports to us must be far more valuable than our exports to them. It's like Omar's: "I often wonder what the vintners buy one half so precious as the stuff they sell" . . . It's not too bad, is it? Of course it's only *vin ordinaire*, but it costs four-and-six a bottle. It used to cost only two shillings.'

'I know.'

'Would you mind passing me the bottle? I think I'll have another glass. Do help yourself first.'

'No, thank you. Why don't you eat something? You should do justice to the excellent dinner your cook has sent up.'

'Oh yes, she is a good cook. But so immoral. My dear, I must tell you. She has taken to sleeping with a soldier. I don't object morally, though considering that she gives him my food and I dare say my wine. . . . What should I do? I don't feel safe with a man like that about.'

'Do? Take no notice. Your cook is a most patient woman, obviously. Also she is far too good to lose because of a stray *amour*. Do you remember that story of Saki's about the civilised gentleman who burnt the evidence that his chef had committed a murder, because he couldn't afford to lose anyone whose . . .'

'Yes, yes. But that's really nothing to do with my cook, who's not such a good cook as all that, and who gives me only bread and cheese and sardines when she is entertaining her lover. I'm quite aware that you're so civilised that you consider it wrong to object to immorality. It's a curious thing I've always noticed, virgins and spinsters are supposed in books to be vinegary and narrow-minded, but mostly they go in for being terribly broad-minded, just so, I suppose, that no one will suspect them of being virgins.'

'I'm sorry; I'd better not say any more.'

'Oh dear! Now I've offended you! How dreadful! Do please forgive me.'

'Of course. There's nothing to forgive. Do please go on eating your food. Have a little more cauliflower?'

'Yes, I think I will. It's the meat that's so tough. Don't you find it so?'

'No, I don't. It's very good. Did you see Miss Phillips yesterday?'

'Did I? Yes, I think so. What day was yesterday?'

'Today is Sunday, so yesterday was Saturday.'

'I expect I did then. She only comes on Saturdays now. It's too terrible. She just comes in and writes cheques which I sign, and pays Kathleen and has a talk with her in the kitchen. And then off she rushes again. I've told her that I can't bear the loneliness, that she'll have to do something . . . oh, I know what I was going to say to you. After all you're my oldest friend, and a literary woman. Couldn't you and your sister move here? I'd only charge you for your food. You could have the spare bedroom, and you could write in the back study that Wallace used, do you remember? I'd put a desk in there for you.'

'My dear woman, my writing days are over.'

'Then you wouldn't need the study; but you could have it

for writing letters . . . or if you suddenly thought of a title for a book. I'm always thinking of good titles, and then I make a note in my diary.'

'What's the good of that? Doesn't the subject precede the title?'

'Oh, I think a title can inspire one. It opens doors, doesn't it? But what I wanted to ask you was will you, and your sister, of course, come here and live with me? I would only charge you for your food.'

'You ask me this every time I come and see you, and I've told you over and over again I have no intention of moving till I make my last move. And that will be done for me. Now, if you've finished, shall I ring the bell, and start to clear away the dishes?'

'Have I asked you before? I'm so sorry. I know that my memory is simply outrageous. But why won't you come? Because it would be cheaper for you. . . . Where are you going?'

'I'm just getting up to ring the bell. To let Kathleen know we've finished.'

'Have we finished? I'd like some more wine if I may?'

'You haven't finished what's on your plate, but I suppose you've had enough.'

'Yes; eating is so tedious unless the food is really superlative. And then one should eat in silence.'

'Which you've never done, my dear.'

'Oh, how little you know. I have all my meals alone now, or nearly all. Sometimes as a great favour cook allows me to have dinner with her. And with Mrs White, who comes to do

the washing every Monday. Then my oldest friend, Edith
Barlow, comes every second Sunday to lunch.'

'I am quite aware of that. Could you pass me the sauce
boat?'

'Oh, you *are* Edith, aren't you? For a moment I thought you
were my companion. My dear, I'm so sorry. It's this appalling
memory of mine.'

Miss Barlow came back to the table and sat down, pending
the rumble of the lift with the second course. She said, ignoring
the appealing gaze: 'Have you seen Eleanor Riding lately? She
rang me up last week to ask me something about this new book
she's writing. It was a fact she could perfectly well have verified
in a book of reference; however, she was quite amiable and
chatty. . . .'

'Eleanor? I haven't seen her for months. She's treated
me so badly, and considering that I discovered her, Wallace
and myself, and brought her out to begin with, and I lent
her several dresses that time she was so hard up, and going
to have her baby. And, do you know, when she returned
them . . . '

'You've told me over and over again. There were
perspiration marks under the arm-holes.'

'I'm so sorry I repeat myself, but I do wish that you'd
behave more like my guest, and less like my governess,
Edith. It's so discouraging always being with people who order
one about, and put one in one's place. One continually has
the same sensation as a poor naughty child who has been put
in the corner, and told to stay there for ever and always. Please
forgive me if I'm saying anything that's rude, because I know

how very kind it is of you to come all this long way every second Sunday and see me.'

'Ah, I think our pudding, or whatever cook has sent up, has arrived,' said Miss Barlow, glad to get up from the table, and start being energetic once more. Behind her friend's back Mrs Temple poured herself out some more wine, drank it, and then started to explain the advantages and history of the service lift, another old and very much repeated story, so that Edith Barlow tried not to listen, feeling that if she did she might say something very sharply. Instead, getting back to her place she observed pleasantly: 'What a nice-looking jam tart!'

'She makes pastry very well, but that doesn't prevent her from entertaining soldiers at my expense. Did I tell you that she has a soldier in nearly every night, or one night a week, to sleep with her?'

'Yes, you did tell me. Are you going to serve the tart?'

'I'm waiting for the cream. Isn't she going to let us have some cream? Will you ring the bell?'

'She hasn't sent any cream, because there is none to be got. The government has forbidden farmers to make it.'

'How extraordinary! Well then, we shall have to eat it without. Let me give you a piece.'

'Thank you. Now have some yourself.'

'I don't think I want any. I think I'll have some more wine.'

'You've nearly finished the bottle, you know. Why don't you keep some for another time? And really you must have some tart.'

'Must I? All right.'

'You see, if you don't eat, your memory will just go on getting worse and worse. You won't make enough blood to feed your brain, you know.'

'I know what you mean. You mean pernicious anaemia. I do try and eat, but it's so lonely having all my meals by myself. It's like living in a cave without any scenery about one. People have always been my scenery, you see. The props and the *décor*. Remove them, and really what's the good of having the play at all? I always so disliked those horrid little repertory theatres with no orchestra, and everything done in the dark or else in the kitchen. Cook does occasionally let me have my meals with her in the kitchen. Would you and your sister come here to live, and then we could all have our meals together? It would be so nice.'

Edith paused a moment, and drew a deep breath. Then she said:

'Apart from everything else, my sister wouldn't dream of moving further into London with the increased risk of bombs.'

'I thought only the lower classes were afraid of bombs. They go into shelters and down the Tubes. Does your sister go into a shelter?'

'No, she doesn't, because we haven't got one.'

'Poor Lisa gets frightened. Oh, where is Lisa? I must find her.' Mrs Temple rose with a distracted air.

'Sit down, Claire. You know we agreed some time ago that when I came to lunch on Sunday the cat should be kept downstairs. Don't you remember?'

Reluctantly, Mrs Temple sat down, and reached for her

glass. 'Of course, you're one of those people like Lord Roberts, who can't bear to have a cat in the same room. How clever of cook to remember.'

'What I can't bear is for you to be up and down the whole lunch-time looking for your precious cat. It makes conversation, difficult enough at any time, quite impossible. . . . You're surely going to eat some more of your tart.'

'I don't really like it. It worries me when I don't know where Lisa is. Cook lets her stray out into the streets, and if she were run over then I should have no one. But I mustn't go on talking to you about it: I know it bores you intolerably. Are you having a good lunch? Do let me give you some more of something.'

'No, thank you. I've enjoyed my lunch very much. I'm only perturbed that you've eaten so little.'

'What about coffee? Has she brought the coffee?'

'No. Do I ring?'

'You mustn't get up. You're my guest, not my companion. There! I'm sure she'll let us have some coffee. She makes quite good coffee; it's such a pity she's so brutal. Also she is very familiar.'

'That's probably because she's Irish. Irish servants consider they are part of the family more than English servants.'

'You mean they are faithful then?'

'I wouldn't say that. They have their own standards, which are hardly our standards. Personally, I dislike the Irish because they have so little sense of style. As individuals. Everything is soft and smudged. One sinks, as it were, into a bog, and bogs are treacherous.'

'That's what you dislike in me, that I have no sense of style as an individual, isn't it?'

Miss Barlow found this sudden flash of intuition disconcerting. It contained, as Claire's flashes often contained, so much truth. For Edith Barlow could give her friend no marks for the qualities she most esteemed. Long ago she had pigeon-holed her and disposed of her under the heading 'Victorian Female'.

Her pretensions to be a *grande amoureuse*, for example. What did Claire's much-talked-of *affaires* amount to? They were only two in number, and they both merited Edith Barlow's favourite word of scorn: 'Injudicious'. In her youth she had vastly troubled her parents and sisters and shocked her old family friends by becoming the mistress of a married man. Well, that might have been excused by reason of youth and impetuosity. But when the married man had promptly married someone else as soon as his wife died, Claire should have learnt something. Instead, she had submitted to an attack of the vapours called a nervous breakdown, travelled on the Continent, and then returned to write a number of novels all about herself, her lover and her friends. Critics had been more friendly than otherwise, but who ever heard of her books these days?

Then, when she was old enough to know better, she had surrendered even more injudiciously. Wallace had been a second-rate man of letters with a pronounced lack of integrity, many years younger than herself. He had, of course, used her, and then deserted her. And Claire's pretence of being married to him was so ridiculous that one wondered how she

could impose on herself, let alone anyone else. But, once again, she was being true to type as a Victorian female who considered marriage the necessary crown of her existence, and after Wallace had gone she had transformed herself into another Victorian institution, the Widow. One acquaintance had remarked that it was rather touching the way Claire still received all Wallace's press cuttings, still talked incessantly about him – even though she could no longer remember whether he was dead or alive – still assumed that everyone would be interested in such a great man. It was very much surely the attitude that Queen Victoria would have assumed towards the Prince Consort, had Albert been less good, and she more bitter. Certainly, the sum total of Claire's *affaires de cœur* did not add up into a romance and song for poets and sweet singers.

Then she was supposed to have had wit. Well, Edith Barlow allowed, it had, in a measure, existed, but wit not of the head but of the more feminine personal order, a wit which pounced, like a bird upon a crumb, on some weakness, some idiosyncrasy of a friend. Such wit is the appetiser of the moment; it has no lasting quality having no iota of universal quality. When it is conserved, it is conserved only under the heading of malice, for of the scene which gave rise to the words, to the phrase, the individual, the appointments and the cues being all laid away in the dusty warehouses of time and forgotten, nothing remains but the empty husk, over which the moralist in us all shakes his head and murmurs: 'How unkind'.

She had watched that frail feminine talent function, nourished by no such coarseness and urbanity as fed the

full-blooded *esprit*; she had nodded not unappreciatively when friends repeated to her what Claire had said; and for a long time now she had seen it wither under the too-plentiful showers of self-pity. A shoot or two might still unexpectedly appear, but that was all.

Then her looks? Could she be considered tolerantly as a one-time beauty who, having fallen into the sere and yellow, must still be allowed a modicum of flattery and pity, because, after all, she had been so much admired? As when a rich man falls upon penury, his friends remind themselves that, of course, for him poverty is so much more difficult than for those who have never known wealth. Edith Barlow had shaken her head. She had never allowed her friend beauty: 'Not with that ill-shaped nose, so broad at the nostrils,' she had replied firmly, denying thus to her friend for ever a place in the gallery of those who having once been beautiful are in their old age among the tragic and ill-fated.

There remained nothing to the Claires of this world, Edith considered, but dignity before their inevitable disaster, and Claire of all people had the least dignity of anyone she had ever known. She had sold out this most important human heritage; crying over herself like an ill-behaved child. Bewailing her loneliness to all and sundry, even to strangers she picked up in the streets.

Thinking of her friend, and indeed she had spent a good deal of time thinking about her, she had once decided in a flash that she resembled the Red Queen in *Through the Looking-Glass*. She had run so fast in her life that she managed to make other people feel giddy. But like the Red Queen with all her running she had always stayed at the same place. She had had to run to keep there.

But her friends had not stayed in the same place: they had moved on, and they had moved away. So when this Red Queen looked round, the once-crowded scene was deserted.

'And, of course, you have never had any great opinion of my novels, have you?' her hostess inquired while she still fumbled for the answer to her first comment. 'I remember your once saying that my madcap heroines so full of defiances would date. I think you were right about that.'

Edith Barlow shrugged delicately. 'We have certainly moved into an age in which there are no taboos worth mentioning,' she said, 'and to that extent perhaps . . . but they were enjoyable and fashionable at the time. And well worth writing,' she added, putting more emphasis than usual into her voice as is the way with naturally truthful and egoistic people when they tell a lie or half-lie for the sake of the other person's feelings. To consolidate the position, she added: 'It's like the time you were caught up in the Suffragette movement, do you remember? When you sold papers for the cause in Kensington High Street and wore a rosette or something. I always felt that was truly admirable, especially for a woman so feminine as yourself. And it remains admirable, even though the pioneers of the Suffragettes are now outmoded. Indeed, more, they are comic figures to a generation which believes they spent their time slapping policemen and scratching them . . . in so far as they have ever heard of them.'

'I suppose I was a Suffragette because Rose Bartlett who was frightfully keen dragged me into it. And it was fun having

intellectual parties in which one mixed the pros and the antis
. . . one enjoyed the sensations of a tight-rope walker. Do
you remember my introducing Mrs Humphrey Ward to
Christabel?'

'I do indeed.'

'But all over, as you say my novels are. My novels must
be all over because no one will reprint them.'

'Paper shortage, you know. . . . And your uneasy stories,
you know I have always had a great admiration for them. You
should have written more, and then you would have made a
sure place for yourself in that gallery which contains Poe,
Sheridan Le Fanu, Algernon Blackwood and Arthur Machen.'

She stopped because the door had opened to admit
Kathleen with the coffee-cups, but her thoughts went on. For
it was very true what she had just said. Look at Claire now, her
small wrinkled sunken face, flushed with wine, underneath the
fine wild white hair . . . look at the fragility of her, her wrists
so thin. Yes, her arms and legs were like broomsticks, so it
would be really suitable if she took up her abode among ghosts
and shadows and bogeys; if there was something eerie in her
continual flitting from room to room. Bedlam itself would
have been a fitting house. But no, that solid Victorian in her
which had believed in the conventions sufficiently to get
thrills out of breaking them, that side of her which went on
clamouring for people and conversation though she was now
past all conversation save in snatches, held her to the earth,
held her there desperately. Now she was being almost servile
to Kathleen, praising the coffee she made, watching her face
anxiously.

'Yes, I know she makes good coffee. Let's see, you haven't a grinding-machine, have you? They do it for you at the shop, don't they?'

'No, Madam. The machine broke down on us. But I only get small quantities at a time, and that makes it keep fresh.'

'How wise!'

When the door had closed behind Kathleen, Mrs Temple said: 'If I'm nice to her, she'll probably let me have supper with her in the kitchen. So I always try to be.'

'I don't think it does them any good, that sort of thing. I do think you ought to have your meals properly in this room, and not keep begging to be let into the kitchen. It's not very dignified, is it?'

'No, it's not. I know you despise me for not having more dignity. But when one is as lonely as I am you do disgraceful things . . . it's like when you are starving and grab crusts of bread from dust-bins. That's what my life has come to, grabbing garbage out of dust-bins.'

'Don't be silly. Making melodrama out of your state doesn't help it. You really need a companion. A lady. Why doesn't Miss Phillips advertise for someone?'

'Yes, I know I do. But can I afford one? I paid that wooden secretary a pound a week, but now she has left me to get more money on a government job.'

'Yes, you told me about that. Well, there is that pound a week, and then she would live in. I shouldn't think she would want very much more. There are probably elderly women still obtainable. Won't you pour out the coffee while it is hot?'

'Oh, I'm so sorry. How forgetful I am. If I had a companion, then she could do things like that. But I would like her to be fairly intelligent. And to have manners. Not the kind that keep thrusting themselves into the conversation. And insist on talking to my friends as if I weren't there. I had one ghastly woman like that . . . do you remember her?'

'Yes, she meant well, you know. Your loss of memory makes it very difficult sometimes.'

'Oh, I know that so well. But I have an idea. Why couldn't you and your sister come and live here with me? I'd only want your company at meal-times. Perhaps in the evening now and then? And I'd only charge you for your food.'

Edith Barlow drained her coffee-cup before replying. It was worth investigation, she thought, the way repetition drove one to such interior impatience that one had to clench one's hands before replying. It resembled a Chinese form of torture . . . they relied on the cumulative effect of a continual drip of water. . . .

'Would you be able to come? I should so love to have you. Are you thinking about it as you look out of the window?'

'No, I'm not thinking about it, Claire, for the reason that I've already replied to your kind invitation . . . about three times, I think. And on every occasion I visit you.'

'I've asked you before? I'm so sorry. And you don't think you can come?'

'No, it's quite impossible. . . . May I have some more coffee, please?'

'Oh yes, do. I'm so glad you can enjoy the coffee. Perhaps it makes up a little for my being so wearisome.'

Edith passed her cup without replying. For really, she was thinking, what could one reply? What good indeed was she doing by her visits since she invariably lost her temper once or twice before she left? These visits were purely sentimental, like the visits paid by dull provincial people and peasants to cemeteries and graveyards: a clinging to something that was dead and done with. Such people invariably wore their best clothes, generally those most unbecoming to them, and carried flowers that were beginning to droop or, in some cases, were artificial. She, too, she realised, wore her most unbecoming clothes when she went to see poor Claire – the clothes of a mentor, as Claire had put it, a governess. Stiff and ill-fitting, for she was not really like that. It was Claire and her silliness, who made her like that. Claire was really not her cup of tea. Claire really never had been her cup of tea.

She wondered vaguely why she could not feel more pity for Claire, why impatience was so strong within her, and half-glimpsed the answer. Sad stories of the deaths of kings and fair frail ladies were one thing, patient following of the circles which an old woman's conversation made was another. A drab may win the love of the realist who stays to look deep enough; but the romantic choose the tragedy by its brave or delicate colours.

But since Edith Barlow, devotee of the Age of Reason, had never admitted she was a romantic, she stopped just short of the recognition that attendance at death-beds when the patient was an unconscionable time a-dying, was not her forte. Instead she blamed the patient.

'Is your clock right? I shall have to be going soon.'

'Oh, please don't go yet. Can I give you some more coffee? If there is any. Oh dear . . . I'm afraid there isn't.'

'I don't want any more. I've had two cups.'

'I wonder if there's some brandy, or some whisky about?' In a second Claire was out of her chair, wandering restlessly about, poking in a china cupboard, murmuring: 'I thought I hid some brandy in a tiny bottle here. . . . Where can it be?'

Changing her seat to the fire, Edith said: 'Please don't bother. I'm sure your budget can't include brandy these days. Besides, I don't want any.'

'Well, if you don't want any, I do. "Dost thou think, because thou art virtuous. . . ." Still I can't find it, so I suppose cook has taken it away. She is so cunning, cunning as well as cruel, a horrible combination. Oh, I do so want just a tiny glass.'

'Why don't you ring the bell, and ask your cook if there is any?'

'Oh, I couldn't possibly. I wouldn't dare. You don't understand. When she has brought up the coffee – she did bring it, didn't she? We have had coffee, haven't we?'

'Yes, we've had our coffee.'

'That's all right. I was so afraid, for a moment, that I'd forgotten. She mustn't be disturbed afterwards; she does the washing-up, and then she has a rest. I never ring the bell; I have to go to her; she's the mountain and I'm Mahomet. But I mustn't go to her unless it's urgent. And specially not when she has her soldier lover here. If I did, she'd walk out and leave me all alone. Did I tell you about her having a soldier in at night?'

'Yes, you did. Please sit down.'

'There's still a little wine left that we can have.'

'Not for me, thank you. If you finish that, you won't have any left for this evening.'

'It doesn't matter. I get it from that funny old dear in Wardour Street: he used to charge me only two shillings, but now it's gone up to four-and-six.'

'I think I'd better be putting on my coat. It takes me so long to get home, and then I like to lie down on Sundays.'

'But you can lie down here. Will you lie down on my bed? I'll ask her to bring you a hot-water-bottle. She will for you, because she always takes care to be polite to visitors.'

'Please don't trouble. I'm just going to put a little more coal on the fire for you. Then you can have a rest in that comfortable chair. I'm sure you must be tired.'

'I'm not at all tired. I'm never tired. Please don't go yet.'

The large eyes turned upon hers seemed as if at the next moment they would fill with tears. Edith Barlow sighed: this business of getting away was almost the worst of all. But she thought of the long bus journey as a hurdle that must be taken. And then there would be tea and toast, even if it were margarine and not butter. And *The Sunday Times* and *The Observer*. And then the new Sitwell, which The Times Book Club had sent, for the couple of hours before their light supper had to be prepared. Dull, would some say? That was all she wanted: the civilised dullness suitable to her age and tastes before she closed her eyes finally in the perpetual sleep of death. If only the bombs would leave No. 1, The Ridings, alone, and refrain from making their entrance into that final sleep an ill-conditioned, inelegant affair. That was her sister's chief trouble, for her sister was nervous of the raids, lacking her own sense of fatalism. It was due to her sister that they had already sorted out their things, had indeed done some packing, so that if havoc descended they would be ready to move to that address in Bournemouth where they had had such a pleasant summer holiday before the war.

'I'm sorry, my dear, but I must. You know my sister doesn't like being left alone very long these days. Besides, you forget that I'm a very old woman, and quite lacking your amazing energy.'

'I suppose your sister hates being alone, as I do. Do you think I could come and stay the night with you some time?'

'You know perfectly well that you hated it when you came to stay with us a year or so ago. You upset Anna by not liking her cooking, and going out and buying wine, which, as I explained beforehand, we were sorry we couldn't afford to give you.'

'But I couldn't understand why you minded. I think suburban life needs a lot of wine to make one forget the narrow hall, and the smells of cooking, and having to wait on oneself, and having to put kettles on all the time for something or other. . . . But truly, I didn't mean to be rude. Have I offended you?'

'No, you haven't offended me. You've said all that before. Scores of times. I'm quite aware that our inconvenient sub-urban villa can't dispense the hospitality to which you used to be accustomed. You've only been used to staying with rich people and that's spoilt you.'

'Oh, I'm not spoilt any more. There's been no one to spoil

me for years. That goes when one's last man friend has gone. I don't mind anything now except being so lonely. Oh, here's Kathleen!'

'Excuse me, Madam, but I just wanted to know if Miss Barlow was going to stay to tea?'

'Yes, she will, won't you?'

'I'm afraid not. As I've just told you, I've got to go now.'

'Very well, Madam.'

'Thank you for the nice lunch.'

'I'm glad you enjoyed it, Madam.'

'Kathleen, have you got the cat downstairs? My dear Lisa! If Miss Barlow is going, I can have the cat again.'

'I think she's downstairs; I'll look.'

'And I'll use your bathroom, if I may?'

'Oh, yes. Let me show you the way.'

'I should know it by now. Please don't get up.'

Before Miss Barlow descended the stairs she glanced into Claire's study. It certainly looked dusty and neglected, but then it was impossible to expect one woman to do the work of the whole house and also be at Claire's beck and call. A companion was the solution, and she decided firmly that she would write to Miss Phillips the very next morning about it.

Perhaps tonight. But she felt too tired. This fortnightly expedition was really becoming too much for her strength. She would tell Claire not to rely on it. And a sense of farewell arose within her as she went slowly down the stairs, glancing at the signed portraits. She had met many amusing and interesting and infuriating people in this house; and on the whole, she had rarely been bored. But for long past the house had betrayed her, provided her with nothing but boredom and depression. One gets into it, and then sinks into a muddy pool. . . .

'Edith, is that you? Oh, I thought you must have gone down to talk to Kathleen.'

'And why should I go down and talk to Kathleen?'

'She generally tries to collar my friends, and tell them how dreadfully I behave. Why are you getting your coat?'

'Because I'm going home.'

'Oh, you can't go yet. Don't go. Stop just ten minutes longer. Then we'll have tea; Kathleen can make such good scones.'

'Now goodbye, my dear. Thank you for the very good lunch.'

'You will go? When shall I see you again? Isn't this Sunday? Not till next Sunday?'

'I usually come every second Sunday, but you mustn't rely on me, as I've told you before. My sister is in a very delicate state of health, and I fear merits your contempt, as she is terrified of the air-raids. I'll ring you up and let you know.'

'Will you? But won't you fix a day now, and then I'll rush away and write it down in my book. Couldn't we go to the London Library together one afternoon, as we used to do?'

Edith Barlow shook her head. 'Goodbye. Once again, many thanks. I'm going to do my best about getting a companion for you.'

'Are you? How very kind of you. Do forgive me for anything I've said that I shouldn't.'

'Of course.'

She turned at the gate to wave her hand and say: 'Do go in, or you'll catch cold.' Her last glimpse was of a small figure in black looking after her in silence as if . . . almost as if they wouldn't ever be seeing each other again.

CHAPTER FOUR

Once upon a time Mrs Sara Berkeley had been one of Claire Temple's secretaries, and she had always 'kept in touch'. For Mrs Berkeley, like many others, divided the world into Somebodies and Nobodies. The criteria are, of course, different: with some it is their own family that matters and the rest of the world is plunged into outer darkness; with others it is Money that counts: Big Business and Millionaires receive their respect; with others again of all classes it is Social Eligibility that is the test; and there is quite a large number who feel sincerely that it is only they themselves who are really and truly of importance.

But Mrs Berkeley shared none of these tastes: the people who were Somebodies in her esteem were literary people, 'people who wrote', and she was catholic in her admiration. It had been at Claire Temple's that she had met really celebrated literary people, and after her fashion she was faithful to the source of the lights which had temporarily shone on her. It was quite true that nowadays 'nobody' except her old friend Edith Barlow came to see Claire, because, poor dear, she couldn't remember anything and kept saying the same things over and over again. It was very sad, thought Mrs Berkeley, for

a Somebody like Claire Temple to have to suffer these things, and she considered it her duty to go and cheer the poor thing up. If sometimes her hostess was quite rude to her, well, Mrs Berkeley made allowances. It wasn't as if Claire had ever been an ordinary person.

Thus at least it had been in pre-war days, but this afternoon, as Mrs Berkeley crossed over the road from buying a cake near Barker's, and started to climb the familiar hill, she was prompted in her visit to Claire less by kindness of heart, directed towards the succour of a member of her most favoured division of human beings, than by a patriotic passion. What she wanted from this afternoon's visit was paper to be salvaged to help the war effort. There were, she knew, files and files of old newspapers, loads and loads of press cuttings, old notebooks and worthless typescripts and manuscripts piled away in cupboards and drawers in Mrs Temple's house. There was a time when she would not have used the adjective 'worthless' as applied to notebooks and typescripts; she would have felt towards them as the romantic feel towards a neglected orphan: one day he might grow up to be President of the United States or whatever equivalent is favoured.

But the war had changed her viewpoint. Lesser suns had declined in her esteem. Mrs Berkeley, who had been born Sara Bernstein, had previously never quite understood what people meant when they used the words 'holy' and 'sacred'. Now she understood, for the war, that is the war as waged by the British people, and soon, she hoped, by the Americans, was to her a sacred and holy cause. The war, she felt, was the

vindication of her race – a race that in the piping days of peace she had only half-acknowledged, keeping, as it were, on nodding terms with it, but being careful not to fraternise overmuch. She felt towards her people as if they were poor relatives who mustn't be encouraged too much in their claims towards one. But now the great might of the British Empire had risen in its wrath to avenge the cause of these poor relatives, and had thereby placed them on the visiting list of the most socially powerful and respectable. One might be excused in normal times for overlooking some of the family, who, after all, lived in ghettos, or who insisted on being 'orthodox' when it was no longer done to be 'orthodox', but now, of course, one remembered that blood was thicker than water and rushed forward to grasp the hand of the martyrs of Hitlerism.

To Mrs Berkeley then the war was very especially her war, and she showed her enthusiasm for it in various ways, not least by never failing to switch on the radio and listen to the news at eight o'clock, at one o'clock, at six o'clock, at nine o'clock, and sometimes even at midnight. When she listened to the BBC announcer, her face, with its full lips tightly pressed together and the corners of her mouth slightly turned down, wore very much the same expression as many people feel it incumbent to assume in church.

There was only one aspect of the war, one of the many inconveniences that it had brought, which Mrs Berkeley found it difficult, and small blame to her, to suffer gladly. That, of course, was the bombs. She and her friend had their Anderson Shelter in the garden, and it was something to be able to

huddle there together when the Terror was abroad. But now, after six months of heroic endurance, she was beginning to feel that she couldn't stand very much more.

Even now, just before she turned in at Claire Temple's gate, and hearing the sinister throbbing note of a distant aeroplane, she was saying farewell with infinite reluctance to her dearly-loved salvage work for the WVS. Of course it would only be for a time; and even in the country no doubt one could find some work to do for the Cause. Any work, so long as it were not fire-watching. 'I want to help,' she would say. 'Anything so long as I can help.' And: 'We are so glad to see you,' they would say, and 'Thank you so much for coming. That's the spirit'.

She was so deeply occupied in her meditations that she had turned into the garden before she saw that her hostess was standing on top of the steps, apparently waiting to welcome her.

'My dear, they've only just told me you were coming to tea. So I've been up and down the steps for the last ten minutes. Are you going to be my secretary again? I do need someone so much. How nice you look! Just like an over-blown rose; so becoming. To you, that is.'

'You always tell me I look like an over-blown rose, and I know you mean it as a compliment. Shall we go indoors? Aren't your feet cold in those bedroom slippers?'

'Oh, no, they are most comfortable. I walk everywhere in them. And they don't wear out! I suppose they will, because everything wears out. Except me. It's terrible the way I can't wear out, but go on feeling in my heart, feeling everything.

I forget how old I am, but it's quite old, and I shouldn't feel as much as I do at my age. It is rather terrible, isn't it?'

'I shouldn't like not to be able to feel,' said Mrs Berkeley gravely. 'I had better ring, hadn't I? Unless you've got your key?'

'Yes, do ring. I haven't got my bag. I came out to meet you, and then I forgot you were coming, and thought I was going for a walk.'

Kathleen answered the bell promptly. 'So there you are,' she said to her mistress. 'And I put you in the dining-room to wait there for Mrs Berkeley.' She glanced towards the visitor behind Mrs Temple's back, shaking her head slightly, pursing her lips and rolling her eyes, by which she intended to convey that Mrs Temple was worse than usual. And Mrs Berkeley smiled back, an understanding compassionate smile.

'*Put* in the dining-room! Kathleen talks about me as if I were a doll. Or a child. That's how she thinks of me, of course. Will you bring us some tea, please? I suppose you did know Mrs Berkeley was coming?'

Kathleen went away without bothering to reply. She felt there was no need to keep up appearances before Mrs Berkeley, as with some of the occasional visitors. Mrs Berkeley had been Mrs Temple's secretary, and, like all her secretaries, couldn't fail to know what she was.

Mrs Berkeley went into the dining-room, looking about her, as she went, with appraising eyes, though she did not know them to be appraising. Whenever she visited Mrs Temple these days she saw the furniture grouped as it might be at a preview of an auction sale, for, she felt, it couldn't be very much longer now. Moreover, there was the question of bombs: some of the literary mementoes should be of value, and it was distressing to think that they might all be destroyed. She was surprised that someone didn't do something about them, and her curiosity as to who was going to benefit prompted her first question after she had sat down:

'Do you ever see your nieces nowadays?'

'No, never; they are so dull. Besides, they don't want to see me. I don't think they can bear me.'

Mrs Berkeley shook her head. Feeling rich in her discovery that all Jews throughout the whole world were her relatives, she felt it sad that poor Claire couldn't even get on friendly terms with a couple of nieces.

'A pity! Well, I must tell you what I've come about. Apart from wanting to see you, of course. Paper.'

'Paper?'

'You know, dear, how urgently it's required for the war effort. Paper makes shells, you know. And we're not getting it now as we used to do.'

'Aren't we? Well, it doesn't matter. I don't think I shall ever finish this book I'm writing. I've only the one servant, and I have to make my own bed, and do lots of things. I can never settle down and concentrate. Will you come and be my secretary again? I am afraid I can only pay you a pound a week.'

'You forget, Claire, that I'm now very busy with the WVS, the Women's Voluntary Service, you know. I've told you all about it, but I suppose you've forgotten. At the moment I'm doing salvage; I'm going round from house to house making arrangements for the collection of paper.'

'What an extraordinary thing to do! Is it interesting?'

'It's not extraordinary at all. You mustn't forget we are at war, and that paper makes all sorts of things besides weapons against the Huns. As to being interesting, no, I wouldn't say it is particularly. But one does what one can to help.'

'How kind of you. I've always said that about you. She may . . . she is a really kind woman, I've always said. One of the very few I've ever known. I'm not kind myself, but I'm not really cruel. Now my cook is a cruel person.'

'I'm sure she's not. That's just your imagination. Now when you realise, and you do realise, don't you, that we, that is the British Empire, is fighting for its very life. . . .'

'Is it? No, I'm afraid I don't realise it. I'm too unhappy to bother. You don't know how lonely I am. Will you come and be my secretary again?'

'I couldn't possibly. I'm far too busy. As I was telling you, if you will listen. But what I will do is to come and help you to clear out all your rubbish. I mean those old newspapers that you have filed away in the study. And those old typescripts and notebooks. You can tell me what you want particularly to keep.'

'I'm keeping them all. They will go to my literary executors. You are not one, I don't think. No, I had men. One is. . . . Oh, here's the tea at last. She has been a long time. You would like some tea, wouldn't you?'

'Thank you, I would,' said Mrs Berkeley. She got up and settled herself firmly in a chair at the table, and waited. Claire seated herself at the head of the table, and stared round her with dissatisfaction.

'Is there anything you want?' asked Mrs Berkeley.

'It's such an odd-looking tea-table. No cakes or anything.'

'But, look, there is some nice hot buttered toast. And really the cakes are not worth buying. I've bought one in the High Street to take home, but really I know it won't be worth the money I paid for it. But like you, my friend, Miss Bates – you remember her, don't you?'

'Do I?'

'Of course you do. You've been to tea with us several times. She's very fond of cake.'

'Who?'

'Miss Bates.'

'Does anyone mind if Miss Bates is fond of cake or not?'

'Now don't be tiresome, darling. Shall I pour out the tea for you?'

'I don't see why you should. I am still in my own house, aren't I?'

'Of course you're in your own house. I was just trying to be helpful. I thought you might be tired.'

'You are kind, I know. Please forgive me.' Mrs Temple stretched out a penitent hand towards her guest. 'Let me see, do you have sugar?'

'No, I used to, but I've given it up for the war.'

'Will that help? You do have milk, don't you?'

'Yes, please. Milk isn't rationed yet, you know. Though it probably will be.'

'I wish you could come and be my secretary again,' said Claire, passing the cup. 'There's something comforting about

you. It's not what you say, but what you stand for. I'm trying to say something I can't quite express.'

'So sweet of you, darling. I wish I could help you, but I've absolutely no time. The WVS, you see. And I do think that everyone who can, who is able-bodied that is, should be helping in this war.'

'I'm too old, aren't I? And I'm a woman. Besides my husband is at the front. No, he's dead, isn't he? I think he was killed.'

'Mr Temple is dead. You know that. You must be thinking of the last war. This war is quite different.'

'Different from what?'

'Have some toast. Different from the last war. Much worse, but much more inspiring. We are all together at last.'

'Are we altogether? I'm not altogether. But I agree: it's not such a cheerful war as the last war. In the last war, one sold flags, and the soldiers sang as they went by. And in the last war we could get cream. Now cook tells me we're not allowed to have it.'

'No, this war is much better managed. We have equality of sacrifice. Everybody is rationed. So that the rich can't take unfair advantage.'

'Equality! I suppose that's why it's such a dull grim war. It can't really be fair, you know, because the poor always get advantages: they go about with babies in their arms, and, the woman who washes here every Monday tells me, misconduct themselves in the black-out on sandbags.'

'What nonsense! The great thing about this war is that since Dunkirk at any rate all the petty personal things are over. The nation is standing together as it has never done for centuries. Not since the Napoleonic wars. Do you mind if I have some more toast? Thank you.'

'Dear Sara! How interesting you make it all sound. Or if not interesting, so moral. That is another reason why there is something so grim about this war. It is an uplift affair, and uplifting things are generally dull and dowdy. Of course, you belong to an uplift society, weren't you telling me?'

'Oh, you don't understand, Claire. But you should try and understand enough, as an Englishwoman, to realise the . . . the importance of helping. That's why I'm asking you for your paper.'

'Newspaper?'

'Yes, newspaper. And everything in the way of print.'

'But the only newspaper I have now is the *Telegraph*. And before I've seen it Kathleen whisks it away to light the fire with. And it's got so small. There's really nothing in it that one wants to read.'

'Of course. Now you can understand that there's a paper shortage. That's why it's small. But I don't mean your daily paper: I mean old papers. Could I have another cup of tea, please? If you can spare it.'

'Oh, I can spare cups of tea. Anyone who wants a cup of tea. That is if Kathleen doesn't mind. But we haven't any newspapers. Do you take sugar?'

'No, thank you. You have plenty of paper, you know. All those files. . . .' She paused to rescue her cup, which was spilling over. 'Thank you. All those files in your study.'

'But you don't want those. They have reviews or articles by

myself or my friends. Or there are references to events which meant something in my life. You see, if I should write another autobiography it is important to be able to verify my dates. I haven't a secretary now, because the last one went away because she could get more money. Oh, I know why I asked you to tea. Won't you come back and be my secretary again?'

'I've told you over and over again I can't. But I would come, say, Thursday afternoon, and help you clear up all your papers. You know if this house were bombed you'd never be able to verify any dates in your files.'

'No, but then, presumably, I should be bombed, too, wouldn't I? So it wouldn't matter. It is only when one is alive that one feels one must have all one's things around one. When one hasn't any more friends, then one makes friends with one's chairs and tables. I say, "Well, at least *you've* stayed with me all these years." I get up at night sometimes and come down here and into the drawing-room with my flashlight; and then when I see my Morris table, I know I am still in my own home.'

'It's not very good for you to go wandering about the house at night like that. It's a wonder you don't catch pneumonia.'

'Oh, but it is. Very good for me. You know with my bad memory I'm not always sure where I am when I wake up; and then if I get out of bed and go downstairs, after a minute or two I begin to see things I recognise. Pneumonia isn't nearly as bad as not knowing where you are. I think I shall have another cup of tea . . . why doesn't it pour? Because there isn't any more! And she hasn't brought any hot water. What a pity!'

'I'll go and ask her to give you some,' said Mrs Berkeley, seeing a door open for her enterprise.

'Will you? How kind. You see if I ring the bell, she doesn't answer.'

Kathleen was sitting having her own tea when Mrs Berkeley came in, and said brightly: 'I don't want to disturb you: we do need some hot water, but I really wanted to ask you something. About salvage.'

'Salvage?'

'Yes. You know we want as much paper as we can get. To make shells. And you know I'm a member of the WVS and I'm going round to houses collecting. Now I know Mrs Temple has oceans of waste-paper, carbon sheets and old note-books and press cuttings that she doesn't really want, all stuffed away in that huge cupboard in the study. And newspaper files. They are only accumulating dust and make the house dirty. Can you speak to her about them? Or just have them ready and let me know. I do want it done before I go away, and I may be going away soon.'

'I daren't for my life touch any of her papers, Mrs Berkeley. You don't know the wild fury she gets in if she thinks any of her old rubbish is after being touched,' said Kathleen, getting up to put the kettle on the stove. She foresaw that Mrs Berkeley's suggestion would mean extra work for her, and work that would provide her with no thanks.

'But, Kathleen, she wouldn't know. You can't persuade me that in her present state of mind she would miss, say, the carbon copies of books that have been published more than twenty years ago. She's always had a mania for hoarding.'

'Ah, you don't know her. She's a terror the way she goes on if anything in her study is touched. Or in her bedroom. She won't even let me dust in there; she's supposed to do it herself, but, of course, she never puts a hand to it, and that's why there's all the blackness and dirt up there, as I told Miss Phillips. It isn't either as if I could open a door in this house without her knowing. You don't know the artfulness of her.'

'But if you took a little at a time, Kathleen. When she is out. I wouldn't ask, but, after all, that paper is urgently needed for the war. You must have seen the Government appeals?'

'I seen them,' said Kathleen, nodding her head.

'I know you Irish are neutral, but haven't you a sweetheart in the war? You were telling me about getting married last time I was here. Every piece of paper we give to the war effort . . .'

A clear voice called: 'It is Mrs Berkeley down there, is it, cook?'

'Yes, she's here, Madam,' replied Kathleen promptly, taking up the kettle and pouring the water into the jug.

'I'm just coming. I was waiting for the water to boil.' She turned to take the jug from Kathleen's outstretched hand. 'Will you see what you can do?' she murmured. Kathleen nodded, and stood listening till Mrs Berkeley had mounted the stairs. Then she heard:

'Isn't it rather odd to run off and leave me in the middle of tea so that you can gossip with my cook?'

'I wasn't gossiping,' she heard Mrs Berkeley say before they moved into the dining-room and out of earshot. At the table she added: 'I had to wait till the kettle boiled again, hadn't I?'

'Of course Kathleen loves people to go and talk to her. It gives her an opportunity of making up lies about me. But I had really hoped that you, my secretary, wouldn't listen to them.'

'She didn't say anything about you, honestly.'

'What did you say then?'

'I was asking her if she thought there was any spare paper about. I told you that the WVS are collecting it for the Government.'

'I don't know what the Government has told you to do; but I would really prefer you didn't give orders and question my servants in my own house, behind my back. You're not my secretary now . . . are you?' Claire stopped as those all too familiar doubts, black question marks whose function was to push her into a chaos of uncertainty about everything, shot up like demons. 'Why don't you answer? Are you my secretary? I used to have that wooden woman, but she left.'

'There's no need to be sarcastic, Claire.' Mrs Berkeley took up the last piece of toast. Then she went on: 'It is like this. I happen to feel that in these terrible days of England's trial it is the duty of all to see that there is no waste; in fact, we are supposed to report people who hoard food or wilfully waste valuable materials.'

'Are you going to report me?' inquired Mrs Temple. 'Do you go round telling people to put their lights out? Air-raid wardens, they are called. Kathleen says they are the people who will report me unless I'm careful. I do try to be careful. I told the last one who came that I was terribly sorry, and luckily Kathleen found some whisky, because as a rule we never have any whisky. He ended up by being quite nice.'

'No, I am not an air-raid warden,' said Mrs Berkeley. She sighed. It was evident that unless Kathleen did help, nothing could be done about the paper. She sat listening with apparent attention while Mrs Temple started to tell her about another air-raid warden whose mother had turned out to be at school with her in Notting Hill, but she was really wondering if she should ring up Miss Phillips. She would see the importance of it. On the other hand, she didn't want anyone else at the WVS to get the credit for such a big haul of paper. And if they were going away. . . .

When she next looked at the clock, she was surprised to see how time had fled: 'My dear, I must be going: I had no idea it was that time.'

'You can't go yet.'

'I must. Supposing there is an air-raid.'

But it was no easy matter to make her farewells as brief as she wanted them to be. And even as she stood in the hall, that sound occurred which struck terror to her heart: 'What's that?' she asked, pausing with upheld finger.

'I expect it's a dog howling. There's one that lives down the road with a very melancholy disposition.'

The wail became louder, filling the world with its desolation: 'That's no dog,' said Mrs Berkeley. 'It's the Warning.'

'Warning of what?'

'Of German aeroplanes. Oh, my goodness, why didn't I go a few minutes ago? I promised May I'd be home before it got dark, and I thought I'd just do it. If you hadn't kept me. . . .'

Kathleen, coming up to do the black-out, said: 'Aren't they early tonight?'

'I've never known them so early,' said Mrs Berkeley with bitterness.

Kathleen went into the dining-room, and then stopped to listen: 'There're planes overhead,' she called back to the others.

'Oh dear! And you haven't a shelter, have you?' Mrs Berkeley wrung her hands. She couldn't help it. Now that she could hear the sinister grinding moan of the aeroplane engines, it seemed certain that they were rushing straight for her; they were going to aim at the one spot on which she was standing. 'We'd better go down to the kitchen or underneath the stairs. That's the safest place.'

Kathleen, hearing, reappeared: 'Those will be our airy-planes,' she informed Mrs Berkeley. 'Else our guns would have opened up.'

'How do you know? To me they sound just like the Germans,' said Mrs Berkeley. She turned to shout at Claire, whose hand was on the hall-door latch: 'What are you doing? Keep the door closed. We must go to the kitchen.'

She led the way, and Claire, surprised but obedient, followed. 'Have you heard a bomb?' she inquired.

'Not yet.'

'How nice and cosy it is in here,' said Claire, entering the kitchen with pleasure. 'I do hope Kathleen won't mind us being here.'

'Of course she won't mind. I'm so troubled about May. She will be so anxious about me. And there she is, all alone.'

'Ask her to come here. I am sorry for all lonely people, because I know what it is.'

'Don't be silly! How could she go out in this? I wonder if I should telephone her.' Kathleen came in, and she turned to her. 'It's my friend, you see. She'll be so worried to think of me out in this.'

'You can telephone her if you like. But it's still quiet. There's no gunfire yet. You'd be home before they started with any luck.'

'Oh, you mustn't go if you're frightened of the Zeppelins,' said Claire. 'Do sit right up to the fire. Perhaps I could find you some whisky.'

'It's *not* the Zeppelins. It's *not* the last war. The Germans send over hundreds of aeroplanes to shower bombs. Now, listen!' She held up a finger, transfixing the other two in an attitude of attention. 'That was a bomb, I believe.'

'No, it wasn't,' contradicted Kathleen. 'It was gunfire, but very far away.'

Mrs Temple flitted out of the room and up the stairs. 'Where's she gone?' inquired Mrs Berkeley. 'Do come back, Claire,' she called.

'I'd better go and see what's she up to,' said Kathleen. 'This is when you have to be watching her all the time, for her one idea seems to be to rush to the window and draw back the curtains.'

'Oh, don't let her do that,' implored Mrs Berkeley. 'Go at once!' Huddled in her chair, she wondered once again how she had managed to let herself in for such a situation. She would not have minded so much with some people, but to have to stay with Claire Temple – who was now so much of a lunatic that she would draw the curtains to stare out of the window

while an air-raid was in progress – never putting out the light, never thinking of anybody else, and so giving a full invitation to the Germans to shower their bombs down on the house – was the height of folly. Moreover, supposing the police, supposing the air-raid wardens came, they would blame *her* as accessory after the fact. Claire would get off because of her age and mental condition; and Kathleen was an Irishwoman, and only the maid. But she, she was an Englishwoman and a Jewess, on behalf of whom the war was to some extent being fought. She went to the bottom of the stairs and called up: 'Claire, do come down here. Claire, where are you?'

'I'm here,' said Mrs Temple, reappearing. 'I couldn't find any whisky, but I've found Lisa. Isn't she beautiful?'

'Claire, for goodness' sake, stay quietly here. Don't go near the windows. Supposing a bomb fell even yards away, the windows would all be splintered, and plenty of people have been killed that way.'

'How interesting! Lisa is in one of her naughty moods: she won't stay with me; she wants to go upstairs again to Kathleen.'

'Don't let her go. If you sit quietly down in the chair, she'll stay. I am surprised, with your imagination, Claire, that you don't seem to realise that at any moment we may be killed.'

'Killed at any moment,' said Claire, her attention arrested sufficiently to sit down. 'Well, for myself, I really don't mind. It's obvious that I've lived quite long enough, since I am left alone with no one to talk to except an Irish cook who bullies me. And one or two dull people who used to be my secretaries

and who are certainly very kind, but kind hearts don't make their possessors good company. Quite often, on the contrary. No, I shouldn't mind dying at all.'

'You might be maimed,' said Mrs Berkeley, with some viciousness. 'Or blinded.'

'Might I? Yes, I see. But I don't know that that would make a great deal of difference. For having lost my memory so badly, I am, in a sense, maimed already. I have come to be a bore to my friends just as invalids are bores to their friends. But people feel that they have to go and see invalids, that it would be unkind not to do so, while they don't have the same compulsion about people who have a screw loose in their minds. I've often wondered why that should be so . . . what are you listening to?'

'Guns! Can't you hear them?' rapped out Mrs Berkeley.

'Yes, I do hear something.' Kathleen came back into the room, and Mrs Temple turned to her: 'Kathleen, can't you find anything for Mrs Berkeley to drink? Just a drop of whisky or something. She feels she may be killed at any moment, and though I think that's a stimulant in itself . . .'

'I told you, Madam. We haven't any whisky.'

'It's May I'm worrying about really. She'll be so anxious about me. I wonder, should I telephone?'

'Why don't you?' inquired Kathleen.

'Because the Government has asked us not to telephone while there's a raid on.'

'Oh, I wouldn't mind that. They just have to be saying those things, do you know?'

'That's not so, Kathleen,' said Mrs Berkeley, aroused. 'The

point is that the lines must be kept clear for urgent calls, for the fire services and ambulances.'

Kathleen said nothing. She had done her best; she had said what the person really wanted you to say, and then, in the contrary English way, they turned on you for doing it. She was sorry for Mrs Berkeley, but she wished she would go home out of the way.

Mrs Berkeley was indeed to be pitied. For her own words had convinced her that obviously she couldn't in decency telephone. Her personality was resolved into two irreconcilable components: the WVS patriot, who laboured resolutely on behalf of a great and inspiring cause; who did everything the Government asked her to do, including the recent sacrifice of an almost new aluminium saucepan; and another Mrs Berkeley, the instinctive one, who was just a shuddering bundle of instinctive fear, the animal sniffing the scent of the slaughter-house. Her need, like that of the animal, was to moan out her fear; instead she put her hand over her mouth, closed her eyes, and remembering the advice about taking deep breaths in any emergency, proceeded to follow it.

'I remember they brought one Zeppelin down near where one of the Willses, Mary Wills, lived,' said Mrs Temple. 'She's been dining out on it for weeks. What if they brought one down near us, and the Germans came here? I could speak to them, and you know German, don't you, Sara?'

'I certainly wouldn't speak to a Hun,' said Mrs Berkeley, momentarily interrupting her exercise.

'You don't like them? No, I don't. Not altogether. But I did feel when I was in Germany that I was surrounded by a kind of peace, not a peace that passeth understanding, but the peace which attends a good digestion. My husband had a German mistress, as, of course, you know. . . .'

'No, I don't. I never met your husband. Listen!' She stared over at Kathleen. 'Can't you hear? There's a plane right overhead. His engine has slowed.'

After a listening pause, Kathleen said: 'It's going away. Oh, they're not really here yet; it'll be much worse later.'

'Do you think so?'

'Of course. It's nothing at all yet. If you feel worried about the other lady, now's your chance to be getting quick back to her.'

'Do you still live in that maisonette where I came and had tea with you and your friend, Miss what's-her-name? I know how devoted you are to each other.' Mrs Temple paused, hoping for a fervent declaration which would, she felt, clinch matters. But, as none came, she went on: 'And such an odd Italian woman came in, do you remember, with brown, dirty, wrinkled hands carrying loads of rings. I remember her catching hold of my sleeve. Everything, all the rugs and hangings, everything so intimate, so . . . oriental. I adored it. May I come again?'

Mrs Berkeley was forcing herself to a resolve: 'Do you really think it will be worse later?'

Kathleen nodded. 'Why, there's nothing here now,' she said. 'They've gone away over to the Docks. You won't hear a sound yourself.'

Mrs Berkeley listened. It was true. Peace seemed momentarily to reign.

'Well, I'll go. I've got my things on, and we do live near the District. I'll run down the hill and get in at Notting Hill Gate . . .'

'And you'll be home in the shake of a cow's tail,' said Kathleen, rising. 'I'll go up with you; then I can put on the light in the hall, and turn it out just as you open the door. You have a torch, have you?'

'Yes, I have my torch. You do think that's the best, do you?'

'Much the best.'

'You're not going?' cried Mrs Temple, who had followed this conversation with some difficulty.

'Yes, I must. May will be so anxious. I can't bear to think of her in the shelter all alone. We make ourselves a cup of tea, you know, and it's all so cosy.'

'Kathleen will make you some tea. Yes, let's all have a cup of tea. It is a pity that there isn't any whisky. Shall I try and find some again?'

'No, stay here,' cried Mrs Berkeley in alarm. Kathleen said: 'You don't understand, Madam. Mrs Berkeley feels she ought to try and get home while it's safe. The guns may start again at any moment.'

'But you won't like that, will you? I should think the best thing is for you to stay the night. You can sleep in the room next to mine. I'd love you to.'

Mrs Berkeley momentarily hesitated. But she caught Kathleen's eye, which seemed to convey that while Mrs Temple must be humoured, it was a preposterous notion for anyone to consider staying under the same roof as her.

'Kind of you, Claire, but I've made up my mind. I must go.'
Mrs Berkeley turned resolutely to the stairs.

'Of course I know how devoted you are to the friend with
whom you live. Are you still in that old maisonette? Where
I came to tea. And met that old Italian woman who tugged
at my sleeve,' cried Claire, fluttering up the stairs after her.
'May I come and see you again?'

'Yes, certainly. Any time. No, we may be going away,' said
Mrs Berkeley distractedly. Kathleen switched on the light,
and now she was pausing in front of the hall door suffering
in full the agony of that moment when she would go out into
the dark, with death raining furiously in a delirium of noise
at her any moment, any second, from the skies.

'Are you going away then? Why are you going away? Shan't
you come and see me then?'

'I don't know. I'll ring you up and let you know. We shall
have to see.'

'Have you your torch ready?' cried Kathleen. 'Now then,
I'll turn off the light, and you slip out quickly.'

'Wait a moment,' cried Mrs Berkeley. 'I heard something;
if it wasn't a bomb, it was guns.'

'Is there an air-raid on?' inquired Mrs Temple. 'Don't go if
you're afraid of the Zeppelins. Stay the night. We have plenty
of room.'

It was probably the word 'Zeppelins' that decided Mrs
Berkeley to cry: 'Now', to slip back the latch, and step out into
the unknown as the shivering soul launches itself upon
eternity. But she really couldn't stay any longer in the vicinity
of one who imagined this war to be the same as the last war.

'She's gone,' said Kathleen, turning on the light again. 'Come on back to the kitchen, and I'll make us some tea. If I'd given that one tea, she'd never have gone.'

'So oriental, isn't she?' said Mrs Temple, following her. 'I went to have tea with her and her friend, and their maisonette was festooned with carpets. And there was an Italian woman with rings on her dirty brown fingers who kept plucking at my sleeve. . . . Of course she and her friend are Lesbians.'

Putting the kettle on the stove, Kathleen paused to ponder over this word which she had heard used with some frequency by her mistress, but whose meaning, though considering its source it was bound to be something bad, had escaped her. She didn't like to ask Harold, and, of course, she wouldn't betray her ignorance to Mrs Temple. Now she said in a detached voice: 'Isn't she a Jewess?'

'Profoundly and utterly so,' cried Mrs Temple. She sat down with Lisa in her lap. 'She bored me more than ever today with something about an uplift society which she has joined. The Government is now her lord and master; they tell her to do things, and she goes and does them. The Government is the Sultan and she is one of the favourites of the harem . . . isn't everything very noisy?'

'That's the battery in Kensington Gardens,' said Kathleen. 'They've opened up on the German airyplanes.'

'It's really very enterprising of the Germans to come over and bomb us like this, isn't it?'

Kathleen, setting out cups and saucers, paused. 'Mother of God, wasn't that a bomb?'

'Yes, I think it was,' nodded Mrs Temple. She sat stroking

the cat and listening to the noise of the guns. While the air-raid was on, she was thinking, Kathleen would let her stay down here; she even listened to her conversation with some attention.

'And do you know,' said Mrs Berkeley much later to her friend when, the All Clear having gone, they prepared for bed, 'poor Claire is much worse. Quite batty. She doesn't for one single moment realise that there's a war on.'

CHAPTER FIVE

I

Had he made a mistake, Mr Francis Maitland wondered, as his cab turned from the romantic degree of London's early-autumnal black-out falling on one of its main arteries in which the shrouded lights glowed pensively against the gathering dusk, into the darker side turning. It was all pretty enough now, but what about getting home? Would they be able to find a taxi? Going out to dine now that the summer was over was an adventure not to be undertaken without due expectation of reward and profit.

And that was where his misgivings came in. He had been warned that old Claire had gone completely ga-ga, that it was too embarrassing and quite too dreary to go and visit her these days. Of course if it weren't for the war and the black-out, and everybody being so busy – and then there was the point about not eating other people's rations – one would feel it was one's duty to go. But as it was. . . . Besides, his chief informant had told him, Claire, like the Bourbons, had forgotten nothing and learnt nothing, and in 1941 there was not even museum space for such relics.

It was at this point that a spark of sympathy had been struck in Mr Maitland's breast. For these days he, too, carried with him an uneasy feeling that he was outmoded. He had been so long out of England that his friends seemed nearly all dead and scattered. His escape from the South of France on a coal-barge was a topic that was now exhausted, just as he had exhausted his stay with the Lett-Wilsons in Cornwall. It was obvious that now the raids were over, at least for the present, he must live in London, where at least there was his club, and one could get books. But people, they were more difficult to find! And so he had resolved on looking up Claire.

'If you should go, in spite of being warned,' his adviser had told him, 'be sure and ring Miss Phillips. It's no good speaking to Claire: she is certain to forget all about it.'

He had done that. And Miss Phillips had also told him that while Mrs Temple would be delighted to see him, he would find her very changed. Protesting the endurance of old friendship, he had fixed a date. So at least he might rely on a meal awaiting him. But, for the rest, Mr Maitland, who prided himself on ordering his life by eliminating, so far as they could be eliminated, such unpleasant facts as hunger, cold, fear and boredom, wondered now that the moment had come if he not made one of those inevitable miscalculations that have such a lowering effect on the spirits.

The cab stopped, and Mr Maitland got out. 'Are you sure this is it?'

'That's the number, sir. And I think it looks as if you was expected. The lady didn't ought to leave the door open with the light showing.'

He glanced up: it was true. A light streamed downwards, and a figure was standing by the open door. Hastily he paid off his driver, and went through the gate, a prey to a sudden onrush of trepidation. How much better had he done to have dined quietly at his club, and let the two young men call in on him there.

'Francis, is that you?'

He did not reply till he was abreast: 'Claire! Do let's go in so that I can see you properly.'

He closed the door behind them, and he was looking at a small figure in a black embroidered fringed shawl, saying, as he took both her hands: 'My dear, how wonderful to see you again! After all these years! And how little, yes, how little you've changed.' And, to an extent, what he was saying was true, he thought, as he awaited her reply: the large eyes were still brilliant; her cheeks delicately flushed, and she hadn't sprouted hairs on her face, the worst monstrosities of female old age.

'How nice of you to say so. But I have changed. I've lost my memory, and that makes me very tiresome. But you haven't changed at all. Still handsome, still distinguished! What are you doing now? Are you publishing anything? Or writing? I can't write at all scarcely. I have to run the whole of the house by myself. Just a cook, and a woman who comes in now and then . . .'

He took off his overcoat and laid it carefully on the chest while she chattered. As he remembered she had always chattered. The chatter had often been quite amusing, but now was it going to be amusing? For his part he had always favoured that trick of silence by which women imposed on men a temporary belief in their feminine pliability and understanding.

It might, as one usually found, after one had made love to them or married them, be only an illusion and a sheath over crass stupidity, but in middle life – he did not care to use the word 'old' yet – it made for a certain restfulness. Besides, he could do what talking was required.

'Do come in to the fire, and have a glass of sherry,' she was saying. 'I only use this one room now, because that is all I am allowed. I am simply at the mercy of my cook. You have no idea.'

'War-time, war-time. I shock everybody in this country by saying out aloud how I hate the war. Not for the proper reasons, you understand, the humanitarian reasons, but because it is making civilisation untenable for any of us.'

'I am so sorry there is nobody coming to meet you. I did try, or Phil tried, to get someone – whoever was it? – but then she rang up to say she had got flu or something. It is dreadful for you just to have me . . .'

'But it's what I'd so much rather. After all these years, there is so *much* to talk about. But, by the way, I have taken the privilege of an old friend, and my son – he's in the Air Force, you know – has been dining with an American friend of ours. At least I don't know him, but his mother was a great friend of mine. She had a very nice villa near Cannes, and one used to run in every day for cocktails . . . can I help you? Are you looking for something?'

'The sherry! But I've found it: this is it, isn't it?'

'Yes. Can I open it?'

'No, I've got the corkscrew. Do go on. You were saying . . .?'

'So I feel bound to do something for the son, who's over

here on Intelligence or something Hush-Hush, you know. He's dying to meet you, my son says; so I said they might come round after dinner, about nine, you know, to pay their compliments and fetch me home.'

'But how nice! Only why didn't they come to dinner? I should have been delighted. I do hope this sherry is all right.'

'Thank you. Let us drink to happier days in store.'

'They are not in store for me, but I will certainly drink to the aspiration. Is it passable?'

'The sherry? Very good. Very good indeed.'

Kathleen came into the room wearing her most aloof air, and unburdened her tray containing a small joint and accompaniments. Miss Phillips, who had rushed in on her way home from the office to see that everything was all right for this new man visitor, had asked her not to use the lift: 'You know how helpless men are over that sort of thing, and Mrs Temple would be sure to spill everything, or forget about it.' Kathleen had decided to omit soup as too much trouble, and she now cast a look over at her mistress to see how she was behaving, for Miss Phillips had also fussed *her* up, impressing on her that Mr Maitland was an old and dear friend, and had lately come back from abroad, and must be welcomed properly. She had got the mistress into a proper dither of excitement, and Kathleen was sure that, as a consequence, and with the bottle of burgundy and sherry, the fat would be in the fire before the end of the night. At the best the queer one would get drunk and probably cry. And, she decided, this Mr Maitland was a small wisp of an old man who didn't seem worth all the commotion.

'Dinner is served, Madam.'

As Kathleen left the room she heard Mr Maitland say: 'Now I'm going to be very interfering and take this bottle of burgundy, that I see you have warming in front of the fire, away and put it on the table to cool again. The temperature of the room is quite sufficient, but how few of our domestics or indeed women generally – I except you, of course, Claire – can be made to understand that.'

He went on talking while Claire carved the joint, and carved it, considering her age, considering everything, quite efficiently. Really, people, he was beginning to think, had exaggerated. Of course she still had her old way of cutting in on what people were saying with something completely irrelevant. But then many women were like that; they just couldn't listen. That was why they rarely learnt anything. 'Now do tell me about our friends. London is a desert to me; you've no idea. I've kept such little track. Oh, I must tell you how sorry I was to hear about Edith Barlow.'

'She's my oldest friend.'

'Yes, but you know, of course, about her death.'

'So she did; she did die. I know! I was fearfully upset. I cried about it. Even though she really despised me, she was my oldest friend, and she came every Sunday, or nearly every Sunday, and bullied me.'

'What I heard was that their house was bombed; and so they moved to Bournemouth, and there, apparently at her age the shock was too much for her, she died. But perhaps you can tell me more. The press had scandalously little about it. There was a short obituary in *The Times*. A woman, you know, who really had a mind. You ought to have written something for one of the weeklies, say *The Spectator*.'

'Oh, I should, shouldn't I? After all, I've known her for years. She came every second Sunday and bullied me. Ought I to write something? Shall I do it now? I mean tomorrow.'

'I'm afraid it's too late now. She died some time in June, didn't she? But she really wrote some readable things.'

'She never got over Byron's incest, do you think? She dragged it into everything.'

'Oh no. Not really! I protest! Of course she was in love with Byron: Byron was the great love of her life, *undoubtedly*. And I suppose she was jealous of Augusta. Though fond of her, too. But you do remember that lovely story of the little girl who was lost at a picnic, oh, but you *must* remember. . . .'

She didn't remember, but she was beginning to remember, as she observed him with brilliant perplexed eyes, more about this man who was dining with her. A picture was forming: of course he had published in rather an amateur way; he had two wives; she had known his wife, a rather mousy little thing, who had divorced him. Then he had married again, and lived abroad. But before he had gone abroad he had come to quite a lot of parties that she and Wallace had given. . . .

She broke in on what he was saying: 'Do you remember the champagne parties Wallace and I used to give? We just had a few sandwiches and Wallace made the fillings himself, and they only cost about five pounds.'

'Don't I? Delightful occasions.' He paused. Evidently one mentioned Wallace: indeed they had told him she loved talking about the man whose most famous mistress she had been.

'I was so amazed to hear of his death. Just before the war, wasn't it? In Dinard? Or was it Trouville?'

'I don't know. He is dead, isn't he? Poor old Wallace. But he owes me so much money.'

'I met his last lady-love, you know. The one who was with him when he died.'

'What did you think of her?'

He shrugged: 'May I help myself to more of these delicious, but delicious beans? A very earnest young lady who took him, you know, *au grand sérieux*.'

'I would so like to meet her. Won't she come and see me? Do ask her if she'll come and see me.'

'I am sure she'd be delighted. But she's gone to New York, or somewhere. To be candid, and one can always, as I remember, be candid with you, Wallace did rather impose on people, don't you think? As a man of letters, I mean. It was only the Americans who took him seriously. My American friends, the mother of this boy who's coming this evening to meet you, tell me he gave such bad parties in New York on one evening in the week. I mean the drink was bad . . . but I'm chattering too much, and you're not eating a thing.'

'Oh, I am. It's not very good, is it? Do refill your glass. I'm neglecting you.'

'Let me give you some more first. This will be better because it should have cooled off by now.'

'Won't you have some more meat?'

'No, thank you. I got out of the way of eating much meat in France. I must get into it again, because, of course, the

English climate demands loads of roast beef. My dear, you don't know how I'm dreading this winter!'

'Oh, so am I! In the summer it's much better. One can walk about the streets. And I spend hours sitting on that seat opposite. Because now and then people come and talk to me. Quite sweet people. I was talking to a very nice woman, who was a refugee, she said, this afternoon.'

'London is simply full of them. It teems with them. We shall be no better than New York by the time the war is over. But London can't absorb them, the way New York does. They stand out like wens on a face. I think they've disfigured the scene far more than the bombs, don't you? Don't let's talk about them; now who else did we know?'

'Are you publishing anything now? I do wish I could be published in that paper edition. They sell in their thousands and thousands, I believe.'

'No, I'm doing absolutely no publishing. Or, of course, I should *insist* that you write more memoirs for me. As for that Goose or Pelican or Duck, or whatever they call it, I don't think it will last.'

'But everybody buys them because they are so cheap.'

'How you would shock George Moore. He would turn in his grave if he heard you. You know, he'd never let his publishers . . .'

'Is George Moore dead? I never met him. Of course I knew Yeats. One entered a Frigidaire when one met Yeats. But so handsome. And then did I tell you I once met Parnell? I had tea with him on the Terrace of the House. He was so word-bound. But Kitty O'Shea thawed him out. Men like that are always one-woman men. Now the men in my life have always liked lots of women. That's been so unfortunate for me. . . . How is your wife?'

'Now I wonder which wife you mean. It was Hilda you knew, wasn't it?'

'Yes, poor Hilda. I suppose she wasn't smart enough for you?'

'I didn't mind that: it was her stupidity that repeated itself too incessantly. But Elizabeth, though a change at first, was, I soon found, a change-over merely to another form of stupidity: and one that seemed even more trying. She could not resist Russians, especially if they had a beard; if she had met Rasputin, she would have sat at his feet, hoping thereby to be raised to his bed. Still . . .'

'Are you publishing anything? I do wish you could get me into one of those sixpenny paper editions. Don't you think *Weary Leaf* might be suitable?'

Mr Maitland, feeling irritation surge up, checked it by laying his knife and fork neatly together, taking another sip of wine, and wiping his mouth before he answered. This was evidently the snag: she would go on saying the same thing over and over again; asking the same completely absurd question.

'I told you: I'm not publishing; I'm not doing anything. I'm just the dilettante, the poor faded butterfly, if butterflies did fade, come home to perish in London fogs and snows. My dear, may I say how grateful I am that you haven't asked me about Michael Arlen and Willie Maugham? My friends give me a brief glance; say something polite about being glad I am safe; and then plunge with eagerness into that topic. Of course now, thank heavens, their fears are allayed.'

'But why should I ask you about them? Has anything happened to either of them?'

'Nothing; that's it. Nothing at all. Everybody escaped; everybody, even if covered with coal-dust, is completely safe.'

Of course she wouldn't understand a word of that. But it would be too tedious to explain. That familiar sensation of weariness was descending upon him. One did one's best; one tried to entertain, but if there were no response, then, more and more, one felt inclined to give up bothering, to steal quietly home to one's electric fire and warm bed.

'Michael Arlen covered with coal-dust!'

He hurried on: 'But how nice not to talk about the madding war! I must congratulate you about something else; you're the only person who has not told me long stories of how nearly they were killed. After the fifth account of how the windows were all broken and so on and so forth, one looks at them, you know, and wonders – would it have mattered so much if they had been? I won't say one does; one just sees out of the corner of one's eye the temptation approaching, so that there is time to say: "Get thee behind me, Satan." But I was really sorry to hear about Edith Barlow; though, as you so rightly said just now, her continued liaison with Byron did begin to pall.'

'She was my oldest friend. She came here every Sunday, no, every second Sunday, to lunch. And bullied me. But she's dead, isn't she?'

'Quite dead. She was one of the ones to whom it really did

happen, even if only at a second remove. You don't seem to be enjoying your food at all. It's my fault; I'm talking too much.'

'No, you're not. I'm so dull myself; I never go to theatres or do anything interesting. I've lost my memory, you see. . . . Oh, how dreadful of me. Your plate is empty. Won't you have any more?'

'No, really, thank you very much.'

'Then would you mind ringing the bell? I've got such a bad-tempered cook. And if she has to wait, and the savoury is spoilt . . . have we kept her waiting long?'

'No, indeed: a mere trifle of time.'

She watched him return to his seat and raise his glass, and more of his identity became plain to her. Eagerly, she said: 'Oh, do you remember the time when we were both staying with the Lett-Wilsons, and you came into my bedroom to read me some manuscript, and I heard a sound outside the door, and I opened it, and there was Mrs Clarke-Thompson standing just outside? Of course she'd been trying to see through the keyhole. She thought you had been making love to me.'

Kathleen came in with the tray just as she spoke these words; and thereby stopped Mr Maitland from making the rejoinder: 'I wish I had been.' Instead he looked surprised, and said meditatively: 'How strange! I don't remember that at all.'

'But you must do. Oh, this looks nice. Kathleen can make such good savouries.'

Mr Maitland watched Kathleen leave the room without showing by a flicker of the face that she had heard any of the conversation. Rather a pretty young woman, and he was regretful that now she would probably have the notion for the rest of her life that he was a wicked old roué.

'Is there some more wine?' his hostess was asking him.

'Yes, let me fill your glass.'

He observed her drinking eagerly, and made a note that the bottle was now probably one of the poor creature's consolations. She set down her glass, and after taking a mouthful of food, said, leaning towards him eagerly: 'Do you remember the time when we were both staying with the Lett-Wilsons, and after we had all gone to bed, you came in to read me a manuscript . . .'

On and on it went; really he couldn't bear it. He had to interrupt. 'Yes, dreadful woman, I remember she . . .'

'She always stole about in bedroom slippers or her shoes had rubber soles.'

'Talking of bedrooms, do tell me how our *enfant terrible* is getting on. I mean, of course, Christine. Someone told me she'd become a pacifist, the kind that shouts about it, I mean. So credible! That is the trouble about all those who commit adultery for the sake of adultery, isn't it? Their earnestness comes out into everything. I mean they sin with such good intentions that it has to be proclaimed from the house-tops. Whom is she sinning with now, because everybody must know?'

'But I don't know. You see, I don't see anybody; I don't hear any gossip.'

She was speaking excitedly now, fixing him with her eyes that glittered, he decided, just like those of the Ancient

Mariner. Feeling a premonition of disaster, he said hastily: 'But, anyhow, who cares? She tried to "make me" one time. You know, or perhaps you don't know, the Americans have such a blunt phrase about the overtures of seduction. They call it: "Making a person". But I . . .'

'I never see her. And she used to give me such good dinners, and behave so demurely, that one felt she wore her reputation rather prettily, on the whole.'

'Oh, but you saw the best side of her. You didn't have to listen to the love letters she insisted on reading one. Pages and pages. And, honestly, no one would ever believe me, but she did tie them all up with blue ribbon.'

'She gave me such good dinners, but now she never invites me any more. I'm quite deserted. I live on an island, because I'm shipwrecked.'

'Nonsense. *You* to talk of being shipwrecked. What a good savoury this is! You still have a good cook, and I congratulate you.'

'She is a good cook when she troubles to be, but she is frightfully cruel to me. I am shipwrecked alone with her on a desert island. Miss Phillips, you remember Phil, only comes every Saturday. But how dreadful of me talking about myself! I mustn't do it. Have you got a wife now?'

'No, I'm deserted too, just, if you will insist, like yourself. One has nothing to do but huddle by the fire and remember ghosts and read old books. And really there is a kind of pleasure about it all; a gloomy pleasure perhaps, but still a pleasure. One gets into that Browning sort of mood: *Since there my past life lies, why alter it?*'

'I don't get any pleasure out of it, gloomy or otherwise. I find it terrible. I'm so unhappy that I don't know how to bear it.'

Mr Maitland felt his skin contract coldly with distaste. So it had come at last, that cry of the heart; those emanations of naked misery. One of the doors which, during the course of a fairly long life, he had generally been successful in creeping past, head carefully turned in the other direction, had opened emitting its full blast of the fogs and vapours of depression. And now what to say? If he spoke it would be merely to say something completely banal. Such as: 'Come, come. It can't be as bad as all that.' And he had always felt it due to himself to avoid the banal, even before the uncritical.

'Let me give you some more wine,' he said instead. And, of course, he thought, as he poured the last of the bottle into her glass, that was the one thing he ought not to have done. He should have kept it for himself. For the more tipsy she became, the more maudlin she would also become.

She had sensed his disapproval; she was saying: 'Do forgive me. It is such bad manners to be so *triste*. I should hold my tongue. There is no excuse for me.'

'The excuse that you have retained your sensibilities, whole and entire. At least as regards yourself.'

He stopped, shocked at himself. Why had he added that rider? Was it cruel? He awaited her reply with some trepidation.

'You mean that I'm a tiresome egotist, only concerned with myself. That I haven't done what the Christians tell us we should do, die to ourselves. But you haven't either, have

you? I know you are much younger than I am; but you are dependent on other people, at least for conversation, aren't you? I remember your telling me that. Of course you haven't lost your memory; that makes the difference, doesn't it?'

So Claire could still understand something, and understanding, strike back. Had she struck home? Surely, surely there was a greater difference between them than the fortuitous circumstance that his brain still functioned equably, that the visible world still palpably existed, that events marshalled themselves in their order of time and season under his observing and not unappreciative eyes. Twiddling the stem of his empty wine-glass, he let his glance dwell with apparent casualness upon his hostess. He noticed that now her face was flushed with the dry flush of age, that her shawl had slipped down over one shoulder, and that some grey woollen garment had ridden up above the line of dress. A strand of white hair had also escaped from its pin; her neck didn't look any too clean either. She might be any semi-drunken old drab, except that, to be fair – and Mr Maitland prided himself on his fairness – there was the brilliancy of those large appealing eyes, the still beautiful line of her jaw.

'I certainly haven't died to myself,' he told her. 'Why ever should one? Oneself is the last and most ubiquitous company one has, and therefore one should try to entertain oneself to the very best of one's ability. I have never claimed to consider other people interesting except as they interest me. But, my dear Claire, I wasn't in the least criticising you. We are both subjective people creating our own worlds . . .'

He paused, partly because he felt he was rambling and not

succeeding in holding her attention; partly because he heard steps outside. Kathleen appeared. 'Are you ready for your coffee, Madam?'

'Oh yes, we are, aren't we?' Kathleen disappeared, and she said: 'Do you mind having it here? I'm only allowed one room these days. You see, I have only one maid, and I have to do everything for myself.'

'Don't apologise. The war is gradually stripping us of all our dear creature comforts. But we are not going to talk about the war, are we?'

'No. What were we talking about? Oh, I remember. My losing my memory, and you haven't. Henry James told me once not to rely on perennial charm. And he was so right. But for a woman, what else is there? I mean I can't go and write a book about mathematics, because I don't understand mathematics. My charm, if I ever had any, of course, went along with my memory, so that is why I am now on a desert island . . .'

Mr Maitland had stolen a glance at his watch. It was twenty to nine. They might be arriving soon. He had better do something more in the way of preparation.

'By the way, forgive me for interrupting you, but when my son – whose name incidentally is John; I think you saw him when he was in his perambulator, just about the time I was behaving *so* badly to poor Hilda, you *must* remember?'

'How is Hilda?'

'You must ask John. He knows about her. I believe she's perfectly well, and lives somewhere in Devonshire. . . .'

'I wish she'd come and see me. Does she ever come to Town?'

'I doubt it. When John comes, ask him. He is going to bring a young American with him. . . .'

'But why didn't they come to dinner? I should have been delighted. Have we had dinner? Yes, of course, we have. Here's Kathleen bringing something else. Oh, coffee. Do you mind our having coffee here because . . .'

'Not a bit. When they come, they'll probably be here at about nine, you must talk to this American – Lance Burroughs is his name – about Henry James. And AB and HG and Oscar Wilde, and Uncle Tom Cobley and all . . .' he finished, feeling again that mounting sensation of weariness. The maid was making up the fire. Just an excuse to listen, probably. If so, it was just as well that she should take in that people were coming. Else they'd probably be turned away at the door or something. . . .

'Black or white?'

'Black.'

'But who is this? Is this someone who knew Oscar?'

'Oh no. He's far too young. Young enough to like to listen to someone who did. He's simply longing to meet you.'

'When is he coming?'

'Soon. In a few minutes.'

'No! But have we got enough to give them to drink? Kathleen . . .'

Kathleen, busy now at the side table with her tray, turned. 'Yes, Madam?'

'Have we got whisky or anything?'

'There's only a very *little* whisky, Madam. I was just going to bring it up.' (Kathleen did not add that acting on Miss Phillips's instructions she had, as usual, added water to the decanter. 'He'll have to put up with it,' Miss Phillips had declared. 'If Mrs Temple drinks whisky that isn't diluted on top of the wine and sherry he'll be likely to find her a good deal more trying.')

'Oh, isn't that too bad! I do really think that if people manage my affairs for me, they might be managed a little better. Bring what you have. Try and find some more of something. There are two men coming.'

'It doesn't matter a bit,' interposed Mr Maitland. 'You see, we can't stay very long . . .'

'But I want you to stay.'

'You see, because of taxis and the black-out and . . .'

'You can telephone for a taxi from here.'

'Even so, it might not come for a while, so one has to ask for it in plenty of time. Besides, ever since I returned from the now unhappy land of France, I find I've been sleeping very badly. . . .'

He stopped. There had been a ring at the bell. They were early.

'Do tell me,' Mrs Temple asked. 'Who are these people who are coming? I've forgotten their names. My memory!'

'My son, John. And a young American friend of ours, Lance Burroughs,' he answered briefly. He was occupied in preparing a readjustment of himself. Young people, it was one of their many disadvantages, entailed such a readjustment. Since they thought of one as old, one had, in a measure, to become old; that is to be more decorous, more stylised. He

chose his role: as anyone could see that Claire was half-mad, or if they couldn't see it, would soon hear indisputable testimony that such was the case, he would be the gravely courteous old friend, covering up her blunders as far as possible. Americans always appreciated chivalry.

Kathleen came into the room with the tray containing the whisky decanter and glasses as the bell rang again. Mrs Temple cried urgently: 'Do answer the door. Didn't you hear the bell?'

'I was just going to, Madam,' answered Kathleen rebukingly, but wishing that she could rap out: 'I haven't two pairs of hands, have I?' She went reluctantly and frowningly to the door. Three visitors at once were unheard of, and she hoped they'd go soon and not keep her waiting up till all hours. And probably she'd have to make more coffee!

II

Both the young men who came into the room, the one, John Maitland, short and fair, in the blue uniform of the RAF, and the American, tall and dark and sallow-complexioned, in mufti, were agreeably surprised at their introduction to Mrs Temple. John especially, who had been warned by his father that the old woman with whom he was dining had once been a literary celebrity, but had now fallen into dotage, had anticipated some mumbling toothless Kensington dowager. And thus he had warned his more open-minded friend, to whom everything in the English scene was still grist to his mill, and to whom the carelessly uttered remark: 'She was supposed

162

once upon a time to have known everybody, and been a literary somebody,' was not without its appeal. 'The best thing to do,' John had said, 'is to arrive early, cart the old man home as soon as possible, and then we can go on some place.' And so it had been arranged.

But they both were unprepared for this rather untidy, frail little creature, old, of course, with white hair, but who nevertheless flitted about the room with the vivacity of a young girl, wondering if they would take coffee and apologising for there being so little whisky.

'And what there is, isn't good, is it?' she had added, one of her sudden intuitions making her observant of a momentary something which had crossed Mr Maitland's face as he set his glass down. She clasped her hands. 'I'm so sorry, what can I do?'

She seemed so upset about it that John had hastened to reassure her, the more especially as his father had sat glum, and didn't seem to be in very good form.

'It doesn't matter a bit. In fact, speaking for myself, I dare say I've had as much as is good for me. To tell you the truth, we didn't quite know where this house was, and we were early, so that on our way we turned into quite an attractive pub at the top of the hill.'

'I know. They call it The Goat and Compasses. Someone who came here took me to it once. It was such fun. They had such *good* whisky. Do tell me, Mr Burroughs, isn't it? Can you really get whisky there?'

'You certainly can. If you pay for it,' said Lance, amused and interested.

'Should we go there then? Do let's.'

Mr Maitland judged it time to intervene. 'Nonsense, Claire. We are enjoying your hospitality enormously. It's dark outside, and you'd hate to go wandering about.'

'But I always go wandering about. I love it. If there is anyone to talk to.'

'It's not dark,' said John. He had decided that it was rather a good idea to take this sporting old lady into the saloon bar, the more particularly since his father in his usual way was vetoing everything. 'The moon's up.'

'There you are! It's not dark. And I have my torch. I always carry my torch about with me. It's such a *good* one.'

'There might be an air-raid warning, and you wouldn't surely like to be away from your home if that occurred,' said Mr Maitland, speaking in the indulgent tone one uses to a forward child so as to impress upon the others the way matters stood.

'But I don't mind air-raids in the least. The bombs might fall anywhere. I can't understand the way people run to shelters or must be in their own homes.'

'There's a good deal in what you say,' said John, speaking with the authority his uniform entitled him to. 'At the end of the war we shall probably find that, taking into consideration the number of people killed when a bomb goes through a shelter as they often have done, it would have worked out at evens if we'd never built any shelters. Some of them are pretty jerry-built affairs, too, I can tell you.'

'Don't talk nonsense,' said Mr Maitland, letting his weariness and irritability get the better of him. 'Of course people are safer well below ground. Hampstead Tube, for example, is how many feet underground?'

'I didn't say anything about the Tubes. I said: "Shelters".' He turned to Mrs Temple. 'If you'd like to go out and have a drink at your local, I'm the man to take you.'

'I'd love to go. I'll go and put on my coat, shall I?'

They stood up as she flitted out of the room. Francis said to his son in a low, angry voice: 'Now you've done it.'

'Done what?'

'Let it be on your own head. Can't you see that she is . . .' he tapped his forehead.

'I didn't notice,' said John in a distant voice. The snub still rankled. Mr Maitland turned his back, and then remembered his duty towards an American. 'I don't know if you're interested in furniture, but this table was designed by William Morris . . .' he raised his voice as Claire came back, 'I'm just showing Mr Burroughs your table.'

'But is he interested? I've only put on my old black coat. It's not very grand, is it? Shall I disgrace you all? Had I better go upstairs and find something else?'

'That'll do fine,' said John, stepping forward. 'Now we'll get on our things. You are coming, are you, Sir? Or would you rather wait for us here?'

'No, I'd better come,' said Mr Maitland. Following the others into the hall, he thought that he wouldn't mind some real whisky at least. He'd had just enough to drink to be edgy and fretful. Nor had the dinner been really up to much. Well, it would be the last time. And, since John seemed to have taken charge of Claire, he could explain the position to Burroughs as they went along. He didn't want this son of his dear and hospitable friend, Mrs Burroughs, to get a wrong idea about him.

John did take charge of Claire, guiding her down the steps, and she repaid him with excited chatter:

'Over there, you can't really see, but that used to be my mother's old house. It's nothing but a ruin now. They said that a land-mine had done it.'

'It must have been pretty near you. Weren't you frightened?'

'I forget whether I heard the noise or not. My memory's simply shocking. But when they told me in the morning, I did cry. And just where we are coming to, a famous singer, whose name I forget, tumbled right down the stairs when he was drunk. It was so exciting because there were so many cabs coming and going, and the police . . .'

'Be careful. There's a step here. What happened to him?'

'He just disappeared. But his house is still there. Only my mother's house which we have passed isn't there any more. There was a land-mine. And all that corner disappeared in a night. I cried when I heard about it. Isn't this fun! I'm so glad you came and took us all out. I was having a rather trying visitor, Francis Maitland . . . of course you'll know him, won't you?'

'Yes, I know him. But I know my mother much better. You knew my mother, too, didn't you?'

'Do forgive me. I am sure I knew her. But what is her name? My memory, you see. It makes me blunder about like a blind person trying to feel his way into places and out of places . . .'

'Her name is Hilda. Here we are. Let me go first.' He held the door back for her. And then they passed round the black-out screen into the lights and voices of a small, fairly crowded bar. Heads turned and remained turned, for even the half-aware attention was disturbed by the feeling that the old lady, not an old woman but an old lady, with her head carried high, and hollow, flushed cheeks, who was looking so curiously around her, didn't belong. The only remaining seats were along a bench at the side of the wall, and they heard her say in a clear voice to the Air Force officer who indicated a space to her:

'Do I sit here? Isn't this nice? I mean, to see everybody drinking so happily together.'

Francis Maitland came in just in time to hear the words and observe the covert grins which greeted them. He assumed a remote expression, and sat down as far as he could away from Claire, nodding his head when John asked him if he would have whisky.

This action provided Lance Burroughs with an opportunity of slipping into the space between them. 'I'd like to say how happy I am to have the privilege of meeting you, Mrs Temple,' he said shyly. 'I'm sorry I haven't read any of your novels, but . . .'

'No, of course you haven't. How could you? They're nearly all out of print. I do want to get *Weary Leaf* into one of those paper editions that everybody buys.'

'Mr Maitland has been telling me that you knew Oscar Wilde and Frank Harris and I was particularly interested because there was a play on Broadway about three years ago, written by an Englishman, which relied a good deal on Frank Harris's account of Wilde's last days in Paris. I wondered if . . .'

'Of course I knew Oscar. Dear Oscar! He asked my father if he could marry me. But then he never followed it up. My father said so sensibly that he'd better ask Claire, me. If I had married Oscar, of course I was very young then, and didn't think of marriage to anybody as anything but a joke, but if I had married him, would my whole life have been different? Of course it would.'

There was an interruption while John handed them both a glass of whisky. 'No room for me, I see. Well, I'll let you have your innings.'

Lance nodded gratitude. 'That's very interesting. Do you agree that he was in such penury in Paris, and that . . .'

'It was dreadful, wasn't it? Everything that happened to poor Oscar was dreadful. I can't forget the time I saw him in Boulogne: he was coming down the hill looking just like a country squire, with such a red face. His face lit up when he saw me. And then this woman I was with pulled me away. "You mustn't bow," she said. I didn't want to go, but I went. You see, I was staying with her. But wasn't it dreadful! His face lit up when he saw me, and then the light went like a blind being drawn.'

'I can understand you felt pretty bad about that,' said Burroughs gravely.

'Isn't this whisky nice? Can I buy some? Oh, I've come out without my bag.'

'Ladies mustn't buy drinks: it's my turn now.'

As John Maitland came nearer, his father intercepted him.

'I really don't think it's wise for Lance to get her another drink. She's not used to it, and she was a little, you know, when she left the house. She won't be able to walk home,' he said in a low voice.

'I can't do anything about that: Lance is bringing the drinks right now.'

'And they look like doubles. . . .'

'Of course they're doubles. What does it matter if she does get a bit tight?'

'Here you are,' said Lance, stopping beside them and offering glasses. 'Isn't she a wonderful old lady?'

'Yes, but she really shouldn't drink any more. We had better get her out of here quickly, before we attract any more attention. I wonder if we could get a taxi. And then we could take it on.'

Lance left the old man to fuss over things with John and went back to Mrs Temple. 'Thank you so much for this wonderful whisky. The only thing that's worrying me is that I've left my bag behind me, and I haven't a key, so how will I get into my house?'

'But there's someone there, isn't there? What about that pretty girl who let us in?'

'My cook? Yes, she is pretty, isn't she? But so cruel; oh, she is so *cruel* to me.'

To his horror Lance saw two large tears appear in Mrs Temple's eyes. He said hastily: 'Don't worry about her. We'll fix her for you. Tell me about . . . Henry James.'

'He told me I was not to rely upon perennial charm. Wasn't it true?'

'Not at all. I mean you've still got charm. Loads of it. You knew him very well, didn't you?'

'Yes, but there was a time when he was very unkind to me. He hated getting his feet wet; being dragged into anything. He was a kind man really, oh, a dear, but he hated getting his feet wet. Are you an American?'

'I certainly am.'

'Americans are so nice, though sometimes they need more oiling. What other Americans do I know? I met Louisa Alcott when she came over here.'

He waited: she was twisting the empty glass in her fingers and staring about her with a puzzled air. He said: 'Would you mind elaborating on that? It's all pretty interesting to me, you know.'

'Elaborating? On what?' Her attention had left him, and had gone to a woman who was squeezing in on her other side. 'Don't want to crowd you, Missus,' the woman said to her in a friendly manner, 'but there's a bit of a crush here tonight.'

'Oh, but you are not crowding me a bit. Do make yourself comfortable.' She turned back to Lance: 'This is a public-house, isn't it? I do think it's so pleasant to see everybody sitting together and drinking. Why don't I come here more often?'

'Thinks she owns the blasted place,' said a man standing beside the counter, who, as Francis had observed, had been listening and watching them with frowning hostility. 'Who does she think she is?' Mr Maitland looked away and hoped that John, who had gone out in search of a taxi, wouldn't be very long.

'Do you come here often?' Claire was saying to her new neighbour.

'Now and then. Makes a change, doesn't it? Better than staying at home and wondering if them syreens will go.'

'Syreens? What are they? Do they frighten you or something?'

'Don't suppose I'm more frightened than anyone else,' said the woman, all her friendliness gone. She was realising that the old lady was a toff, and the ones with her were toffs, and that the men standing up by the bar, including her own husband, were listening to them critically.

'You were saying? About Louisa Alcott?' prompted Lance from her other side.

'*Little Women*? One of the very few good books there are. There are so few good books, aren't there? Do you know that I'm afraid that I've come out without my key. I wonder if Kathleen, that's my cook, you know, who is so unkind to me, will let us in. It is an excruciating position, isn't it, to be left entirely at the mercy of one's cook? But that is my position.'

Francis was keenly aware that her words had aroused a movement of ridicule up at the bar. He heard a voice say: 'Won't be so much of that after the war, mate. The chaps coming home, they won't stand for it.' Leaning forward over Lance, he said: 'It's all right, Claire. My boy has gone to fetch a taxi, so that we'll be sending you home soon.'

'How kind of him. Who is he? Oh, you're Francis, Francis Maitland! I thought you'd gone. I must apologise for the wretched dinner I gave you. You did dine, didn't you? This evening?'

'It wasn't wretched. It was very good.'

'I so enjoyed meeting your son. Has he gone?'

'He's gone to find us a taxi. But perhaps we'd better not wait any longer. It's difficult, you know, in the black-out. Shall we go? Do you think you can manage the walk?'

'Oh, yes, perfectly well. It's a mere nothing. You mustn't waste your money on taxis. Not for me, I mean.'

'I'll take your glass back to the bar. If you'll allow me.'

When he returned, he was relieved to see that she was on her feet, and that Lance was opening the door. But immediately he was embarrassed by hearing her say, looking round, and as a sort of general benediction: 'Good night. It's been very pleasant.'

The woman who sat next to Claire mumbled a 'good night', and the barman, who was also the proprietor, called over: 'Good night, Madam, and thank you.'

It was given to Francis to hear arising from the general watchful silence the voice of the man who had previously spoken: 'After the ruddy war, people who think they own the ruddy earth will have to get off, see? And the quicker, the better.'

He hastened after the other two, and came out into what seemed total blackness to hear Claire complaining: 'Isn't it dark! I can't seem to make my torch go. Perhaps we'd better go back into that nice lighted place we were in.'

'If we get you between us,' said Lance, 'we're going to manage fine. Could you take her other arm, Mr Maitland? Now then.'

Francis took her arm, but she stood motionless, swaying slightly; then he heard her say clearly: 'It's most tiresome of me, and ridiculous, but I don't feel I can walk a step. I must be tipsy. Do you think that's it? I can't be paralysed, can I?'

Someone passing by laughed, and a woman's voice called: 'Take more water with it next time.' Mercifully, Francis Maitland, into whose mind the spectacle of police, ambulances and jeering spectators moved as a horrible prospective nightmare, heard Lance say: 'Hold on: I see a cab stopping.' And he raced away.

'Was that woman speaking to me? What is happening? Where am I?'

He tightened his grip on her arm. 'It's all right, Claire. You're with me. Francis Maitland, you know. Our young American friend seems to have spotted a cab. We are going to take you home.'

'Are you Francis Maitland? But I thought he'd been living abroad for ages. Oh, no. He came to dine with me. I feel so confused. I do wish I knew where I was.'

'You're only a few yards from your own home. Ah, here it comes. Lance, you're a marvel! You hold the door, that's right. Now, in you go.'

It was a wonderful feeling, having got her behind closed doors, where she wouldn't make a spectacle of herself. He gave the number to the driver, and then got in himself. Lance followed and sat in the turn-down seat opposite. 'Pretty swift work,' he said complacently. 'There were other people after it, you know.'

'Where are you taking me?' asked Mrs Temple urgently.

'I couldn't see a thing myself,' said Francis. 'I'm no use in the dark.'

'It's not so dark really.'

Mrs Temple rose in her seat, and shouted: 'Let me out. I must get out at once. Let me out!'

Francis pulled at her arm. 'Sit down. We're taking you home. My dear lady, we're taking you home.'

She wasn't listening to him; she was screaming, scream after scream, which attacked Mr Maitland's stomach; he sat frozen in a sick paralysis. He heard Lance speaking to her. 'My dear . . . it's all right. You're nearly home. Honestly. The cab's stopping.'

It was stopping, but perhaps, thought Mr Maitland, it was stopping because the driver thought they were cutting the old woman's throat, robbing her, raping her . . . no, it seemed all right. Lance was opening the door, helping her out. She wasn't saying anything; quite extraordinary for Claire not to be saying anything. . . .

He roused himself, remembering the need for action. If he didn't pay the man, then he might take them on.

'Can you wait just a few minutes? We have to see the lady in. She's not very well. And then we're coming on. Or I am.'

'Where do you want to go to, sir?'

'Only to Knightsbridge. Banns Place. Do you know it?'

'All right. But you won't be long, because . . .'

'Only a few moments. I promise,' said Francis. He followed

the other two, and then heard steps and paused. It was John, who said: 'Oh, so you managed to get a taxi. I couldn't get one anywhere; I went right to Notting Hill. . . .'

'Why didn't you come back and tell us?'

'I did. They told me at the pub you'd just left. So I footed it on here. Is the taxi waiting?'

'Yes, so we must just say goodbye quickly. Do you understand? Mrs Temple isn't well.'

'Oh dear, I'm so sorry.'

John's voice was correctly commiserative, for they had gone up the steps, and he saw the old lady hovering in the hall. Mr Maitland said: 'We must close the door because of the light.'

'Here's my bag; it was here all the time,' said Mrs Temple. 'Kathleen's just found it for me.'

'Aren't you feeling well? I'm so sorry.'

'But I'm quite well. I've had such a lovely time.'

'Ah ha,' Lance greeted John. 'Who couldn't find a cab? And who did?'

'Very smart, aren't you? The American way of life?'

'Looks like you've got to rely on it when you want something done.'

'Why are we all standing here?' asked Mrs Temple. 'Do come in, everybody, and I'll try to find something to drink for us.'

'No, my dear,' said Francis firmly. 'I'm so sorry, but we can't possibly. I promised the taxi man that we wouldn't be a moment. He is taking us on home.' He followed Mrs Temple into the dining-room, where she was opening the sideboard cupboard and said: 'It's really "good night" this time. And I want to thank you for a wonderful evening.'

'Has everything been all right? Have you all got to go?' She turned to John, who had followed. He said soothingly: 'It seems a shame; but taxis *are* taxis in these hard times. But may I come round again, and talk to you about my mother? I haven't been able to get a look-in the whole evening with you.'

'Oh, please do. And give her my kindest regards. I do wish she'd come and see me.'

'I am sure she would if she were in London. But she'll be so interested when I tell her I've seen you.'

'Isn't she in London? . . . Oh, goodbye . . . I'm so stupid, I've forgotten your name.'

'Burroughs, Lance Burroughs. But it doesn't matter a bit. It's been wonderful meeting you. Thank you very much.'

'And you'll come again, won't you?'

'I certainly will; first chance I get. But I'm flying back rather soon. However, if I get over again . . .'

'Do get over again.' She was in the hall looking from face to face wonderingly. 'Where have you all *been?*' she asked urgently. 'All this time?'

Francis Maitland said quickly: 'I've been abroad, you know, Claire. And my son, this is the first time he has had the privilege of meeting you.'

'You've been away? But you're back now?'

'Yes. Good night. Look after yourself. I'm closing the door because of showing the light. Once again, thank you so much.' He pulled the door to with a firm hand.

III

'Well, well,' said Francis, breaking the silence, after the cab had moved off. He turned to Lance: 'I must apologise profoundly for letting you in for that painful scene. Of course, it was a mistake in her condition to have taken her out. I did my best, but John here was mulish.'

'Why, what was wrong?' asked John. 'It did her good.'

Lance said quietly: 'Would you tell me why she screamed?'

'Why? Because she thought we were taking her to the lunatic asylum,' said Francis fretfully. He found his cigarette-case and took one out. 'Will you smoke?'

'Thank you. So that was it, was it?'

'Did she scream?' asked John. 'When?'

'In the cab. When we were taking her home.'

'It was really very disturbing,' said Francis. He added vindictively, 'though, of course, that's where she should be. It's obviously a case for certification. She's as mad as a hatter.'

'I think you're exaggerating,' said John. Burroughs said: 'She repeats herself, of course. I soon realised that. But I found what she said very interesting. In America, we'd be inclined to look on an old lady like that as a kind of institution. . . .'

Francis interrupted. 'You see, neither of you had very much time with her. I did. I suppose it wasn't . . . let me see, as I arrived rather late, it wasn't much more than an hour and a half or so, but what I went through! To begin with, she didn't know who I was most of the time; when she did have occasional gleams of recognition, she went back to a passage in our acquaintanceship in which she practically and archly accused me of going to bed with her. That went on repeating itself over and over again.'

After a pause, Burroughs said: 'You're quite sure she screamed because she thought she was being taken to some place for people who have gone nuts? That seems pretty ghastly to me.'

'Oh, that was it! All the paraphernalia was there, you see. That is, for the stereotyped mind of the novelist. Woman finding herself in a cab in the darkness – the black-out helped, of course – with strange men; we were all strange to her at that moment; being taken she knew not where.' He stopped, spreading his hands.

'How long did she go on screaming?' inquired John.

'It seemed an hour, but it was only a matter of seconds. The cab mercifully stopped, and Burroughs here assured her she was at her own home. Of course, immediately she stepped out on to her own familiar ground, she forgot all about it.'

'It's something then she must always be afraid of?' asked Lance.

'Oh, of course. It happened to one of her relatives, I believe. And she's always been an eccentric woman. But though I was warned I had no idea she was as bad as she is. Years since I've seen her. I suppose she's nearly eighty now.'

'Yet she doesn't strike one as an old woman. I mean there's no suggestion of senility about her.'

'Senility; no, it's more what Burton in his *Anatomy of Melancholy* defined as *phrensie*. The active and wearing form of dotage.'

He sat back, struck by his own words. No, it wasn't senility:

senility sat back heavily in its arm-chair, saw little, and heard little, was lifted into bed and out of bed. Claire never relaxed. And that was probably the main reason for her loss of memory: she had lived at a continuous tension; there had been a continual striving to be amusing and entertaining; now, she was an old actress, running about, mouthing her lines, gesticulating and weeping on an empty stage in front of no footlights, no audience. She had considered her whole life a drama to be served out as entertainment. Certainly, she had made the most of her two love affairs from the point of their conversational value; but then time had played upon her the trick that it plays upon most of us, of running faster than she had. For how outmoded were her two grand passions in an age which spoke of affairs, and not even love affairs! Yes, the curtain was down, had been down for years, and she couldn't bring herself to realise it: That *where have you all been?* Ghastly. He roused himself: 'Yes, a most depressing evening, for she used to be quite entertaining in the old days. Still, it wasn't so bad for you two, I mean to meet, for once in a way, a specimen of pre-war – I mean pre-last war, of course – literary-cum-social hostess.' As neither of them made any reply, he peered out of the window. 'I believe we're nearly there. Yes . . . we're passing the mews. Are you taking the cab on or will you come in and have a nightcap?'

John said quickly: 'We'll just go on to Piccadilly and have a final beer.'

'Do. By all means.'

The taxi stopped, and they all got out. Burroughs said, after the altercation about paying was settled: 'I still don't get it. I think Mrs Temple should have a companion. Wouldn't that help things, don't you think?'

Francis said somewhat irritably, for he hated standing in the street to resume a conversation that was really over: 'A companion? My dear, they've been tried over and over again, but none of them stays. And now it's war-time, when that kind of person is very difficult to discover.'

'Still, isn't somebody trying to do something about it?'

That gentle persistence was really a very trying American quality: 'You haven't really taken Claire's measure. The ordinary sort of companion would just increase her frenzy. She's never been able, like myself, to suffer fools gladly. Goodbye. So nice meeting you.'

As he let himself into his flat, Francis Maitland was conscious of some mental jar, of some remaining depression that he was momentarily unable to define. It was his own words, 'like myself', that gave him the key when he had settled in front of the electric fire. Yes, of course! Claire had drawn a comparison between them which still rankled.

Was it in any way true? No one had ever called him eccentric, so far as he knew. He had always conformed to the laws of the society he had frequented. It was true that like her own his intelligence was an intuitive one, working on living material rather than on facts, the facts of politics, economics, engineering, motor-cars, but . . . besides, even if men possessed, to use the trite phrase, the artistic temperament, they always kept a better balance than did women, a greater sense of proportion, of objectivity.

His mind turned down another line: he hadn't made a very

good impression, he felt, on Lance Burroughs. Burroughs, in his solemn American way, no doubt felt he had talked too harshly of old Claire. He smiled to himself. It was easy for youth, still with sufficient surplus emotion, to indulge in the facile pleasure of pitying others. When one was old and gray, but not, alas, full of sleep, one's fears for oneself occupied one so much less pleasantly.

But he would never become like poor Claire. He would watch himself, watch himself all the time. Perhaps there was something in that Pelman system they used to advertise so much. He might try it. They said it strengthened the memory. He *would* try it. For one thing it would be something to do in the long evenings.

PART THREE
THE DARK NIGHT OF THE IMAGINATION

CHAPTER SIX

Miss Phillips read the copies of the testimonials Miss Jones had received from previous employers with the feeling that she was committing an old-fashioned solecism. In war-time one felt that all that was necessary was the presentation of identity card, insurance card and labour exchange permit. But still we were not yet quite living under a soviet or gauleiter, and Miss Jones, thought Miss Phillips, darting an apparently absent-minded glance which took in the full rather puffy face, the grey hair pinned into a small bun upon which rested a heavy brown felt hat, and remembering the almost ankle-length skirt, was certainly pre-war, pre-soviet, even pre-last war. For to be a companion at all surely dated one as an Edwardian.

She brought her wandering thoughts to bear upon the reference she was reading. Like the others it informed her that Miss Jones had been found willing – one had said helpful – and cheerful. She remembered that the first one she had read had stressed her kindness. Kindness and cheerfulness. Did those qualities make the balm that Claire required? Well, in these days employers couldn't be choosers; and Miss Jones would certainly need all her kindness and all her cheerfulness if she took on the post.

'Fine,' she said in her deep voice, and Miss Jones started slightly, for she always felt nervous with women who cropped their hair closely, and wore tailored suits, crediting them with a share of the commanding and intellectual qualities more usually, Miss Jones considered, and more rightly, possessed by men. She restored an agreeable and expectant expression to her face, which gradually faded while Miss Phillips said:

'Your side of it is, of course, most suitable. I'm glad to see, for example, that you've had some nursing experience. But it is only fair to say that if you take the post, you'll find Mrs Temple a rather difficult person to deal with. She has been . . .' Miss Phillips broke off to look for inspiration on the table . . . 'you could almost say a brilliant woman. In her day. She wrote, entertained a good deal, and so on.' Miss Phillips paused, and to fill in the pause, Miss Jones said: 'A writer? How very interesting! I'm a great reader myself.'

'I don't suppose you've read her books. They've been out of print for a good many years. Nowadays her mind, I won't say it's unhinged, but she's lost her memory to a very large extent, and you'll find that she says the same things over and over again.'

'I understand,' nodded Miss Jones. 'I just shan't take any notice.'

'Most people find it tiresome. I do myself. It's curious how maddening it can be. Then, and this *is* trying, and that is why I said I'm so glad you've had nursing experience, she has lately let herself go about keeping clean and dressing herself properly. She forgets about interior cleanliness, you see, and so sometimes she's incontinent. It's not very nice to talk about;

but I have to warn you. The poor dear is very upset when she realises. You'll have a lot of tears to contend with, I expect. That's rather tiresome, too.'

Miss Jones's heart sank. It didn't look as if this job was going to be all honey and jam. She had cleared up so much for other people in her life, consoled them through so many afflictions, that she had hoped that now that she was getting on, something nice and easy would come her way. Depressed, she for once took the initiative.

'I assume she has some staff. How many servants are there?'

'Only one. Kathleen, the Irish cook who has been with her about three years. And a woman who comes in to do the washing every Monday. She did have a secretary, of course. But last winter, about Christmas, she left to do war work. I come in every Saturday morning to do the accounts, and pay Kathleen her wages and so on. Just a weekly tidy-up. We can't let Mrs Temple have much money, as she'd just go out and either give it away to anyone who asks her or spend it. So Kathleen, or if you accept the post, of course you would, sees that she just has a shilling or two and a few coppers kept in her purse.'

'And there are no relatives?'

'There are, but she doesn't have much to do with them. It's chiefly a sister and two nieces and a nephew. The nephew's abroad; the nieces are married and live in the country. So does the sister, but she hasn't been on speaking terms with her for years. To be frank, Mrs Temple was the emancipated woman of her time, and rather shocked her more conservative sister.

I don't mean that she did anything that would shock anybody these days.'

'Oh, I'm sure not. We are all so much broader-minded now, aren't we?' said Miss Jones, a little mechanically. She was thinking that that was one good thing, anyway. To be in a post without interfering, always critical relatives was something. It was a good deal.

Miss Phillips handed her papers back to her, saying: 'I quite understand that you won't be able to decide till you've seen Mrs Temple. Have you the time to come along now? It's only a short walk.'

Miss Jones considered. She believed it never did to let people think that you had plenty of time at your disposal. She looked at the watch, which was a very nice watch, having been given her by Lady Hartlett – dear kind Lady Hartlett, would she ever meet anyone as nice and warm-hearted again? – and said in grudging assent: 'Yes, I am free this afternoon.'

As they went down the stone stairs leading from Miss Phillips's flat, another important question suggested itself, and she walked in silence for a while, trying to wrap it up, so that it didn't appear an offensive question. No wrapping except such as disguised the significance of the question altogether occurred to her, so she gave a little cough and plunged: 'Excuse me, but is Mrs Temple inclined to be violent in her conduct?'

'You mean does she attack people? Oh, no. I've never had any complaints of that.'

They turned a corner. Miss Phillips added: 'She is, as I tried to convey, excitable. She cries a lot because she is very sorry for herself, and she might shout in some moods. By the way, I should say that she really oughtn't to drink.'

'Drink?'

'I mean spirits. Whisky or brandy. Well, for one thing, like most of us, she can't afford the present prices, and for another, it's very bad for her. You'll find that she asks for it, because having in the past entertained a lot and gone about a good deal, she just can't understand why there isn't plenty of stuff around. She's not an extravagant woman; in fact, I should say she's naturally on the thrifty side. I generally get in a bottle of whisky a month, and it's sent up in the decanter very much watered. It's the only way.'

'I'm not a total abstainer, but I take very little of anything myself,' said Miss Jones, with a vague feeling that testimony of her own sobriety was perhaps required.

'Don't you? I drink what I can get, but it's very difficult to get, apart from the ruinous prices. Do you know this part of London well? I've lived for years round about here.'

Miss Jones replied at some length, giving a summary of the districts of London she knew and also of those she didn't know so well, or had just passed through. Miss Phillips listened with responsive attention; she knew that Miss Jones was so suddenly eloquent because she felt nervous, now they were nearing the house, and without analysing it, she appreciated the reason for her nervousness. They were about to enter that world which is lit by the unstable moon. The moonlit world with its corners and shadows and grotesque shapes and extravagances of cruelty and anguish that had no counterpart in the workaday sunlit world. There were evil and wrong in

both, but under the moon there were no rules to explain away or exact retribution for what happened. The writ of the Policeman, of Societies for the Prevention of Cruelty to Children or Animals, of Governments, did not run, and there were no weather forecasts. Both women, for different reasons, did not wish to dwell on the existence of that world, Miss Phillips for the practical one that it did no good, Miss Jones, because it wasn't a gentlewoman's province. Psychoanalysts, she had been told, could explain it all; her part was to have ready soothing words, cups of tea, basins of hot water and plenty of soap; to insist that there was nobody behind the curtain really, and to trust that the skies would soon clear.

'Here we are,' said Miss Phillips, opening a gate, and leading the way up a stone-paved path to steps that mounted to the front door.

The house was fairly large and just detached, and it was still quite a good neighbourhood, Miss Jones told herself. A good address meant something, even in these days. It was better to write to one's friends from Kensington than, say, from Brixton.

Kathleen answered the door-bell, Kathleen in a pink print dress and a clean apron, at whose impassive face Miss Jones looked anxiously. So much depended for one's comfort on the servants or servant. Kathleen, for her part, summed up Miss Jones without appearing to do so, thinking as she welcomed Miss Phillips: 'I doubt if that old one will stand much; there doesn't seem much fight in her.' To Miss Phillips, she said: 'She's upstairs; I'll tell her.'

The next moment there was a flurry of steps, and Mrs

190

Temple was running down the stairs calling: 'Is someone there? . . . Oh, it's you, Phil! I'm in such trouble; I can't find Lisa anywhere. Kathleen's let her out again. Is this a friend of yours?'

'I want to introduce Miss Jones, Claire. This is Mrs Temple.'

'How do you do? How nice of you to come and see me. I'm so sorry I didn't expect you, but I have very few visitors.'

'I rang up and told Kathleen to tell you we would be coming. Shall we go into the dining-room?'

'Yes, why not? What did you say your name was?'

'Jones. I'm Miss Jones.'

'Isn't it curious that though Jones is supposed to be such a common name, I mean a name by which a lot of people are called, I've never known a Jones before. I don't think so. Have I, Phil?'

'I don't know. Not that I know of. Will you sit in this chair, Miss Jones? I think it's fairly comfortable. We've come on business, you know, Claire.'

'Business? But you do all my business. I sign cheques; that's all I do. It's very odd, but . . .' she turned to Miss Jones: 'they tell me my memory's too bad for me to manage my affairs. So what can I do? Of course, it's most kind of Phil . . .'

'You remember you've said over and over again that you wanted a companion. And your friends think you should have one. So I've brought this lady along to see if you both could come to some arrangement.'

'Do I want a companion? You mean a *paid* companion, I suppose?'

'Of course!' said Miss Phillips impatiently.

'But I thought I was really looking for someone who'd come here and pay me. I've got a spare room that I don't want. And I've got quite a good cook. She can't get cream, but then nobody can get it, can they? Or enough butter.'

'The rations part will be easier when there are three of you,' said Miss Phillips. 'But don't be tiresome, Claire. It is very necessary that you should have a companion, because Kathleen says she can't go on with things as they are.' She turned to Miss Jones: 'Mrs Temple doesn't like being left when Kathleen goes out. And the woman must go out sometimes. As it is she hardly ever gets an evening off, because with Mrs Temple's memory being so bad, she forgets about things like the black-out.'

'I understand.'

'I know I've got a very bad memory these days, and it's so inconvenient for me, but I don't know why everyone should blame me for it. My cook is most impertinent about it.'

'No one's blaming you. The question is if Miss Jones feels she can come. She has, by the way, excellent references, including one from Lady Hartlett. We shall be very lucky if . . .'

'Who is Lady Hartlett? I have never heard of her.'

'She lives in Dorset, not far from Charmouth. She's such a nice woman,' said Miss Jones warmly.

'I dare say she is. But that doesn't tell me anything *about* her.' She turned to Miss Phillips: 'I'm always surprised when the . . . let's say the unprecise mind says "nice" it imagines that it has told one something about the person. Do forgive me; I don't mean to be rude.'

'It's quite all right,' said Miss Jones. 'Wouldn't you like to read the copy of her letter?'

'Is it about you? A kind of reference?'

Miss Jones nodded, taking the paper carefully out of her handbag. To Miss Jones the letter addressed: 'To All Whom It May Concern' had the quality of a great and beautiful poem, and no poet's inamorata could have cherished a laudatory sonnet more carefully. Her time spent with Lady Hartlett had been the happiest time of her life; she had lived in luxury with a sweet-tempered woman who had been delighted with the least thing she had done for her. Of course it was only a copy that she took out of her bag, but even so, she handled it reverently. But Mrs Temple waved it away.

'Oh, please not. I think there is something so . . . grubby about reading other people's references. And rude, too, if one does it in front of them.'

This was a new point of view for Miss Jones, and she looked towards Miss Phillips for guidance.

'Well, I've read it. It says the nicest things. You'll be very lucky indeed if Miss Jones agrees to come to you.'

'Do you want to be my companion? Everyone tells me how dreadfully tiresome I am. And then I'm poor, too. I can only pay you a pound a week.'

Again Miss Jones looked towards Miss Phillips: she had been told, and told apologetically, that she would get thirty shillings a week. A pound was *really* too little. But she was met by a slight, but expressive shake of the head which reassured her.

'I've told Miss Jones all about that, and she's been wonderfully kind at understanding the position.'

There was a pause. Then Mrs Temple got up, and rushed to look under the table. 'Where is my cat? I was looking for it. Kathleen must have let her out again. It's really rather beastly of her. When she knows . . .'

'Oh, please sit down, Claire, and don't bother about the cat for a moment. We really must get this settled. Miss Jones hasn't all the afternoon to waste, you know. There's plenty of work for everyone these days.'

Miss Jones observed with relief that Mrs Temple sat down meekly. She evidently wouldn't be very hard to manage, she decided, if one set about it the right way.

'I know there's a lot of work. I have to make my own bed and dust and everything. I can't do my own work at all.'

'If Miss Jones came, she might be able to help you there.'

'Would you help me? How very kind of you! But I can only pay a pound a week.'

'We've been into that,' said Miss Phillips, rising and walking over to the window.

'Oh, you're not going, are you? Please don't go. Why aren't we having tea? It's tea-time, isn't it?'

'No, we can't stay for tea,' said Miss Phillips, coming back. 'Miss Jones has plenty to do, I'm sure, and I must get back. I was here all this morning, you know.'

'So you were. It's Saturday then, isn't it? How very kind of you to come and see me again.'

'It was really Miss Jones who brought me out again. Naturally, she wanted to meet you before deciding if she could accept the post.'

'What post?'

'If you decide to come, when could you come? Would Monday be possible?'

'Well . . . Tuesday would be better.' 'You can tell me as we go home,' said Miss Phillips with an understanding nod. She got up, and Miss Jones also rose.

'Are you going? What do you mean about Tuesday? Who's coming on Tuesday?'

'This lady may come, but she has to think it over. Goodbye now, Claire.'

'But will you like it here? I think there will be too much work. And you're rather old, aren't you?'

This comment, coming from a woman so very much older than herself, failed to remove the kind and tolerant smile with which Miss Jones was regarding Mrs Temple. For she had made up her mind about her. She was difficult, of course. But in the way a child was difficult. If she were humoured, she didn't think she would have a great deal of trouble.

'Oh, I wish I could find Lisa,' said Mrs Temple turning away from the smile. Miss Jones said: 'Now I wonder where your cat can be. What a pretty name Lisa is for her!'

'I call her that because all cats are older than the rocks, aren't they? And this one is so disdainful. She likes Kathleen better than she does me, though Kathleen is always chasing her out of the kitchen.'

'Oh, I'm sure she doesn't really.'

'Goodbye, Claire,' called Miss Phillips passing through the door.

'Are you going?' cried Mrs Temple, following. 'Has something been settled? You said you came on business, didn't you?'

'I hope it has been settled,' said Miss Phillips. She glanced towards Miss Jones: 'I hope Miss Jones feels she can come here, and be comfortable.'

'If she comes she'll be quite comfortable, because I've got quite a good cook.'

'I think it will be all right,' said Miss Jones in a low voice, answering Miss Phillips's questioning look.

'Good! I'll just tell Kathleen about preparing your room then.'

'Now where is she going?' asked Mrs Temple, her eyes following Miss Phillips's retreating figure.

'I think she's gone to have a word with your cook.'

'Is that necessary? I wonder what she's gone to talk to her about.'

'About my coming here, I think.'

'Really. Are you coming here? To live?'

'Well, let's say just for a little while,' said Miss Jones, still speaking in a grandmotherly tone. 'To see if I can be of help to you, or not.'

'You sound very kind. But I don't think I can afford to pay you.'

'Never mind about that.'

'But I do mind. I'll just go and speak to Miss Phillips. She really is managing my affairs very strangely.'

Left alone, Miss Jones stepped quietly back into the dining-room, and made a brief survey of the furniture, which on the whole met with her approbation. There were two comfortable chairs near the fire, and to have a comfortable chair to sit down in was, Miss Jones knew, one of the important things. Another was the fire: that afternoon at least it was a good fire. She wished she might have seen her room, but probably it wasn't ready. She might leave some of her things on Monday, and that would give her a chance to look around without the presence of the somewhat intimidating Miss Phillips.

Meanwhile, down in the kitchen, Mrs Temple was saying: 'You don't mean to thrust this woman upon me, do you?'

'If she'll come, it will be a godsend,' said Miss Phillips firmly.

'But she's so dowdy. I know I'm only rags and bones and a hank of hair myself, but she's dowdy in such an *emphatic* way.'

'My dear Claire, women who look like fashion plates are not usually after jobs as companions to other women. Well then, that's all right, Kathleen. *Do* do your best for her, won't you?'

Miss Phillips led the way upstairs. Kathleen followed, murmuring: 'I'll just remind her about bringing her ration book. Maybe she should get an emergency card.'

Miss Jones was waiting for them in the hall. Kathleen said to her: 'You won't forget your ration book, will you, Miss?'

'Indeed I won't. So important these days, isn't it?'

'It'll be better for you to come in with us for the butcher; so you'll have to get an emergency card.'

'Shall I? Oh, yes.'

'Why has she to get an emergency card?' asked Mrs Temple.

'And I'll have your room ready on Tuesday then,' added Kathleen, with a reassuring nod.

'Thank you so much,' said Miss Jones, grateful for that assurance and the friendly smile, and not knowing that the friendliness might be compared to the benevolent impartiality of a spectator watching one of the Early Christians awaiting his turn to be thrown to the lions. Miss Jones turned to Mrs Temple: 'Goodbye then for the present.'

'For the present? Do I see you again?'

'Yes, on Tuesday,' said Miss Jones, with her most affable smile.

'But I don't think . . . did I ask you?'

'Of course you did,' called Miss Phillips from outside the door. 'Goodbye, Claire.'

Mrs Temple watched them go out of the gate, and then turned to Kathleen. 'Is that preposterous person coming to stay here?'

'It's wonders to relate, but looks like she is,' said Kathleen. She ran down to the kitchen singing 'But I'd rather be where the Mountains of Mourne sweep down to the sea.'

CHAPTER SEVEN

I

Just before Miss Jones reached the house where she was now going to be employed, she half-paused and looked around her somewhat in the same spirit as a sentenced man may snatch a glance at the outside world before the prison cell opens to receive him. Half-seeing she stared at the sky, at the smoky red gleam of the winter sunset filtering over the Kensington roof-tops, while the gentle melancholy of those winter-time moments before tea when the day lags in its going like a reluctant child not yet ready for bed, hiding its identity in a withdrawn silence, lapped about her. She sighed and opened the strange gate, yearning for the familiarity of St Ermyn's Private Hotel, Earl's Court, where with all its drawbacks, and there were many drawbacks, the pleasant young manageress hardly ever failed to have a friendly word with you if she was about when you came in. She hoped just before she rang the bell that Mrs Temple would be friendly: even though she was 'mental', and therefore Miss Jones considered in such a case that nothing could really be expected from her.

The maid whom she had seen before, and whose name

she had made a point of memorising, opened the door promptly:

'Good afternoon, Kathleen. You were expecting me, weren't you?'

'Oh, I didn't forget,' said Kathleen. 'Come in. It's cold, isn't it? Go into the dining-room, in to the fire for a minute, will you?'

Miss Jones complied, while behind her Kathleen stood at the foot of the stairs listening.

'It's all right,' she then said, coming in. 'She never heard the bell, though she's been expecting you the whole afternoon. Not for one minute did it go out of her mind, and that's strange, because she forgets everything. Sit down there and warm yourself.'

Miss Jones sat down, and not altogether happily watched Kathleen seat herself in the chair opposite, in the attitude of one embarking on a confidential chat.

'Tell me, are you used to mad people?'

'I've had some experience of a mental case. It was a fairly slight one.'

'Slight? Oh, she isn't slight. She's a handful, I can tell you, and she gets worse every day. I notice it. Myself I'm well used to mad people. But I couldn't have gone on any longer, not with one pair of hands. Now that you and I can work her in together – I mean if you want to go out in an afternoon, then I can go out in the evening, d'ye see? – I am hoping you'll be able for it. But it's only right to say that she's the maddest one I ever struck, and mad in a peculiar way.'

'I shall try to do my best,' said Miss Jones, endeavouring to speak with some coldness, and yet not sound too stiff. She was sitting on the edge of her chair, ears strained. For it didn't do, it never did, for one's employer to arrive and find one hob-nobbing with the servants or servant. Once again, and more quickly than usual, she was impaled on the horns of the eternal dilemma: your employer hated you to be familiar with the servants, to spend more time than was absolutely necessary in the kitchen. But if one wasn't on friendly terms with the servants, then *they* hated you. They considered you stuck-up, and all one's creature comforts depended on not being considered stuck-up by the servants. Miss Jones had had a full taste of what it meant to have tepid hot-water-bottles stuck just in the side of the bed; of one's morning tea – if one got it – being almost undrinkable; of fires that were slacked down, or let go out for want of fuel, as soon as she was left by herself.

'I've done my best for you,' said Kathleen, bending forward. 'I've told her if she doesn't behave with you, you won't stay, and she'll be left on her own with nobody to do the work of the house. I didn't say, but, of course, she knows very well inside herself what that'll mean, for, mind you, and that's one of the things you'll find out, she's often not as mad as she lets on to be, d'ye know?'

'I quite understand.' Miss Jones sought for a way of con-cluding the conversation. She opened her handbag: 'Oh, here's my emergency card. I shall have to go to the Food Office about re-registering, shan't I?'

Kathleen took it absently. 'You will so. There's no hurry. I've got a nice chop for you and her tonight. She would have her supper with me most times, but, as I told her, she'll be having it up here with you now. Her worst time is in the evening; in the morning – though of course there's the trouble you'll have in getting her to wash herself – she'll just be wandering about, letting on to be dusting and making her bed. Or if you go out shopping, then you take her with you, and she likes that, and it keeps her quiet, though she makes you look a fool with her talking so loudly that people look at her, and then they look at you. The thing to do is to take no notice. . . .'

Kathleen stopped suddenly, and listened. Then she jumped up, and hissed: 'She's coming.' In a loud voice, she said: 'Very well, Miss. Will you have your tea now, or will you go up to your room?'

'Whichever is convenient,' said Miss Jones, who had also stood up, and was looking towards the door. Mrs Temple came in, wearing the same thin black dress she had worn before, and stared hard:

'Oh, is this the lady?'

'This is Miss Jones,' said Kathleen in a reproving voice.

'Why wasn't I told that you had come, I wonder?'

'I've only just this minute arrived, and I was giving my ration book to Kathleen.'

'You are my new companion, aren't you? You have come to stay, have you?'

Miss Jones said: 'Yes.' She tried to think of something more to say, but nothing occurred to her. She felt isolated, because both women were watching her with the detached curiosity of animals towards strangers who have not yet earned their right to acceptance in the household.

'Why don't you take off your hat and coat then? Or do you want to keep them on? Are you going out again?'

'No, I'm not going out again. Unless you want me to get anything for you. Perhaps if I took my bag up to my room?'

'I'll show you after tea,' said Kathleen. 'When I do the black-out. I'll leave this one for you to do; it's only to be careful to pull the curtains right to.'

'I'm so glad it's not a difficult one.'

'Righto, then,' said Kathleen, leaving the room. Mrs Temple said: 'My cook is an extraordinary character. She loves talking to my visitors in front of me. It's really not for her to give instructions, but she's very badly trained. Unless she likes to pretend otherwise before people, of course. What are you standing for? Do sit down.'

'I'll just take off my coat and hat, shall I? And leave them in the hall?'

'Certainly. That's what people generally do. You have come to stay?'

'I hope so,' said Miss Jones, trying to keep her flag up. But in the hall, she felt depressed. Somehow, Mrs Temple seemed much more intimidating than when she had seen her before. She took as long as she could before she went back to the room, to find Mrs Temple sitting bolt-upright in a listening attitude.

'That's right. Sit down by the fire. Have you come a long journey?'

'No. Only from Earl's Court. It was really very convenient being so . . .'

'What's happened to your luggage?'

'I sent a trunk by Carter Paterson. They came for it this morning, so I don't expect it will be here for a day or two. One must expect everything to take longer these days, I suppose.'

'Oh, why?'

'Well, the war, you know.'

'Oh, yes, the war. It's always made the excuse for incompetence, isn't it? I remember it was so in the last war. Do you know shorthand?'

'I'm sorry, I don't.'

'How tiresome. I particularly wanted someone who was a good shorthand typist. You see I'm a writer. Did you know that?'

'Yes, Miss Phillips told me.'

'Dear Phil! She presides over my life like the statue of an angel. I mean she's so good and calm, just like the statues in a Catholic church, but nothing ever moves her. One prays and supplicates and weeps . . . have you known her for long?'

'Not long,' said Miss Jones. She had decided on giving those evasive answers which she believed were suitable fare for mental cases, drunkards and children.

'What do you mean "not long"? How long is that?'

Mrs Temple's attention was distracted by the entrance of Kathleen with the tea-tray, and instead of pressing for an answer she said graciously: 'Here's tea. You'll be glad of it after your long journey.'

'I'm always ready for my tea,' said Miss Jones, with some emphasis.

'I'm bringing up some toast in a minute,' said Kathleen to them. 'I expect Miss Jones likes toast.'

'Oh, I do.'

Mrs Temple said nothing. When Kathleen had gone she said coldly: 'She's very officious today. That's because you're here. Let me see, you were having quite a conversation with her, weren't you, when I came in? I suppose she was telling you all about me. She loves doing that.'

'No, indeed. She was just asking me for my ration book, or rather emergency card. I have to change over to your butcher.'

'Have you? Why?'

'Well, mine's at Earl's Court, and Kathleen thinks it would be better if we had the same butcher because of getting more meat.'

'You mustn't pay too much attention to cook's opinions, you know. She loves bullying and bossing people. I must really warn you about that.'

Miss Jones bent her head. She was used to being warned by number one against number two, and number two against number one, and though the position had its apparent strategic advantages, she had found that these advantages were somewhat illusory. So now she had a discouraged sensation.

'That is, if you are going to be my companion? You are my new companion, aren't you?'

'I've taken the post. For the present at any rate.'

'For the present? Have you got another engagement later on?'

'No.'

'Oh. You rather implied you had, didn't you? Do you know shorthand and typing?'

Miss Jones shook her head.

'Oh, the tea's on the table,' said Mrs Temple, suddenly noticing the tea-pot. 'Would you like a cup?'

'Yes, please.'

'It's a drawback your not knowing shorthand, because then you could take down some of my ideas. I am writing a book, but I've so much work to do that it's difficult to concentrate. Do you take milk?'

'Yes, please.' 'And sugar?' 'Yes, please.'

Kathleen came in with a covered dish, and having put it by Miss Jones said to her: 'You'll have to help yourself.' In a louder voice, she added: 'I'll draw the curtains, shall I? Now I'm up. It'll be more cosy so.' Without waiting for a reply she went over to the window.

Mrs Temple made a despairing gesture with her hands, and turned round: 'Do we have to have the curtains drawn now?'

'You don't *have* to. Not for another few minutes. But it's as well done, isn't it?'

'So now in the middle of tea we must sit in darkness, must we?'

Kathleen said nothing. After a further rattling with rings she went over to the door, and switched on the light, and then went out of the room. Mrs Temple said: 'She really is a most curious woman, isn't she? Don't you think so?'

Miss Jones made a non-committal sound. Her eyes, which were weak, were dazzled by the artificial light, and she blinked slightly before focusing them on Mrs Temple. Mrs Temple was sitting back looking at her with such a penetrating regard that she immediately averted them again and bit into her toast.

'Do tell me. Why are you a companion? You *are* my new companion, aren't you?'

'Well, some of us have to be, I suppose.'

'Was it the usual reason? Because your father or mother died when you were nearly middle-aged, and there wasn't any money to live on without your doing something. And you'd never married, and so . . . it's rather sad. Sad in a dreary, lifeless, straight-lined sort of way.'

'Oh, but I enjoy my work. One meets different people, and that's so interesting. I shouldn't like to be idle.'

'Wouldn't you? I think you look as if you need rest, and going for long walks. Don't mind my saying this to you. I suddenly wondered, when Kathleen put on the light, and I really saw you coming out of the darkness, I wondered if two women who have absolutely nothing in common could make each other less lonely. Perhaps we have something in common? I haven't any furniture in my life either.'

'Oh, but . . .' Miss Jones glanced around her.

'You are taking me *au pied de la lettre*. People were my furniture. Now there are no people. I keep running from the empty attics to the empty basement, and wringing my hands over the desolation. I do wish I could stop running. I'm afraid you're going to find me very trying. People do, you know.'

'Oh, I'm sure I shan't . . . May I pass you some more toast?'

'Thank you. Do have some yourself. I'm glad you're hungry. Have you come a long journey?'

'No, only from Earl's Court.'

'I wonder if we could do something about each other. I went steadily up at the beginning of my life; you see I was praised a lot, and artists painted and drew me, and I wrote articles and knew people. Then I had bumpy bits: my love affairs were like switchbacks; it was exhilarating going up, but going down one felt sick. And now I'm right in the valley. Sometimes I think it's so dark that it must be the Valley of the Shadow of Death. You have read the *Pilgrim's Progress*, have you?'

'I did when I was a little girl.'

'Do you like reading?'

'Oh, yes. I'm a great reader.'

'When people say that they are great readers, it means always that . . . oh, I mustn't be . . . I mustn't *sound* rude. I don't mean to be, but I often sound rude, and that has lost me so many friends. Have you ever had a lover?'

Miss Jones looked down at her plate. She thought such an indecent question should go unanswered, but the silence insisted on an answer. She said: 'I've had my chance of marriage, if that's what you mean.'

'Have you? And why didn't you accept him?'

This time she was determined not to answer. With others, one might explain, embroidering a little here, adding a little there, making quite a romance. But one did not talk intimately about oneself to a mental case. She said: 'Oh, that's a long story,' and gave Mrs Temple a condescending smile.

'Won't you tell it me?'

'Perhaps I will some time.'

Kathleen opened the door, and came in just in time to hear Mrs Temple say: 'You don't look a passionate woman. I shouldn't think you've ever been passionate?'

'When you're ready perhaps you wouldn't mind showing me my room,' said Miss Jones, goaded to a direct question to the maid.

Kathleen nodded slowly. The nod also expressed her pleasure that the new companion was getting a taste of the badness of the mistress's mind so quickly.

'Kathleen will show you, or I will show you in a minute. I'd just like to finish my tea, if you don't mind, cook.'

'I thought you'd finished.'

'No, I haven't.' She turned back to Miss Jones. 'Are you religious? You don't look a religious woman either.'

'Oh, no, I'm not religious,' said Miss Jones. 'That is to say I don't go to church much, if that's what you mean. But I like to listen to a good sermon on the wireless. And when I was at Ealing, where I had my own wireless in my bedroom, I often used to tune in to "Lift Up Your Hearts". That's a very nice little five minutes' talk they give just before the eight o'clock news.' She looked about her. 'I suppose you have got a wireless?'

'A wireless set? No, I'm afraid not. One or two people, especially a woman named Mrs Berkeley – that is what she has named herself – who used to be a companion-secretary of mine, and is so kind and looks like an over-blown dark red rose, she wanted me to have a wireless. But that's because she's obsessed by the war. She kept telling me that I should listen to the news. But I have the *Daily Telegraph* every morning, I can't afford *The Times*, they tell me, and so I can read the news there.'

'Isn't there a wireless at all in the house?' asked Miss Jones, looking hopefully towards Kathleen, who was putting the things from the table slowly, one by one, on her tray.

'There is not. I don't mind much myself, because I've never bothered much with them.'

Miss Jones sighed. In her disappointment she addressed Mrs Temple in her natural voice: 'But don't you find the evenings very long? Apart from the news, there are such interesting programmes nowadays. Talks and Discussions on Important Things.'

'I should find them so much longer, listening to tinned culture. I should be face to face then with the bankruptcy of myself. It would be too terrible. I believe some of the people who used to be friends of mine, and in fact were discovered by my husband and myself, broadcast. But they don't let me know when they are broadcasting, so really I don't think it's worth spending a lot of money on this machine, clever though it is.'

'You used to be able to get them on hire. Perhaps you still can. I could make inquiries if you like.'

'Ah, no,' said Kathleen. 'You can't get them any longer. Can I take your cup now, Madam?'

'If you're in such a hurry.' Mrs Temple pushed back her chair, and then looked at Miss Jones with an air of rediscovery. 'Have you come a long journey? Would you like a bath or anything?'

'No, thank you.'

'Has Lisa had tea? Where is Lisa?'

'She's down in the kitchen,' said Kathleen, going towards the door. 'I put her down a saucer of milk, but she's giving herself great airs, and won't look at it.'

'Oh, then she's ill,' cried Mrs Temple, following her at a rush. 'My poor Lisa. I must come and see to her.'

Miss Jones heard Kathleen say: 'You'd better go down

the stairs in front of me if you're in that hurry.' She sat on alone, waiting for Kathleen to return and show her her bedroom, sitting as one sits in a dentist's waiting-room, filled with premonitions of pain and discomfort.

II

The setting down in detail of Miss Jones's first weeks as companion to Claire Temple would make a record of such inflicted humiliations, that the one real problem for the inquirer into her welfare would be – how could she stand it?

For, as her personality grew increasingly displeasing to her employer, she had to accustom herself to direct and indirect forms of insult. Indirectly, for example, she had to practise the deaf ear when Mrs Temple, having insisted that she should give Miss Phillips's telephone number to the Exchange, took the receiver from her with a cold: 'Thank you, will you leave me now?' and then proceeded to complain of her . . .'This woman you've thrust on me, she really must go. Not only is she an imbecile, but she's also a liar: she is incapable of speaking the truth about one single, solitary thing.' And much else, to which Miss Jones gathered that Miss Phillips made soothing replies. Indirect also, since Mrs Temple did not presumably mean Miss Jones to overhear, were the remarks upon greetings and especially upon the leave-taking of the infrequent guests to the house: 'Do forgive the way my companion butts into the conversation.' 'I can't tell you how infuriating I find this new companion I've had forced upon me.' 'I must warn you, there's a dreadful woman here who insists on having dinner with us.' To the list should also perhaps be added the occasions when Mrs Temple, forgetting that she was addressing the person referred to, complained to Miss Jones of Miss Jones: 'My dear, you can't imagine how dreary she is; she must always have lived in regions immune from the sun, the moon and the stars . . . the genteel English virgin made entirely of grey india-rubber.'

Directly, Mrs Temple did not for some time go as far as she did when she believed or took it for granted that Miss Jones was out of earshot. It was rather the tone of voice in which she addressed her, the tone of one sorely tried, who was holding on desperately to her patience, or the sharper voice in which, patience having slipped, she was asked: 'Do you mind leaving me alone? Must you always be here?' Or alternatively: 'I pay you to be my companion, not to use my house as a hotel, from which to do your shopping.' 'Have you no conversation at all? Did nobody bring you up to make yourself agreeable?'

It was Miss Jones's simple and comprehensible faith that Mrs Temple, being 'mental', everything she said was rendered innocuous and, to a sensible person like herself, of no account, that made for her a bridge over all that was unflattering. Much more difficult at first was the accustoming of herself to Mrs Temple's nocturnal prowlings. On the first occasion when she was awakened by hearing the door next to her own being opened and the sound of descending footsteps, she shiveringly decided it was her duty to see what Mrs Temple was doing.

She found her in the dining-room, flashing a torch upon the table: 'Do you want something? Can I find it for you?'

Mrs Temple turned the beam on to Miss Jones, and after a

moment remarked: 'Oh, are you the companion?' and turned it away again.

'Don't you think you'd better come back to bed? You might get cold.'

'Allow me to manage my own affairs. I don't require you at the moment.'

'Very well, but . . . would you like to have a cup of tea? The only thing is I'm afraid I don't know where anything is kept.'

'Don't you? Perhaps you can light a fire, can you? I've been thinking of how beautiful everything was when I was a little girl. I opened the window or the door, and looked out and everything was dressed up, do you know what I mean? So that you wanted to clap your hands, and run out. I suppose it's the Wordsworthian mood of regret: "If-I-could-feel-as-once-I-felt", and yet I do still feel. Shall we light candles and sit down, and talk about when we were little girls, because I suppose even you must have been eager and ardent once. Did you have pigtails?'

'If you'll excuse me, and if I can't do anything for you, I think I'll go back to bed. I get cold rather easily.'

'I remember all about you now. You've only just come and you've had such a long journey, haven't you? Yes, you must be tired. I wish I could be tired. *Tired out* is what I really mean.'

Miss Jones had returned to bed, but not immediately to sleep. What could Mrs Temple be doing down there, she wondered. Suppose she set the house on fire?

In the morning she had consulted Kathleen as to the danger of these nightly wanderings. Kathleen said:

'It's just as if she were a ghost, creeping up and down and looking at her old junk. I don't pay heed to her now, for since the fright she gave me, walking in one time, I keep my door locked on me. It's best to let her be till she tires herself out.'

'It's very worrying though. Suppose she did set fire to something, why, we should all be burnt in our beds!'

'Ah, she wouldn't do that,' said Kathleen, turning away. Then, gazing out of the window she paused to say, dreamily: 'Though there's no telling what that one mightn't do with the queerness that's in her.'

It wasn't very satisfactory, but then Miss Jones soon decided that Kathleen's whole attitude was very odd and unsatisfactory. Kathleen spoke with a relishing gloom of Mrs Temple's madness, and that, though for her there was no smack of relish, was something she could understand. But then, other times, Kathleen would retire into herself and into the kitchen or her own room, sending up meals with an absent-minded air; and should Miss Jones descend in search of advice or sympathy, make it clear that she considered the problem of their employer as really Miss Jones's concern and not hers. Her explanations, too, of Mrs Temple's whims and whimsies, were more dark than helpful.

'Going out in her slippers is nothing to what she can do. I wouldn't mind about that.'

'But it looks so bad. People will think I shouldn't let her do it.'

'How can you prevent it, and she the way she is? I hope that you'll never see her the way I've seen her.'

'What do you mean?'

'Oh, I wouldn't soil my lips to say. You'll find out soon enough. I have to write a letter to my husband; he's a great one for bothering about letters, if you'll excuse me.'

No, Kathleen wasn't much of a help. All the same, considering it was war-time, the meals sent up by Kathleen, if sometimes uneven, were much better than those she would be eating at the private hotel.

The warm fires and the cooking were indeed the major compensation of Miss Jones's life, and must be taken into full consideration in estimating the reasons which made Miss Jones stay on with Mrs Temple, despite the unmerciful treatment which she received from her. One might rate almost equally high the pleasant and unusual feeling of being to a degree her own mistress. She might be living sometimes at an address that was next door to Bedlam, but for that very reason there were rare callers and no relatives to propitiate. The telephone – and Miss Jones was always nervous of the telephone – rang but rarely. There is an atmosphere of siesta about houses and rooms to which the noises, conversations and doings of everyday life sound but in a muted or diverted shape, and Miss Jones, without realising that she relished this invisible drawn curtain, found it soporific to her nerves. The time she enjoyed best was when Mrs Temple was out of the house altogether, wandering about the hills and terraces of the neighbourhood, for then there was no chance of this remote calm being disturbed for a while. But there were, at first, other times when her employer occupied herself with reading old cuttings, with turning pages, perhaps making occasional notes upstairs in her study, while Miss Jones, huddled over the fire,

knitted, read her library book, or half-dozed the afternoon away. In these intervals it was as if she lived on a deserted island, in which the consciousness of war abroad and the claims of life outside the windows hardly existed. Downstairs she would occasionally catch the sound of Kathleen singing some old Irish ballad, or a snatch of one of Moore's melodies, 'She is Far from the Land where her Young Hero Sleeps', and that, too, was soothing, emphasising her sense of being marooned, but safely marooned from outside dangers and perturbations.

The evening, of course, was the worst time, since it was then that Mrs Temple was so urgently desirous of company, and, not finding what she sought in Miss Jones, inflicted the irritability of disappointment upon her. Miss Jones could not then relax any more than one can relax before the eruptions of a volcano. But increasingly to Miss Jones Mrs Temple's behaviour to her, like such eruptions, came into the category of the insensate acts of Nature or Providence, and therefore to be accepted by the sensible person as inconveniences, sometimes considerable inconveniences, but not productive of anger or hurt to one's self-love. If somebody not 'mental' had treated Miss Jones as Mrs Temple treated her, even the insecurity of her scanty financial means – the few dividends she received had dropped considerably since the war – would not have been sufficient inducement to keep her in her thankless labours. But Mrs Temple couldn't be held responsible: 'She doesn't know what she's saying,' 'Poor woman, how dreadful to have so little self-control!' were typical of the comforting assurances with which Miss Jones armed herself against the most unpleasant or irritating manifestations of Mrs Temple's dislike.

And since to pity with detachment can be productive of comfortable feelings, the more when fortified by the conscious-ness of good works, Miss Jones could feel a pride in the way she was standing up to the job. Miss Phillips was, for a woman who was not by nature effusive, lavish in her encomiums, and sincere in her expressions of gratitude when she came on Saturday mornings, a time when Miss Jones was able to do her own shopping and treat herself to a cup of coffee and a cake in Kensington High Street. Even Kathleen, to whose advantage it was that Miss Jones should stay, offered her a due meed of flattery: 'It's wonderful how you put up with her; the strength of patience you have in you for her goings-on is wonderful,' she assured her. And Miss Jones would reply gently: 'In a way, you know, it's my form of war work. I'm glad if I can do some good to the poor woman, because she can't help being so trying.' To which Kathleen made no reply at all, having made up her mind long since that there were many remarks made by the English that were so daft that no reply was possible.

Who then can blame her if some complacency of spirit sat with her as she sat and knitted, if there was a slight unctuous flavour in the epithet 'dear' which she had slipped into the benevolent habit of replying to her employer:

'Do you mind not calling me "dear"?'

'Very well, dear. I won't if you don't like it.'

'You did it again. Just now.'

'Did I? Now *wasn't* that silly of me?'

It was Mrs Temple who hurried angrily from the room, muttering something Miss Jones didn't hear, but was probably the expression of a desire for the company of her cat, and Miss

Jones who sat on comfortably. A meek answer should turn away wrath; if it didn't it was not the fault of the person who had obeyed the scriptural injunction.

CHAPTER EIGHT

I

Mrs Temple was one afternoon startled into the consciousness of a peculiar phenomenon. The clock on the other side of the street said ten-past four, but the big stores had pulled down their blinds, and barred the doors. Moreover, she was caught in a sudden rush of people who were pouring down to the main street from a side entrance. It was a rush of women and girls trying to catch bus, tube and train, girls and women of all kinds, but still, on the whole, smarter in their appearance than the shoppers upon whom they had recently waited.

Mrs Temple, however, did not note details. She only knew that the clock said ten-past four . . . nearly a quarter-past now, and that therefore it was too early for the shops to close. But since undoubtedly the big shops had closed, something very untoward had occurred in the reassuring sequence of familiar things. It was with her as with someone who, rarely looking outside their own walls, had suddenly observed one day that midnight was persisting, that the sun had not come up. Or as one surprised out of her passionate grief at the loss of a lover by noticing suddenly that all the furniture in one's bedroom had also disappeared. One understood, even if one couldn't accept the personal loss, since there is always evidence that we are born unto trouble, as the sparks fly upwards – but the other was not in nature – not without some intimation beforehand. Surely the 'sure and firm-set earth' remained, however much one's footsteps upon it weakened, faltered and strayed.

She stopped one of the hurrying young ladies: 'Excuse me, but is that clock right?'

'Quarter-past four. Yes, exactly right.'

'Why has Barker's closed then?'

'That's the time we do close now. I mean we close at four. Because of the black-out, you see. It will be half-past four next week, though.'

'Will it?' She wanted to add: 'Why?' but the girl had gone.

The 'black-out' would probably again have been her answer.

The 'black-out' was what Kathleen was always doing . . . and that in turn meant *the war*. And, of course, bombs, for now she remembered about the land-mine and her mother's house, were also *the war*. The war had changed everything: certainly it had changed Kensington almost while she slept.

How shabby and tired and disagreeable, too, everybody looked, now she came to notice them. Nobody smart, nobody cleverly made-up any more. And how odd that girl looked, wearing breeches and leggings, as if she were a stable-girl, yet having long golden hair hanging to her shoulders. The woman in front of her was much too old and stout to wear trousers. And why wear trousers when she went shopping? for she carried a basket, on top of which could plainly be observed a tin of Vim. She remembered that they didn't wrap up things any more, because, of course, Miss Jones was always keeping paper bags and scraps of paper. She had thought it was one of Miss Jones's many personal peculiarities. But in that, at least, she had apparently misjudged her companion.

'O London, where have you gone?' she cried out in her heart. The London she had known, of smart tea-shops, of taxis which appeared when one raised one's finger, the London of theatres where one sat in a stall, and waved to one's friends, and went over to talk to them in the interval, the London of book-shops, where one had only to ask for the manager, and say who one was, to be treated with respect. She had imagined that it all went on, though, of course, without her, because she was now shabby and old and, having lost her memory, had lost her friends. But the clock that said ten-past four had opened a crack in her world through which she viewed with horror for a few moments an abomination of desolation that was all about her. If she got on one of those red buses travelling east, she would see, she believed indeed she had seen, sandbags in Kensington Gardens. Kensington Gardens, sentimentalised by dear Barrie into a nursery for Peter Pans, Wendys and Nanas in perpetuity. Or so one had thought. But Kensington Gardens had not, after all, been made secure by Barrie. Was Barrie dead? Very probably, since everyone she had known, or even known of, seemed to be dead.

She crossed the street and stood on the centre island, waiting while a charge of red buses went by, and pursuing the thoughts that the mention of Barrie had aroused. It was not smart to approve of Mary Rose, but one had ached with the same desolation, understanding how lost she had been: to have remained young, and found everyone about her old, including the man who had been her young lover. And now she understood still better, she thought, glancing at a lorry of soldiers going by. For though I am old, and look old and fearfully shabby, yet my heart still flows with pain just as when I was young, only now there is no one to run to, no letter to expect, no possibility of the long estrangement ending, no one to say good night to, except the woman who looks like a dirty flannel dressing-gown, whose name is Jones. I hope I've never told her she looks like that, because then she might go, and then cook would go, and then there would be silence, or . . . *but that way madness lies; let me shun that.* People were crossing, and she must follow them. As she went she caught sight of the policeman directing the traffic: he had a stolid reassuring face under his helmet, and she felt a momentary lightening of her heart. She was glad she had observed that there were still policemen in London. There would be still some law and order then.

All down the passage of her life, she reflected, as she walked along the pavement to her own turning, policemen had always been so kind to her, calling her 'Miss' when she was old enough to be flattered by it, and in her youth, when she got out of cabs, coming home sometimes unescorted at an hour that was improper in her time for a solitary girl, they had turned a blind or benevolent eye. Now that she was old, undoubtedly they would still be kind and take her side against her cruel cook and the imbecile companion who did nothing but knit. She must remember that these planks existed, planks for the shipwrecked. And if anyone was shipwrecked, it was she . . . her thoughts were safely back on familiar ground, as she rounded the corner.

Then she came to a stop, for someone walking behind her had drawn level, and was speaking. She was a poor woman, wearing a pulled-down hat like dustmen wore.

'I beg your pardon?'

'I was asking, do you know a doss round here, mate?'

'A doss?'

She looked at the other perplexed; and then she darted to the meaning of the word. Pleased with herself as an emancipated woman, she said: 'Of course. I know what you want. You want somewhere to sleep?'

The woman nodded. 'I thought perhaps you was going somewhere.'

'So I am. I am going home. Have you no home?'

The woman shook her head. She said after a moment: 'Can I doss in with you? I can pay you a bob or two.'

Good heavens! This poor creature thought she was another such as herself. She *must* be looking shabby. Or was it one outcast, one of the shipwrecked, hailing another? Staring at the swarthy dirty face under the mushroom-hat, she plumbed dark seas at the thought.

Then, before she reached the depths of those seas, so cold, so terrible, so perhaps salutary, she rose, borne to the surface of things by the memory of her slippers that looked to the uninitiated like bedroom slippers.

'I wear these shoes because I walk a lot, and they are so comfortable.'

The woman looked down and nodded mechanically. The clear decisive voice was just beginning to make her sense that she had spoken to the wrong person, but being of a brooding melancholy disposition, much alone, living in and to herself and directing her outward-going thoughts solely by the recurring necessity of securing a night's shelter and some food, her mind did not extend itself to further comprehensions with ease. She had a minute ago, as she walked behind her, sensed in the old woman's carelessly-worn clothes, in the aloofness of her walk, the aura of someone who like herself was an exile from the freemasonry of those who looked respectable, whose outward-glancing eyes informed them of where they were going, who always had some place where they were going.

'Do you walk much? Haven't you a home?'

Now the woman was almost sure she had made a mistake, for the manner was tied up in her mind with that of the lady at the charitable organisation who sometimes gave her a pound, and besought her to try to find work and keep herself clean. It was the sort of thing they asked.

'No. I'll be getting on to Hammersmith.'

'What shall you do at Hammersmith? Shall you go to the workhouse? Don't you want to go? Are they unkind to you?'

She didn't answer, but turned her head away. Claire realised that she was about to lose a companion, that the tale was hardly told. She said: 'If you walk home with me, I'll give you some money. Half-a-crown, would that help you out?'

The woman nodded, and said: 'Thank you.' Without reluctance she attached herself to Mrs Temple, convinced now that she was something to do with the Charity Ladies.

Walking side by side, they were oddly contrasted. Mrs Temple kept darting sharp interested looks at her companion, who for her part looked neither right nor left, but walked with sunken head, replying slowly or not at all to the questions that were fired at her at intervals.

'Have you a husband?'

'Yes.'

'Isn't he with you? Doesn't he help you?'

'No. I don't know where he is.'

'Do you miss him very much?'

There was no answer, though Mrs Temple repeated the question. The Charity Ladies had not asked her that, so there was no precedent for a reply.

'I miss mine very much indeed. Though he was often unfaithful to me. Was your husband unfaithful to you?'

No answer.

'Can you do any work? Perhaps you can help me. Are you working now?'

'I got a job yesterday, washing up at a canteen.'

'Do you like it?'

No answer.

'Where do you generally sleep? Do you always . . . doss?'

'I had a room at Shepherd's Bush. But they turned me out.'

'Why did they turn you out?'

'Because I hadn't the money for my rent.'

'What a shame. Because now you work in a canteen you could pay them, couldn't you?'

'Not till the end of the week.'

'You could sleep at my house, but I'm afraid my cook, she's

a very hot-tempered Irishwoman, won't let you. She won't do anything I tell her; if I say anything she threatens to go. Can you cook?'

'No.'

There was a long pause, while Mrs Temple stared, and then tried to fathom the secret of some profound indifference which reached her.

'I'm very unhappy. Are you?'

No answer.

'Perhaps the police will find you a room for tonight. Why not ask them? There's such a nice comfortable sort of a man who directs the traffic in Kensington High Street. Do you know whom I mean?'

For the first time the woman shot her a dark suspicious sideways glance. 'I always keep away from them.'

'But why? You shouldn't. I've always found them so helpful in any emergency. I was thinking just now, just before you came up and spoke to me, that they are the only people who haven't changed in this horrible dreary London, that looks nowadays like a broken-down bargain basement at a second-rate auctioneer's. Don't you think so?'

The woman was silent, but this time Mrs Temple didn't wait for a reply, because they had arrived at the gate of her house. 'This is my house. I think I'd better go in first, and get you the half-crown, because if my cook saw you she might come out and send you away. I have a companion, and I'll ask her. A Miss Jones, and unbelievably stupid! In a way, I'd rather have you as my companion, because you don't chatter, and, I feel, have had a sad life. Miss Jones hasn't had a sad life: she's only had a dreary life, and it does make such a difference to people, doesn't it?'

She observed that the woman was looking at the house in silence. It was the silence, Mrs Temple thought, of a wild animal who scented danger. She understood. If she were taken by some stranger to an unfamiliar house, she would also scent danger. She said quickly: 'You needn't come in. I understand how you feel. You wait just inside the gate, and I'll be back in a minute. Will you?'

The woman nodded. She stood patiently, holding her blue coat, which had no buttons, closely round her.

This time Mrs Temple had her key with her, and she hurried into the dining-room where Miss Jones was enjoying her afternoon by the fire. 'Will you give me half-a-crown from the money that Miss Phillips left with you for me, please? At once.'

Miss Jones, surprised, put her head on one side, and said archly: 'Now I wonder, what do you want half-a-crown for?'

'Don't be silly. I want it for a poor woman who's waiting outside for it. She has nowhere to go to sleep. She offered me two shillings, so if I give her half-a-crown that will be enough for her to go to a very cheap hotel, what they call a doss, you know. Or probably you wouldn't, as you know nothing of real life.'

'Oh, a beggar! I wouldn't give as much as half-a-crown, dear. Sixpence will be enough.'

'No, it won't. Will you do as I tell you?'

Miss Jones left the room, and went upstairs, while Mrs Temple hurried back to the open door and called reassuringly:

'She's just getting my purse. Would you like to come up and warm your hands? My companion always keeps the fire loaded with coal for herself.'

'It's all right. I'm not cold.'

Kathleen, emptying rubbish into the dust-bin at the back, heard voices, and came along by the side of the house to investigate.

Mrs Temple, who had descended the steps, explained: 'Oh, here's my cook. I wonder if she has a piece of cake for you.'

'There's no cake,' said Kathleen, looking dreamily at a point beyond the woman's head.

Miss Jones appeared with half-a-crown, and handed it to Mrs Temple. 'Here you are, dear. Though I do think . . .' She stopped, seeing Kathleen.

Mrs Temple ran forward to the gate with the eagerness of a child performing a pleasant errand. 'Now you can get a cheap doss, can't you?'

'Thank you.' The woman turned swiftly away, and with head still down, retreated.

'Do come and tell me how you get on, will you?' called Mrs Temple after her, disappointed that it had all ended so quickly. But there was no reply. 'Goodbye,' she shouted, hoping in vain that the head would turn.

She turned back to hear Kathleen say to Miss Jones: 'Fancy letting her give half-a-crown. Miss Phillips won't be pleased.'

'It's not your business, cook. I want that woman given some more work to do, because she needs it.'

'She hasn't been doing any work. Not for us.'

'I know she hasn't,' said Mrs Temple quickly. Her mind had gone completely blank after the recent strain of curious observation imposed upon it, and she ran into the hall, and then upstairs, impelled by the feeling that she must enclose herself in her bedroom, that is, if her bedroom were there. Miss Jones said: 'It was too much, I know. But really she was so insistent, and it isn't as if she's much pestered by beggars. It was kind of her, too.'

There was a lot here for Kathleen to answer; especially, she must rebut the suggestion that Mrs Temple was kind. 'It's not kindness; she's as mean as mean really. Do you know how much she wanted to give me for my wedding present? Five shillings. Of course, Miss Phillips made her give a pound. But even a pound after all I've done! Beggars don't ask her as a rule, because of the sight she looks, but there was one, a real bad woman, who was always after her, till I put my foot down. She gives away just out of craziness when she feels like it; another time she wouldn't part with a ha'penny. There was an old man selling bootlaces came up to her when she was in the garden one time and "Go away", she said to him. "I'm too poor to give you anything, and I don't want any bootlaces." I heard her myself, and that was someone it wouldn't hurt to give just a copper or two to. But in her fundamental nature, d'ye understand me, I mean the way she really is underneath all the palaver and forgetting, she holds on to her things like a miser. I'm telling you what I know.'

'She's variable, of course,' said Miss Jones, who wanted to get back to the fire. 'That is to be expected.' She looked pensive and then disappeared through the front door, while Kathleen

looked up at the sky as if to toss away the folly of one and the stupidity of the other before she returned to the kitchen to make the tea.

II

Mrs Temple sat silently most of tea-time, making a much better meal than she generally did. It was only after her third cup that she began to talk, and then, to Miss Jones's surprise, it was on an unfamiliar topic, the devastation of London, which, apparently, she had just noticed. Miss Jones decided that she must be improving, since her complete indifference to and incomprehension of the fact of the war was, of course, a manifest symptom of her being 'mental'. She assented sympathetically to all that was said, agreeing that it was very sad.

A slight divergence of views indeed occurred when Miss Jones ventured that it was saddest of all in the East End. 'In Stepney and Whitechapel,' she informed Mrs Temple, 'there are hundreds, perhaps thousands of people homeless because of the Blitz.'

'Really! But that doesn't concern us, does it? If anything, it must be quite a good thing that the Germans have cleared away the slums for us. But I saw sandbags in Kensington Gardens. And women with Edwardian figures going about in trousers. Really shocking.'

'They are probably women doing their bit. And trousers are more efficient,' said Miss Jones, priding herself on the way she kept up with the times.

'And Barker's and Derry and Tom's close at four. I don't think shopkeepers should be allowed to do things like that. I know it's the black-out. A girl told me that. So inconvenient for the public. I haven't anything to spend, so it doesn't matter for me.'

'We all have to make sacrifices,' said Miss Jones pushing back her seat, preparatory to putting the things together for Kathleen to clear. 'And I think the way all classes have united in making sacrifices proves how sound we English are at heart.'

'Oh, I'm not talking about sound hearts. I suppose the Germans have sound hearts, too, haven't they?'

Miss Jones smiled in a superior way as she reached over for a plate. 'Not really. They are *made* to do things, you see. We do them willingly.'

'But we *have* to do things. We have to do the black-out, and we have to keep our torches down. And we can't have cream. There's no difference that I can see.'

Miss Jones looked kindly at Mrs Temple. No, poor thing, she couldn't see. That was one of the sad things about her. Changing the subject, she said: 'I'm sure that poor woman must have been very glad of the half-crown you gave her.'

'What half-crown? Oh, yes, I remember. I gave someone half-a-crown, didn't I? Was that this afternoon?'

'Yes.'

'I remember. She wanted somewhere to have a doss. Poor thing. Why shouldn't she come here?'

Miss Jones made no answer. She went over and rang the

bell, while Mrs Temple perused her own thoughts. She said suddenly: 'I must telephone Phil. Will she be there?'

'I should think she'll just be back.'

'Will you write down her number on this piece of paper, please?'

Miss Jones, after an interval spent in finding a pencil, did so. She knew now that it did Mrs Temple good to telephone, for she was often quite friendly to her afterwards, in a rather guilty way. It was Kathleen who, on her way into the dining-room, stopped to listen, and heard:

'She is sad and poor, but not dreary like this woman you've got me. And that would suit me so much better. I think her husband deserted her. What do you say? I can't hear . . . I don't think I know her name. Oh, I do hope I put her address down. I'll go and see, and then I'll let you know. . . . But you must find someone else. This one is a bladder of lard with a sound heart – she keeps talking about sound hearts . . . I'd rather have a poor woman . . . this one's not a lady, only a "lydy" . . . all right. Goodbye . . . please come and see me soon.'

She put down the receiver, and turning saw Kathleen: 'I suppose, cook, you've been listening to what I was saying. I do think it's most contemptible of you. To think I can't telephone in my own house without being spied upon!'

Kathleen swung round upon her: 'What do you mean . . . *spied upon*?'

'You for one.'

Inside the dining-room, Miss Jones, hearing the angry voices, raised her head to listen, thinking sadly: 'Oh dear, now Kathleen is going to have a row with her, and that'll upset her for the rest of the evening. I do wish she wouldn't.'

'If you mean, did I hear what you were saying, I did hear, for the reason that I was coming up to clear away, so how could I help hearing? And if you didn't say things that you should be ashamed to say, you wouldn't mind. It's you that goes behind people's backs, as you well know.'

'I shall say what I like in my own house. That's final. It's no business of yours.'

'It wouldn't be any business of mine in the ordinary way,' said Kathleen, lowering her voice to normal and opening the dining-room door. She looked over at Miss Jones, giving a half-wink, which Miss Jones avoided noticing.

'What do you mean, "in the ordinary way"?' cried Mrs Temple rushing upon her from behind.

'What should I mean?' said Kathleen, setting the tray on the sideboard, and then taking up the crumb-brush, and looking at it thoughtfully.

'That's what I am asking you. You mean something, you beast!'

'Now, now,' said Miss Jones pacifically. 'Why don't you come and sit down by the fire, dear?'

'Miss Phillips told me I'd better watch out in case you did something dangerous, didn't she?' said Kathleen, starting to sweep almost invisible crumbs on the table-cloth.

'Something dangerous! You're mad.'

'Oh, it's me that's mad? Of course. I forgot.' Kathleen folded the table-cloth with a slight secret smile.

'You see how she talks to me? You see how she hints?' Mrs Temple swung round on Miss Jones.

'Kathleen doesn't mean anything, do you? I wish you'd sit quietly down.'

'I'll sit down just when I want to sit down. I don't pay you to tell me to sit down.' She turned back to Kathleen. 'As for you, get out of this room at once.'

'I'm going. For the good reason that I've finished what I have to do here. Have you got enough coal for the night, Miss?'

Miss Jones looked in the coal-scuttle. 'We could do with a little more.'

'Very well, then. I'll bring it up in a few minutes.'

As Kathleen went out she heard Mrs Temple say to Miss Jones: 'It's hardly your place to give orders to my cook in front of me, is it?'

'She asked me, so I told her that we do want some more.'

'She's a wicked beast, and does that on purpose to enrage me. And she said things that were wicked, and cruel, too.'

'It doesn't do any good to excite yourself,' said Miss Jones, busy with her knitting. 'Kathleen doesn't really mean anything.'

'Of course she means something, you fool. And you know what she means. Sitting there while she threatens me. What are you paid for? Do you mind telling me?'

Miss Jones shook her head and sighed.

'You are certainly not paid to give orders to my servants or to connive with them. Monopolising my fire seems to be all you do.'

'There's plenty of room for us both if you'd sit down,' said Miss Jones, knitting faster.

'But there isn't plenty of room for me. Not with you. That's one of the things you don't understand.'

Miss Jones's expression grew a little more remote, her lips pressed together rather more closely. Mrs Temple averted her eyes from the spectacle, which had the effect of making her want to throw something, and wandered about the room, and then out into the hall, sighing and muttering. After a while, she came back and said: 'Where's Lisa? What have you done with Lisa?'

'I haven't done anything with her. I expect she's downstairs in the kitchen, with Kathleen.'

'Of course. That beast will have taken her.' She ran out of the room, and down to the basement with the feeling that she was, for some reason she had forgotten, braving the infernal regions. But she must rescue poor Lisa. However there was no fight awaiting her. Kathleen was washing up in the back kitchen, and singing softly, while Lisa, lying on the rug, was quite content to be taken up and borne away.

Somewhat soothed by her unexpected and bloodless victory, Mrs Temple passed the next half-hour pleasantly enough, fussing over Lisa, placing her in her basket, and then getting her out again to sit on her knee, making Miss Jones move further back from the fire, so that there would be more room for the basket, and so forth.

But just as a child after a happy interval with her doll, whom she has imagined to be her baby, and therefore has dressed and undressed with care and with soothing words, begins to tire, so that the doll becomes only a doll to be cast aside for a fresh diversion, so Mrs Temple began to tire of the somnolent Lisa. Imperceptibly, that dreaded and dreadful sense of silence crept into the room, and finally possessed it.

She pressed her hands tightly together, and tried not to look at Miss Jones opposite, but the consciousness of her moving hands holding the grey segment of wool, the faint click of the needles, and sometimes the sound of her silly little cough, became increasingly irritating. On her left there was the secret life of the fire going on, ever apart from human concerns, on her right the closed door, at which she now and then darted appealing glances, hoping that someone, anyone, even the cruel Kathleen, would come in. If Kathleen came in, there might be a row, but shouting meant life, and was better than this deadness that surrounded her. But the door remained implacably closed.

From the outside there did at last emerge the grinding moan of an aeroplane. Miss Jones heard it. For a moment her fingers paused, and her head went on one side in a listening attitude. Usually she would have been inspired to comment. But tonight she said nothing. She had decided that Mrs Temple was in one of her very nervy moods, and then anything she said, even the most harmless thing, and especially the most harmless thing, would be sufficient to set her off again. She was like a sizzling fire; she couldn't help sizzling, but was then best kept away from.

Mrs Temple spoke. She said: 'Perhaps that's a German, and the maroons will go soon.' She was hoping that it would be an air-raid, and then they would go downstairs and sit in the kitchen. Kathleen always had to let them sit with her on such an occasion, she remembered.

'Oh, no. That's just one of ours. There's nothing to be frightened of.'

'I'm not frightened. Why should I be? I've nothing left outside myself to be frightened of.'

The aeroplane went away, and the silence came back. It was an encroaching significant silence that made her heart cry out in anguish at the loneliness it brought with it. She looked round the room with apprehension; she bent down again to Lisa, but Lisa was fast asleep, withdrawn from her, as everything else was withdrawn.

In the distance a dog barked, and she concentrated on the sound eagerly. Then it stopped. So it was with all the sounds she could hear in the room. They appeared like little mice suddenly from their holes, stayed for a timid moment, and then disappeared, swallowed up in the fearful gulf of silence.

Now a rumble came from Miss Jones's interior. 'Pardon,' she said, and shook her head in reproof at herself. Then she went on knitting.

If it were not for Miss Jones, her mind might slip away to the other house, to the house of the past, and dwell there in expectancy, awaiting the arrival of someone, about to set out somewhere. But the presence of Miss Jones was a clamp riveting her to the empty present, so that her very bones ached in the agony of restlessness which possessed her.

This was the moment when she would generally rush to find her torch, and go rambling into the other rooms till supper came. But tonight the adventure of the afternoon had left enough impression on her mind for her to cast an imploring thought outside the curtained windows.

It couldn't be like this everywhere in London. It couldn't

be like this everywhere in Kensington. Somewhere there must
still be drawing-rooms where, into that dry dullness which
settled like dust upon the spirit whenever two or three or more
females were gathered together, a reviving wind came into
the room with the presence of a man – even a very old man,
even a very young man, even 'one of those'. One didn't hope
or expect or even desire that man to make love to one or to
be flattering. So long as there existed that friction so stimu-
lating to the mind and the spirit – which, alas, exercised their
hungers long after the flesh had become quiescent – which
sets in automatically when the two halves of humanity meet.
Yes, even an intensely stupid and dull man did something to
disturb the dust.

Or even leave men out of it – and heaven knew that they
had been out of it long enough so far as she was concerned
– were there not still drawing-rooms where someone played
the piano, and the tinkling notes effected a kind of recon-
ciliation between the abiding loneliness of man's spirit and the
vastness which surrounded him? Perhaps it might be a valse,
causing the dry leaves to flutter, transporting one to the sweet
pains of nostalgic memories. And more and more, so that the
past rushed in upon the present, and everything was alive
and everything was joyful and everything was sad, as it used to
be when one was young. Only much more so, for now it was
all illuminated by the poignant light of a sunset that said:
'Never more.'

She couldn't go and call on anyone. Not at this hour. But
she could pass slowly along the pavement, listening, hoping
to hear something from behind those curtains. And there

was always the chance that someone might speak to her, ask her something. . . .

The grinding whirl of the aeroplane was overhead again, and this time Miss Jones was about to comment when Mrs Temple forestalled her by rising and saying: 'I am going out now.'

'Oh dear. I do wish you wouldn't,' said Miss Jones, distressed.

Miss Jones was always distressed when this announcement came, but the distress of the first occasions, when it seemed all wrong for an old lady who was 'mental' to be wandering about in the black-out, was now mitigated by knowing that prayers and expostulations were of no avail, and that hitherto she had turned up again safely. But she had done her best to detain her. And following Miss Phillips's advice that the one thing was to distract her attention, had suggested on a previous occasion a game of patience.

But Mrs Temple wouldn't play cards any more than she would accept Miss Jones's offer to teach her to knit. In Miss Jones's mind there had indeed stirred the conviction that had Mrs Temple known how to knit, she would never have become 'mental'. It was after all the most suitable – being also so useful – way of passing the time that existed.

As for Kathleen, she had been even more discouraging: 'The only way to keep her in would be to take the keys away from the doors and bolt the windows. And at that she'd scream the place down, and smash the windows.'

'I'm worried about her getting run over.'

'Not she. It's to innocent poor people that accidents like

that happen,' Kathleen had said in the resigned voice of one
confronted with the inscrutable ways of the Almighty.

Miss Jones had come to the real point: 'Well, I won't be held
responsible. I refuse to be held responsible.'

'Since she's not certified, you couldn't be held responsible.
For it's not your fault, is it, that she's not certified?' said
Kathleen, in the voice of one now turned lawyer.

It was not very comforting, but then Kathleen was never
very comforting. So in the present instance all Miss Jones
did was to follow her employer into the hall, watch her put
on her coat, and warn her: 'It's really dark this evening, you
know. There's no moon, as there was when you went out
last time.'

'I've got my torch.'

'Are you sure you wouldn't like me to come with you?'

'Of course not. That's one of the reasons I'm going out.
Stupidity is so stifling; you can't breathe. I must have some
air.'

'I'll turn off the light while you open the door, shall I?
You've got your torch ready, have you?'

Without replying, Mrs Temple stepped out into what
seemed a complete darkness, except for the faintly bright circle
thrown by her torch on the stone steps. But, characteristically, instead of standing and accustoming her eyes to the
blackness, she went on following the gleam of light. It was
dark; for once the woman had spoken the truth; the dark
that brought bewilderment which must be controlled or else it
would become panic. The only way she knew how to control
that panic was to keep on moving.

Safely through the gate she turned to the right, and then saw in the middle of the road the stationary light which gave her enough confidence to cross over to it, thereby putting the maximum distance between herself and the house she had left. Besides, her seat was on the opposite pavement.

She left the island as one embarking upon unknown seas. But luck was with her, for the stir and moving light of an approaching car helped her onwards. As it approached she had a momentary vision of trees standing ghostly sentinel before silent houses, and above all the grey sky.

It was gone as quickly as it had come, leaving deeper blackness behind her. But she was safely on the opposite pavement, walking on to find her seat.

Footsteps were coming behind her. Soon a man's voice said: 'Hold your torch down, will you?' She turned round, and waited, obediently directing the light on the ground: 'Was I holding it up? I'm so sorry; I was looking for a seat that should be about here.'

He came abreast, and said: 'Oh, it's you, is it?'

It was an air-raid warden, and evidently someone who knew her. She didn't know him, but he sounded quite kind; and alert to grasp the opportunity of speech, she said: 'Oh, I'm so glad it's you. There's a woman warden, a Mrs Hobson, you know, who knows me, too. I don't know why she feels it necessary to hound me, just because I used to go to school with her mother. But she has turned so disagreeable.'

'Well, the women are sometimes a bit . . . but, as I've told you before, Madam, you really mustn't hold your torch so high. It's against the rules.'

'I am sorry. I will try to remember. I did have tissue-paper put in it, you know. Was it you who told me to?'

'I told the maid at your house. I brought you back one night when you couldn't find your way.'

'So you did! How kind of you! I am sorry to be such a nuisance. But I'm quite near my seat now, aren't I?'

'I'll show you. But there are no stars to look at tonight, you know.'

'I don't mind. I've been driven out to escape the excessive overwhelming stupidity of my companion.'

'Your companion? It was your cook you were telling me about last time.'

'My cook is cruel, yes. But she doesn't get in the way all the time, like the other. And she looks quite attractive, and sings as she works. But, of course, she is cruel. She bullies me and terrorises me, and then she goes away and I'm left with the other.'

'That's bad,' said the warden, with only a faint trace of irony perceptible in his tone. Indeed, being of a meditative disposition, he was interested in the odd old lady, as he was interested, since he had taken on this job, in all those whom he felt to be in his care who lived behind the still dignified Early Victorian facades of the biggish houses near his post. Toffs mostly, but he had discovered that there were great differences among toffs. This old lady, for example. She certainly wasn't a stuffed shirt. By her own account she was a kind of fairy princess, incarcerated in a castle with a cruel cook as gaoler. This evening another dragon had appeared, he noted. The cook, of course, had told him she was mad when he had brought her back, and again when he had had to call about the black-out. But it wasn't, he had decided, the usual sort of madness, and he liked the impression even someone as old as she was gave of being so trustfully dependent upon his masculinity.

'Here you are,' he said, and shone the beam of his own torch upon the seat.

She sat down, seeking eagerly in her mind for a topic that might detain him. She had told him about her cook, and besides, one mustn't, no one MUSTN'T talk about oneself. Being an air-raid warden, he'd be interested in bombs and things.

'There are a lot of houses gone, aren't there? Poor old Kensington. It had an aroma, you know.'

'We shall build them all up again,' said the warden, whose name was Mr Mills.

'But you can't. Do you remember that Henry James, in one of the dullest of his books, says something about the air of London being sanctified by the past, so that one breathes in the smoke and the soot and the fog as if it were the most delicate of scents? Of course, he was an American, and therefore was able to find his Holy Grail in Bloomsbury. When he walked, he walked on holy ground. But there is something in it, don't you think?'

'Perhaps there is.'

'There is always, I believe, something more in the romantic view than in the factual or realistic one. The pudding is richer, the sandwich has a more savoury filling. But I was thinking that now he could only smell decay; the stone has rolled away and let in the evil odours of the dank marsh on which London is built. The past is being wafted by the present. Witches and bad witches, sweeping busily with their brooms. Is that fanciful?'

'No,' said Mr Mills agreeably. He added, after a moment: 'I don't hold any brief for the present, but I have hopes for the future.'

'Have you? But then you are so much younger. I'm too old to expect any future, you see. I knew Henry James well. Do you know his work?'

'Might do. He was an American, wasn't he?' asked Mr Mills cautiously.

'Of course. But he became naturalised, because of this war. A New England spinster really. And so unkind to me when . . . I mustn't talk about myself. I'm so sorry.'

'Go ahead. It's all right.'

'Is it? I do bore people so. It's difficult to explain, but if I'd remained in my own class and married suitably, a country squire, like my sister did, and not mixed myself up with artists, and been an artist myself, well, then, I should not have been left like Cardinal Wolsey, given over in my old age. Only he said it about serving God, didn't he?'

There was a pause. Mr Mills then said: 'You mean toffs stick together?'

'How clever you are. That's just what I do mean,' said Mrs Temple delighted. She waited expectantly, but Mr Mills's eye had been caught by a distant light from a window. He said: 'Excuse me, there's a light showing up there. Been on a whole minute. I must go and see about it.'

'It's so reassuring to know that other people are forgetful, like me,' said Mrs Temple. 'Don't send them to prison, or anything like that, will you?'

'Maybe it won't come to that,' said Mr Mills. The sound of his retreating footsteps made her feel like a shipwrecked mariner seeing a ship sail away. She thought: 'I do hope he'll come back. I do hope he wasn't bored. What did I talk about? I think it was Henry James. Next time, I must ask him about his wife and children. That's what nice common people like that prefer.'

She remembered after a few moments that he had gone to see about a light, and strained her eyes across the road. But no answering gleam rewarded her. She was all alone in the darkness, now that to please Mr Mills she had left her torch turned off. There were no windows. Everyone was shut in upon themselves.

Another vehicle was running towards her; she watched its headlights, which were but dimmed half-lights, making its smooth passage as mysterious as if it were driven by a ghost upon a ghostly errand. When it had passed, renewing the intensity of darkness, she drifted into a dreamy state, in which she was one with the insubstantiality of the world about her. Her ego burnt low in a cavern where there was nothing to do but wait, a cavern situated in the region whose existence she had always fearfully glimpsed. 'There are cracks in the world,' as even Sydney Smith had written to Miss Martineau, and with an accepting chill in her heart she had copied the words into one of her diaries.

For the cracks opened for her on no regions of light and

beatitude, but first on desolation, and behind that desolation on terrors which were the terrors of nightmare. She was sitting so still, so, if he had known, unwontedly still, that Mr Mills thought she had gone when he approached her seat once more. He switched on his torch for a brief moment, saying: 'Still here?'

'Who is that?'

'The warden. Don't you remember? The nice one.'

'I don't remember. Do I know you?'

Mr Mills was a trifle hurt. Then he thought: 'It's because she's touched,' and said kindly: 'Yes, you were talking to me just now about Henry James.'

'Henry James? Oh, yes! He said, "cultivate loneliness". I never have. That has been one of my mistakes. If you don't, if you run away, as I always ran away, then it is so terrifying when at last it catches up with you. How nice of you to let me talk to you! Are you a warden or a policeman?'

'I'm a warden.'

'Oh, yes, you go about seeing that people don't pull back their curtains and show lights. Do you get lonely walking about?'

'Can't say I do. I rather enjoy my own company. If I do, I go and have a glass of beer with one of the other chaps.'

'It's so easy for men. Even if they are pompous old bores – I don't mean you, of course, because you sound so nice – but men can always find someone to listen to them, can't they? They have their clubs and public-houses.'

'Well, you have a nice house, haven't you? Don't you think you ought to be getting back there? You might get pneumonia or something sitting here. It's cold, you know.'

'I never get cold. I only get miserable. Because I'm so lonely.'

'Let me see you across the road.'

'It's very kind of you, but I'd rather wait here a little longer. Are you a policeman?'

'No.'

'I was just thinking about a poor woman I met once who asked me where she could "doss". It's very sorrowful, but it's less lonely when I think of the tramps who sit out all night on the Embankment, and watch the lights of the Savoy and the Cecil and that whisky advertisement. I think that I know how they feel. Shut out from everything.'

'You have a good roof over your head, remember that,' said Mr Mills, mildly reproving. 'I've got to go back to the Post now; I wish you'd let me see you across the road first.'

'Very well. Thank you very much. Can I put on my torch?'

'I'll use mine. Will you take my arm?'

'Thank you. I suppose I am very lucky to have a house to go to, as you say. But I think, I can't quite remember, but there is someone staying with me whom I dislike. I suppose she must be my companion.'

'Look out: here's the kerb.'

'It's so kind of you to help me. Do you know where I live?' A sharp suspicion pierced her mind. 'I think I had better go on alone now.' She drew away from him, switched on her torch, and raised it high, searching in sudden panic for some familiar sign that she was near her own house.

'Please yourself,' said Mr Mills, hurt once more in spite of himself. 'But keep your torch down.'

'Oh, there's my gate,' she cried out in relief. 'For a moment I was quite lost.'

'Keep your torch down. You'll get into trouble one of these days, you know.'

'I'm so sorry. Are you an air-raid warden?'

'Good night,' he said briefly, passing on, and leaving her there, stricken by a sudden consciousness that she had said or done something to offend. 'Thank you so much,' she called after him, but he made no reply, leaving her to turn sadly in, thinking that if only she'd been younger she could have followed him, using, as she had so often used, her femininity to make the apology for her. A touch on his arm, a 'Do forgive me: I feel I've been stupid.' But she was old, and it was very dark.

Miss Jones opened the door. 'I'm glad you've come back. I've been so worried. I was just coming out to look for you.'

Mrs Temple stared vaguely at the figure that had risen up before her, and brushed past her without replying. In the hall Miss Jones switched on the light, saying: 'It is dark. I was so afraid you'd get lost.'

'Are you staying with me or something?'

As Miss Jones was never sure whether such a question was satire or genuine ignorance she generally evaded a reply, as she did now. She went back into the dining-room, and poked up the fire. 'Here you are,' she said, when Mrs Temple came in. 'Sit down and get warm.'

In the hall Mrs Temple had heard Kathleen singing: 'It was not for her beauty a . . . lone', and the snatch had brought back to her consciousness of her companions. So now, after a long look at Miss Jones, she looked for something else: 'Where's my cat? I suppose you drove poor Lisa away as soon as my back was turned?'

'I didn't drive her away; she's probably down in the kitchen, with Kathleen.'

'I must go and get her. Poor Lisa!'

Left alone once more, Miss Jones looked into the fire, and shook her head.

CHAPTER NINE

I

The movement towards violence in a nature gentle if quickly emotional is slow, and to the exterior eye as imperceptible as the momentum by which a breeze in temperate zones becomes a wind, as the turn of twilight into night. For years Claire Temple had known that her memory was fallible, had admitted that therefore she had become increasingly a bore to her friends. She admitted, too, with tears and bitter private shames, that old age had brought to her, hand in hand with that loss of memory, certain physical weaknesses. But further than that she could not, must not go. She must keep her back turned to the existence of the waiting monstrous shadow or be engulfed by it.

Her chief way of escape previous to the advent of Miss Jones had been into the past, to that past in which, though often unhappy and hurt, she had been admired and entertained, scolded and watched over. She could be the girl contriving a network of circumstantial lying to hide from her parents where she had spent her evenings, or weekends; then there was a hiatus, for she could never reach beyond the fearful

knowledge that her first and true love was dead beyond reach
of any happy ending. But she could live again with her second
love, whose death had come too late to inflict a mortal scar. She
could live again through their occasional happiness, through
their quarrels, through the long years of estrangement,
because the hope remained that one day he would return, that
they could talk together again, that his rare praise would be
hers for something she had said that released a spring in his
own mind. With him the long lonely arduous task of creative
writing, so much a strain on her own volatile nature, would
be transformed into something exciting and adventurous.
Perhaps they might yet write a book together, for he had
said, had said at the beginning at least, that she had helped
him, that she was the match to his flame. So she could imagine
herself within his nimbus, waiting for a telegram, waiting for
his knock, waiting to hear who was his latest literary discovery
to be invited to lunch. She could live again, too, the sorrow
of his desertion. It had always been a story that fell fresh and
vivid from her lips whenever she entertained more recent
acquaintances. So she could re-live the past with herself, and
talk of it to any listening sympathetic ear.

As fewer and fewer people came to listen, more and more
she retreated herself into that house where all that had been
of pain and joy, of triumphs and humiliations, friendships
and the long tattered ends of friendships, were bestowed.
There was nourishment for her mind there, and while she was
thus fed, she need only occasionally remember the existence
of that shadow, that way that like King Lear she must shun.

But now when even her vitality was weakening, when she

was getting tired, when more and more she craved some stimulant, whether it was a glass of whisky or the visit of an acquaintance, or stranger, to make her tingle with the consciousness of all there was in the storehouses of her memory, there came Miss Jones. And Miss Jones, with all her virtues, was no stimulant. Like a wall of iron with no resilience, she barred the entrance to that house of the past. She might escape for an hour, but soon Miss Jones's voice or her presence would come, calling her back, putting her in full mind of the unhappiness of her present lot.

The shadow spoke urgently to that present. It was ever at her side warning her: 'If you're not careful, they'll put you into a mental home. You have lost your memory, and that's what they do to people who have lost their memories.' Forced into an existence where she sat generally for breakfast, always for lunch, tea and dinner, with Miss Jones, it became her constant preoccupation to wonder if she, if Kathleen, knew of the shadow. She had to watch them all the time, so the shadow warned her. And that watching imposed the most continuous strain she had ever known.

When Miss Jones went downstairs to see Kathleen with some such reason as that she wanted to bring up the laundry, or get a glass, she had to remember to watch the clock, and see just how long they remained together talking. When Miss Jones helped Kathleen to make the beds in the morning, she must remember either to stay with them, or to contrive to be on the landing or in the next room. She must do her best to overhear what they were saying, while leaving them in ignorance of her strained ears. Imposing upon herself these

so unnatural burdens, she grew increasingly to feel as dark enemies the two women who shared her roof. She would sit tense, listening to footsteps on the stairs; an unexpected sound would make her start and then brace herself afresh for her task. But it was Miss Jones she feared as the greater enemy. For Miss Jones, her intuition told her, was concerned about her in a way that Kathleen was not. Kathleen sang about her work; Kathleen left the house in her new spring suit as much as she could, even to Claire's eyes bent more on pleasure than on plottings. It was Miss Jones who was the continual gaoler; and it was Miss Jones whose silence, whose placid acceptance of insults began to be tinged for her with a sinister quality. For Kathleen, who had objected to her open pestering, also objected to her more creeping appearances. She would swing round smartly upon her with: 'What are you doing there?'

'Nothing.'

'Why don't you keep warm by the fire, and not be following us about?'

'I know that is what you'd like me to do.'

'What do you mean by that?'

'You know quite well what I mean. So does she.'

'Ah, you're crazy. It's no good talking to you.'

Crazy! She would ponder over the word which always seemed to be on Kathleen's tongue. Did it mean that Kathleen was fully aware of the shadow, and was she now daring to threaten her openly? Suspense in a highly-strung nature must eventually take voice, and one morning when Kathleen was in ill humour, and therefore inclined to shout at her mistress, the fatal word was said. It started with a query about Miss Jones.

'She's out,' bawled Kathleen. 'As well you know.'

'I didn't know.' Mrs Temple shouted because Kathleen had shouted.

'You held the door open for her when she went, so you *ought* to know. It's just an excuse to bother me.'

'If she's not here now, she generally is. Plotting with you behind my back.'

The word 'plot', like the word 'spy', always had a dynamic effect upon Kathleen. She left off brushing the stairs down, and turned round to shout down to Mrs Temple: 'Plotting what? I'm sick to death of your insinuations. Plotting WHAT?'

'Plotting to have me put into an asylum.'

There it was out! She heard the harsh noise of iron gates clanging behind her; she passed through a door, and turned just in time to see the bolt drawn behind her; she screamed; someone muffled her mouth with a huge hand and dragged her on; dragged her into a padded cell, where no one would hear her screams. . . .

For a moment her mind was too full of the horror of the scene to take in what Kathleen was answering. But she heard the concluding words: '. . . you're going the best way about it.'

'About what?'

'Making them have to put you away. I'm warning you for your own good.'

'I'm going to the police. That's what I'm going to do.'

'Don't be making more of a show of yourself than you do now. The police will only laugh at you.'

'That's what *you* say.'

'Go then. I don't mind. I've warned you. I've warned you time and again.'

'You've threatened me, you mean, you beast,' said Mrs Temple. And then both women turned at the sound of a key in the lock. The next second Miss Jones came in looking rather worried, for she had heard loud voices. Mrs Temple said: 'My cook has had the impertinence to threaten me while you've been out amusing yourself.'

'I wasn't amusing myself. I've managed to get some tongue for our lunch. Won't that be nice? Shall I take it down to the kitchen, Kathleen?'

'You can give it here to me,' said Kathleen, bored with her sweeping. She pushed her hair back with a dirty hand; seized the dust-pan, and came down the remaining stairs at a clatter, waiting only long enough to take the white paper packet Miss Jones handed her. One enemy having betaken herself off, Mrs Temple was left to do what she could with the other:

'I've told that woman that I'm going to the police.'

'Nonsense, dear.'

'It's not nonsense. She threatened to have me put in an asylum.'

'I'm sure she didn't.' Miss Jones, having left her coat on a peg, went past her into the dining-room. She wanted to write down exactly what she had spent for Miss Phillips to see. But she had hardly found her pencil when Mrs Temple interrupted her: 'It may be a small matter to you, but naturally I am interested. Is that what you are working for . . . to have me put away, as cook calls it?'

Miss Jones glanced up, and Mrs Temple's face was so flushed, her manner so tense, that she answered with genuine warmth: 'Of course not, dear. Nobody is thinking anything about such a thing.'

Her sincerity communicated itself to Mrs Temple, and she sat down, puzzled. 'What do you want then? I mean, why are you here?'

'To be company for you, and to help you.'

'But you are not company for me, and you don't help me.'

This time Miss Jones did not reply. Her face became remote; and then she started writing on a piece of paper. Mrs Temple sat opposite trying to understand the mystery. A murmur which reached her: 'I forgot the prunes; they were one-and-four,' suggested a possible clue.

'I've made my will,' she announced.

'Pardon?' said Miss Jones, without curiosity, putting away her pencil.

'I said I've made my will. And I haven't left a penny to you.'

'I never expected you to,' said Miss Jones, somewhat huffily.

'Not a penny. So you don't gain anything by staying on here, you know, hoping that I shall die.'

In silence, though with an appearance of aloofness, Miss Jones was bowing her head over the ashes of a dream which had coloured many years of her life. The dream of being left a sufficient legacy never to have to work any more. It was always the same, though the opening gambit was different. Sometimes it was a solicitor's letter: 'Dear Madam, if you will call at . . . you will hear something to your advantage. . . .' Or dying hands clasped hers: 'My dear, never in all my life have I known such unselfishness; you will find when I've gone that I've remembered you, though nothing I could leave you would be adequate payment for all you have done. . . .' Or, all unknown to her, some rich gentleman had watched over her from afar, had marked how hard she had to work . . . she opened a letter . . . she opened a parcel containing a box of chocolates . . . a parcel containing a book. There fluttered unexpectedly into her hand a cheque for two thousand, one thousand, five thousand pounds. And a note: 'You don't know me, but all these years I have admired you from afar . . .' Miss Jones hadn't played this game so much lately, but when Mrs Temple spoke, she breathed an unconscious sigh in remembrance.

'Did you hear me?'

'Yes. I told you. I don't expect anything from you in your will.'

'Well, then, will you state plainly, if you can, what are your intentions towards me?'

Miss Jones got up. She said: 'I must take these things down to the kitchen,' and went out.

After a minute, Mrs Temple rose and treading very softly went to the head of the stairs, and stood listening. It was Miss Jones she wanted particularly to hear, but, alas, Miss Jones's voice was too soft to be overheard at that distance. In a minute she heard her approaching, and she turned, and as silently withdrew. But the morning had not been entirely wasted. She had made one of them come out into the open with her threats. She must think of what she should do. Perhaps not the police yet. Perhaps the doctor first.

II

Two mornings later, after the usual tussle with Miss Jones about a bath, Claire Temple suddenly remembered quite clearly that she had made a plan. She expected opposition, but Miss Jones said: 'Yes, dear, certainly,' when told that she must ring up Dr Fairfax and make an appointment immediately.

It was true that when Mrs Temple, instead of going off and forgetting about it, kept at her side and began to show signs of restiveness, Miss Jones decided that this was one of the occasions when Kathleen must be consulted. The more since Mrs Temple had said: 'But I don't want cook to overhear.'

However, Kathleen, in one of her detached moods, merely shrugged her shoulders and said: 'It'll take her off for the morning. If he'll see her, let her go. What harm?'

'She said I wasn't to tell you.'

'For the reason that she wants to relieve herself by telling wicked stories about me. But sure the doctor won't believe a single word she says. He'll see the way she is, and maybe he'll give her some medicine that'll quiet her.'

The appointment was made for eleven-thirty that morning. And for once Miss Jones, impressed by the importance of not putting a doctor to inconvenience, was forced to hurry Mrs Temple rather than restrain her. For she did things that on her own initiative she was unaccustomed to do; brushing her hair, changing her stockings, insisting that her shoes must be found and polished, looking out a different coat and hat. And because these things were so unaccustomed, she did them slowly, moving sometimes in a dream, sometimes in a twitter

of excitement. It was a relief to Miss Jones when at eleven-twenty she saw her go out of the door, having even meekly accepted, in view of the uncertainty of the weather, an umbrella. Looking after her, Miss Jones thought she looked almost like an ordinary elderly woman, if smaller, more frail and wispy than most. And that was the highest praise she had ever, or would ever, bestow upon her employer.

Dr Fairfax, a good-looking man in his early sixties, was familiar with the varying address of the women who entered his consulting-room. There were those who came in fear and timidity, as coming before a judge and savant; there were those who entered haughtily: he was the one to be put on trial, to be tested by the sufficiency of his response to their precious – precious because they were theirs – idiosyncrasies. And there were still those, despite his grey hair and bald pate, who thought of his being a Man before they thought of his being a Doctor, and acted accordingly.

Claire Temple, he knew of old, belonged to the third species. He therefore apologised for having had to keep her waiting for a few minutes, and fussed over her pleasantly. Indeed, his purpose was twofold, for there was, he had noted, a dangerous glitter in her eye, an eagerness for once to over-look the social preliminaries and burst into excited speech. She must be soothed and flattered before he gave her rein; and it was due to him that when he waited for her report of herself she spoke not in anger but more characteristically as an aggrieved child.

'Doctor, it's too dreadful! Those two women between them – I have a terrible companion now, you know – are driving me out of my mind. I know I'm partly out of my mind, but I'm not *quite* out of it, am I? Do tell me.'

Dr Fairfax took up his fountain-pen and studied the nib. He knew that the interview was bound to be painful; he must act so as to make it as little painful as possible. Therefore the way of sympathy must be trodden with circumspection. Already the moving nature of her own question had brought tears to her eyes.

'Surely not,' he said meditatively, and half-questioningly, as she waited.

'I'll tell you why I ask. This cook I have now, a horribly cruel creature, though she makes good savouries, threatens me night and day with the asylum.'

'At night?'

'I mean she makes me *think* about it at night. No, *she* sleeps sound o'nights. She locks herself in her room, so that she won't be disturbed whoever else is. But I can't sleep; I have to go wandering about the house. Dr Fairfax, you won't . . .?'

'Won't what? I'm afraid you're not taking the bromides I gave you last time. Are you? You see, you must rest your brain, and not give it so much work to do. I spoke to your companion on the telephone, didn't I? I must ring her up again about that.'

'It's no good telling her anything. She's unbelievably stupid. One of those half-bred, half-educated people, you know. A "lydy"!'

'Everybody can't be a piece of quicksilver, as you've been, all your life. You must be as patient as you can with her.'

'I pay her a pound a week, but she does nothing. I've

dismissed her, but she won't go. She's always there. I thought it might be the hope of getting something out of me, so I've told her I shan't leave her anything. Over and over again. But still she doesn't go.'

'Did Miss Phillips engage her? How is Miss Phillips, by the way?'

'Yes, she engaged her, I think. Phil comes to see me on Saturday morning: that's all. She's in some sort of a job on other mornings. When she comes she just looks at figures, and writes cheques for me to sign, and then hurries away. I've told her about Miss Jones, but she doesn't take any notice. She doesn't see the danger.'

'What danger?'

'Well, the extraordinary thing that this woman, pale and flabby, with chilblains on her hands, who calls me "dear" all the time, won't go when she's told to go. What does she want?'

Mrs Temple was becoming excited. Dr Fairfax said quickly: 'She doesn't go because obviously Miss Phillips has begged her to stay. You see, the position is that, owing to your loss of memory, it is inadvisable for you to be left alone. In war-time, with all the bother of black-outs and so on.'

'But Kathleen does the black-outs. She's the one I've really come to you about. She's cruel and determined, and she threatens me. Please, Doctor, we're old friends, aren't we? and if she comes, if they come to you, you won't . . .' She stopped for a moment, for it required courage to go on with the Shadow waiting to be brought into the open: 'You won't certify me, will you?'

She looked at his face anxiously. She was both relieved and disappointed that it remained so expressionless. So the idea didn't come to him as a shock.

'That is not likely to happen. But there are places, you know, not asylums, of course, where you would be looked after. . . .'

'I'm not going into an Old Ladies' Home, if that's what you mean. I know I am old, but I'm not old in the way they are. I'm not senile.'

'The whole point is that there must be someone with you, and if you want to stay in your house . . .'

'I'm determined to stay in my house. It's the only thing I've got now. It's been very lonely since Wallace left me, but . . .'

'You must have someone to look after the house, and cook your meals, mustn't you, then? If these two people were to go, what would you do? It's very difficult to get either nurses or household helps these days. And, do forgive me for saying this, because your memory is not trustworthy you are not likely to be an easy person to look after, are you?'

'I know I'm not easy. I bore people to distraction. But I don't see why I should have to grovel to these two vulgarians, one so cruel and heartless, the other . . .' She stopped, her mind weighed with the recollection that there was some sinister mystery about the other. What was it?

Dr Fairfax was saying: 'I don't want you to grovel. What you must do is to think about them as little as possible.'

'How can I not think of them when they are there all the time?'

'Answer this question,' said Dr Fairfax more sternly. 'What would you do if they were not there? Think!'

She saw the picture he intended her to see of the house quite empty except for herself, wandering from room to room, her feet echoing in a silence that grew increasingly menacing. There was a parable in the Bible about it, seven more devils entered, worse than the first. With the tears pouring down her cheeks, she answered: 'I should die of grief and loneliness.'

He touched her arm comfortingly, and then passed her his handkerchief. He rose to look out of the window at a big bloated silver balloon shaped like a legless cow that was adrift from its moorings. Behind him he heard her say:

'I am dying of loneliness now. Like one of those neglected pot plants outside the window of a slum tenement. You see them when the trains go out from Waterloo.'

They were back at the impasse; at the grief that could not be carried away. Macbeth's question raced through his mind: *Canst thou not minister to a mind diseas'd, pluck from the memory a rooted sorrow, raze out the written troubles of the brain . . . cleanse the stuff'd bosom of that perilous stuff which weighs upon the heart?* and the Doctor's answer: *Therein the patient must minister to himself.* Turning round he looked at her in sadness. She mistook the meaning of that look.

'I am so sorry. I know I am keeping you. Here's your handkerchief. Forgive me for being so foolish. Men hate tears, and ever since I was a little girl I've cried when I was hurt. It's a stupid habit, because afterwards there are so many times when there is no one to run to for comfort.'

'I am just sorry that I can't help you more. You are not keeping me; you are keeping the next patient. I am going to write you out a prescription that I want you to be sure to give to your companion to take to a chemist. I'll ring her up also, in case you forget.'

'I won't forget. I promise. I'll go straight home with it.'

'And I want you to rest as much as possible. Your heart isn't too strong, you know. Is it any use to suggest that you should relax, think of green fields, silent trees and cows grazing. . . . I suppose not?'

She shook her head. 'No. People have been my furniture, with all the heartbreaks they bring. But you have been very kind. I wish you would come and dine with me.'

He blotted the prescription. 'I never go anywhere these days. Too old and too tired to be any sort of company.'

'But you don't look old,' Claire cried vivaciously, her social instinct rising dominant, so that this important moment of a farewell between the sexes should be clothed with fitting grace. 'And you are so soothing, and so clever. Why don't you write your reminiscences? It would make such a good book. I can't write now, but . . . but you should.'

'If I ever do and manage to get published, I shall send you a copy inscribed: "To my most distinguished and charming patient." Goodbye.' As his secretary, answering his bell, came to stand by the open door, he bent to kiss her hand.

She walked out of the square in which he lived with a swift light step, and comforted heart. He had been so kind that she must remember, yes, she must try to remember, not to go and see him again for a long time. She wanted him to remember her as being – what had he said? *Charming*. If she went again her tears might blot that impression out entirely.

III

'I wish you would tell me where cook has gone.'

'I've told you half a dozen times,' Miss Jones answered. 'Kathleen is having a day off.'

'Why a whole day? Surely maids have afternoons and evenings off. Not the whole day. I didn't give her permission.'

'Her husband has come back on leave. You wouldn't like her not to see him.'

'The soldier? The one she used to sleep with before she got married?'

Miss Jones made no reply. Mrs Temple watched her as she spread a coloured cloth on the kitchen table, marking the resigned droop of the lips. With every movement the woman killed, she thought, all life in the air about her. Kathleen was hateful, but Kathleen at least answered questions, standing with hands on hips, or with head thrown back in most arresting and vivid poses. Where Kathleen was, there was life, even if it were an angry infuriating life that made you throw dignity to the winds and want to scream and shout. One quickened into a communion that made one forget at least one's isolation, the vivid communication of fighting fish-wives. But Miss Jones was pale death; you went on trying to touch her; you wore your tongue and your heart out, trying to reach her.

'You are Miss Jones, my paid companion, aren't you? Do you mind answering me when I speak to you?'

'I didn't know you asked me anything.'

She had asked her something, but now it was gone. She hurried over the lapse of memory. 'What exactly are you doing? Why are we having lunch in the kitchen?'

'Because there isn't a fire upstairs. Kathleen hadn't time to light one.'

'And you are incapable of doing it. Is that so?'

No reply. After watching her with bright angry eyes, Mrs Temple remembered Lisa lying at her feet, and bent to lift her up. As she held the cat close to her, she said: 'It's extraordinary how much closer I feel to this animal than I do to you. It is alive; you know that it is greedy for fish and rabbit, and likes being stroked and prowling in search of a mate. But you? I know you've never slept with anybody. But have you any animal nature at all?'

Unanswering, Miss Jones moved about the dark kitchen, setting knives and forks and plates down. It was like attempting to strike matches on a damp box, reflected Mrs Temple. No answering flame; only the tearing sound of her own voice.

She had to strike across the silence again, and in despair she cried out: 'Golly, I don't think I've ever disliked anybody as much as I do you, and I've disliked so *many* people. Naturally.'

'Now, now,' said Miss Jones, bringing up a chair to the table. 'And I've got such a nice luncheon for you.'

Mrs Temple stared at the table. 'Where?' she demanded.

Indeed, there was some excuse for her question. The main dish was evidently that which contained rounds of grey, brown liver sausage. There was a loaf of dingy government bread, a slab of flabby cheese, and a green glass dish containing a refined segment of margarine.

But Miss Jones replied brightly, showing no outward signs of her realisation that Mrs Temple was going to prove 'difficult': 'Here! And we are going to have a nice cup of tea and a piece of cake afterwards. If you sit with your back to the fire, that will keep you nice and warm. Oh, I forgot the water. Do you want some?'

Mrs Temple made no answer. She got up and took the chair offered, watching Miss Jones intently as she placed two rounds of sausage on her plate. While Miss Jones went into the back kitchen to get the water, she tasted what had been put on her plate. Miss Jones returned to find her spitting it out.

'Oh, don't do that! There's your serviette. What's the matter?'

'Horrible filth. I've asked you not to use that word "serviette". Why are you trying to poison me?'

'Don't be so silly. You are really very naughty. Do try to eat it, because there isn't anything else.'

Mrs Temple pushed her plate violently away. 'Are you going to eat it?'

'Of course. Eat the other piece. That was the outside one and it's rather stale. That's why you didn't like it.'

'I see it all now. You are trying to poison me, but doing it with the maximum of stupidity. Will you get me some grease-proof paper, please?'

'What do you want grease-proof paper for? Not to eat, I hope.' Miss Jones gave a little laugh.

'If you don't get it, and stop your nervous giggling, I shall get it myself.'

Mrs Temple sounded so angry that Miss Jones judged it advisable to humour her. She got up and started to rummage in the pantry, while Mrs Temple stared at her stooping plump back, clad in a brown cardigan, with intent eyes which were yet focused on nothing.

'Is this what you want?' inquired Miss Jones, returning with a piece of paper which had contained three-quarters of a pound of margarine.

Mrs Temple took it from her, held it up to her eyes; then wrapped it round the offending piece of liver sausage. She next rose, and without a word walked out of the kitchen and up the stairs.

'Where are you going? Do come back and finish your lunch.'

There was no answer; after waiting just long enough to devour a couple of mouthfuls of food, Miss Jones went upstairs, to find Mrs Temple putting on her coat in the hall.

'You mustn't go out now, dear. I want you to come back and finish your lunch. Perhaps we can find something else, if you don't like the liver, and I'm just going to make you a nice cup of tea.'

'Can say "nice" and still be a villain,' murmured Mrs Temple with, to Miss Jones, complete irrelevancy.

'Do come back to the kitchen. It's such a nasty cold afternoon.' Miss Jones laid her hand with intended persuasiveness on Mrs Temple's arm. Her touch seemed to arouse a sleeping demon.

'Don't touch me. How dare you! After what you've just tried to do! Are you really too stupid to understand that I haven't left you anything in my will?'

'I don't want to be left anything. I just want you to come downstairs and have your lunch.'

For answer Mrs Temple ran to the front door, opened it, and banged it behind her.

Miss Jones waited for an uncertain moment or two. Mrs Temple had stormed out of the house before, and one only made a fool of oneself by running after her, and being snubbed and shouted at to the amusement of passers-by. Besides, Kathleen always said that there was nothing like a walk for cooling her off. So she went slowly back to the kitchen, and to the liver sausage, which, she could not help agreeing, was not very appetising. Sitting there, facing the melancholy bare branches of the sooty oak tree in the back garden, she shivered a little and her heart sank. Of course, it was absurd for Kathleen to talk about Mrs Temple as being wicked, but the atmosphere in the kitchen now that the scene was over was certainly oppressive. There seemed something menacing about her that had not been there before. She decided she was being fanciful, and for that the best remedy was a cup of tea.

Mrs Temple had rushed out of the house with such haste that she found herself going north to Notting Hill rather than south to the nearest police station she knew. But she went on at great speed, knowing that if she did not maintain and even stimulate the uprush of anger within she might forget or misplace the object of her errand. The little packet she carried in her hand was evidence, and she kept looking at it, as the highly-strung traveller keeps a nervous watch on the whereabouts of his or her ticket.

Yes, Miss Jones had tried to poison her; one would not have thought it of such a paltry and pasty-looking woman, but now she understood the reason why she had crept into her house and stayed guard upon her.

How wicked, she thought again, as she turned towards Holland Park. Wickedness without a purpose, for she had told her over and over again that she was going to leave her nothing in her will. But murderers like that were born in every generation; there was Jack the Ripper, there was some Frenchman . . . yes, she had known all her life that beneath the rattle of teacups and glasses, of agreeable voices retailing titbits of gossip and compliments, a dark and sinister world existed. Give the devil his due: he existed! Miss Jones, as she called herself – there was, of course, something suspicious enough in that: the name was too common – was a devil. Devils could come in queer forms, wearing ugly brown cardigans, and having chilblains and a sniffling cold, and calling her 'dear', and saying 'pardon'. Miss Jones, she had once thought, cherished her cold over the fire as another woman might cherish a great passion.

She reminded herself that she didn't know quite where she was going, and paused to ask to be directed by an approaching middle-aged man in a bowler hat. If he had been at all impressed by her question, she would probably have delayed to tell him the story, but he gave her directions casually: 'Turn right, and then keep on till you get to a pub called The Mitre. It's only a few doors from there.'

'Thank you so much.'

He probably thought she was on her way to inquire about a lost umbrella or a lost cat. She had been several times to the nearer police station in search of Lisa. He was not to know it was . . . *what*? O God, let her remember . . . what? It was something dreadfully imperative. Murder? Of course! She sighed with relief. Miss Jones had tried to poison her, and she was carrying the poisoned meat in the little packet in her hand. 'Murder, murder,' she whispered over and over again, as she hurried on.

Ah, there the police station was right before her, when she hadn't really been looking for it. Was her hair tidy? It was a pity that her shoes looked so much like bedroom slippers. People did misunderstand things like that if they were the usual prosy kind. As, of course, policemen were. Not poetry, but prose made their lives. *Body Found Drowned; Woman Missing From Her Home; Anyone Witnessing Accident Please Communicate* . . . There was one of them, passing her quickly without a look. But the sight of him carried encouragement. He was a symbol of law and order. People were NOT allowed to try to murder each other. She was in London and not in the Dark Kingdom where bogeys, witches, warlocks, vampires and ghouls made their home.

Inside the building she asked a plain-clothes man peremptorily:

'Where's the Superintendent, please? I must see him.'

'Through that door on your right,' he said with a glance which had an obscure effect of stripping her of all privilege, of all prestige.

She opened the door. There were several desks with men sitting at them. When she started to speak the man nearest waved her on with a jerk of the thumb.

Angry now, she did not wait for the grey-haired man to look up from his writing. Besides, if she didn't speak soon she would forget what she had come about: 'I've come to see you about a very serious matter. I have a companion whose name, she pretends, is Jones. Just now she tried to murder me.'

He looked up, and because his face was agreeable, she relapsed unconsciously into her femininity: 'Please tell me what I am to do.'

He gave her a long look from head to foot. 'Another of them,' he was thinking. 'How the barmy ones rush in here.'

'Now what makes you think that?' he said kindly, as to a child.

His levity struck her like a blow. Her hand closed on the packet: 'It's all right. I know policemen have to have evidence. I've brought it. I've got proof.'

'That's right, ma'am. Can't do anything without proof.'

'Look at this filthy mess, then! She gave it me to eat for my lunch. My cook has taken the day off, and that gave her the opportunity.'

The police officer took the piece of paper which she held open before him: 'Looks like the dog's dinner,' he said facetiously.

'It looks disgusting, doesn't it? But it wasn't intended for the dog; it was intended for me.'

He sniffed at it. 'Come now; it's not so bad. War-time has its horrors, you know, Madam. Bit of liver sausage, isn't it? And not so fresh as it might be. Still . . .' he raised his voice. 'Anyone feeling hungry?'

A red-faced man just going off duty came over: 'I wouldn't say no to a nice piece of roast chicken.'

'This lady thinks this is poisoned. If you want a George Medal, Fred, here's your chance.'

Claire said earnestly: 'Please don't eat it, either of you. I spat mine out.'

'Ah, but then we coppers have cast-iron stomachs, haven't we, Fred?'

'Can't speak for you,' said Fred. 'But mine isn't what it used to be. My wife served me with dried eggs and a piece of this foreign bacon last night for supper. I said to her: "What's this?" "Why, eggs and bacon," she said. "Surprising how different it tastes," I said back. "Trying to poison me, are you, and get the insurance?"'

She had listened intently, but when the man at the desk laughed, she realised their facetiousness. Or rather she felt the atmosphere of farce about her, of stale kippers, of Wigan pier, of mother-in-law jokes.

'I'm quite serious. This isn't a joke. I've suspected this woman for some time of peculiar designs. She was foisted upon me against my will, and I've repeatedly asked her to leave my house. But she won't go. She thinks she is going to benefit under my will. She calls herself "Jones". That in itself . . .' She paused, looking for understanding, but the Superintendent's face was now impassive. 'However, whatever her name is, is beside the point. Have you to have this meat analysed, or what are you going to do?'

'Where do you live, Madam?'

She told him.

'I suggest you go home now, and tell her you've complained to the police, so that she had better give you something more tasty to eat.'

'What I want to know is what are you going to *do*? I have laid a grave charge.'

'Do? Well, I don't know. Perhaps if you wrote to Lord Woolton it might help.'

'I don't think I know Lord Woolton. Is he the head of your office or something?'

The two men laughed spontaneously. Then the red-faced man, seeing the clock, said: 'Well, I'll be getting along.'

'Right you are, Fred.'

A pale young policeman came up to the desk and said in an excited voice: 'A woman here says she has some information on the Hedgerley case. Will you see her?'

'Okay. Just a moment. Now, Madam, I think I can assure you this meat's not poisoned; it's only gone stale. Quite wise not to eat it, because it might give you indigestion. But I wouldn't worry any more.'

'How do you know it's not poisoned? You're surely going to have it analysed?'

'Right you are. We'll have it analysed, and communicate with you if we find any more foreign matter than usual has been inserted. I've got your address. Good afternoon.'

She wanted to stay, but his will was superior, and she found herself standing disregarded at the door, while he beckoned onwards a woman of the working-classes with a white deter-

mined face, who went eagerly forward. 'This is the way out, lady,' said a voice, and she found herself looking into the pale grey docketing eyes of the man she had seen before in the corridor. She said, passionately: 'I think you're dreadfully casual if not rude here. I came to lay a most serious charge, and I am not at all sure that you are going to take any notice of it. I thought English policemen were supposed to be the best in the world. I shall take the matter further, I warn you. I presume you have something to do with the police. Are you a detective?'

'It doesn't matter what I am, Madam,' he said, looking at her steadily, and taking a step forward. Head erect, she moved away as from a wall, stirred by an unusual emotion of pity, pity not for herself but for all those who were weak in their losing fight against those who were strong, whether by their own right or by right of the authority invested in them.

She went out into the street, and also she went out into a world which was colder and greyer and more implacable than she had ever seen before. 'What a horrible man,' she muttered to herself. 'An iceberg that watches. I shall never go there again. And yet the policemen at the other place were so kind about Lisa, when I lost her.'

Her brain wearied as she tried to struggle with this new problem. Nice about cats, but not about poisoned meat. They had made music-hall jokes, and swept her out, as if it were she who should be put into a dust-bin. Of course, they were common men, with no habit of courtesy.

The street down which she was walking matched her disillusioned mood. About her was the dinginess of houses that

had come down in the world, but yet kept themselves to themselves with lowering respectability, a respectability that was menaced and badly frayed at corners by the thrust of swollen Victorian public-houses, by small but assertive vegetable and ironmongery shops, displaying their wares outside the windows on the pavement, by a group of clamorous children with skipping-ropes.

Claire Temple, however, did not notice detail; she felt only that she was abroad where she had no business to be. Enough of spaciousness and dignity still lingered in the hills and terraces near her own house for her personality to feel, except for occasional jars, that ordered and placid lives were still the rule outside of her own bitter loneliness. But this was another world, not strange to her, for there was a nearby open market where she had gone with Kathleen to pick up bargains in the way of kettles and saucepans. But to go slumming for fun was one thing. To expose oneself to rudeness was another: it was like the time when she had sold the Suffragette paper, but that had a glow like the glow of being a naughty child. Now there was no glow.

She tried to remember what had prompted this chill of discouragement: what had happened at the police station? She believed, though uncertainly, that they had promised that the meat would be analysed. It had been their attitude that had affected her rather than what they had said. She should have dressed up, that was it. If you were a woman you had to dress up to go to see policemen, otherwise you were accorded no respect. And again far off, like the suggestion of gentle rain, there fell upon her heart that strange impulse of impersonal

pity, pity for those who couldn't dress up, who were hustled through the world like a tramp moved on from a seat in a park.

It dulled and was wiped out, as her own image and the sense of her own sufferings imposed themselves, rousing the response of anger and resentment. Whatever others did, she, Claire Temple, was going to fight to the end. She was not going to do what they wanted her to do. Other old women – and seeing herself through the detective's eyes, she was now conscious of herself as an old and perhaps crazy woman – might huddle behind their doors, peering out of windows with eyes still greedy for life, yet afraid to venture, but she would still go out. All her life, from the time she had been a girl, she had gone out when she had wanted to go, however other people, her mother and father, had criticised. She was going to fight for her own individuality to the end, and, with a sense of adventure, she thought as she came to the shops of Notting Hill that she would go into a tea-shop, and order herself a meal. If she went into a completely strange tea-shop, somewhere she had never been before, it was unlikely that her enemies would be before her with their poison tricks.

But she must have money to pay. Luckily, she had remembered to bring her bag with her. She stopped and removed her purse. It contained only three coppers. All her peering, all her searching in the different compartments of her bag, failed to bring any further money to light.

They had stolen her money from her was her first thought, forgetting the meagreness of her allowance, which had been drained on the previous afternoon by random purchases at a haberdashery counter, when she had been out with Miss Jones.

Outsoaring that sense of her poverty which had been stressed so frequently by Miss Phillips as the reason for her lack of spending money, she was conscious now only of the ignominy of her plight. She had had no food since the early morning, and now she had not the wherewithal to go into the cheapest tea-shop. For even in the cheapest tea-shop it would not have occurred to her to omit a tip. Miss Jones had not only tried to poison her, but she was also engaged in pilfering money out of her bag. Her anger mounted, and gave her strength to climb up the hill out of the High Street. 'Robbers as well as murderers,' she muttered to herself over and over again as she went.

Her key was in her purse, so she let herself in, banging the door behind her to give full notice that a fighter had come to the wars. With some surprise she noticed that the dining-room was empty, and she swept on with fear as well as anger to the top of the basement steps: 'Cook, are you there?'

There was a rustle beneath her. Then Miss Jones called back: 'Is that you, Mrs Temple? Kathleen is out for the day. Won't you come down here by the fire?'

She went down, asking angrily: 'Why isn't cook here? Did I give her permission to go out?'

'Of course you did. Now shall I make you a nice cup of tea, or did you get something when you were out?'

Remembrance swept back upon her. 'Of course I didn't. I have only threepence in my purse. That is what I want to speak to you about. I assume you've been stealing from me.'

'Don't be silly,' said Miss Jones, with some sternness. This was a new and unexpected charge against her. 'You haven't any money because you insisted yesterday on buying all those reels of Silko that really you don't want at all.'

Impelled by fatigue Claire sat down. She did remember something about buying pretty reels of coloured cotton. Or had Miss Jones made it all up? There was certainly something very wicked Miss Jones had done, if she could only think of it. She dropped her head on to her hands, and then started to massage her hot forehead with cold fingers. If only she could think clearly. But she was quite sure that Miss Jones was an enemy.

'I can see you are tired,' said Miss Jones. 'But you really must understand that you mustn't accuse anybody of stealing. It's a very wrong thing to do. I'll make you some tea, and cut you some bread and butter, shall I?'

Claire said nothing, so she busied herself with preparations. After a while she asked: 'Did you have a nice walk?'

'I didn't go for a walk.'

'Where did you go then?' said Miss Jones, with that kind smile which intimated that she accepted the irresponsibility of her employer.

'I went to the police,' said Claire, delighted as recollection returned. Another and more depressing intimation came to the surface of her mind. 'Of course, I should have worn better clothes. Aren't you my paid companion? You should surely have seen that I changed my shoes.'

'What did you go to the police for?' asked Miss Jones, pausing on her way to the stove, where the kettle was not boiling.

Mrs Temple made no reply. She was observing with interest the sudden tension in Miss Jones's figure. It was not often that

Miss Jones awaited with interest a reply to any question, and while she pondered over the reason for this curiosity, she said with more emphasis: 'Yes, I've been to the police station.'

Miss Jones proceeded to make the tea. When she brought in the tray and set it down, she said in a worried voice: 'I do hope you haven't done anything silly. Are you sure you went to the police?'

Mrs Temple was silent, watching Miss Jones fixedly. Something was coming back to her, something to do with Miss Jones's wickedness. Tired of the silence, Miss Jones passed her a plate, and then handed the bread and butter she had cut, saying: 'I expect you are hungry. Have some bread and butter while we wait for the tea to draw.'

Mrs Temple took a piece of bread and butter, still watching Miss Jones, who now said with more brightness: 'I'll bring this small table over to you, and then you can put your cup and plate on it, and needn't move away from the fire. . . . Now I think the tea will be ready. Shall I pour out for you?'

'Go on.' said Mrs Temple.

She muttered the two words, for the scene had become a stage setting. The kitchen where she sat was no longer a familiar apartment in her own house: its walls had dissolved, for the foundation of concrete familiarity had gone. There were only two people facing each other in the last act of a play, the victim and the murderess.

'Drink it while it's hot,' suggested Miss Jones, placing cup and saucer on the table.

The next moment there was a crash. Mrs Temple had sent the table flying to the floor. The cup had broken; the tea-pot

lid came off, and hot liquid stung Miss Jones's foot, as she stared down in dismay.

'What have you done? Oh, my goodness! Really, I do think . . . I shall have to go! I can't manage this any more.'

Mrs Temple, too, had been surprised by the crash. First, her mind went completely blank, and it was only after a few moments that familiarity came back into the scene, and she saw Miss Jones bending to pick up a broken cup, and then recede from her into the scullery to find a cloth. 'What did you do that for?' she heard her ask.

She heard herself saying: 'I'm not going to be robbed and poisoned. Perhaps now you will understand that.'

Miss Jones said nothing. With lips pressed tightly together she went into the scullery with the tea-pot. It was as if, with her going, she took Mrs Temple's last remains of energy with her. Though she cried out petulantly against the disapproval of that back – which her sensitiveness related to some general social disapproval of herself – 'It's not fair that I should be robbed and starved and poisoned; I'm going to my room now,' the movement with which she got to her feet was for once a slow and heavy movement:

'I should think that is the best thing you can do,' said Miss Jones over her shoulder.

IV

Miss Jones went to bed early that evening, but she couldn't sleep. At half-past eleven she decided she would go downstairs and see if Kathleen were back. Kathleen must be told what

had happened, which, after all, Miss Jones considered, was nothing less than the sudden conversion of Mrs Temple from being 'mental' into becoming a maniac.

Kathleen, who had just come in, listened with a yawning half-attention to the narrative. She was tired, and more concerned with making herself a cup of cocoa than anything, interrupted Miss Jones sharply to ask: 'Where's all the milk gone?'

'The milk? Oh, she came down at the end of the afternoon and drank it all.'

'I do think you might have quelled her. Now what are we going to do for breakfast? Don't you know well that the milk doesn't come till eleven?'

'Stop her! I kept away from her. I didn't want anything else thrown at me, thank you. She thinks I'm trying to poison her or something. I expect that's what she told the police.'

Frowningly taking out a tin of condensed milk from the cupboard, Kathleen said: 'So you think she really did go traipsing off to the police, do you?'

'Yes, I am quite sure she did. And she accused me of taking money out of her bag. It's really too much for flesh and blood to stand.'

Kathleen looked thoughtfully at the dumpy figure in the green flannel dressing-gown. She had never seen Miss Jones so indignant, and she supplied her with a sop of reassurance: 'Sure the police would only laugh at whatever she said. They'd know her for what she was as soon as ever they clapped eyes on her.'

'That's not the point. I'm not going to have accusations

made against my character by whomsoever they are made. Nor am I going to have scalding tea-pots thrown at me. My foot is really bad. I'll show it you if you like.'

'Just wait a moment,' said Kathleen. She went to the stove and poured boiling water on the cocoa. When she had stirred it well, she settled herself into the chair opposite Miss Jones, and took up the role of a sympathetic judge who was examining a rather stupid witness.

'Hasn't she thrown things at you before, tell me?'

'She's thrown a towel. And once her sponge, that time she accused me of making her have a bath when she didn't want one. But now that she's started being really violent I tell you I've finished. I'd have rung Miss Phillips up and told her this afternoon, only I know she's gone away for a week. When I first came I told her: "I'm not going to stand for violence." I don't mind a mental case in the ordinary way, but violence is a different matter. I'm not going to be a warder in a lunatic asylum, no, not for anybody. I hope I haven't come to that yet.'

'I tell you what, I'll read the Riot Act over her, that's what I'll do. The devil's in her, and no mistake, but she's afraid of losing *me*. And I'll tell her I'll go, that I won't stop a single solitary moment after you've gone.'

'Please yourself about that,' said Miss Jones, getting up. 'I'm certainly going to look out for another post, and I shall tell Miss Phillips so when she gets back from her weekend on Monday. It's too much responsibility.'

'Will you have a cup of cocoa?'

'No, thank you,' said Miss Jones, with some coldness. She

considered Kathleen might have offered her some before. 'Good night.'

'Good night, and I'd sleep on it, if I were you.'

Miss Jones retreated without answering, leaving Kathleen to reflect that when the worm, as she considered Miss Jones to be, turned, it might stick to its turning, and in that case she must try to do something about it.

She put her plan into operation the next morning, when, Miss Jones having come downstairs with the information that Mrs Temple wanted her breakfast in bed, she cooked bacon and scrambled egg with care. When she handed the appetising tray over, she asked: 'Tell me, was she in a cross mood with you?'

'She didn't seem to know who I was. She called me by another name, Mrs Jessup.'

'That was the one that was here last year. I'm going up now to make a good fire for you, and I tell you, I'll fetch down the tray myself. You needn't bother. Have a good read of the paper, and make yourself comfortable.'

'Thank you,' said Miss Jones, without fervour. It didn't need a great amount of intelligence to see that Kathleen was trying to get round her. Nevertheless, she intended to give the maximum of attention to the advertising columns of the *Daily Telegraph* rather than the news of the war.

Half an hour later Kathleen entered Mrs Temple's room and stood surveying the bed and its occupant, and also the tray on the floor. Tea had been spilt, but everything she had sent up had been eaten.

'Have you finished your breakfast?'

'Oh, that's you, cook. Yes, thank you.'

'Did you enjoy it?'

'Very nice, thank you, cook . . . will you tell Mrs Jessup to come upstairs and take a letter?'

'It wasn't poisoned by any chance?'

'Poisoned? What do you mean?'

'Your breakfast. Was it poisoned? I'm asking you,' said Kathleen, raising her voice.

'No, it wasn't, was it?'

'I'm asking *you*.'

'I think you are being silly, cook. If it were poisoned, I suppose I should be feeling ill. And I'm not ill, but I'm very, very tired. As if I'd taken too much wine. But I don't think I did. Because we don't get any now, do we? That's what I want Mrs Jessup for, to write a letter to that dear old man in Wardour Street and ask him to send in a bottle or two of whisky. Or brandy, and some sherry. There's such a sense of gloom in a house that has nothing of the friendly juice of the grape. And don't you want sherry for cooking? I know we're very poor, but surely we can afford one bottle of cooking sherry?'

Kathleen placed her hands on her hips, thrusting her elbows forward preparatory to her next lines.

'And isn't it well for you lying there at your ease, and talking about sherry and brandy and whisky, and knowing well what you've done to bring disgrace on this house and yourself? Most of all on yourself, for, mind you, we're not responsible for what you do. Making a holy show of yourself the way you did. Oh, I know all about it, don't think I don't.'

Mrs Temple raised herself from her pillow; the slumbering

embers of anger within her stirred, as if a poker had been applied. 'Really, Kathleen – you are Kathleen, aren't you?'

'Full well you know I am Kathleen, and no other.'

'Don't talk to me in that tone of voice, please. You're my cook, and here you come bursting in on me with some accusation. Will you speak out? but don't shout . . . there's no need to shout.'

'Oh, there isn't! Not after you've been to the police and levelled charges against anybody and everybody of poisoning you. Miss Jones told me. Running off with the bit of meat and making a fool of yourself showing it them. That meat wasn't poisoned. I got it myself, and that's why I'm asking you. Do you accuse me of poisoning you? That's what I'm asking you.'

Recollection illuminated Mrs Temple's mind. 'Yes, I did go to the police. Miss Jones – of course her name isn't Miss Jones at all, too absurd – tried to poison me, and she's robbing me. Let me see my bag, and I'll show you.'

'Now, who's shouting? If a lawyer heard you, you'd be had up for libel instantaneously.'

'I'm not shouting. If I am, it's you making me shout.' Mrs Temple paused, remembering the tradition of bad-tempered cooks. 'All the same you've got it wrong. I'm not accusing you. My breakfast was cooked perfectly. You are very good at savouries, I know. You're too good a cook to poison anybody. It would be like a good artist painting a bad picture. It's against the nature of the beast.'

'Are you calling me a beast?'

'No, I'm not. Don't be silly, cook.'

'So I didn't poison you, but Miss Jones did. Is that it?'

'Yes, I think she did. Anyway, the police are going to have the food she gave me, perfectly filthy food, I can tell you, analysed. Another thing, she let me go out in my slippers, and she's robbing me.'

'And *you* never did anything? You never threw a tea-tray at her, I suppose? Scalding her foot, so that this morning she can hardly set foot to the ground. She could get big damages off you for that, you know. Oh, she's well on her way to make her fortune.'

'Don't talk nonsense, cook. I haven't anything to give her. I'm a poor woman, and if she goes to law she won't get anything. Besides, I never scalded her foot. It's all nonsense. You're a very wicked woman, I've always known that.'

'It's not *me* that's wicked.'

'Yes, you are, because you're trying to send me mad.'

'I'm trying to prevent you, that's all. But I can't do much more against your wickedness. Oh, I'm not talking about the men you've lived with and you never married to them, and only letting on to be married, as you know you do. That's not my business. But now you're going too far altogether. Taking away people's characters and throwing tea-pots at them will have you up in a court of law, and you know what the end of that would be?'

Mrs Temple banged the pillow wildly with her hands. 'How dare you? Leave this room.'

'I'll leave this room when I please and not before. What I say is this, and calm yourself to listen, so that it may do you some good. You'd better apologise to Miss Jones, and give her some decent present – and when I say "decent present", I don't mean half-a-crown, for I know your stinty nature well, but something worth the having. Otherwise, you'll be up in the courts, and certified as a raving lunatic. Now, I'm going . . .'

'Yes, you'd better, or I shall kill you,' shouted Mrs Temple. She jumped out of bed, and seized the knife from her tray. But when she turned and flung it, it hit the door, which Kathleen had closed smartly behind her. Shivering and shaking, and sobbing the tearless dry sobs of hysteria, she stood there in her nightgown, trying to remember what it was she must do, trying to remember what it was all about. . . .

Downstairs, Kathleen poked her head in at the dining-room, and said with gloomy relish: 'Oh, she's very bad; she was going to attack me just now, but I was too quick for her. I wouldn't go near her for a while if I were you.'

'Very well. I am going to write some letters. There are one or two things here that might suit me.'

'All the same, I wouldn't do anything in a hurry. You might get yourself out of the frying-pan into the fire, do you know? Some that thinks themselves sane are often worse than them that do be mad.'

Miss Jones said nothing at all, and Kathleen went on her way meditatively.

CHAPTER TEN

I

Between them during the next few days they sent her to Coventry. It was true that Miss Jones's was a mild method of turning her back. No longer did she bother to make conversation at meals. But she was still punctilious in the difficult matter of persuading Mrs Temple to take a morning bath; she still followed her about with brush and comb; she still reminded her of other daily necessities. But once Mrs Temple was up and dressed, she withdrew herself; no longer did she persuade her to come shopping; no longer did she draw chairs up to the fire for her; no longer did she call her 'dear'. Mrs Temple might have been gratified by the lesser evidence Miss Jones gave of being part of her life, had it not been for Kathleen; and Kathleen, ignoring her mistress, inquired assiduously now after Miss Jones's comfort. It was 'Miss Jones, could you do with a cup of tea? I'm making one for myself.' Or 'Your hot-water-bottle is up, Miss, if you want to go to bed.' Useless for Mrs Temple to protest angrily: 'Really, Kathleen, I am employing you, not this lady.' Kathleen would take no notice, and Mrs Temple was left to rush out of the room, murmuring angrily to herself.

She would have done more than protest had it not been
that between them they convinced her that she had done
something terrible. She tried to lift the curtains of memory
to discover what it might have been. But the only clue she had
was that once Kathleen said something about the police, and
looked at her significantly. Did that mean that they were
thinking of handing her over to the police? Had she hurt
somebody? Had she run out of the house naked? Had she
committed arson? She tried to pump Miss Jones, as the more
amenable of the two, for at least she was not full of dark and
dreadful sayings, like Kathleen. Nor did she shout at her.

'Why are you so quiet? Has somebody died?'

'Not that I know of. Of course a lot of people are dying.
This dreadful war.'

'You sit as if you were at a funeral. You used to talk more,
didn't you?'

'Did I?' Miss Jones gave a little laugh. 'Perhaps I haven't
very much to say.'

'No, you haven't. But that didn't stop you chattering,
did it?'

'Well, now I've stopped chattering.'

'Can't you tell me exactly why? You may think I'm mad,
but I'm not an imbecile.'

'I told you. I haven't anything to say.'

'So different from me,' said Claire, drawn once more down
a much traversed path. 'I've so much to say, but there's no one
to listen to me any longer.'

'Oh.'

'I'd like to tell someone about the way I'm treated in this

house. Hunted and harried like a wild beast. Why? Have I done anything I shouldn't?'

'Your memory's not very good, is it?'

'No, I know it isn't. But is that a reason for being continually insulted in my own house?'

Miss Jones said nothing. There always came the point when Miss Jones refused to answer. Claire would look at her grey-skinned closed-up countenance, and think how smug it looked. What dark design did the veil conceal? She resumed her watching; she listened when Kathleen and Miss Jones made the beds together, but she obtained no further satisfaction than the realisation that Kathleen was much more friendly to Miss Jones than she had once been. 'They are as thick as thieves,' she thought, and the phrase stayed in her mind as an enlightening one.

But Miss Jones was not a thief. As one day she proved when Kathleen went into her room when she was dusting, and in her new friendliness sat herself down on Miss Jones's bed.

Miss Jones said: 'I'm giving this room a good turn-out. So that whoever comes here next, if there is such an unfortunate person, will have at least a clean place in which to sleep.'

This remark was at least partly directed at Kathleen, who considered that dusting was a supererogatory act. She, personally, she would have told anyone, had no time for it. And considering this to be understood by anyone with sense, she did not perceive Miss Jones's intent. The menace of the remark, she considered, was the intimation it gave that Miss Jones still intended to leave. To leave her, that is to say, in the lurch.

But Miss Jones mistook her silence for resentment, and, feeling that the subject had better be speedily changed, said quickly as she flicked her duster: 'I do like this pair of prints, don't you? They are genuine Baxters, you know. Worth quite a little, I should say.'

Kathleen said slowly, but casually: 'Why don't you take them?'

'Take them?'

'Yes. She'd not miss them in a hundred years. If she did, you need say nothing but that you never noticed them. And if she asked me I'd remind her that she gave them away or sold them. And she'd believe it, you know, because she's scared at giving herself away. I've often had it to do. "Have you forgotten?" I ask her when she's on the cry about missing something. "Of course I haven't forgotten," she raps out as quick as quick.'

'But, Kathleen, that would be stealing. And telling a lie. I really don't quite understand you.'

'How would it be stealing? And you having to put up with all sorts the way you have. I gave her a hint to give you a decent present, or else you'd go. But she's too mean to take the hint, do you know?'

'I'm going in any case, Kathleen. Just as soon as I get fixed up. I had a reply to that advertisement in the *Ladies' Companion*, and I'm going to see the lady this afternoon. It's in the country, but then one is safer in the country supposing air-raids start again. I certainly shan't take . . .'

She stopped, for familiar steps were running up the stairs, and in a moment Mrs Temple came in. 'So here both of you

are. Now what are you plotting about? Why don't you have the courage to come out with it? All this stealing into corners!'

It was Miss Jones who looked a trifle confused. Kathleen said calmly: 'Plotting yourself it is. Your suspiciousness is something terrible, and will turn on you yet. I've given you a clean sheet, and there's not another in the house, so . . .'

'If you're not plotting, why does she look so guilty?' asked Mrs Temple, pointing a finger towards Miss Jones.

'So she mayn't dust her room now, is it?' inquired Kathleen, walking out of the room. Drawn as by a magnet, Mrs Temple followed her: 'I'm looking for Lisa. Where is she? I've been in the kitchen, and she's not there. I suppose you're trying to keep my cat away from me now.'

Miss Jones heard Kathleen say: 'Oh, cat yourself,' and then Mrs Temple: 'Don't speak to me like that.' She closed the door, and stood for a moment looking, as she vaguely felt, over that abyss which separates the middle class from the lower class, those who had been brought up with rigid ideas about the sacrosanct nature of property and those whose motto was: 'Finding's keeping, but be careful not to be found out.'

It looked very much, Miss Jones could not help thinking, as she resumed her dusting, as if Kathleen was engaged in feathering her own nest. But though she deeply disapproved, she dismissed a faint suggestion that it was her duty to say something to put Miss Phillips on her guard. It never really paid, she had learnt, to do anything but keep one's mouth shut in such matters. She had heard the disgraceful way Kathleen shouted at Mrs Temple – after all, it was disgraceful, whatever the provocation – and she didn't want that same tongue to be turned on herself. Besides, it wasn't as if Kathleen had actually admitted she had taken things. . . .

But, oh, reflected Miss Jones, how glad she would be to get out of this dark and dirty house, where her companions were an old mad woman and an ignorant and . . . well, not too particular Irish servant who seemed, the way she went on, really to enjoy scenes.

II

Miss Jones returned from the interview that afternoon, as Kathleen was quick to notice, in a mixed frame of mind. A few sympathetic queries elicited the information that while the post was Miss Jones's for the asking, it was less in the capacity of companion than working housekeeper that her services were required. 'They didn't put it that way,' explained Miss Jones, 'but as they only have a woman in twice a week for rough work, it seems to me that that is what it would come to. And am I strong enough? That's the point.'

'You're not,' said Kathleen with conviction. 'A week or two and you'd be killed with it.'

'But the pay is good.' Miss Jones stopped, for after all it was going a little too far to confide the question of salary to a servant. She did not want to confide in Kathleen at all, but when there was no one else . . . 'And the lady is very nice. There is only herself and her little girl. Her husband is an officer in the Forces.'

'A child! There's always lashings of extra work where there are children.'

'She goes to a kindergarten every morning,' said Miss Jones, and sighed. 'If I could only see the house, then I'd know better. But I said I'd tell her definitely tomorrow.'

'You can't be expected to make up your mind that quick. It's unreasonable. Besides, you could get that sort of job any moment.'

'Do you think so?'

'Of course. Thousands asking.'

Miss Jones gathered up her belongings, and went slowly upstairs, carrying with her that great burden of having to make a decision immediately. Meanwhile, Kathleen decided that she too must act quickly. It was obvious to her mind that Miss Jones was tempted by the salary. So if she could only make the queer one hand her out those two prints she had taken a fancy to, and perhaps something else into the bargain, then the danger for the moment might be passed. This time she would go to Mrs Temple less in the capacity of a prophet of disaster than as an ally and friend. She would make her see that it was in all their interests for Miss Jones to be induced to stay. And since it was evident that Miss Jones was too soft to take advantage of the opportunities her position gave her, she, Kathleen, would have to fight her battles for her. After all, and she could not help being flattered by the knowledge, the queer one would rather deal with her and be with her than with Miss Jones, for all that Miss Jones was the kind that couldn't say 'boo', whereas she, Kathleen, was not one to put up with other people's nonsense.

She tackled her the next morning, walking into the study, where Mrs Temple was for the moment quietly disposed in reading one of her old diaries. The dramatic way in which she shut the door, and then stood looking gloomily out of the window, was sufficient to engage Mrs Temple's uneasy attention immediately.

'What's the matter?'

Kathleen brought her regard slowly round. 'Matter?'

'Yes. Do you want something?'

'I was only thinking.' She glanced back at the door, as if to make sure it were shut. 'I'm afraid of what's going to happen.'

'What's going to happen?' inquired Mrs Temple, looking round in a fevered way, as if to read the writing on the wall.

'I'm afraid Miss Jones has got it into her head to take herself off.'

'Is that all? I can tell you, cook, it would be a tremendous relief to me if she did. I pay her a pound a week, and she's quite useless. I've told her to go over and over again, but she sits and knits and knits and sits, and lately she has done it in such a gloomy way. If she were more picturesque to look at she might be one of those women in the French Revolution, an attendant on the guillotine.'

'It's all very well for you to be talking, but if she does go, and I happen to know she has the offer of a very good job with double the money and more than she gets here, what are we going to do?'

'Why, I shall advertise for someone else. Or get Miss Phillips to. This time I shall insist on a woman of some literary taste and at least average intelligence.'

'And how are you going to get such? Don't you know well,

haven't you been told over and over, that in war-time they're paying such high wages that the miserable pound a week you give Miss Jones wouldn't tempt anyone in their right senses? Not with what they have to put up with when they get here.'

Mrs Temple disregarded the last unpleasing remark. 'We managed before this ponderous old creature came, and I dare say we can do it again. Mrs White can come more often, can't she? If she's paid? I'm quite ready to pay her more, because at least she is respectful, and that is something in these days.'

'Put that notion out of your head. Mrs White can only come on Mondays, and more, she's failed us once or twice. And it's no good your saying: "Get another woman," for there isn't one in the whole of London to be got. It's not me that's saying this alone; ask Miss Phillips, ask anyone.'

Mrs Temple turned her head restlessly, aware that some net was being spun for her enclosure, but unable to see its pattern. 'We shall have to manage alone then, cook. I met a nice refugee the other day; she might come. . . .'

'Manage alone!' said Kathleen in a shocked voice. Puckering her brows, she went on slowly: 'And you don't imagine, do you, that I'd be willing, and able, if I was willing – for everybody human has to have their time off, and my husband wouldn't allow it if he got to know, as he would – to work this big house all by myself, with Miss Phillips saying that you mustn't be left much the way you are, or heaven knows what you might do. Before Miss Jones came I had to pay Mrs White out of my own wages, so that I could get an evening off in a blue moon. Ah, no. I couldn't do it. If Miss Jones takes to her heels, I'll have to go myself, and that's all there is to it.'

The horror that sprang to life within Mrs Temple demanded immediate utterance.

'You don't mean you'd leave me all by myself in this house?'

'What else? Can't you see it yourself? I wouldn't be able for it, and my husband wouldn't allow it. I shall have to tell Miss Phillips, that is if Miss Jones has her mind made up, and I think, between ourselves, she has.'

'Her mind made up to go. Well, tell the old beast she needn't go. Tell her I say she can stay.'

'But she doesn't *want* to stay. I keep telling you. She's got a good offer, and if she doesn't take that, it will be something else. And it being war-time, she'll be snatched up in the twinkling of an eye.'

'You make it sound like the anthropomorphic conception of Judgment Day,' said Mrs Temple. But she sat still now, her eyes fixed on Kathleen. In a moment she would see the pattern emerge . . . she would escape though; she would beat her way out somehow.

'I'll tell you what I'd do if I was you,' said Kathleen, ignoring this. 'I'd give her a bit of a present. She has a great liking for them two old-fashioned bits of pictures in the next bed-room she is in. The ones over the mantelpiece, do you know? If you made her the offer of them, in a nice way, I'm sure that would go some way in pacifying her.'

'I certainly won't make her any offer. Those were my father's.'

'And then the little crocodile-skin dressing-case. You've no use for that, as you never go anywhere. Ask her if she'd like

it. Say you want to make her a good present, as you know she has a lot to put up with, you being the way you are. I know that you can't altogether help it, but there it is.'

Mrs Temple clenched her fists, gazing in front of her as a picture formed itself in her mind. She was to be left alone, but left alone in a completely empty house. The robbers packed their booty before they left. At night as she slept everything would be piled into sacks. . . . Hot heady anger mounted.

'I see. Yes, I see perfectly.'

'Well, will you do that? Will you go down to her now? She's below making up her mind whether to take this job or not. Go in to her and ask her to stay. Take the pictures with you and just give them to her.'

'That's enough. I'm not an imbecile. You've plotted together to rob me. Before you hand me over stripped and naked. King Lear's daughters over again. I'm not going to allow myself to be robbed. I'm not the imbecile you think me. I am going to the police now, to tell them what you've said. And I'm going to have your boxes searched.'

Kathleen let go of diplomacy. 'Police! You dare to talk about the police to *me*. You know what happened when you went before? They just laughed at you. If you go again, they'll come along to know the reason why a mad woman like yourself is not kept under lock and key.'

'Get out of here! Get out of here at once,' shrieked Mrs Temple. She sprang from her chair and seizing a heavy paper-weight on the desk beside her, hurled it at Kathleen.

It struck her a heavy blow on the mouth before it clattered to the ground. 'My God!' she screamed, clapping her hand to her mouth, and then turned and fled as books came flying across the room towards her. Down the stairs she ran full pelt, while Mrs Temple shouted something angrily after her. She burst into the dining-room and, as Miss Jones looked up amazed, cried to her: 'Lock the door. She's out to kill.'

'Oh dear, oh dear,' cried Miss Jones, complying with this order.

'Look what she's done on me!' Triumphantly, Kathleen exhibited blood-stained fingers from her cut lip. 'Dripping with blood I am.'

Miss Jones approached fastidiously: 'Haven't you got a handkerchief? You'd better have mine. This ought to be bathed.'

'It's a wonder she didn't break my teeth on me. I think the front one is loosened. Oh, my God, I never saw anyone in such fury before. I flew like the wind. I was in such terror.'

'How did she do it?'

'She threw a tremendous hard object at me, I didn't see what it was; and me talking to her as pleasant as you like before . . . and then a storm of books came across the room.'

'She's thrown things at me, you know. Now perhaps you know what it feels like.'

'Is she outside? Listen.'

They both listened. Somebody was speaking, and Kathleen's curiosity overcame her fear. She tiptoed dramatically to the door, and unlocking it, opened it noiselessly. Then she beckoned Miss Jones. 'Come downstairs with me. Not a sound.'

As they tiptoed through the hall, they heard Mrs Temple

speaking on the telephone: 'I said I wanted the police. Any police. Can't *you* get the number?'

'Oh, the wickedness of Her,' murmured Kathleen, as they proceeded down the basement steps. 'Assaulting me with violence, for which she could be put into prison, and then having the audacity and the cunning to telephone to the police.' She went over to the sink, and dabbed at her mouth, disappointed to notice that the flow of blood had already stopped. 'This'll swell out,' she informed Miss Jones, 'and that'll be evidence.'

'I wonder if I went up and quietened her,' said Miss Jones in a worried voice. 'How did it all start? Did you say something to annoy her?'

'If you want to know the way it was,' said Kathleen, with some complacency, 'I was trying to do you a good turn.'

'Me?'

'I was telling her she should make you a present of those two pictures you fancied, and another thing or two. That's what got her. Because of her meanness. It sent her off raging demented. Would you believe a person could be that mean?'

'Really, Kathleen, I wish you hadn't done it,' said Miss Jones sharply. 'I don't want anything from Mrs Temple.'

Kathleen wasn't listening. She said: 'Now what must we do? She might get the police.'

'I ought to get Miss Phillips.'

'How can you, and she at the telephone? No, I tell you what. Run straight out for the doctor. That's what Miss Phillips said we should do any time she worked herself up, and she couldn't be got. Go to Dr Fairfax, and tell him she's gone stark staring mad.'

Miss Jones considered. The advice seemed sensible.

'He could give her a sedative,' she said slowly.

'But be quick,' urged Kathleen. 'You'll have to go out the back way, or she'll see you.'

'But my coat's in the hall; I've got my handbag here, but my coat and hat are hanging up.'

'Wear my coat. She'll be down on us if she sees you. You can use the public telephone, can't you? The one at the end of the terrace. Then you needn't go all the way to the doctor's.'

Miss Jones meditated, while Kathleen nearly stamped her foot with impatience. 'Oh, do be quick. I daren't be left alone with her. She might set fire to the house, while you wait.' She got out her best coat from her bedroom, and urged it on Miss Jones's shoulders. 'Have you got tuppence? Here you are. I am going up to bolt the door at the top of the stairs. I'm not going to have her come down to me.'

Miss Jones went out of the back door, and round to the gate. She cast an apprehensive glance back at the windows, but there was no sign of Mrs Temple. It was a relief to be walking along a quiet street away from the horror that threatened. And for a moment, as she met the casual glance of a woman passer-by, Miss Jones was faintly touched by a sort of pride that, though no one might guess her errand, she moved on the heights of tragedy. As a sequel there came, too, the thought that those ordinary-appearing men and women upon whom her eyes rested unseeingly might also be abroad on sad or secret and romantic missions. But whatever the errand its end was tragic – because of our common mortality. Even the aeroplane droning high above Kensington, whose flight would have been

without interest to her half an hour ago, took its place now, and with cause, in the unceasing tragic and significant motion of the round earth. Apprehension had touched Miss Jones for a moment into that mood of imaginative sensibility which finds expression in the great cry of Christian humanity, *Miserere nobis*. Then she saw the telephone booth ahead of her, and rehearsed her opening words: 'Will Dr Fairfax please come at once to Mrs Temple's house? Her illness has taken a turn for the worse.'

III

A busy doctor answers a professional call minus the anticipations which accompany a social engagement. He considers the possible requirements ahead of him when he packs his bag, but in general his mind, so crowded with knowledge of the varying claims made upon him, disengages itself waiting till his ring is answered, and the moment comes for which his skill and advice are required. It may be a matter of life and death; much more often it is nothing that a few days in bed will not set aright.

But as he walked up the hill to answer the call to attend on Claire Temple who, according to the woman's voice which spoke to him when he had come to the telephone himself, had behaved 'violently', Dr Fairfax did ponder over his patient. An injection of hyoscine would settle matters for the time being, but what of the future? Was there any future?

He was going to see, he knew, a deeply unhappy woman, none the less unhappy because she cried out her pain into

indifferent ears. To be old and alone, deprived even of the supports of congenial friendship, that was the fate of many. And with the added burden of poverty. Yet how differently each man and each woman accepted that fate.

Claire's cry: 'I am so lonely,' for instance. He had heard it often enough from the lips of women of her generation – the individualistic Victorian whose whole life had been composed of the threads, subtle or simple, as the case might be, of personal relationships. With husbands dead or divorced, children grown up and with their own interests, into what an aimless valley their lives often narrowed and shrank; and this, whether they lived in hotels, searching for a bridge game, pouncing upon stray scandals attached to strangers, or whether, like poor Claire, they lingered on in their old homes, quite lost in a world where the telephone rang but rarely, and the postman's knock was seldom heard. There were two main divisions: either such women sank into apathy of mind and body, or else they maintained a feverish clutch on whatever they could reach to attach to themselves. But Claire, once considered amusing, once courted, once granted her temporary meed of literary celebrity, took old age harder than anyone he had ever encountered. Of greater sensibility than the ordinary, so was she more greatly injured. The inquiring mind thus paused by her as the theatre spotlight singles out the chief performer.

To Dr Fairfax some of the answers to the problem of restless old age seemed to be a reflection on the whole of that great creed of individualism which had reached its apogee when Claire had been a girl living in the reign of the Queen, who for so many years had also been a bitterly lonely old woman. That same individualism which had appropriated to itself the high-sounding names of Liberty and Democracy and for which so many good people believed we were fighting this world war! But in the event, in the fires and scourges of war, had it not also been tried and found wanting?

Dr Fairfax was not a communist. Still less was he a fascist. The sacrifice of the individual to the claims of the state, the race, or the hero leader, implied a short-cut return to barbarism, attended by cruelties unknown before the age of the machine. But neither did he think the slogans of so-called liberal democracy were enough. He could not when he considered the facts help agreeing with a definition he had read in a book by the Russian Berdyaev: *Liberty has become the protection of the rights of a privileged minority, the defence of capitalistic property and the power of money.*

'The tree is known by its fruit,' and one of its fruits was Claire Temple, who had been privileged to be herself all her life, and at the end had found that to be yourself was not enough. The creed of individualism by itself, and as an aim in itself, did not make for ripeness, and if ripeness was all, then it had failed. Thinking this, Dr Fairfax's face wore a faintly preoccupied expression as he went briskly up the steps of Mrs Temple's house and knocked a loud rat-tat.

But the expression was wiped out and replaced by one of intentness as he heard the approach of steps halted by an angry voice. Lifting the flap of the letter-box and applying his ear, he heard Claire shouting: 'It's the police and I shall let them in myself. Don't dare go near that door.'

Dr Fairfax acted promptly. He shouted through the letter-box: 'This is Dr Fairfax. I was just passing, and I thought I would call on Mrs Temple if she's in.'

There was a moment's silence. Mrs Temple said less angrily: 'Who is it? I can't hear what he says.' An Irish voice said: 'It's the doctor.' Then Mrs Temple said: 'I am going.'

When she opened the door, her face gazed at him without recognition, but he observed she was clasping a poker tightly: 'Are you from the police?'

'Of course not. You remember your old friend, Richard Fairfax, whom you always said wasn't much of a doctor. I've been visiting in this neighbourhood, and I thought I would come and beg a cup of tea off you.'

'No, I don't remember you. Have you come to take me away? I'm not going to be taken away. Understand that, whoever you are.'

'No one's going to take you anywhere, but you are not going to shut the door in the face of an old friend, are you? That would be very unlike Claire Temple.'

She was staring at him: recognition gradually appeared. 'Aren't you Dr Fairfax?'

'Of course. Do forgive my bursting in on you like this, without giving you warning, but I was calling on Mrs Collins . . .' he had purposely mentioned the name of a neighbour whom she had once known . . . 'and she asked me how you are. She wondered if she might come and see you.'

'How kind!' Claire burst into tears: 'Tell her I'm in such trouble, I don't know what to do. All my friends must help me. There are two women here who are going to rob me and then

306

leave me quite alone. I've asked the police to come. Will you see that they do come? They'll listen to a man but not to a woman unless she's dressed up. I tried to dress myself, but I was too *distraite*.'

'Let me come in, and I'll see to it all for you.'

Across the threshold he saw an elderly woman and the Irish servant he had seen before standing at the back of the hall, and behind Claire's back nodded to them, and made a gesture of dismissal with his hand. He then took off his hat, and leaving it on the chest, said in a social voice: 'Let's see, you sit in the dining-room now, don't you? So I go in here.' He opened the door and she passed in front of him reacting automatically to his lead. Inside, however, she paused: 'You see! They've let the fire out. They are going to barricade me out of existence.'

'It will soon be lit again. I shall see to that. First of all I want you to sit down quietly, and relax. Then you can tell me all about it.'

She sat down, but then suspicion caused a sudden stiffening of the spine. 'Did they send for you?'

'No. I was calling on Mrs John Collins. She sent you such affectionate messages. Between ourselves, my dear, she doesn't wear as well as you do. For you were at school together, weren't you?'

'Yes, at that little place in Notting Hill. I never liked Mary Collins much. But, oh, Doctor, I'm in such trouble. There are two women who have come into this house, and they are trying to rob me, and then kill me. Or leave me quite alone in the house.'

'Mrs Collins was telling me how lonely she feels these days. I always wondered why she didn't marry . . . who was it? Some cousin of the Forbes-Robertsons?'

As she didn't reply, but gazed at him fixedly, he went on chatting, mentioning to her familiar names. Gradually, her posture relaxed, as she assumed the habit, with which he was providing her, of a hostess receiving an afternoon caller. The interruptions by which she sought to attract his attention to the terrors which surrounded her became couched in the calmer terms in which one refers to griefs that have been companions for a long, long while. As when she said, leaning forward:

'Do you remember what Hazlitt said: "Since I have got into notice, I have been set upon as a wild beast." Mostly in my life I have been treated as a monkey, forgiven everything because I was entertaining. But now the cage is round me: those two women treat me as a wild beast, and bolt the basement door to me, where I can hear them whispering below. If they treat you as a wild beast, you become one. I had to take a poker once. . . . I think it was today. What time is it?'

'It's just after two o'clock.'

'Cook never gave me any lunch. I suppose she wanted to punish me. She's always punishing me for saying something that annoys her.'

'That's the one I met before. Isn't her name Kathleen?'

'Yes, she's an extraordinary character. So cruel. Yesterday or one day I went over to the Carmelite church to see a priest about her. I thought he might stop her from being so cruel.'

This was interesting: *More needs she the divine than the*

physician. 'What did he say? Some of those men are excellent psychologists.'

'Yes, and, you know, Catholics of the ignorant type my cook is are supposed to be influenced so much by what their priests tell them. It was a Brother in a brown robe I saw, and he had a very gentle manner. He would have made some woman a very good husband. I think I told him that. But he didn't think he could do anything about Kathleen; he didn't seem to know her. I don't think she goes to Confession.'

'What else did he say?'

'I can't remember. Oh, he asked me if I believed in God; he said I should pray to God.'

'And you told him that you didn't believe in God?'

'No, I didn't. I do believe in the power that maketh for righteousness. That's what I told him. I quoted Matthew Arnold and said: "I believe in the enduring power which makes for righteousness."'

'And that doesn't help much,' said Dr Fairfax in a low voice.

'That's what he said, yes. Of course, I don't believe in a personal God, I said. "Then I can't help you except by praying for you," he said. He was very sweet. But he was no good. The police aren't any good either. I rang them up, but they wouldn't answer. And I don't think my doctor is much good either. Old Fairfax, you know. He has attended on me and my friends for years, but though he has good manners his medicines are no good at all.'

He said mildly: 'You mustn't say that to me, because, you see, I happen to be old Fairfax, and though I may not be much good, I do try to do my best for you.'

She leaned forward impulsively: 'You are Dr Fairfax? Of course you are. I can see you are. One of my oldest friends. My dear, please forgive me. It's my memory.' She stretched out a hand for reassurance, adding plaintively: 'And I'm so tired. I ache all over with tiredness. Could you do anything about that for me?'

'Of course I can. I've just been giving Mrs Collins an injection for insomnia. I'll call your nurse companion.'

'I warn you she's the dreariest creature. No conversation at all.'

Her eyes were closed when he came back from the kitchen. She opened them to smile at him and say: 'How kind of you to call. Have I bored you terribly with my troubles? I always do, I am afraid.'

'Not a bit. Here comes Miss Jones, and we'll just give you this injection, and then you'll go upstairs to your bedroom and have a long sleep.'

Miss Jones approached timidly, but Mrs Temple contented herself with a faint grimace at the doctor, as from one equal to another when an interloper arrives, and held up her loose sleeve obediently.

'And now Miss Jones will take you up to bed. She's put you in a hot-water-bottle, so you'll be comfortable.'

'I do feel very tired. You are going to stay, aren't you, because I don't think I am very well?'

'No, you're not very well. You've rather overdone yourself. I shall be round to see you very soon.' He opened the door, and watched the two women, one so solid and set, the other such a frail wisp of a creature, go up the stairs together.

IV

But though Dr Fairfax felt very tired, he knew that his work was not yet done. It was not likely to be very long before Mrs Temple's tired heart ceased to beat, but the last lap was often the most trying to the caretakers. He must satisfy himself more precisely as to the nature of the two women upon whom the main burden would fall.

Kathleen was pleased to be summoned to the doctor's presence. She came into the room with grave mien as befitted one who moved in dramatic circumstances, and after sitting down in the chair indicated to her, folded her hands.

'I want you to tell me about this morning. I understand Mrs Temple got very excited. Why?'

'She got in a dreadful state, sir, and threw a hard object across the room at me, and then she started hurling books. She cut my lip on me. You can see it's swollen.'

'What made her so excited?'

Kathleen shook her head. 'I can't really understand it, sir, because I was only just speaking to her in the way of giving her advice about being better behaved with Miss Jones, the companion lady. Otherwise, she'd lose her, because, you see, Miss Jones has the offer of a much better job, and with all she's had to stand from Mrs Temple, you couldn't blame her for taking it. It was for Mrs Temple's own sake I spoke.'

'I am sure you meant well, but can you remember what you said exactly? You wouldn't mean to excite her, but it is obvious you did upset her.'

Feeling herself blamed, Kathleen allowed indignation rein:

'I can tell you what I said that she didn't fancy, but 'twas her bad nature and nothing else. I just raised the suggestion that she might make a little present to Miss Jones. That was what had her infuriated past all reason. It's the meanness that's in her. You wouldn't know, and nobody that hadn't to do with her every day would know.'

'Did Miss Jones ask you to do this?'

Kathleen shook her head. 'No, 'twas my own idea entirely, to patch things up. You see, if Miss Jones left I'd have to go, because I couldn't manage her on my own.'

'You've been here a good while, haven't you? So I assume that in the ordinary way you can get on with Mrs Temple, even though she is, of course, very trying. We all know that. When someone as old as she is loses her memory it must be trying for the other people in the house.'

'I don't mind her being mad,' said Kathleen earnestly. 'I have got on with her, for the reason that I don't mind mad people the way some do. You can ask her yourself, and she might say anything, but the truth is, as Miss Jones will tell you, she'd rather have me do things for her any day than Miss Jones. She's taken a real dislike to her, the poor creature. But what does vex me is her wickedness and the things she'll say. You yourself heard her just now say that the pair of us were trying to rob her and kill her, and we doing everything we can to satisfy and fulfil her every whim. The other day off to the police she went, all about Miss Jones trying to poison her. And the police are not going to stand much more of her pestering them. Another thing, I believe she had the . . . I believe she went complaining over to the Brothers in Church

Street about me, and that's a thing that's not very nice for me.'

'All those wild notions are part of her mental derangement. She can't help being suspicious. It's a very usual form of her mania.'

Dr Fairfax paused. The pretty and now flushed woman opposite him was not convinced by his words, and he was intrigued to know why. 'You do understand that she's not responsible altogether for her actions, don't you?'

'Yes, but everyone's responsible in a way, sir. Aren't they?'

'That's an interesting point.'

'I mean, sir, it's different if you don't see her often, because then it's only that she goes on saying the same things over and over again. But it's my belief that there's real devilment in her, or else she wouldn't say the wicked things she does.'

'You think it's a case of demoniac possession?'

'A devil has her by the throat, if you mean that,' agreed Kathleen darkly.

Dr Fairfax was finding the discussion interesting, but he heard steps coming down the stairs. He said: 'Well, however that may be, I sincerely trust that you'll try to stay with Mrs Temple a little longer. We don't want to have to resort to other measures.' He opened the door: 'Come in, Miss Jones, will you?'

'I'm willing to do all a reasonable person can,' said Kathleen. 'But I don't want to run the risk of being murdered. This lip . . . in the ordinary way I'd be given compensation for assault and batter, wouldn't I?'

'Oh, you'll find that won't give you any trouble,' said

Dr Fairfax casually. 'Just bathe it in any mild disinfectant you have, and I'll look at it when I come again. And for the rest, I think I can promise you that from now on Mrs Temple will be mostly in bed. She has tired herself out.'

Kathleen understood she was dismissed, and went reluctantly out of the room. Miss Jones said: 'Mrs Temple is sound asleep, Doctor. That's a good thing, isn't it?'

'A very good thing,' said Dr Fairfax, wondering why women of Miss Jones's kind always favoured browns and beiges and ugly greens for their clothes, thereby doing their complexions much disservice. Their Latin sisters were wiser in their generation in choosing black, which imparted to their maturity a quality at once formidable and feminine. But Miss Jones, he guessed, had never been either formidable or markedly feminine. Her strongest desire was probably to be as comfortable as she could. Splendours and deep sorrows had passed her by; on the other hand, she was not sufficiently an egotist to be touched by malice and cruelty. Easy enough to understand how she had roused Claire's hostility, and yet no one less deserved it.

'I'm afraid this has all been very trying for you. Mrs Temple is a very old friend of mine, and if she were her real self, I know that she would be deeply grieved to think she had behaved . . . badly.'

Miss Jones leaned forward: 'Do tell me frankly, Doctor? She's quite "mental" now, isn't she?'

Jarred by the meaningless use of the word, Dr Fairfax paused a moment, so that his voice should not sound cold, before he replied:

'I should hardly say that. The derangement of her mind, her dotage in the old use of the word, has taken a turn for the worse. She suffers from delusions, and feels that people are her enemies, especially, of course – that's inevitable – those who come into daily contact with her, like yourself. But from what the cook has been telling me – you might keep this to yourself – she did irritate her a great deal before this morning's scene. She doesn't usually act in such a violent way, does she?'

'Not with Kathleen. But she has thrown things at me before, Doctor. Once she upset a tea-tray and my foot was scalded. Quite recently that happened. And I told Miss Phillips before I came that I couldn't stand violence. I really am not strong enough at my age.'

'I do understand. Believe me when I say I understand fully what a difficult charge she must have been for you. It is as an old friend of Mrs Temple's that I ask you to stay on for a little while longer with her, if you possibly can. Before you answer I can, I think, assure you that your sacrifice, and it would be a real act of charity, won't be required for very much longer. Her heart is very much strained. I must send a night nurse in, for she must be kept in bed. I don't think she'll even want to get up, except at those times when her delusions master her. In such an event, I'll come along, and give her a sedative. As you know I am in easy reach.'

Miss Jones nodded comprehension. Then her face grew absent, for she remembered that she had promised the woman who had interviewed her that she would let her know that morning if she would take the post. The time had now gone by, since, other events intervening, she had not telephoned before twelve.

'I tell you what, Doctor. I promise to stay for a little and see how it works out. It will be much easier if only she can be kept in bed. But, of course, Kathleen will be here to do the housework, won't she?'

'I'm fairly sure that Kathleen will stay on if you do. Thank you very much indeed, Miss Jones. You will at least have the satisfaction of knowing that you are doing a great kindness to a very unhappy woman – even if she is not able to appreciate it for herself – by attending to her a little longer.'

'I'm very sorry for her, you know,' nodded Miss Jones. 'She can't help being "mental", and it's a great affliction.'

Dr Fairfax rose. Glancing at her, he asked: 'Then you don't think she is a wicked woman? I rather gathered that the cook thinks she is possessed by a devil.'

'Oh, Kathleen has some very funny ideas. Of course, she's Irish, and they are superstitious, aren't they?'

Dr Fairfax nodded, and went into the hall. 'All the same,' he murmured, as he struggled into his overcoat, 'the idea of demoniac possession is a very old one. You remember the allusion to the kind that is not cast out save by prayer and fasting? I shall be here about eleven tomorrow morning, Miss Jones, and luckily, I know of a nurse who's just disengaged, that I hope to send round tonight. I shall give her full instructions. Goodbye for the present, and thank you very much.'

Miss Jones turned from shutting the front door with a complacent smile on her face. 'The doctor begged me to stay. As a personal favour, and I hadn't the heart to refuse.' That was what she was going downstairs to tell Kathleen.

V

Dr Fairfax had time to ponder on the diversity presented by the three women, Mrs Temple, her companion and the maid, as his visits to the house became a matter of daily routine. It seemed to him that there was irony in the pattern which had brought them together, as indeed the man interested in his fellows finds irony in so many patterns composed by the interdependence of individuals. It was like the old parlour game, he thought – animal, vegetable and mineral.

Kathleen, of course, was animal, and the animal which she resembled most closely, though not in its most simple derogatory significance, a cat. She had the disinterested detachment of the cat, who so long as there is a comfortable corner remains surveying, but not essentially moved by any of the alarums and excursions round her. And like a cat how she appraised titbits, how unerringly she pounced on those things which were essential to her. Dr Fairfax had more than a suspicion that she derived emotional satisfaction from the contemplation of her mistress's more spectacular exhibitions of frenzy, that she found the present situation, when for long intervals Mrs Temple lay comatose under the drugs he gave her, lacking in savour.

And so she turned her back, busying herself about her own concerns. His arrival at the house caused in her no such flutter as it did in Miss Jones. From a brief conversation he gathered that her anticipations were of the future, when he should become raised to the status of the harbinger of death:

'I don't think it will be much longer, sir, do you?'

'Probably not. But it's impossible to say.'

'I wouldn't give her much longer myself, and I've had great experience of the dying. Madam is the kind that, having once taken to her bed, only leaves it as a corpse, and that at no distant date.'

It was a shrewd enough diagnosis, though Dr Fairfax made no comment. But he was struck by the ease with which the mind of the Celt moves from the particular to the universal. Mrs Temple, as a dying individual, held, he felt, little interest for her; Mrs Temple on her death-bed, and as a corpse, might wring tears, and even prayers for the eternal rest of her soul, from one who thought of her in life as either a nuisance or as wicked.

Miss Jones was vegetable: vegetative in the Leibniz sense of the word, the spermatic individual, whose force is quiescent, whose quality of perception dim. Unlike Kathleen, she formed no judgments about Mrs Temple; it was true that Kathleen looked through her own darkened windows, since her judgments were without understanding or compassion. But did Miss Jones, Dr Fairfax wondered, look through any windows at all? Had she any but the most superficial curiosity about her fellows? With her Mrs Temple was 'mental' and there was an end of it. Kathleen's idiosyncrasies were dismissed as 'Irish', and there was an end of that. He himself, he knew without being flattered by the knowledge, ranked in the 'very nice' class. For the reason that he was always pleasant and courteous to her. Miss Jones and her like looked out into a world composed of *culs-de-sac*. Theirs was the negation of imagination.

And yet only the dull and the superior would despise Miss Jones. A world without the Joneses would be a world without ballast, a world without its washing days, its suet puddings and the remorseless punctuality of its trains – in short, an inconceivable world.

Then Mrs Temple, his patient. If she were mineral, it could only be one mineral, quicksilver. And there he had to take leave of his childish fancy.

For the true question over which he perplexed himself was why had the last state of Claire Temple the power to wring the heart, even the heart of such a battered old mildly philosophical medico as himself, one who had become so used and hardened to the spectacle of human folly and human suffering? It was not as if he had ever been really fond of her as one is fond of an old friend. For years he had thought of her very little, and then only as a sometimes tiresome, sometimes amusing woman. Then why did he come away from his visits after listening patiently to her complaints and her wandering remarks – not amusing any more, poor Claire – with such a heavy heart?

He tried to answer his own question by imagining either of the other two women in her place. Kathleen's derangement would have its perturbations at least as fevered and angry as Mrs Temple's: she would scatter curses; she would nurse more bitter malevolences. For, like Mrs Temple and like the great majority of us, she was dear to herself, though not for any such profound reason as that advanced by the theology of her own Church, who laid it down that the salvation of one's own soul was a matter of supreme moment. But once her wits had strayed, no such sweetness, no such occasional self-criticism, would soften the edge of that distrust and that anger with which she would express resentment and suspicion.

He thought of Claire's sweetness. How moving were some of her remarks: 'You are so kind to me, and I know I am giving you so much trouble.' 'I awoke this morning with the feeling that I had done shocking things, that I had tried to hurt people. If I have offended anybody, will you tell me, and then perhaps I could write a note of apology explaining that I am ill.'

Miss Jones he saw, should her mental control forsake her, not in anger, but undergoing the process of brain softening as a cabbage sheds its leaves. He saw her with a fixed smile looking at nothing, now and then whimpering, but on the whole, an esteemed patient, since she gave the nurses little trouble. There were many such.

Neither of these two imaginations was a comfortable one. Yet one accepted them without that something which cried out in protest when he thought of Claire Temple. So many fairies had attended her christening, carrying notable gifts, imagination, personal charm, grace of bearing and a most uncommon vivacity, and in the end they had all dwindled to such a sad and joyless measure. Shakespeare had expressed it with his 'Sweet bells jangled, out of tune and harsh'. Cause indeed for tears, and carrying the quality of tragedy, even if it were minor tragedy.

Or the prose terms of his favourite philosopher could be applied. Claire had been given potentialities which she had not realised. Her sensitive soul had failed to raise itself in the

hierarchy, and become a rational soul. She had omitted to learn what Leibniz called 'general and necessary truths'.

And of those general and necessary truths, one in her case was certainly that voiced by Christianity: *Lay not up for yourselves treasures upon earth, where moth and rust doth corrupt, and where thieves break through and steal.*

Yes, one could find answers and good enough answers. But something was always omitted, since it was not given to the individual to judge, lest he, too, should be judged. Or so thought Dr Fairfax, as he made a note on his pad to send some flowers to Mrs Temple. There were so few friends left to perform this last offering from the living to the dying.

VI

What scars on the heart, what hidden wounds of the mind, do not the dreams of even those who feel that their lives have run to a placid and conventional measure, reveal! And the dreams which came to Claire Temple, whose life had never been placid, during her uneasy or drug-induced slumbers, bore such witness to pain, that the young night nurse was drawn too often for her liking to the bedside of her patient to utter soothing words. 'She's like a fractious child of three or four who can't understand why she suffers,' she had thought on returning to her own couch.

Aroused to a partial consciousness of the present, Claire herself wondered why she should dream of people and events which even by her uncertain measurement were buried under long years. Hugh and Violet, for example, they had surely

been out of her life so long that their estrangement from her was a thing that one no longer needed even to shrug away.

But in her dream about them, she had suffered the pain of separation all over again. Then suddenly, to her joy, she found herself sitting at the same table; other people were there also, but their faces were indeterminate. She was sitting next to Violet, and she told herself as she waited for her old friend to turn and recognise her: 'Now I will be calm: Violet always told me I should be more restrained, so I shall wait for her to speak.' Violet had half-turned, then she had looked away. And while she had sat still tensely waiting she had felt the resolve in Violet form and harden, that she was *not* going to speak to her. She had awakened as one who had received a blow, and tossed and turned, battling with the old grief, grown as lively as it had been a quarter of a century ago. 'Violet won't have anything more to do with me.'

Smaller woes, vanities she had thought to have outlived, aroused themselves, too, from long slumbers. There was a studio party, and there was the great modern portrait-painter: 'As soon as he meets you he'll be mad to paint you,' they had said. But he looked right past her; the interest in his eyes was for another woman. 'Of course you wouldn't really be his type,' someone carelessly remarked. Then she and Arthur Whitwell – whom she hadn't thought of for fifty years – were in the same room together with other people. She had believed he was her particular beau, but he had drunk too much wine, and he stretched out his arms to her, while his eyes roved restlessly. He had wanted a woman, but, she realised with a hurt that had gone unconfessed through the years, any woman, any of her inferiors, would serve his intentions.

Not all her most vivid dreams were unhappy. In one of them Wallace had come back to her. And though they were in a crowded place he was so happy when he saw her that he threw his arms round her and hugged and kissed her. She was greatly surprised, for in their relationship he had never been demonstrative, and, she had often thought, would have died rather than display any token of tenderness towards her if other people were present. In her dream she had said to him: 'Oh, Wallace, what has happened to you! How you have changed!' But he had only kissed her again, drawing her down to sit beside him, and then stroking her cheeks. It was she who had said, remembering other people's presence: 'We must go; if you have forgotten your dignity, I must remember it for you.' He went with her as happily and easily as a child, and then she awoke, still feeling that new happiness warm against her breast.

But gradually the happiness disappeared. For her came that grey heavy dawn which always awaits to dispel with increasing clarity the sweetest dream. Cheated, one discovers that the pot of gold at the foot of the rainbow has turned into dead leaves.

As Claire struggled back to some recollection of the present, she was pierced by another foreboding. Not only had Wallace not come back, but now he would never come back, for they had told her, hadn't they, that he was dead? When Miss Phillips had years before informed her of Wallace's death, had showed her the newspaper cutting, she had been surprised by

Claire's lack of anything but a momentary interest. Now she beat her hands on the pillow in agony.

Someone approached her. A night-light was burning by her bed, and she saw a nurse with a pink clean face bending over her. She asked: 'Is Wallace dead?'

'Oh, no, I'm sure he's not. Now go to sleep.'

The face withdrew, and she pondered the answer. It was not, she made up her mind, a real answer. It was uttered with the bright sticky emptiness of a careless falsehood. The person who had spoken it had probably never heard of Wallace Temple.

'Who are you, and what are you doing here?' she forced herself away from the tug of sleep to ask. But there was no answer, and she was too tired to compel one.

And so once again she slept, and once again she dreamed. Backwards and forwards in her span of days she went visiting houses and seeing people once familiar to her. Sometimes it was pleasant, but at one place she was cut. Backs were turned, and then she found herself out in a long street whose doors were always closed to her. If they would only open she would make them understand that she was really married, that it was only his beast of a wife who said she wasn't. Then all that had disappeared; and she was making a story of it to amuse people. It was like, she was telling someone who was sympathetic and amused, being that Archbishop's wife visited by Queen Elizabeth before the Protestant Reformation was in full saddle. 'Wife,' the sandy-haired Virgin Queen had informed her hostess, 'I may not call you; mistress, I will not; but I thank you.' Then in the odd twist dreams may take, she was herself the Archbishop's wife, rising from a low curtsey, and watching her Sovereign and the long retinue sweep away from her along grassy terraces under a blue midsummer sky.

From her dreams she awoke to be increasingly confused as to where she was. The night nurse always brought her a cup of tea before she went off duty, and the sight of this young woman who had no connection with any part of her life, who was completely strange, made her feel that she was in some No Man's Land territory – probably an hotel. Over and over again she asked her: 'Who are you? Are you a waitress?'

'No, I'm a nurse.'

'Am I in hospital or a nursing-home?'

'No, you are in your own home. You are not very well, you see. Drink your tea while it's hot.'

And then she disappeared. Claire would try to solve the puzzle while she drank her tea. It did not seem to her that she could be in her own home, for there were differences. Why was that couch there? She was sure she had never seen it before.

Next, Kathleen would come clattering up with a coal-bucket and sticks to do the fire, and add her complications to the puzzle. 'Are you the maid?'

Kathleen might merely answer by a grunt. Sometimes she would elaborate a little. 'That's right. I'm your maid, though you always speak of me as "cook". General bottle-washer, that's me.'

'I seem to remember your name. Is it Kathleen, and you're Irish, aren't you?'

This remark would generally freeze Kathleen to silence. She had always considered it an impertinent habit of the

English to fix your nationality for you as soon as you opened your mouth, and she believed that Mrs Temple was merely exhibiting a new form of contrariness.

So that when she left, Mrs Temple was still undecided as to where she actually was. It was given to poor Miss Jones at the beginning to arouse her to some sense that she was in her own house, but attended by one who had, in some mysterious way, proved herself an enemy. Miss Jones might have been more fortunate, but it fell to her portion to perform such thankless tasks because they disturbed the patient as remaking her bed, washing her face, assisting her to the stool, and airing and tidying the room before the doctor's visit. It was true that Mrs Temple had no longer the strength to voice the furies which arose within her, but at first whatever she could do to hinder and render difficult the performance of the morning's rites, she did. The rest of the day passed more easily, for Dr Fairfax's visit always had a soothing effect, since it restored to Claire the feeling that wherever she was she was being taken care of by her own doctor.

But as time wore on, as spring replaced winter, and almond-blossom burst its buds in Kensington squares, Claire Temple came in her own mind to her last halting-place on this earth. She believed she was lying in the old Devonshire farmhouse, where she had spent long summers as a child, and the night nurse became for her apple-cheeked Sylvia Lynton, who had been the daughter of the house more than sixty years ago. A bird twittering outside her window carried the sounds and scents of the English countryside all about her, and when she struggled to get out of bed, but found that she could not rise,

the explanation which satisfied her tired brain was that she had been naughty, and had been sent to bed as a punishment. As her fingers clutched the hem of the sheet and smoothed it in the last motions of the dying, it seemed to her that soon her punishment would be over, and that she would be allowed out into the sunshine to play with her sister, to run down lanes, and look at the low rolling purple hills that were, she knew, just outside the window. All adventure awaited her, but just now she was too tired, because, as it would appear, people had been very angry with her and made her cry so much. Soon they would forgive her, for when one was a child, and hadn't meant to do wrong, all was as surely forgiven as the coming of sleep wiped out all noisy angers and every hurt.

It was half-past six of an April morning when all that was mortal of Claire Temple sank gently and peacefully into oblivion, and outside her Kensington window an early-awakened bird trilled its first call to the rising sun.

AFTERWORD

ᐳᗕᗺᗕᗺᗕᗺᐸ

'This is the saddest story I have ever heard' – the opening words of Ford Madox Ford's novel *The Good Soldier* are quite as true of Norah Hoult's novel *There Were No Windows*, yet the saddest aspect of her novel is its truthful depiction of an all too familiar, all too unwelcome feature of modern life: the tendency of our minds to fail before our bodies do. As the novel's central character observes, when warned that she will catch pneumonia if she scurries around the house at night, 'Pneumonia isn't nearly as bad as not knowing where you are' (p128). Hoult's story of the last days of Claire Temple, former woman of letters whose mind is failing her, recalls comparable and comparably sad, non-fictional endings – among them, those of Iris Murdoch and of Helen Gardner. It reminds us, too, of loved yet burdensome relatives, and of our own possible futures – futures that we cannot necessarily escape. This is not only a sad story, but a frightening one, and not only for its chief victim, being based on familiar experiences that we might prefer not to think about. Its clear-sightedness is redeemed by its generosity, understanding and insight.

Norah Hoult transforms her dark materials into a powerful, rich and evocative fiction set in London during the Blitz

– a moment of national as well as individual danger, of social as well as personal chaos. It begins as an explosion catches Claire Temple's attention, drawing it towards 'that No Man's Land territory in which she found herself marooned between the old house and the new, the past and the present' (p3). We soon discover that the noise was caused by a time bomb, and its action anticipates Claire's own final explosion of terror and anger at the end of the novel. She is locked in upon herself, yet her sense of what has happened in the past and what is happening in the present is now either too distant or too close, and always treacherous and unreliable. Her recurring uncertainty as to where she is and what is going on around her fills her with painful anxiety. She is suffering, as so many old people do, from short-term memory loss, as she readily acknowledges, yet she has lost none of her feelings and sensibilities:

> And . . . everything wears out. Except me. It's terrible the way I can't wear out, but go on feeling in my heart, feeling everything. I forget how old I am, but it's quite old, and I shouldn't feel as much as I do at my age. It is rather terrible, isn't it? (pp121–2).

The novel is carefully structured to reveal Claire's ordeal from without and within. Divided into three parts, the first, 'Inside the House', is largely devoted to recreating Claire's vision of the world through her stream of consciousness, though her thoughts are interrupted by the incomprehension of Mrs White who does the washing (Claire asks about her

recently dead husband as if he were still alive on three separate occasions in the first twenty-five pages), as well as by the impatience of Kathleen, her Irish cook. In part two, 'Outside the House', Claire receives visits from three old friends, fellow writers Edith Barlow and Francis Maitland, and her former secretary, Sara Berkeley. Their several judgements on her include Edith's lofty contempt for Claire's self-deceptions about her past and disgust at her present loss of dignity, and Sara's irritation with Claire for refusing to recognise that there's a war on, and she ought to be contributing to the war effort. Francis Maitland is first embarrassed by her and then horrified as she screams uncontrollably in the taxi, but his young American friend is oddly touched and impressed by this 'sporting old lady', by her courage and her vivacity. He sympathises with her hysteria: 'You're quite sure she screamed because she thought she was being taken to some place for people who have gone nuts? That seems pretty ghastly to me' (p178). And he is fascinated by her reminiscences of the past – she has known everyone on the literary scene over the last sixty years.

As the third part, 'The Dark Night of the Imagination', begins, it has been decided that Claire Temple must have a companion. Accordingly, her former secretary, Miss Phillips, is interviewing Miss Jones, who has applied for the post. She explains that 'Mrs Temple [is] a rather difficult person to deal with. She has been . . . a brilliant woman. In her day. She wrote, entertained a good deal, and so on' (p186). At the same time, she has lost her memory, and 'says the same things over and over again . . . Most people find it tiresome. I do

myself . . . sometimes she's incontinent. It's not very nice to talk about . . .' Despite these warnings, Miss Jones accepts the post, confident that Mrs Temple will only prove 'difficult in the way a child was difficult' (p195), and so will be easy to humour. But once Miss Jones has moved in, she finds herself subjected to so many 'inflicted humiliations, that the one real problem for the inquirer into her welfare would be – how could she stand it?' (p211).

One source of her discomfort lies in Claire Temple's flashes of undiminished intelligence, sharp observations or insights that had once been considered witty, yet (thinks Edith Barlow) hers had been 'a wit which pounced like a bird upon a crumb, on some weakness, some idiosyncrasy of a friend' (p105). Even in her heyday, Claire had been sharply critical, and from a 'modern' standpoint, she is full of Victorian prejudices. The visit of her Jewish ex-secretary, Sara Berkeley, is coloured by the irony that while, for Sara, the war is being fought by the British on behalf of the Jews, thus allowing her to think of herself as a British patriot at last, Claire is still indulging in the anti-Semitism of her generation, commenting as she departs, 'So oriental, isn't she?', and adding, for good measure, 'Of course she and her friend are Lesbians' (p141). Nor do servants seem to her fully human, and she mentally relegates Kathleen to a comic sub-plot, in which she becomes 'the vile-tempered cook entertaining her lover in the kitchen. Mistress Doll Tear-sheet sort of scene' (p84).

Yet she can set aside race or class prejudice, if she perceives a particular individual as somehow touched by romance – as is the bag-lady who asks her for money for 'a doss', or Mr Mills, the air-raid warden. Her companion, Miss Jones, so eager to teach her how to knit and play patience, represents the despised lower-middle classes, the 'middlebrows', in whom she can find no romance. At first, Miss Jones is merely dowdy, dreary, the purveyor of 'tinned culture', 'the genteel English virgin made entirely of grey india-rubber' (pp210,212). Later, she appears more sinister, as Claire's dislike is fuelled by her growing paranoia. As the novel approaches its climax, she imposes her own dark fantasies on her colourless companion, resorting to the violence that she imagines is threatening her. Now her house becomes part of a world 'lit by the unstable moon. The moonlit world with its corners and shadows and grotesque shapes and extravagances of cruelty and anguish that had no counterpart in the workaday sunlit world' (p189). One effect of the blackout had been to reveal London to its inhabitants as an unfamiliar and even alarming moonlit landscape.

Claire Temple's inner chaos and fear are echoed by the setting of London during the Blitz, while her ultimate terror of losing her house and her freedom, of being taken to a mental asylum or to an old people's home, might be compared to the fear of invasion in the early years of war; and just as her life has been interrupted, overwhelmed and reduced to meaningless routines by her loss of memory, so everyone's lives in wartime were interrupted, cut off from the past and overtaken by powers beyond their control. On the rare occasions when the outside world impinges on Claire's consciousness, she rages against the petty tyrannies of rationing or the blackout, but the blackout itself becomes a figure for her own inner darkness. After the air-raid warden has left her, 'She was all alone in the darkness, now that to please Mr Mills she had left her torch turned off. There were no windows. Everyone was shut in upon themselves' (p245). The imagery of the dark house, its windows invisible or missing, also stands for the self-absorption of the individual, appallingly exaggerated in old age, yet also characteristic of Claire's two employees, as Dr Fairfax reflects. Kathleen, her Irish cook, 'looked through her own darkened windows, since her judgments were without understanding or compassion. But did Miss Jones . . . look through any windows at all?' (pp318). The novel's epigraph, quoted from the mystic German philosopher Hermann Keyserling, insists that 'Man is not a windowless monad', yet few of the novel's characters escape from their own thoughts or concerns for very long.

One exception is Dr Fairfax, who seems to be as much a student of human nature as of human illness, voicing the novelist's judgment within the novel, if anyone does. Unlike hard-hearted Kathleen, he feels both compassion and under-standing, and not only for Mrs Temple; 'To be old and alone, deprived even of the supports of congenial friendship, that was the fate of many. And with the added burden of poverty' (p304). Yet he also recognises that Claire Temple 'took old age harder than anyone he had ever encountered. Of greater sensibility than the ordinary, so was she more greatly injured' (ibid). His view of her is balanced, and indeed generous, acknowledging how many gifts had been hers from the begin-ning, and how correspondingly high her expectations must have been:

So many fairies had attended her christening, carrying notable gifts, imagination, personal charm, grace of bearing and a most uncommon vivacity, and in the end they had all dwindled to such a sad and joyless measure. Shakespeare had expressed it with his 'Sweet bells jangled, out of tune and harsh'. Cause indeed for tears, and carrying the quality of tragedy, even if it were minor tragedy (p320).

Here the doctor quotes from Ophelia's report of Hamlet's madness, in words that will later apply to her own. Earlier he had remembered Macbeth's question to another doctor, 'Canst thou not minister to a mind diseas'd . . .?', and the disappointing reply, 'Therein the patient must minister to himself' (p263).

'Yes, one could find answers and good enough answers. But something was always omitted' (p321) he muses. Claire Temple had not fulfilled her potential, had not learned Leibniz's 'general and necessary truths', and cannot recognise any unhappiness other than her own. Her loneliness is unbearable to her, and any visitor, even the washerwoman, is better than her own company. She urges all who come to see her to stay, yet she finds the imposed company of her 'companion' equally unbearable. In one of her flashes of insight, she recognises the truth of Henry James's words. 'He said, "cultivate loneliness". I never have. That has been one of my mistakes. If you don't, if you run away, as I always ran away, then it is so terrifying when at last it catches up with you' (p246). A poignantly feminine longing for male company and male attention further increases her sense of loneliness. She envies Kathleen her fiancé, and repeatedly questions Mrs White about her husband. Kathleen puts it down to 'the badness in her nature . . . It's the men that she always wants to be talking about and thinking about' (p50).

Like most women, Claire Temple has learned to judge and value herself in terms of her ability to attract men, and with the coming of old age, finds herself unwanted and ignored. In a desperate *cri de coeur*, she complains to God of the cruelty of her situation ('Why did women spend years learning to be women, becoming adept in flattery and charm?' p26). But then she had lost her memory: 'My memory, you see. It makes me blunder about like a blind person trying to feel his way into places and out of places . . .' (p166). Contributing to her sense of unhappiness is a remaining awareness that she is being boring, being 'tiresome'. Yet however tiresome she is to others, she can never reach a state of being 'tired out' herself. Through all her forgetfulness, she retains the sharp and painful feelings of youth. In a train of thought that carries her from Kensington Gardens to Peter Pan and James Barrie, she remembers the playwright's other drama of eternal youth, *Mary Rose*. Though now considered old-fashioned, she recognises the nature of its sadness, 'For though I am old and look old and fearfully shabby, yet my heart still flows with pain just as when I was young, only now there is no one to run to . . .' (p222)

Why has this happened? How has this happened? The cruelty that Claire Temple so bitterly and plaintively endures is ultimately that of the human condition – of time itself, and the inevitable processes of aging. Uncertain what day it is,

she imagines herself searching for time, but time has already caught up with her. The power of Hoult's vision and the urgency of her heroine's suffering speak to us as powerfully today, when we all live longer, and must look forward to becoming disoriented, losing our memories, and feeling constant anxiety or senile paranoia, as our lack of physical mobility increasingly narrows our horizons, closing window after window onto the wider world. And the loss of physical mobility can bring a loss of mental or spiritual range. As Claire observes, even china plates wear 'so much better than most women wear' (p37). In old age, she can care for little beyond the familiar objects that surround her – her William Morris table, the bureau once used by Robert Browning, the Dutch cabinet. The doctor recalls the words of St. Matthew, 'Lay not up for yourselves treasures upon earth, where moth and rust doth corrupt, and where thieves break through and steal' (p321), while Sara Berkeley has an even sharper premonition, picturing Claire's precious furniture 'grouped as it might be at a pre-view of an auction sale' (p122).

Much of this novel's power derives from its unflinching representation of old age, with its attendant loss of self-command or self-control, but equally arresting is its sharply focused portrait of Claire Temple, a portrait evidently drawn from life. The following letter might easily have been written during the course of the novel:

Dear Douglas,
    Will you and Malin let me know when you will – if you will? — come and dine here? I am all alone with a terrible nurse companion whom I can get rid of for the

evening if you will say when you are coming back. I guess you are away. I am here — for I can't leave the house and am too poor to go anywhere nice.

Love to you both: real love.

Yrs Violet H

She will be out. She is away *now* – thank God!

Violet H[unt] (1862–1942), the daughter of water-colour painter Alfred Hunt, and Scottish novelist Margaret Raine, and a writer herself, provided the model for Claire Temple, as an exchange of letters between Norah Hoult and Frank Swinnerton reveals. There are numerous close correspondences between the details of Mrs Temple's life and writings within the novel, and those of Violet Hunt. Like Violet Hunt (in *Tales of the Uneasy*, 1911), Claire Temple specialises in ghost stories (see pp75,108), and twice during their evening together, she tries to persuade Francis Maitland to help her reprint *Weary Leaf* in paperback (pp152,167); Violet Hunt's most successful novel was entitled *White Rose of Weary Leaf* (1908). Norah Hoult (thirty-six years Hunt's junior), must have visited her in her later years, and been touched and saddened, and perhaps also irritated by her foibles – her forgetfulness, her rudeness, her repeated questions and assertions. Violet Hunt died in January 1942, and Hoult may well have attended the auction of her prized possessions at her Kensington home on 16 April (the event that Sara Berkeley foresees within the novel).

The idea for the novel, or at least for many of its most

telling details, must have been sparked off by Douglas Goldring's memoir of Violet Hunt and Ford Madox Ford, entitled *South Lodge*, and published the following year. 'South Lodge' was the name of Violet Hunt's house at 80 Campden Hill Road, which she had shared for a while with Ford. Reading this memoir, Norah Hoult would have been reminded of many features of the house, such as the signed photographs of celebrities on the stairs (p19), 'of Henry James, of Cunninghame Graham on horseback, and of Robert Browning, bearded and frock-coated,' according to Goldring; and of the service lift in the dining-room (p95), that Ford had installed. For Goldring, there had been 'something macabre' in his last visit, as he watched Violet poring over old diaries, feeling he 'could easily believe that most of her days, and nights, were spent in roaming about her house, in which every piece of furniture, every book and picture, revived memories of long dead and, in some cases, long outmoded "celebrities". . . . Her worries about the ultimate fate of her possessions had become an obsession and a mania.'

Goldring, like the doctor in *There Were No Windows*, recalls Hunt's golden beginnings, and the highlights of her emotional life – Oscar Wilde's proposal; her first disastrous misalliance with Oswald Crawfurd (renamed McFarlane in the novel), and her later, longer, near-marriage to Ford. In Hoult's novel, Ford becomes Wallace Temple, dismissed by Edith Barlow as 'a second-rate man of letters with a pronounced lack of integrity, many years younger than herself'. Ford had died in 1939, and immediately after his death, his reputation had fallen to its lowest point. Today, if Violet Hunt is remembered at all, it is as the model for Sylvia, Christopher Tietjens' unforgiving wife in Ford's masterpiece, *No More Parades*.

Goldring's affectionate account of Violet Hunt in *South Lodge* provided Hoult with many of the details that make her novel so immediate for the reader. From Goldring, we learn of Hunt's involvement in the Women's Movement (talking to Edith Barlow, Claire Temple mischievously recalls 'introducing Mrs Humphrey Ward to Christabel [Pankhurst]' p108), and of her love of cats. He also records the effects of memory loss as she constantly repeated herself, misquoted from poets she loved, or failed to realise who she was talking to, as when, in conversation with Michael Arlen, she told him that she 'used to see quite a lot of Michael Arlen, at one time . . . He's really quite a nice young man – and extremely clever. I wonder why it is that his books are so *awful*.' In Hoult's novel, Claire Temple carefully explains to Edith Barlow that her 'oldest friend, Edith Barlow, comes every second Sunday to lunch' (p100). Hunt's Welsh parlour maid seems to have been metamorphosed into the Irish Kathleen (Hoult herself was Irish, and she creates a quiet comedy by juxtaposing Kathleen's tough pragmatism with the romantic ballads she likes to sing). Goldring recalls that near the end, Hunt became 'entirely deranged and whenever the bombs fell she imagined herself to be with her father, in the Welsh mountains, during a thunderstorm', Claire Temple 'believed she was lying in the old Devonshire farmhouse, where she had spent long summers as a child' (p326).

On Goldring's last visit to South Lodge, its front windows had been blown out, which he found 'curiously symbolical of

the "revolution of destruction" through which we are living.'
For Norah Hoult, those blown-out windows suggested more
than the title of her novel: they symbolised for her the ultimate
terror of old age – to be left alone in the dark, and to be shut
in upon yourself.

Julia Briggs
London, 2005

If you have enjoyed this Persephone book why not telephone or write to us for a free copy of the Persephone Catalogue and the current Persephone Quarterly? All Persephone books ordered from us cost £10 or three for £27 plus £2 postage per book.

PERSEPHONE BOOKS LTD
59 Lamb's Conduit Street
London WC1N 3NB

Telephone: 020 7242 9292
Fax: 020 7242 9272
sales@persephonebooks.co.uk
www.persephonebooks.co.uk